CHANGED
A4444915B

C0-AUT-928

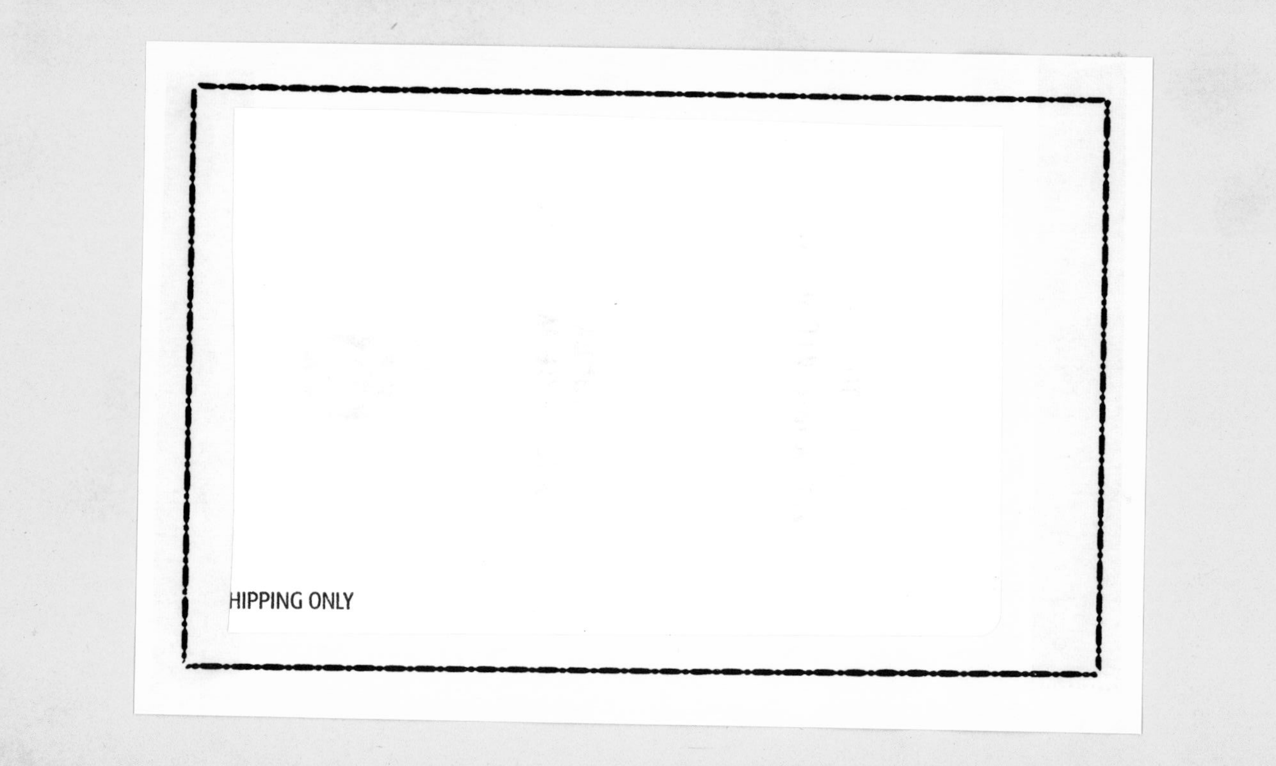
HIPPING ONLY

Other novels by
Robert Payne

The Great God Pan
Red Lion Inn
The Young Emperor
Blood Royal

Robert Payne

The Chieftain

A Story of
the Nez Perce People

Prentice-Hall, Inc.
New York

Printed in the United States of America

Library of Congress Catalog Card Number 53-6363

for

BERTHA KLAUSNER

affectionately

BOOK ONE
THE WINDING WATERS

BOOK TWO
THE BATTLE IN THE TENT

BOOK THREE
THE STORM BREAKS

BOOK FOUR
THE LONG WAY HOME

I returned and saw under the sun that the race is not to the swift, nor the battle to the strong, neither yet bread to the wise, nor yet riches to men of understanding, nor yet favor to men of skill; but time and chance happeneth to them all.

All things come alike to all: there is one event to the righteous, and to the wicked; to the good and to the clean, and to the unclean; to him that sacrificeth and to him that sacrificeth not . . .

Ecclesiastes

BOOK ONE

THE WINDING WATERS

The Beginning of the Story

IN all the world there is no valley so sweet as the Wallowa and no lake so beautiful as Wallowa Lake. The valley is of dark earth soft as shadows under the protecting hills, and a river runs through the valley with trailing vines along the sandy banks. They called it, at the time when the Indians lived there, the valley of the winding waters; and so it was, for there was hardly a stretch of the river which did not curve and twist among the grassy slopes, or break in waterfalls over blue rocks. On all the rolling meadows of the valley the grass grows thick and long for the ponies to graze upon. Deer wander in the hills, and the bears come lumbering down from their caves in the high mountains. In spring the meadow larks sing there, and the dove-colored sage hens wander where they please, while the spotted pheasants peck at the grass. In summer blue camas flowers flood the fields until you would think there are blue lakes on the slopes, and violets and roses blossom, and the river is red with the flickering fins of the salmon running, and it is so peaceful and quiet in the valley that you can hear a man breaking rock five miles away; and half the year the golden eagles roam leisurely overhead. Mostly the valley is bright green with sagebrush and succulent grass, but here and there you will see a flash of white from the smoke of waterfalls or from the snow on the peaks.

All through the first seven decades of the last century Wallowa belonged to the Nez Perce Indians. The green lake was the playing ground of the young braves. They enjoyed the lake at all times, running races round it on their speckled white-rumped ponies, or else they went fishing, or wrestled on the sandy banks, or lay on their backs watching the clouds pass. Nearly every morning they raced down to the lake to bathe; and in the evening when the air turned to blue and gold and the wind roared down from the mountains, they were still there. At last, when the dusk was ebbing, and the lake turned from a burnish of silky gold to purple and then to black, they rode off to the lodges on the uplands, throwing their blankets round their shoulders, huddling together before mounting their ponies, and it was good to watch them as they raced up the hills. Sometimes, as they rode, they would play on their bird-bone flutes; the thin eerie music of the flutes sounded like birdsong.

When they reached the lodges at last they saw the lake shining faintly, and all round the lake there would be a gleam of arrowheads or the glint of fish scales left by the braves, or the strange dark patterns in the grass left by their ponies. Afterwards there was chanting by the lodge-fires, or else they sprawled on blankets, and some of them stood in the shadows, their blankets enveloping their girls.

These people were called the Nez Perce, but no one ever remembered a time when their noses were pierced. The custom, if it ever existed, had been forgotten. The young braves were the most fortunate of men. They were good traders; they possessed the best horses in the Territory of Oregon; they were the fastest runners, the makers of the sharpest arrowheads, and they were the best shots. The fattest salmon came up their rivers; their beef herds grew fat in the rich valleys. They lived simply—on camas bulbs, huckleberries, salmon, venison and game. They killed only for food, and believed that inanimate objects possessed life. A Nez Perce Indian, seeing the antlers of a deer lying on the earth, would lift them up and place them in a rosebush in the hope that the life of the tree would bring the antlers to life again. They lived quietly and simply in their sheltered valley, believing that everything mortal was blessed by the gods: there were gods in every blade of glass, every cloud, every thunderstroke and every lightning bolt: most of all they believed that the gods inhabited the human beings who walked the godlike earth.

From the time of Lewis and Clark the Nez Perce Indians were admired by the palefaces. It was not their gentleness only: it was the way they walked, coming to you with a smile on their lips and with open hands. They were the most generous of men. They were also supple and well-formed, the most indisputably handsome of all the Indians who inhabited the Northwest, even though they streaked paint on their faces and walked about in breechclouts. Mostly, their women wore blouses and long skirts, with shawls over their heads; on ceremonial days they put on white doeskin tunics laced with beads and porcupine quills. In summer their children wandered about naked, and often on summer evenings the young women would dress in doeskins for the pleasure of it.

These people lived in paradise and knew it and sometimes wondered whether it would last. Their medicine men told them to beware: there were strange auguries, strange configurations of the stars. In the sixties settlers came to the valley of the winding waters and built log huts on the distant slopes and searched for gold. The Indians were not worried overmuch. They had been taught tolerance, even of gold diggers. They believed the white men could be trusted. They watched the huts springing up and laughed at people who lived in wooden boxes, when it was more comfortable in tents of buffalo skin. Then surveyors came, and they laughed at the men who pointed a thing like a gun a foot long at the surrounding mountains, but no flames spurted from the gun. Then two or three trading stores were opened, and they were glad to buy salt and tallow, kerosene and clasp knives in exchange for deer-skins and buffalo robes. In May, 1869, they heard that the first trans-continental railroad had been completed, and it amused them that there was a machine which could travel on wheels so far and to so little purpose. They should have known that the end was near. In the following year a small company of troopers was sent to keep watch on the Wallowa Valley. All you could see was the shadowy line of tents on the slopes on the other side of the lake, away from the Indians. Sometimes soldiers would ride over to them and give them tobacco, and run races with them; and these tall Indians, who sometimes wore white men's clothes and were quiet in their manner, came to think that the soldiers were there to protect them from the settlers. They were partly right in this, as they were right in so many other things. So they stayed in the valley, coming from the Imnaha in the spring when the salmon were running and staying through the long summer and the flowering autumn, and when they rode to the Imnaha they would leave a few lodges and some horses and a part of their pony herd and a few families as a sign of possession. They told themselves that the valley with the blue crags and the rippling lake was theirs forever, and no one would ever dare to take it away from them.

Standing there, looking down at the immense heart-shaped valley, seeing the white A tents of the troopers and the log huts of the settlers and the painted lodges of the Indians, all of them separate and far removed from one another, you could write a story about these people and it would hardly matter which people you took for your story: the story would be the same because the people in the tents and log huts and lodges were fated to collide. They could not stay in their own worlds, even if they wanted to. In the end they would seek for advantages and battle with one another. You could take Lem Otis or Marcus Woodridge or any one of the traders in the valley, and start from there. You could take Lieutenant Stevens who was in command of the troopers in the tents, and start with him. You could take the old chief Joseph in his lodge decorated with beads and great designs in red paint or any one of the braves and squaws in the lodges, and start with them. It doesn't matter where you start from. What matters is what happens when three great forces collide, and paradise comes to an end.

I

The Trader

THERE were blue clouds like eagles' feathers over the sun, but still the sunlight shone on the high feathers and painted blankets of the Indians skirting the lake. They came in a long column, two abreast, with their travois piled with buffalo robes behind them, and even from the shack you could see that their faces were painted. The sky was a pale chalky blue with a hint of coming storm. Snow had fallen in the night, but there were only a few white patches left in the hollows.

Lem Otis stood on the rise, watching the column making its way along the shores of the lake. The blue crags shone above with a wintry light, for it was now late October; and these Indians, with the blankets wound loosely round their shoulders, feathers streaming in the wind, would not return until March. Lem was sorry. He had been a trader in the Wallowa Valley for two years now, but it was only towards the end of summer that the Indians had come to trust him, buy things from him, crowd into his store. He was tall and lean with a reddish beard cropped close. He had a low forehead which puckered, and thick red lips, and a heavy nose; but he was agile and loose-limbed, and if you saw him walking across the valley you would think he was handsome enough, unlike his brother Waldo, who helped around the store. You would never have guessed that Waldo was his brother. Waldo was big and heavy, with a thick black beard, and his thick lips gleamed like fresh meat, but the most frightening thing about him was his eyes, very large and blue, and they always seemed to be pushing out of his head. His beard was tangled and unwashed and stained with food-drips, and his bony hands were mottled with oblong yellow moles. Lem resembled his father; Waldo was more like his mother. As the last of the column passed round the lake and disappeared down the valley,

Lem braced himself against the fence rail and said: "I reckon that's the first bunch. There'll be more tomorrow. Two-three days there'll only be a handful of Indians in the lodges. We'll sure enough be holed up for the winter."

He said this without regret, like someone stating a fact. High up on the frozen hills he could see the painted lodges and a few fires burning.

Waldo was watching the lake. In his eyes there was a feverish glitter.

"You mean we'll be alone? You didn't tell me about that. Reckon to stay?"

"Yup."

"Reckon you c'n stick it out, Lem?"

"I stuck it out last winter. The lake froze solid. Snowdrifts, too. You can go if you want to."

Lem laughed and pulled at a plug of tobacco. Waldo had come in the spring, bringing his Bible and a small walnut crucifix with him. He had begged his way from Portland, always childlike, going into saloons and saying he had come to bring the sinners to repentance, rarely washing, asking for a bite to eat as though it was due to him, and when no food was forthcoming, he would sit down contentedly and say: "Give me bread and water all the days of my life, dear God, and I'll sing hymns to the everlasting God. But God, if you don't bring me bread and water, how can I sing hymns to you?" It was as though he was daring God to provide him with sustenance. Usually the sustenance came.

"I'm sorry they're going," Lem said casually. "I sure am sorry."

"Sorry for what?" Waldo said.

"I told you. I like the Indians. I'm not like you. I don't go round snarling at them because they're heathens. I've got more sense than to keep on telling them they are going to burn in hell fire."

Waldo gazed accusingly at his brother, the soft light glowing in his prominent blue eyes.

"They're going to burn, Lem, and they know it! They know they're not doing right. They don't care a bloody mousehole for God. That's why you've got to go and let me read them God's word. It ain't my fault if they don't listen to me. They'll listen one day—remember that!"

The sun was fading, and a chill was coming over the uplands. Lem turned towards the shack with its shelves of salt and tallow, calico and cotton cloth and steel chips for arrowheads and the three or four Winchesters he kept hidden in a japanned box under the woodpile: there was good profit in Winchesters. He could still hear the hooves of the Indian ponies, but soon the sound grew so faint that it was no more than an echoing in the ears. He sat down beside the stove, roaring with great yellow flames. He felt suddenly heavy, hating the winter ahead, the loneliness, the craving for human comfort. He hated Waldo, too, though Waldo had his uses—Waldo could ax wood, and feed the hound-dog, and do all the menial things about the store. Half an hour later he rose and sliced himself some bread, stuffed it into his mouth and then went out to tell Waldo he was going to Lewiston.

"What do you want to go for—stores?"

"I'm not telling you."

Early in the afternoon Lem began the long journey to Lewiston. Three days later, cold, savage and hungry, his clothes wet through, he strode into the saloon bar of the Luna Hotel.

The bar was heavy with cigar smoke and talk of gold. Lem listened, yawned, stretched his muscles, listened to the chuck waggons coming down the mud streets. Somewhere a girl was singing to an out-of-tune fiddle, her voice low and hoarse because she had drunk too much or because she had sung too long, but the girl was somewhere else, on the other side of the clapboard, and there were long intervals when the men roaring and talking in the bar drowned her voice. She was singing about the Deep South, the darkies and the deep blue skies, and there was something haunting and soft in the song, something that made him swallow twice when he lifted his glass to his lips. "God help me, where am I coming to?" he murmured, and the old feeling of loneliness came over him like a wave. He wanted to talk to someone, but the gold miners were busy among themselves with their little leather pouches, spreading the thin dusty gold in open palms, sweating under the swinging kerosene lamps, and always the girl's voice coming from another room. The door opened. An Indian in a thick red blanket came in, walked slowly across the room, his eyes darting as though he was searching for someone, but no one paid attention to him, and the Indian went out again, drawing his blanket tightly around him. In a corner an old man with a stovepipe hat and a forked beard was poring over his Bible with a magnifying glass, muttering to himself and sometimes lifting crafty eyes at the miners. You found old men like that in every barroom in the Territory in those days; the barkeepers had black, twirling mustaches, the housemen were whiskered, and old men with forked beards sat in corners lolling over dog-eared Bibles. There were only a few women in the saloon: they were the centers of small compact groups of miners, and there wasn't one of these hussies he had a mind to talk to.

After three neat whiskies Lem called for coffee. His head was reeling. He drank little at Wallowa: some brandy sometimes when he had a chill, and a thimble of whisky after a ride in the hills; he wondered why he had taken the three glasses which stared at him now. Already there were a few drunks, and one of them had fallen asleep across the pool table. The houseman was leering at him, preparatory to throwing him out into the muddy road with the springy sidewalk planks as slippery as the road itself. There were wet traces of mud all over the saloon floor.

The barman was a taciturn man with thinning grey hair, inflamed eyes and swollen eyelids which resembled lumps of fat. You could see his pink skull beneath the grey curls, and there was a bald spot of eczema the size of a silver dollar above his left ear. At first Lem had unaccountably wanted to confide in the man. Perhaps it was the fumes of whisky; perhaps it was just the strangeness of the place, the feeling he had that in a saloon no one remembered anything you said, you could confide in anyone, they'd never hold it against you. Because he knew his feet would not carry him to the hotel, he beckoned to the barman and said: "Know of a place where I can bed down?"

"We got places right here, Mr. Otis. Dollar a night."

The barman was smiling at him, showing thin pointed teeth with gaps between them. Lem wondered how the man knew his name.

"Are they clean?" he asked.

"Couldn't be cleaner, Mr. Otis. Sweet-smelling, too."

The saloon was swimming round. The engraved mirrors were wheeling, and the people in the saloon were rising and falling as though they were floating on a sea swell. Lem stiffened, attempting to get control of himself.

"Believe me or believe me not—" he began, but he could go no further.

"I believe you, Mr. Otis," the barman said in a kindly voice. "You don't have to worry none. We got a place that'll suit you right down to the ground."

"You got one here?"

"Right here."

Lem closed his eyes tight. A feeling of nausea was mounting in him.

Someone was holding him up, and he was being led through a door down a carpeted stairway to a small room where there was only an iron bedstead and a slop pail, but the room was clean and a window opened on a courtyard. He sat on the edge of the bed, groaned, buried his face in his hands, and when he looked up he expected to see the barman, but it was someone else, a tall man with a pale face and a thin red mottled turkey neck and a nose which jutted out like a long thin wedge of wax.

"You'll be all right in our hands, Mr. Otis," the man said.

"I don't know how the devil you know my name," Lem moaned. "It's not as though I get drunk often." He smiled and said: "I don't know what I'm doing when I'm drunk—don't get drunk often, though."

"You just get to bed and we'll wake you in the morning," the man smiled, holding a naked candle in his hand, and when the grease ran over his knuckles, he made no sign. He was about to go when Lem said: "I want to get me a woman."

"For the night?"

"Yes."

"Run you five-six dollars, a good woman would. Get you a squaw for near nothing."

"I want to get me a woman for tonight and tomorrow night and all the nights to come," Lem went on in a singsong voice, still drunk, still holding himself together with difficulty. There was a miserable look in his eyes. He wanted to sleep. He didn't really want a woman. He wanted to put an end to his loneliness, but there was no way he knew.

"It's none of my business to ask," the man said, squinting at him, "but what would you do with a woman, eh? God durn it, you ain't in no shape for a woman, Mr. Otis. How many drinks did you have?"

"Three."

"If you ain't drunk none for some time, three could knock a man out. Go to sleep, Mr. Otis, and you'll be chipper in the morning."

Lem's head sagged, but he lifted it with difficulty. His mind was on Wallowa, on the lonely stretch of upland above the lake, the store which was no more than a shack, old mad Waldo reciting the Bible and lifting his eyes to the roof, while the Lord talked to him out of unheard thunder and unseen lightning. He shivered uncontrollably at the thought of returning there empty-handed, and there was a desperate look in those eyes which were prominent and veined with little red streaks like trickles of blood.

"I've told you what I want," Lem said heavily. "You go get me a woman."

The houseman bent down and whispered into Lem's ear: "I'll git you one tomorrow when you're fresh and chipper. How do you like that?"

"Tomorrow's too late."

"Then I reckon you'll just have to do without, Mr. Otis. There ain't many free women in Lewiston. Cost plenty, too. It's like looking for elephants. You might find an elephant or two in Lewiston if you hunted hard, but it ain't probable you'd find a bunch of them, considerin' there isn't a circus within three hundred miles, and you'd need a bunch of them, wouldn't you?"

"Need a bunch of what?"

"Elephants."

"I'm not talking about elephants. I'm talking about a woman," Lem said obstinately. "Go get me one. You can get one whenever you want, can't you? It don't help to talk about elephants."

Lem sank back on the creaking bed, stuffed with floss, and passed his hand over his eyes. The houseman had left, leaving the candle on a wooden shelf beside the door, and the door was a quarter open. Lem heard footsteps, drunken guffaws, the rattle of glasses and somewhere a rat was gnawing at the woodwork. The bed was comfortable. His mind kept wandering back to Wallowa, the Indians riding beside the edge of the lake, the blue crags, the hot summers when the earth was baked hard and dust rose in columns. He knew he loved the valley and hated the sweltering town with its muddy earthroads and board sidewalks, the stench of sweat hanging over it. He remembered the day when he first wandered out to the valley, a day when the clouds were piled high and the whole valley was paved with sunshine, and how he stood there on the rise and shook his fists and said: "I won't move from here. No, by God, I won't." Someone was coming up the corridor. The candle was still burning, leaving a long black smear of carbon on the striped wallpaper.

"You sure put a man to a lot of trouble," the houseman said, throwing the door wide-open and pushing a girl into the room. "Here's one. She ain't ever had a man, and ain't likely to." The girl was about eighteen, with a pale flabby face, her black hair tied in a bun with loose hair escaping down her back, wearing a pitiful faded grey dress, cotton stockings and moccasins. She did not have a harelip, but her upper lip was pinched in, giving her face a curious emptiness, as though it was not yet finished. She stood there, brushing the hair with the back of her hand away from her forehead, and because the candle was shining behind her, Lem could not see her clearly, only the general shape of her, the look of pitiful sadness and weariness, the way she was waiting for him to say something and dared not speak herself.

"She ain't bright," the houseman said. "For that matter she ain't never been bright."

"Brightness don't matter," Lem said heavily, with difficulty keeping his eyes open.

He felt obscurely that he must make up his mind now, without waiting for morning.

"What's her name?" he asked, and it was as though he was buying a horse.

"Moll Tillery's her name—that's what she calls herself, Mr. Otis. She can't write or read, though. She's got Indian blood down along the line. You can have her for cheap."

"You mean I have to buy her?"

"That's right. She ain't bright and she can't walk straight. I'd say you could have her for fifty dollars. You'll want to strip her down?"

"Why?"

"You want to see what you get for the money, don't you? It's up to you."

Lem said nothing, staring at the girl who was perfectly expressionless. The look of fear on her face when she entered the room had departed. Half-witted, probably deaf, she was content to stay there until someone pushed her somewhere else. Without knowing what he was doing, Lem gave a little nod. The houseman took it as a sign that he wanted her stripped, and he began to undo the buttons which ran down the back of her dress up to the waist. Afterwards he said: "You do the rest, Moll," and leaned wearily against the doorpost, biting his fingernails only because he was sick of the whole affair, while Moll shuffled out of her clothes. When she was completely naked the houseman picked up the candle and stood a little to one side, holding the candle up, then lowering it to the level of her knees. There was still no expression on her face. Her breasts were large, the belly lumpy with fat, her legs too thick, but there was some grace about her and the whiteness of her skin in the candlelight reminded Lem of Wallowa when there was snow on the rolling meadows. Then the houseman, tired of bending, lifted the candle to her face, and then she smiled because she was dazed by the glow.

"Feel her, Mr. Otis. She ain't got such a bad skin. A man likes a bit of fat sometimes—you could lose yourself in a bit of fat, now couldn't you?"

Lem stared, looking up the length of her, the soft curve of the belly, the astonishing ripeness of those breasts. He had never hoped for so much. It astonished him that the tufts of hair under her armpits glowed like silver wires. As she breathed, her flesh rippled a little, and he wanted to carry her to the bed at once.

"That's right, Mr. Otis. You'll find you can lie on her as comfortable as any bed. She may need a bit of breakin' into, but I reckon it's all right once you are in."

"You can shut up your dirty talk," Lem said, reddening. "She'll do. Now you get out of here."

He was wide-awake now, no longer drunk, and he wanted the whole affair over with, the woman in bed with him, the stove burning bright in the store, no one in Lewiston knowing or caring where he was. He peeled off fifty dollars, thrust them at the houseman, and said: "Where's the parson?"

"What parson?"

"I said a parson. It don't matter what parson. I want someone to marry us."

"You don't have to, Mr. Otis. Just take her away and send her back when you've finished."

The veins were standing out on Lem's forehead. He rose slowly from the bed and advanced against the houseman with the intention of striking him down, then his hand dropped and instead of hitting him he struck the man in the chest with a lowered shoulder. It was an ungainly attack born of weariness and horror, and the houseman, who had been afraid at first, smiled weakly and said: "Don't poke my eye out, fellow." The girl was still standing there, facing the bed.

"Well, what about the parson?" Lem barked, slumped against the wall.

"You won't find one at this hour, Mr. Otis," the houseman said. "You'll find folks like parsons are good and proper in bed."

"We could wake one up?"

"I don't think a parson would want to marry you, Mr. Otis. That's fair and straight, isn't it? I'm telling you what it's like in Lewiston.

You could get a judge to marry you. You go and bed with her, and then think about it. Morning's soon enough."

"I want it now," Lem answered stubbornly, thrusting his red beard out. "Now! I don't care who marries me, judge or parson. Tell me the name of a judge."

"There's Judge Shillitoe."

"All right, bring him here."

"I reckon you wouldn't know a judge if you saw one. There isn't enough money in the world to pay a judge to come here."

"Then we'll go to him. I've got money, haven't I?"

"Might work," the houseman said, and his face wrinkled up as he pushed his palm across his cheeks.

When Moll was dressed, the houseman led the way across two streets to the judge's house, enclosed within a high fence and set back from the road. It was raining a little. Moll walked in the middle, behind the houseman, with Lem trailing. There was enough moonlight to see by. The streets were quiet now, and the mud shone in the moonlight as though there were fish lying still and silent in the road. A lamp was burning in the upstairs bedroom, and when the houseman hollered for the judge, the judge himself came to the window in his nightshirt, aiming a shotgun at them, the barrel glinting.

"Put the gun up, judge," the houseman exclaimed nervously. "There's a couple down here aimin' to be spliced."

"There is, is there? Who's the fellow?"

"Mr. Lem Otis. Came ridin' in from Wallowa."

"Who's the girl?"

"Old Moll."

There was a chuckle from the upstairs window.

"Old Moll, eh? So she's aimin' to be spliced? Well, my friends, I'll be down in a nick."

Judge Shillitoe came pounding down the stairs with a kerosene lamp in one hand and the shotgun in the other. He was a heavy man, but he could move quickly, and there was more muscle in him than most men suspected. He had a heavy bulging forehead, small humorous eyes and a mouth not very much larger than one of his eyes. He was lawfully a judge, unlike the attorneys of Lewiston who in those days were allowed to call themselves judges; and even in his nightshirt, with his hanging dewlaps and hamlike hands, he gave an impression of ponderous strength, and no one ever laughed at Judge Shillitoe to his face.

The judge flung the door open and stood there squarely, pursing his thin lips together.

"Come in, friends," he said. "You're mighty welcome."

Moll's face was lowered, and the judge never looked at her without a smile. He led them through a bead curtain into the dining room, propped the shotgun against the table and set the kerosene lamp on a chest of drawers.

"What did you say your name was?" the judge asked, leaning forward.

"It's Lem Otis, judge."

"Where you from?"

"Portland, judge."

"I'm from Kentucky myself," the judge said. "Ever been to Kentucky?"

"No, sir."

"Well, that's your misfortune. I was born and raised in Kentucky. What's your trade?"

"Keep a store at Wallowa Creek."

"Fine place, fine place," the judge said, closing his eyes, and he was evidently trying to place Wallowa Creek.

"Make it short and quick," the houseman said. "I reckon most men ought to be in bed by now."

The judge searched in the chest of drawers for a Bible, then took Moll's hand and pressed it down on the Bible, and then he did the same with Lem. Suddenly his whole manner changed. Stern and upright, squaring his shoulders, staring straight ahead, he said in a surprisingly deep voice, "My friends, ask yourselves whether you have been joined in matrimony before and then further ask yourselves whether there is any impediment to this marriage you desire to undertake. I tell you, marriage is a holy sacrament not to be entered upon lightly—"

"Short and quick," the houseman said testily.

"I'm making it as short and quick as I know how," the judge said without turning to the houseman. "My friends, if you know of any impediment to the marriage, speak now, and if you know of none, then say 'aye.' "

"Aye," said Lem nervously.

"That's all, my friends. I pronounce you wedded man and wife for ever and aye, and it will cost you eight dollars."

Lem paid the eight dollars quickly, and was about to go when the judge touched him on the shoulder and said: "A word with you, Mr. Otis. I want you to know that Judge Horace A. Shillitoe is a friend of every man, woman and child he meets, wherever it may be. I'm out to serve the community according to my lights and my ability. I'm against all underhand dealings. I don't fear man or beast, and I'm against liars. If it should happen I find you've been married before and you are still lawfully wedded to your former wife, then you may reckon on the strong and powerful arm of justice striking you down. Bear that in mind, Mr. Otis."

"I ain't ever been married," Lem said, and he turned to comfort Moll, who was sobbing quietly to herself.

"I was only warning you, Mr. Otis. I'm a friend of the people. If you deal straight with me, I'll deal straight with you. Call on me when you come to Lewiston. I'm at your service, sir."

Then, picking up the shotgun and the kerosene lamp, the judge accompanied them to the door.

II

Waldo

LEM sat by the bank, cooking some jerked meat in a tin pan over a sagebrush fire. He had dug a hole a foot wide, two feet long and two feet deep, and piled the chopped sagebrush in, then set light to it. The pit was full to the brim of glowing coals of sage, and there was no smoke. The silver clouds were turning a dull reddish gold in the sunset, and there was Moll, sitting in the cart with a hood drawn over her shoulders, and the sun caught her, so that her head and shoulders turned the same dull gold as the sunset.

"It's fair fuel," he said, turning from the glow of coals to the glow which hovered around Moll. "The fire will go on all night—won't need replenishing. You can sleep where you like, near the fire or in the cart. It's all the same to me."

"I'll sleep where you are," Moll said quietly, and she dug her fingers in the long black woolen coat he had bought for her, for a cold wind was springing up, rustling the chokeberries and the sage.

"I'm sleeping by the fire," Lem said, without looking up. "Bring them blankets down, Moll."

There was a heap of blankets, all bundled, at the back of the cart. He had bought the blankets to sell to the Indians: they were all in grey wool, and the Indians would dye them in their own time with strange arrow-shaped patterns of bright red, yellow and green. Glancing up from the fire as the shadows came racing across the windy plain, Lem saw her lifting the bales of blankets and noted how strong she was, her firm shoulders, the way the coat tightened over her buttocks when she strained to lift the bales down, twenty or thirty blankets to a bale, and she lifted them, not easily, but without any heavy breathing. She had been pale when he found her in Lewiston, but now the wind had whipped color into her cheeks, and there was about all her movements the heavy grace of a lumbering animal.

"Set!" he said sharply, when she continued to stand beside the bales. "Eat first, then you can spread them blankets."

"I'd prefer to spread the blankets now."

"Do as you are told!"

She obeyed him, but there was an amused smile hiding in her lips. Mostly in the spring-cart he had been silent. Now he told her about Wallowa, the lake, the Indians, the salmon runs, the clumps of cottonwood behind the store, the blue-green grass of summer and the fat ponies gamboling on the uplands, but he said nothing about Waldo. As he spoke there was a rough kindliness in his tone, and he would look up to see her head bent over the fire, attentive yet somehow remote from him, not pretty in any way even when the flamelight came from underneath and softened the puffy contours of her face. He said nothing about Waldo, because he was afraid to talk about Waldo, could not trust himself to mention the name which acted upon him like an irritant. She gave no sign that she was listening except an occasional timid nod or the briefest of smiles.

"It ain't like town life, ain't no amusements, ain't nothing at all but the shack. You'll fetch and carry all the days of your life, and maybe you won't ever leave Wallowa, because I've a mind to stay there the rest of my days. I'm a trader. Remember that. I buy cheap and sell dear, and that's the way it is with you as with everything else. You ain't bright, Moll, but you've got to learn as how I've got a hankerin' for obedience. I don't aim for you to be much more than a servant, obeyin' my wishes. I'd 'uv got me a brighter woman if I wasn't so hurried. Keep your mouth quiet, and you'll do. So I ain't offerin' you no promises, ain't givin' you anything but your food and a bed, and I aim to keep it that way, and I can't help it if you ain't got no lights in your head—you'll have to make do with the lights you have, and God help you, my poor soft Moll."

He said the last words very quietly as though to himself, and he was surprised when she lifted her head and gazed steadily at him.

"You heard?"

"Yes, sir."

"Then that's the way it is, Moll. There ain't no use fightin' against it."

"I don't aim to fight against it—I don't aim to fight against anything at all, Mr. Otis."

"You'd better call me Lem. I reckon if I heard you saying 'Mr. Otis, Mr. Otis' all day at Wallowa, I'd go plumb crazy."

"If that's what you want—"

"I do want it, and I don't want you actin' soft. I'll go plumb crazy if you do everything I say. You've got a strong body. I want you to develop a mind of your own. I believe you can. I believe there's a bit of light shinin' there, and if I blow on it, maybe there'll be a bigger light."

"You're a sudden man, Mr. Otis," Moll said softly, and he wondered what she meant.

"How so?" he asked after a long contemplative pause.

"One moment you say I've got no lights and the next moment you say I've got 'em. I reckon you'd better make up your mind."

Lem was so surprised that he smiled with pure pleasure. Her sass delighted him. It was the last thing he expected. He squinted at her, pretending to be looking at the horses, and then he said: "Better unwrap them blankets, Moll."

"Yes, Mr. Otis."

"Thunderin' Jesus, didn't I tell you to call me Lem? I'm suspicionin' that you call me Mr. Otis out of pure sass."

If she heard him, she gave no sign. She was busy unwrapping the blankets, spreading them over the tussocky earth, collecting stones to weigh down the corners. The sun had set. The purple darkness was coming down like rain, and the dying wind, rattling among the sagebrush, settled at last to a faint murmur like the sound of a running brook. Then the stars came out, clear and frosty, and the sweet smell of the sage hung over them as they both crouched beside the fire warming themselves before they slipped under the blankets.

"Can you read, Moll?" Lem asked, looking at her with an enquiring look, for it had suddenly occurred to him that there was a good deal more in his purchase than he bargained for.

"I can read a bit, Lem."

"And can you sing?"

"I can sing a bit."

"Then sing for me."

In a quavering voice she began to sing, but there was no strength in her breath. The knowledge that Lem wanted her to sing, her desire to sing at her best, the strange nervousness which came over her once she opened her mouth, all these prevented her from uttering a single right note, and she turned her head away in confusion. Then, taking a deep breath and looking out into the distance, far beyond the glow of the fire, her voice faint at first, then rising clear above the murmur of the wind, she sang as she had never sung before:

I gave my love a cherry that has no stone,
I gave my love a chicken that has no bone,
I gave my love a ring that has no end,
I gave my love a baby that has no cryin'.

How can there be a cherry that has no stone?
How can there be a chicken that has no bone?
How can there be a ring that has no end?
How can there be a baby that has no cryin'?

A cherry when it's blooming, it has no stone,
A chicken when it's pipping, it has no bone,
A ring when it's rolling, it has no end,
A baby when it's sleeping, there's no cryin'.

Lem did not call upon her to sing any more songs. He was content, sitting there with the glowing bowl of his pipe in his cupped hands, his face lit by the gleams of the sagebrush fire, the rough face softer than it had been for many years. He said: "Git under them blankets, Moll. You ain't bright, but you can sing."

"You liked it?"

"Sure I liked it. Why shouldn't I?"

"I didn't think you would, Mr. Otis."

Her voice was trembling and her face was turned away.

"Git under them blankets and loosen them skirts a bit," he said quietly, and then he knocked out his pipe and listened to the faint howling of the coyotes for a while before unbuckling his belt and slipping under the blankets beside her.

With Moll's head pillowed on his shoulder, four or five blankets under him, five or six on top and others within reach, he gazed up at the cold stars, losing himself in the immensity of the heavens. There was no moon yet. The air was clean and scented with the honey-smell of burning sage, and it was pleasant to listen to the horses snuffling beside the road some twenty yards away, and to watch the mallards flying up in the black sky. It was many years since he had slept with a woman. In those early days he had been rough and awkward. Now he lay still, waiting for her heat to come warming him, letting it play on him, hungry yet stemming his hunger, not wanting to take her before the warmth of her had penetrated through him; and then when he had pushed his trousers down and he was altogether lost in the quiet warmth of her, he was surprised by his own gentleness, and all he could say was: "You're in my heart, Moll. Ah, you'll do, you'll do!"

He slept soundly, like a child. When he woke up he thought for a while he was back in the store at Wallowa, but there was a pale blue sky overhead and the smell of coyotes hanging in the air—they must have come close to the fire, then left, for their traces were nearby. He knew it was folly to come out without a rifle, but it was more than he could do to think of shooting man or beast on this bright morning, with a white dapple of frost on the ground. The sagebrush fire was still burning. Moll's hair had fallen across her face, and he lifted it up and stared at her sleeping, saying to himself: "You ain't purty, but you've got a good heart, Moll," and then he guffawed with pure pleasure, slipping noiselessly out of the blankets. Then he cooked some more meat over the fire, and fed the horses, and wandered off into the cottonwoods to relieve himself, so pleased with himself that he would burst out into little cackles of laughter for no reason—a bird rising, the blue shadow of a single blade of grass, the rusty-red wheels of the spring-cart, anything at all could give him this momentary sense of inexplicable happiness.

All the way back to Wallowa Lem sang in his heart. He would ask Moll to sing *I gave my love a cherry,* always the same song, for no other delighted him so much, and when they came in sight of the store, he said proudly: "It's all yours, Moll, every bit of it." He expected her to smile, but instead she was very silent, paying no attention to the shack, her gaze rooted on the valley with the blue cliffs and the lake already white with ice. "It's sweeter'n cherries," she said softly, and all the color was drained out of her cheeks.

Lem pushed her into the store. The black full-bellied stove was burning. Waldo sat on a bench huddled in the corner, wearing his long black overcoat, his beaver hat drawn low over his eyes. "That's Waldo," Lem said, as though Waldo was no more than black faggots lying there.

Moll settled down to live in the store. She needed no pushing; saw what had to be done, and did it. She loved Lem. At night she stayed awake, thinking of the miracle of the warm naked body lying beside hers, so fierce and then so limp, and still wonderful. She loved to draw her fingers through Lem's bristling red beard, which he trimmed every morning; loved to be awake before he woke, for then she would see him opening his eyes to the morning light, a bewildered glint in them as he recognized her afresh and drew her down to him. Then, rising, she would sit in the cold bedroom before a cracked mirror and comb her long hair, and Lem loved to watch the muscles of her arms as she combed, the tug of her healthy young body. She was never beautiful, but there was a rough grace about her which was close to beauty.

When spring came, and the Indians returned from their hunting grounds in the Imnaha Valley, she was always out of doors. She collected flowers and filled the hut with them, always wandering through the woods back of the store or tending the vegetable garden. In the evenings she would sit in a basket chair just beyond the rail and watch the braves racing beside the lake. She said once: "I ain't ever been so happy, Lem. I think of you and I think of the lake, and it's all the happiness I can bear."

In a hundred ways Moll changed the look of the store. She hung teas and herbs from the roof beams, baked johnnycakes, gave Lem three square meals a day, and was forever mending his two suits and two pairs of socks. She paid little attention to Waldo, but was always scrupulously polite to him. She liked the Indians who came to the store, and if a young brave came with a fan of eagle feathers, she would stroke the feathers with her finger tips; and if the brave was sick she would feed him on calomel pills and herb tea. There was no coquetry in her. It was simply that she liked the Indians and was in love with the valley.

"Seems you git along with the Injuns mighty well," Waldo said once when he came upon her talking in sign language with some Indian boys.

"I kin git along with pretty near anybody," Moll said, and added tartly: "I kin git along even with you."

For Lem things were turning out as he had a secret hope they would. He loved Moll, and could not think of life without her. Waldo's loud ravings became no more than dark mutterings in a corner. The Indians liked Moll and brought more trade. Once when a young chieftain came to the hut wearing his painted feathers with a train of scarlet and purple feathers down his back, Lem saw her fingering them and said: "Moll, you're in love with them beauties with chicken feathers poppin' out of them, I swear you are!"

Moll's face turned crimson. She had been stroking the feathers and smiling at the young chieftain.

"I ain't in love with no one—only you," she said. It was as though she had been caught performing a forbidden act. She turned her head away, and her lips were trembling, and the young chieftain was smiling down at her.

"I was only joking, Moll," Lem said lamely.

"It ain't a thing to joke about," she answered, and for the rest of the morning she was trembling with indignation.

It was high summer now, the time when the blue camas bulbs are put in sacks and thumped to a powder: you could hear the dull thudding of the camas sticks three-four miles away. The sky was like a sheet of calm blue silk; the lake glittered; and every dawn blue mists crept down the mountains. Lem had never taken Moll up to the lodges. He decided to ride her up. They closed the store and sauntered down to the lake, where Moll collected wild flowers, and then up the river reaches to where the snags dammed the water into deep blue rock pools, then they rode past the pony herds. It was early evening when they reached the lodges, the best time, for then the Indians gathered together beside the storytellers and the medicine men began their long night chants. It was all as Moll expected it to be, the dust rising, the fires glinting, the young women walking about in their doeskin tunics, with daubs of red paint on their cheeks and in the parting of their hair, and soon the young braves came up from the lake, sweat rippling across their chests and down their bare legs. With yearning Moll gazed at the young women who walked so easily and gracefully with necklaces of beads and glass, and from the young women she turned to the brown and naked children who wandered among the tepees. The presence of the children almost made her suffocate with happiness. She clutched Lem's arm and whispered: "It's all a wonder, dear. It's all a wonder." Then she said: "We'll have a child, won't we?"

"About time," Lem said gruffly, not daring himself to speak.

Moll smiled through her tears. They rode on through the smoke of the cooking-fires. While they were still silent, thinking of their child, they saw an old man riding towards them. His skin was the color of bark, drawn tight over the bones; he had dark deep-set eyes and hollow cheeks and thin pursed-in lips and a craggy chin. He wore buckskin leggings, and there was an immense spread of scarlet feathers, and he carried himself with incredible assurance, as though the lodges and the meadows beyond and all the mountains belonged to him. Stiff and upright on the decorated saddle, he rode leisurely, not smiling, not showing by any gesture that he recognized any of the Indians who were suddenly hushed into silence by his coming.

"Who's the old 'un?" Moll whispered, pointing.

"It's the chieftain. They call him Old Joseph. He's old, Moll. They say he's near on seventy."

"God bless him, I say," Moll said, and she made a curious sign like a blessing on the air.

The chieftain passed through the Indian camp. Moll never forgot him. There was dignity and a settled sadness on his face, and great repose. He would not live long. Sometimes the thought of the aged chieftain, so frail, so proud, shadowed the miraculous summer.

All that summer and well into the fall there was a singing inside Moll. When the Indians went away to their hunting grounds and the first snow fell, she was still singing.

One day, when the earth lay deep under snow, Waldo disappeared. For some weeks he had been strangely quiet and secretive. Towards evening they realized he was gone: neither Lem nor Moll remembered seeing him since midday. It was bitterly cold, with a gusty wind blowing, the hills white with snow in the moonlight. Lem took a kerosene lamp and followed Waldo's tracks until they were lost in the sagebrush.

"Better saddle the horse, and ride after him," Moll said, standing at the door of the store.

"What's the use?" Lem said. "The tracks are lost. Let him go."

Moll was breathing hard and twisting her hands in her apron. For her, Waldo was like a child. She knew she wouldn't rest with Waldo out. She went back, shoved wood into the stove, shuddered, imagined him lying dead, muttered prayers for him, the same prayers he had intoned in a corner of the store as he stared at them, his eyes shining and his black beard coiling, as he dared them to say a word against him. She threw a shawl over her head and made to go to the door, but Lem was watching her. The silence was unbearable. There was no sound except the sucking of the stove and the rustle of the cottonwoods.

"I can't stand it," she said, trembling.

"He asked for it," Lem said. "By God, he asked for it." A moment later he said: "You're wasting your pity, Moll. Do a piece of sewin'. He's gallivantin' up them hills and shoutin' the glory of God, and why shouldn't he? It's what he was wantin' all along, ain't it?"

Moll could not keep her lips from trembling. In the moonlight the snow was pure white, gleaming like a knife. Waldo would fall down, and there would be no one to care for him. She imagined his face bleeding. The tin clock ticked the hours away. From afar off she heard the eerie howling of coyotes, and somewhere, from closer at hand, there would come a coyote's sharp vicious bark. He had fallen, and the coyotes were all over him, for she knew how they ravaged and tore at the dead oxen or horses that dropped from the train.

"I can't stand it," she whispered, and buried her face in her apron, shivering, feeling in her own body all the wounds that Waldo suffered.

It was an hour later, near midnight, when she heard a horse coming up the rise. As soon as she heard the sharp hoofbeats she ran out of the store and down to the fence. She could make out an officer riding a horse, and a young brave running beside, and then she saw a great white bundle thrown over the saddle. The young lieutenant with the yellow mustache which trailed round the corners of his lips touched his cap and said: "There's been some trouble, ma'am. Better bring some hot water quick!"

"It's Waldo," Moll said, dazed, not knowing what she was saying and not caring, thinking only of the large bearded man who lay limp over the horse, his face white in the moonlight, his beard and clothes all thickly frosted over. She hardly noticed the blanketed Indian who was attempting to lift Waldo down from the horse.

"What happened?" she asked the officer.

"I don't know what happened for sure, ma'am. Seems he went up to the lodges and started preachin' at them. I reckon they went and threw him in the lake because he wouldn't stop preachin' at them."

"He's dead," Moll said quietly.

But Waldo was not dead, though he was as near dead as anyone had ever seen him. His eyes were closed, his beard was a stiff tangle of ice, his clothes were wrapped round him like curtains of ice, and he hardly breathed, though he groaned a bit. The Indian was trying to put his head under Waldo's armpit and so carry him into the store.

"That's Bird-with-one-eye," the lieutenant said, dropping from the horse and then nodding in the direction of the Indian. "He's a mighty fine feller, too. Helped to fish Waldo out of the lake, and he had to fight off the other Indians to do it."

"Who are you?"

"Lieutenant Stevens—Keff Stevens, in charge of the troops up on the hill, ma'am."

Moll ran to help Waldo into the store. Lem had come out, swinging his lamp. The ice was crackling on Waldo's clothes. Lem's mouth was wide-open. He knew exactly what was happening, but part of his mind rebelled: it was incomprehensible that Waldo should have turned dead white, his beard, his face, his clothes, everything white.

The young brave laid Waldo tenderly by the stove, and at that moment the striped blanket he had been wearing slipped from his shoulders. The Indian was powerfully built, with heavy shoulders and a small beautifully shaped head, dark as a walnut. He was bare to the waist. As he knelt there, looking down on Waldo, his lips formed words, and Lem knew enough of the language to know they were words of healing.

"He wasn't worth bringing back," Lem said, pouring brandy for the lieutenant and the Indian. He looked the lieutenant up and down. "Jesus Christ, why did you have to bring him back?"

The Indian refused the brandy or any reward, and the lieutenant only sipped the brandy. Moll had put a kettle on the stove. She was busy plucking the ice from Waldo's face.

"Dear God, bring him back to us," she prayed, and she was still praying quietly to herself when the young lieutenant and the brave went riding off into the snow.

III

Moll

WALDO thawed by the stove, his face paper white, his blue eyes staring. Moll cared for him, wrapping steaming towels round his forehead, trying to breathe life in him, forever rubbing his chapped hands and feet. She bathed him twice a day, to Lem's disgust. He was terrible as he lay there helpless by the stove, unable to speak, shaking with indignation because a woman's hands were touching him.

"You don't have to do it, Moll. He ain't grateful. He ain't no good to no one. Just leave him be."

"Poor sufferin' soul," was all Moll would say, and though she had risen when Lem addressed her, a moment later she was on her knees again, wringing out a hot towel, comforting Waldo with her own young strength. Lem saw that she shivered sometimes. It was as though the warmth was departing from her and entering Waldo.

As the days passed Waldo grew well under Moll's care. Now the lake was frozen over and the wind howled, but the roaring of the wind gave him strength; that, and Moll's warm hands stroking his face and kneading his body into life again. Moll ministered to the warmth which lay hidden deep within him, coaxed it, brought it up until it lay on the surface of the skin. Five days after being dredged from the lake Waldo was eating again.

A week of warm days followed, and Waldo, lying in the wintry sun, with his Bible within reach, still demanded Moll's attention. But Moll was sickening. Her eyes were swollen and red, she complained of headaches and moved about slowly, and the fever raged in her. She suffered from continual chills. Waldo's face was red from the sun, but Moll's was a strange pearly color.

All morning Waldo shuffled about in scuffers, keeping his eye on Lem. Occasionally he would sit down on a barrel, with the Bible open on his knee, reading hard as though there was little enough time left, and sometimes he would break out singing:

Oh, for my soul's happy,
Glory hallelujah!
Oh, for my soul's happy,
I'm on my journey home.

As he sang, he would pass a hand over his face and watch Lem between his fingers, and all the time he would be smiling a strange twisted smile. He told himself there were things he would have to tell Lem in good time, things that had been revealed to him by the power of God's word, but when he saw Lem looking at him, he would bury his nose in the Bible again, chuckling to himself as though he had discovered the secret of secrets.

"It's all right, Lem. Don't you keep your eyes on me. You know me—just give me a piece of fat meat from time to time, and I won't be in the way."

Lem said nothing. Moodily, he would stand by the muslin-covered window, and wonder how soon he would have to board the window up. It was growing cold. There was a blue sky in the morning, but it was turning chalky-white by afternoon, with snow in the air. The wind rippled across the lake and there were flurries of snow which hid the tepees on the slope. From time to time Lem would go into the cold bedroom where Moll was lying, and then, gazing down at her drawn face, the large eyes, the indrawn lips, he would curse himself for not having brought the doctor to the store or for not having ridden into Lewiston with her. She was sinking rapidly. He knew that. And every time he came out of the bedroom, he knew Waldo was chuckling to himself.

"How is she?" Waldo asked, rubbing a hand over his face.

"Poorly."

"You sendin' for a doctor?"

"It's too late now. There isn't anything a doctor can do that she couldn't do as well herself. Just rest, and maybe the strength will come to her."

"Listen to this, Lem, from the good book—"

But Lem did not listen. He turned away towards the shelves, which he had arranged a hundred times since the coming of autumn, and he would go on arranging them through the winter and the spring, hoping the Indians would come in only because they were more pleasant companions than his own brother. Waldo frightened him. There was something in that stern, unyielding face which made him shiver sometimes. Waldo's eyes were as blue as summer skies, but one eye was brighter than the other: Lem was always looking out for the expression in the brighter eye. But when he thought of throwing Waldo out of the store, a sense of his own loneliness came over him: even Waldo was some comfort when Moll was sick in bed.

The fever had passed, and there was no more spitting of blood, nor any weeping. She lay very quiet now on the wooden bed, sunk in her own thoughts, her face turned towards the window, which was half boarded up, and there were two layers of muslin there, not one, to keep out the draft. It happened that when Waldo burst out singing, Lem would sometimes say: "You'll wake poor Moll. She's sleeping." He would say this even when he knew Moll was wide-awake.

Lem said once with a break in his voice: "I think she's dying, Waldo."

There was no answer from Waldo. Lem hadn't expected an answer. He fried some jerked meat on the stove and some potatoes, fed Moll gravy, pushed a plate across to Waldo and spent the afternoon feeding the stove and turning over the pages of his catalogs. It was growing dark when Waldo began speaking.

"Listen to me," Waldo said. "Without women we'd be livin' in the heavenly glory, Lem. Without women there would be no priests or gods or devils or poverty or crime, nor death either. Life without women—that's the pure life of the spirit and meditation, of thinkin' and broodin' over the immensity of God's handiwork, and His power and His glory. God's takin' her away, and He's going to put a pure heart in you. He's goin' to do it the hard way, because you've got a kind of fondness for fornicatin'. He's goin' to make you a great man. I know that. I've always known it. But first He has to see as how you are pure in heart, and that's why He's takin' her way back to Himself, and He's doin' it for your sake."

Lem listened, as he always listened to Waldo's outpourings, half believing them, half angry with himself for listening. He could not find words to form his thoughts, nor images to hold them; Waldo did it for him. He could hear Moll writhing and groaning in the empty room, and because he knew she was screaming with her hand cupped against her mouth, he made a movement to go in to her.

"Don't go," said Waldo. "Let her die. She'll be at peace then—at peace with God."

"I don't hold with peace," Lem said, the words forced out of him. "I've got to help her."

Waldo lifted up his shaggy hand.

"If you help her, what will God say? Have you thought of that? No, Lem, let her be. Praise God that she is leavin' this sinful earth. Praise the Lord for His goodness and mercy. She had it comin' to her, didn't she? She's been fornicatin' and enjoyin', same as you have, and now let there be an end to it. I tell you this, Lem. I've been thinking God is reservin' something very special for you. I've got it in my mind that all the Wallowa Valley is waitin' to be lorded over by you, waitin' for the purity and grace of your holy hand, Lem. It's a beautiful thing the Lord in His mercy is reservin' for you. You wouldn't want the Lord in His mercy to take away what He is reservin' for you, would you? Let her die, Lem. She ain't no more than a mouth to feed. You'll be glad when she's dead. I tell you this, if it wasn't for women, men would have conquered death. It's all in the good book. 'And the woman was arrayed in purple and scarlet color, and decked with gold and precious stones and pearls, having a gold cup in her hand full of abominations and filthiness of her fornication. And upon her forehead was the name written, Mystery, Babylon the Great, the Mother of Harlots and Abominations of the Earth.' That's what it says, Lem, and it says a lot more about war with the Lamb and the Heavens runnin' with fire, and the spirit of man, the divine spirit of man, being taken and crucified on a wheel of gold. The good book says the flamin' whore of Babylon is runnin' wild in the world, and she sits on seven mountains, and the cities are fallin' in fire and brimstone!"

Waldo was drunk with his own words, with his own visions. He leaned forward, his dark eyes piercing the smoky darkness of the store, while the snow fell outside and the dog barked and the strange shapes of things in the unlit shelves assumed depth and grandeur. It was at dusk and late at night that he had most power over Lem. Moll's mutterings were fainter now, little shrill screams, more like the sound a cat makes when in pain than the voice of a human being. To avoid looking at Waldo, Lem bundled some wood and shoved it into the stove.

"Isn't it true what I say?" Waldo said quietly. "Isn't it true the whole valley will one day be yours? God gives it to you. He says: Climb the cross, and it is all yours. Doesn't God say that?"

There was a sharp, sudden scream of pain from Moll.

"I'm going to bring her in here out of the cold," Lem said stubbornly. "Many a time Moll has kept me warm. I can't let her stay there in the cold."

"You let her stay where she is!"

"I can't, Waldo. It's not in me to do a thing like that. She's dying, ain't she?"

"Ain't that the best thing that could happen to her poor sinful soul? Let her die! There ain't any good in a woman, so help me. There ain't no women in paradise—the good book tells us so—there's only the pure and cleansing waters—"

Waldo rambled on, and sometimes he would spit a slosh of tobacco against the wall, and sometimes he would tug at his black beard, and all the time it was growing dark. Lem's heart froze every time Moll screamed. He said stubbornly: "Some folks have to have women, Waldo."

"It's all filth," Waldo said, muttering to himself. "I'm trying to keep you from the flames of Hell. I'm tryin' my best. God sees us—every mortal thing we do. He sees what our hands do underneath the covers, sees how the woman's legs come squeezin' up to our hands, sees all the filthy things we do for everlastin'. Have done with it, Lem! Rest by the quiet waters!"

There were times when Lem felt himself in his brother's basilisk glare. He could not escape those eyes. He had to struggle with himself to keep his mind clear, and even when he was struggling he hardly knew what he was doing. He knew it was weakness, and fought against it.

Moll heard all this as she lay on the bed; heard it, and could not tell whether this was some nightmare she was dreaming; heard it, and knew that the words were intended for her as much as for Lem. The sweat was pouring down her face, and somehow the sweat made her face colder than ever. Because the fox with the flaming feet and the famished jaws was coming closer, she wanted Lem to hold her in his arms. She wanted this more than anything else. She wanted to lie in the warmth of Lem's arms, and so she would try to turn over on her side and somehow make her way towards Lem, and she wondered why he did not come when she called. She knew the snow was falling, the hound-dog Silver was barking and somewhere on the other side of the lake the moon would be rising soon.

"God blast you!" Lem said at last, and he swung away from Waldo towards the door.

Moll was whimpering, sitting up and throwing out her arms as he came in.

"You're all I have, all I have in the world," Moll whispered.

"I'll carry you into the warm, Moll. You don't have to stay here. I don't know what Waldo's leadin' me to. Come with me, Moll."

He lifted her up, and when she threw her arms round his neck, he knew once again the voluptuous and painful craving for her caresses. She was so light that it was like carrying a child. He laid her beside the stove. Her hair was wild and damp and plastered over her forehead and the hollows of her cheeks were swimming in sweat. Her eyes gleamed like little wet pebbles. He knelt beside her, stroking her, saying over and over again: "Moll, Moll, dear love—" and when she shivered and gasped, he held her tightly, kissing the hollows of her eyes and her lips, and when she began to stroke his face, he burst into sobbing.

"You won't ever leave me?" Moll whispered huskily, feeling the warmth coming back to her.

She opened her mouth to suck in the great warmth which came from the flames. She felt safe now, though there were places in her body where the cold had dug in, and which would never be warmed.

"I'll never leave you," he said, looking over her shoulder at Waldo standing in the corner of the room. "I won't ever leave you, if that's what you want."

"Put your hand on me," Moll went on. "Put it here and here. Bring your warmth to me."

"Don't talk, Moll. Rest and be quiet, and you know I'll never leave you now."

"And send Waldo away."

"Yes, I'll send Waldo away if that's what you want."

"And never let him come between us."

"No, he'll never come between us," Lem said, and he felt strong enough to rid himself of Waldo now that she was lying in his arms.

"You're good, Lem."

"No, I ain't good, never have been. I'm selfish. I reckon I ain't ever done anything much."

"Remember Lewiston, that night, Lem. You were kind and gentle. No one had ever been so gentle with me."

Blinded with hot tears, Lem could not see her. It was enough that she was there, stirring in the light of the stove, her skin golden, her hair silver. She rested quietly for a while, taking in deep draughts of air, her eyes closed, a strange smile on the corners of her lips.

"Dear Lem," she said, "don't ever leave me."

Waldo watched, waiting his time. It was not that Lem hated Waldo. The feeling he had for Waldo had gone beyond hatred altogether. He had now for Waldo the kind of feeling he had for storms, for black clouds, for the days when the earth shook underfoot, for the darkness which spread over the earth at night. It made his head spin to think of Waldo brooding there, huddled deep in the corner, while the red flames from the stove mouth went springing up the length of him; and even with his eyes on Moll, Lem knew Waldo was standing there, sweating, little trickles of sweat falling through his beard. Now that the stove door was wide open, the forced draft made a noise like the loud beating of birds' wings. There was no light in the store except that of the fire that blazed, fell back, and blazed again.

"I'm going to die," Moll said quietly, staring like a mad woman at the flames.

"Ah, you can't perish," Lem exclaimed, the words bursting out of him. "Hold on to me, Moll. I'll keep you with me. I'll breathe in you such love you'll keep alive."

Moll smiled, and the firelight played on her long strong teeth, so that there was something horrible in her smile, something that reminded Lem of a skull.

"I loved you, Lem. You'll remember that?"

"Yes, I'll remember it. You won't die. We'll be loving again when you're better."

"I won't get better, Lem."

"Yes, you will."

"It's snowin' outside, ain't it?"

"Yes, it's snowing, Moll."

"And there's a great trumpeter swan flying overhead, ain't there?"

"I haven't heard it, Moll. Usually I hear things like trumpeters."

"I know it's there, Lem. I've seen it and heard it. Will you hold me in your arms?"

"I'm holding you."

"I mean, the way you used to hold me. Put your hand on my middle, Lem. It comes to me the trumpeter ain't going to leave the house tonight."

Lem did not know what to make of it. Was it true—could it conceivably be true that there was a trumpeter swan flying above the store, and yet he did not hear it? He choked back his sobs. It was strange to him that she spoke these things in a calm voice, as though she had nothing else on her mind but a passing illness. Waldo was making a movement to come forward, lifted an impatient hand, kept trying to attract Lem's attention. He had no time for Waldo.

"I'll love you even in the grave," Moll was saying. "You'll be standing up in the sunlight, but I'll be loving you even in the grave."

"Just keep quiet, Moll."

"I don't have no time to keep quiet, Lem. Put your hand on me. Don't let Waldo come near."

"He ain't coming near—I won't let him."

"You won't let him come near my grave, will you? He's been trying to kill me ever since I came here, hasn't he? He won't be satisfied till he has killed me, but I don't want him near me even when I'm dead. Unhook me, Lem."

With fumbling fingers Lem unhooked the back of her blouse; then with all her strength she pushed her arms out of the sleeves, and pulled down the cheap vest which was worn and spotted with russet-colored stains, until her breasts shone there, pure in the ruddy light of the stove, with little golden rivers of sweat trickling over them, so that they shone wonderfully bright, looking like the promise of some unknown country, at once mountains and rivers of sweetness; and so Lem covered one with his hand and left the other bare, and sometimes he would draw his hand away from the breast and stroke her belly, keeping her quiet, gazing at her body rather than her face, his eyes as hungry as ever. All the time, knowing that she was dying, he suffered a terrible gnawing in his heart; and once when he looked up and saw Waldo gazing at him steadily from the corner, like a cornered beast, it was on the tip of Lem's tongue to scream so loud that Waldo would run away; he did not scream because he was afraid his screaming would take strength from Moll.

And her strength was going. It was something you felt in your finger tips, in the way she stared at the flames, in the weariness that came over her eyes, so that the eyelids would droop occasionally, and then with an effort she would open them wide again. Soon the flames began to die down, until there were only little edges of red lace and white ash within the stove; yet the stove itself kept pushing heat out into the room, and if you touched the black iron ring of metal you would scald your fingers. Even now, when she was resting in his arms, and part of her weight was supported on his knee, she had the look of someone who was desperately seeking the warmth and comfort of a man, and she would turn towards him, and seeing that he was still there, a little smile played about her face.

"You'll be good to the Indians, won't you, Lem?" she said after a long pause. "You'll trade kindly with them?"

"I've always traded kindly."

"You know you haven't, Lem. Sometimes you've traded hard. I want you to be good to them, preserve them, help them in our ways. I've always liked seeing them when they come back from the hunts, haven't I? It's love—that's what you've got to have for them. I don't want to go away till they come back from the hunts. I'd like to stand on the hill and see them as they come round our lake, Lem, with all them feathers flying and the horses racing and the boys running. Except for you, Lem, there isn't anything I've liked so much as the sight of the Indians as they come round our lake."

"It's a good sight," Len admitted, stroking her and gazing down at her, wondering how long it would be before the stove turned cold. Sooner or later he would have to go out of the store and cut logs with the double-bitted ax and push them into the stove.

"But you didn't say it was a good sight, did you, Lem? You didn't tell them. People have to be told. You didn't go up to them and say: 'You're beautiful in the sight of the Lord,' did you? You ought to confess to them that you love them—it always does a lot of good."

"I ain't good at confessing, Moll, and when I think of it I don't know there is anything to confess. I treated 'em kindly. You couldn't ask more than that."

"Oh, I could, Lem. I could ask a powerful lot more. You ought to love them. Oh, love the Indians, Lem, because they're so pretty when they come round our lake."

She smiled, then, and closed her eyes, and Lem was certain she was trying to retain on the retina of her eyes the image of the feathered men beside the blue lake. She breathed more easily now. He heard the snow melting and trickling off the roof, and the dog barked again, and once Waldo made a move to come closer, but Lem raised his head sharply, and immediately afterwards there was a sharp scuffling sound, like the noise rats make in straw, and Waldo had once more retreated to his corner. The light of the flames was dying on Moll's rounded breasts until there was only a crack of faint yellow light falling on them, yet the place was still warm and the stove still made its thump-thump sound, the noise it always made when it was going out. A blanket was lying over the counter, and now Lem pulled it down and wrapped it round her shoulders. He was pleased when she smiled up at him appreciatively.

"You rest, Moll," he said quietly. "I'll go out and cut some wood—"

"Don't leave me with Waldo," she whispered, and there was a quick intake of breath as she turned her head in the direction where Waldo was standing. "You won't leave me, will you?"

"I'll take Waldo with me. I'll make him come out," Lem said with determination.

"You're sure you won't go far away?"

"No, I'll go round the corner and cut some wood and you'll hear me."

He made her as comfortable as he could, propping a saddle under her head and wrapping the blanket more carefully around her, then he stretched himself and lit a candle, and still holding the candle he turned to Waldo.

"You're coming with me," he said, and slowly raised the candle above his head, so that he could see everything in the room, every shelf and bottle, all the saddles hanging on the wall, all the tins and blankets and basilicons of pitch and oil, the waxes and resins and packets of horsemint tea, and Moll looked comfortable enough in all that disorder as she lay sleeping beside the stove. He bent down and kissed her lightly, then turned to face Waldo, and nodded, and he was not surprised when Waldo went meekly to the door. What did surprise him was that Waldo was trembling, and kept looking at the floor.

It was dark outside, with gusts of wind blowing from the direction of the lake. The icy wind, the snow falling into their eyes, the horrible sense of being lost in the darkness, all these forced them back. Lem had thought there was still a little light in the sky, enough to hack timber by, but he was mistaken. Leaving Waldo outside, he returned for a lantern, lit it and then went to the timber pile, swinging his ax. Waldo was waiting for him, looking more shaggy than ever in the light of the lantern. They exchanged no words. Lem simply set to work, and cut eight or nine logs into shape, and Waldo knew he would have to help carry them in. Suddenly, while Lem was working and Waldo was leaning against the store, warming himself against the lantern, they heard a scream. Lem flung the ax down, and in his haste knocked over the lantern and went blundering down the side of the store, unable to find the door, looking for the crack of light which would shine underneath, but he couldn't find it. The scream was repeated. It was the scream of someone in terrible agony.

When Lem found the door, he flung it open with a kick and then ran to Moll. In the faint smoky yellow light from the stove, he saw she was no longer as he had left her. The blanket had fallen away. Her mouth was open, but worse than the open mouth and the shine of her teeth was the smell of burning and the blackness on her cheek. She was kneeling in front of the stove. She had evidently tried to get up, and she must have pressed her face against the stove and been burned. There were black smudges on her hands. She was in agony and her mouth was open, but she could not say anything, though she rocked a little on her haunches. Lem sat beside her, holding her tight, waiting for the terrible silence to end, for she was still breathing but she had lost all power of movement. He saw, too, that her breasts were smudged with black, and she must have thrown herself against the stove either in her desire for warmth or because she thought she was pressing herself against him.

"We'll get the wood," he said stupidly. "Are you all right, Moll?"

There was no answer. A single yellow flame, curling within the stove, lit her cheekbones, her nose and her smooth forehead. Waldo was in the doorway.

"It's God's punishment for all your fornicatin'," Waldo said. "He's takin' her away, Lem, takin' her to His own blessed and bleedin' side. It had to happen, Lem. You know it did. There isn't a thing you can do now except fall on your knees and pray."

Lem rose slowly to his feet and shook his fists helplessly.

"Get out of here! Get out! For Christ's sake get out before I break you like I'd break a stick across my knees!"

Then he turned to the girl lying by the stove and said: "Poor black Moll," and fell to sobbing.

IV

Shades of Night

THE snow was falling, the hills were deep in clean white drifts, and inside the store the black stove blazed merrily away. Moll lay on the straw bed with her hair freshly combed and the black smudges washed off her face, her hands folded across her chest. The muslin curtains had been torn down, and now the faint sun coming through the falling snow lit her pale face and sunken cheeks: there was something almost childish in the smooth silent face, in the way she held her hands to her breast, as though something long-wished-for had happened to her and she was squeezing her hands against her heart in pure happiness.

"You're looking pretty, Moll—as pretty as I've ever seen you," Lem muttered, standing by the bed, remembering how he had washed her all over with water boiled on the stove. Afterwards he had scented her, and then he had gone out cutting wood, and it seemed strange to him that the store was so silent, and never had the soft falling of the snow been so beautiful, with the sun shining through it, making the drops shine gold sometimes, and there were little flashes of blue and green fire coming up from the sunlit snow on the ground. There were two inches of snow now, and Lem wondered in an absent-minded way whether the snow would come creeping up the peeled logs of the store, and maybe bury it. It had happened before, according to the Indians, that there were ten-foot drifts.

As the morning went on, Lem knew he could not delay the burial of Moll, but he wanted to keep her a little longer. He would cut a few logs and then come rounding into the store with an expression of eagerness and pity on his face, thankful because there was no change on her face. He had closed her eyes and bound her jaw with a strip of looped cord, but when he went in to see her, he forgot the cord and pretended to himself that she was sleeping. Waldo had made himself inconspicuous. Once when Lem came in, he heard a scuffling in the cupboard where he kept the canisters of kerosene; he was sure Waldo was there, reading the Bible by the faint light which came through the high slit of a window, holding the book up and shaping the words with his lips. But his mind was no longer on Waldo. He was of a mind to carry Moll in his arms to some place beside the lake, and there dig a grave for her in some sweet and sheltered place, and so he fussed about the bedroom, wanting her to rest there a little longer, arguing with himself about how he would carry her, and all the time he was murmuring endearments: "Dear Moll, pretty Moll—"

At twelve o'clock, when only the faintest shreds of smoky snow were falling, Lem went to the timber shed, and began to sharpen his two-bitted ax, and afterwards he sharpened the cutting edge of his mattock and roped three sapling logs together. Then he carried the sapling logs to the door of the store. He looked anxious, his face lined with sweat, and he would stare across the snow-laden landscape as though afraid someone would come and interrupt him at his labors. He had thought of a place near the lake, not far from a clump of cottonwoods. He went into the bedroom, took a new green blanket from the store-chest and wrapped Moll in it, then carried her to the three logs. She was very stiff in his arms and did not bend. He thought of covering her face with a handkerchief, but she looked strangely peaceful and it occurred to him that she might want to have her last look at the sky. The snow came down on her face, but very lightly.

"It's time, Waldo," Lem said.

Waldo came out of the cupboard, his face redder than ever, his thick beard streaked with sweat.

"You want me?" Waldo said innocently.

"That's right. I called you, didn't I?"

Waldo slipped the Bible into his fathomless pocket.

"You goin' to bury her?"

"Yup."

"Goin' to sled her?"

"No, we're goin' to carry her—you and me. Take up your end, Waldo. Remember, I don't want no hymns, no speeches or sermons. You're coming with me because I want someone to help dig. Understand?"

The muscles of Lem's face were working. There was such a look of authority on him that Waldo did exactly as he was told, taking the end where Moll's feet lay, while Lem took the end which would allow him to look down on her face. At the last moment Lem slid two strips of cord over and under her, below the knees and round the waist, to prevent her from falling off the sapling logs. Then with the sun on their faces they walked down to the lake in a curious jaunty stride, with little shuffling paces, and always careful to keep Moll steady. They walked in such a silence that Lem could no longer believe he was in the world: it was the silence of a dream or nightmare.

It was half an hour before they reached the shores of the lake. Rabbits and birds had left neat tracks in the soft snow: mist buried the hills. Silver came behind them, loping, not barking. The lake was no longer green but white with blue shadows in it, and the wind made patterns on its surface. Sometimes, looking up through the mist, they saw the tepees on the hills and once they saw the orange glow of a fire burning. The brightest thing in all that white landscape was the green blanket thrown over Moll. The only sound was the muffled click of hobnailed boots on snow.

When they reached some cottonwoods after skirting the lake, Lem said, breathing heavily: "We'll put her down here."

"Goin' to bury her here?"

"Yes."

"You can't. There's water under these hills. Bury her here, and she'll be floatin' out into the lake come summer."

"You think so? Then we'll dig higher up."

They went up the hill a little further.

"I don't want you telling me where to put her," Lem said. "Keep your trap shut. She wanted here, and she was all of me, and so we'll put her here."

He was furious because Waldo had made him change the original burial place. His hands clenched and unclenched at his sides. Waldo wore his coat open in the front, like a cape, and the cape flapped in the wind which was beginning to come down the hills, blowing the mist away, and because there was no more snow the lake was turning green again. They set to work, Waldo with the mattock and Lem with the ax. The snow which had fallen on Moll's face was melting. It was so hot, digging the grave, that Lem threw off his coat. He told Waldo not to damage the grass, but to remove it neatly, so that it could be replaced and no one would know there was a grave; and when Silver came near to Moll, the long red tongue lolling, Lem reached out a foot and kicked the hound away.

"You thinkin' of putting a cross up?" Waldo said, when the grave was half dug.

"I don't hold with the cross," Lem answered. "You keep digging, and keep your trap shut as I said. Maybe I'll put up a stone later."

"You could put up a stone in the shape of a cross," Waldo suggested five minutes later.

"I'm fixing to do it my way," Lem said. "I told you to keep your trap shut."

It was hard work, for the ground was frozen and there were heavy stones near the surface. Beside the sapling logs the green squares of turf were propped. From time to time the two men would pause and mop their brows, and sometimes, when Silver came close to Moll, Lem would shy a stone at it with tremendous strength, pleased if he hit the dog. It worried him that wolves or foxes might come near the grave. Waldo was grunting, exerting all his force, mumbling under his breath. During the journey round the lake Lem had found himself silently praying for Moll, but he was praying no longer. Prayer had receded into the distance, like a signpost long passed. He was concerned with other things: whether to stay in Wallowa, whether to keep the store, whether to sleep on the straw bed, whether to go at once to Lewiston and find another woman. He wanted no empty beds. He knew that, and the knowledge did not frighten him. He could look down at the sleeping face of Moll lying on the logs with the green blanket drawn up to her chin, and he could love her, and at the same time he could be thinking of some other woman. Once, in the middle of digging, he climbed out of the grave and kissed Moll on the forehead, because it seemed to him that she must be lonely waiting there, with the dog howling and the mist coming down the hills, and even while he kissed her, he was thinking: "The new one will have to be mighty good to be the equal of her." Then for a space he fell to brooding about how she had cared for and fed him, and how her hair flowed sweetly over the pillow, and how her warm arms felt around his neck, and then he stubbornly returned to digging, somehow comforted by the sharp sound of ax or mattock on stones. They had been digging for twenty minutes when Lem observed that an Indian was standing on a rise above them.

At first Lem thought the Indian was an apparition, for the mist swirled round him. He was a tall man with a copper-colored face and a single eagle feather in his scalp lock, and wore a heavy grey blanket which looked greasy from having been slung too long over a horse, and there were splashes of color on his moccasined feet. The man looked about forty, and there was grey in his hair, but perhaps this was only snow. He stood unmoving and imperturbable, like a statue, and Lem thought there was more than a hint of refusal on his stern face. A bitter, stubborn wind began to grow through the cottonwoods, and he could see the Indian's blanket flapping and feel the coldness of the wind on his own face, and now the lake turned green in the places where the wind hit it. It was time to lift Moll down into the grave, and he was glad the wind had been stilled while she was resting there. Now he would shelter her, lift her down gently, like someone taking another by the hand into a dark place. He could hardly see because he was choking with sobs. A scurry of mist hid the Indian, so that he was only a ghostly dark shape standing on a knoll above them. Waldo was leaning on his mattock, his lips forming into silent words, his heavy eyelids lowered. Taking care not to touch the blanket, Lem untied the knotted cords around her, and then lifted her. When he was on the edge of the grave he paused and looked up at the stretch of pale blue sky directly above his head, and muttered some words of prayer about how well Moll had cared for him and he prayed the earth would receive her, and no wolves would ever dig her up again, and how she had passed her life in usefulness and goodness, and the earth must be good to her. It was all rambling and there were no words enough to say what he wanted to say. When she lay in the grave, she looked as she had looked on the straw bed, with only a faint wrinkled yellow scar on her cheek to show where she had been burned. Suddenly in a loud voice Waldo said: "Our Father which art in Heaven, hallowed be Thy name—"

"I don't want you saying any prayer for Moll," Lem said quietly, overcome by a sense of desolation, by the knowledge that Moll was there but could not hear what was being said, would never again know the touch of his tenderness. And what were prayers?

"She was a good woman—as good a woman as you'll find," Waldo said. "She's pure and sweet in death as she was in life."

The words, coming from Waldo, were so strange that Lem had to hold himself together.

"What are you saying?" he asked, leaning forward, unable to believe what he had heard.

"I said she was good and sweet, and now she's sitting beneath the throne of God."

"It ain't so," Lem said miserably.

"Then where is she?"

"She's here," Lem said, and he began to collect some loose stones and arrange them around her feet. A strange sickly sweet smell was coming from her. The expanding muscles of her jaw were pushing at the cords he had fastened under her chin. Now for the first time the knowledge that she was really dead came to him. It was not the Moll he knew, but something else. Silver was whimpering, pressing up close to the grave. Lem threw a clod of cold earth, and he smiled when the dog went squealing away with its long tail between its legs. Lem, knowing that Moll would like to stay above the earth a little longer, dawdled. While Waldo wandered away, he heaped small stones around her to protect her in some way: it was like building a small stone house around her, before the earth was placed over her. While he was arranging the stones around her waist, a long gasping sigh came from her mouth which opened a little. Lem turned white, and held on to the edge of the grave for support. The thought that she might be alive had never occurred to him. He put his hand to her face, but it was waxy cold, and there was a sickly white dew on her skin, and there was no color now in her lips, which were pale and bloodless. He hurried on with his work; and having covered all of her body except her face with rubble and earth, he closed his eyes and wondered how he could ever bring himself to pour earth over the face he had kissed so often. Then, steeling himself, he placed a long smooth stone shaped like a slate over her head, and when she had disappeared entirely he worked harder than ever, anxious to get away from the place. He was dripping with sweat, and the wind was turning the cottonwoods white and he could hear the creaking of the boughs. The Indian had come a little closer.

When Lem had put all the slabs of green turf back, he smeared handfuls of snow over the grave and then stood very silent for a while.

"You're in your green dress, Moll," he said. "You're green under the white earth, and you have a house. I'd have left some food for you, too, if I thought you could take it. I'll be watching you. Rest in peace, Moll, and remember I loved you more than anything in the wide world."

He could not trust himself to go on, and stared moodily away in the direction of the lake, which was all white and green now like the grave, with the wind whipping creamy whitecaps and the reeds making a clucking sound. A pale yellow sun was shining through the wastes of mist, and it caught the shining back of Waldo's coat. The sight of Waldo standing under the cottonwoods filled Lem with disgust, and so he began to walk away, sunk in his own thoughts, in the direction of the lake. He was still sunk in his thoughts, wandering aimlessly, when Waldo came hurrying after him.

"Where you going, Lem?" Waldo said, out of breath. "You don't look well. You ought to rest a bit."

"Why?"

"I told you. Because you ain't lookin' well."

"What in hell does it matter how I look, or where I go?" Lem exclaimed, pushing his brother back. "You get out of here! You leave me alone!"

"Ain't you goin' to say the Lord's prayer over her?"

"I'm aiming to say no prayers, Waldo. I've got enough on my mind. You leave me alone!"

"Listen to me, Lem. There's a great deal to talk about. I've been thinkin' a lot about you and Moll. She's innocent as the driven snow. She died for you, just as Jesus died for sorrowing mankind. Do you understand that, Lem?"

"She's dead. Let her be. I don't want you talking about her, not now and not ever!"

"You're being hard, Lem. I've been thinkin' how her death was as you might say ordained. I've been thinking she's left you free to come to Jesus Christ and ask forgiveness of your sins. I've been thinking it's time for you to come to baptism. What do you think, Lem? Why don't you open your heart to Jesus? I could take you to the lake and baptize you in God's holy waters. I could make a cross over your forehead, and it will be for a sign. Won't you let me take you to baptism, Lem?"

"I don't want no baptism," Lem said, glaring. "I don't want no high-flown words. You go your way, and I'll go mine!"

"Don't you want me to stay with you, Lem?"

"No, I don't!"

"You're being hard."

"I aim to be hard. I aim to be hard as iron."

Lem turned away. He could not bear the whining voice any more. He told himself he would have to kill Waldo if the whining did not cease. He looked down at his hands, all wet and muddy with earth, and then he walked swiftly away.

For the rest of the morning and all the afternoon Lem walked in the hills, grateful when the mist came down. Sometimes he caught a glimpse of the lake, peaceful below the hills, and then he would pause and ponder the passing of time. Once he passed close to the lodges and thought of asking for food because he smelt the meat being cooked, but something, some sense of his own dignity, made him pass on.

Towards evening, when his trousers were cut to ribbons by the rocks and there was a hard crust of blood on his hands, he threw himself on the earth, dreaming that Moll was close to him: he had only to put out his hand, and she would be there. The great sun was sinking. He warmed himself in its yellow glare. Dark arrows of shade were beginning to fleck over the lake. He lay on his face, his eyes closed, then he opened them and saw a young Indian girl with swinging braids jumping among the rocks. She wore a doeskin smock decorated with porcupine quills; her leggings and moccasins were of smoked orange-yellow buckskin; her braids were sleek with bear oil; her copper cheeks glowed in the setting sun. It occurred to him she must have wandered away from the lodges in search of the colored stones embedded in the rocks. She was soundless as a young animal. He lay there very still, waiting for her to come close to him. He heard her quick laughter, and saw her long shadow sweeping among the red rocks. He heard the scuffle of her moccasined feet on the slippery rocks, and the whisper of her breathing, and when her shadow fell over him he rose and darted after her, scrambling among the rocks. Once, as she ran from him, she shrieked, and the sound went welling out across the lake, reverberating among the hills. When Lem caught up with her, her eyes were wide-open in terror and she was standing against a smooth rock, the sunset full on her face, and her mouth was wide-open, with the sun lighting up her teeth and her tongue, but no sound came from her now. She saw the expression on Lem's face: it was unlike any expression she had seen before, with misery and a wild hunger running across it. "Come," he said, and lifted her in his arms, and went swinging down the slope. She did not fight him. She lay limp in his arms. She was as soft as Moll, and much lighter. When he reached the pasture he threw her down among the sagebrushes. He was panting. She made a little whimpering sound, like the sound a rabbit makes when it is caught in a springtrap, and then she was still. Then they lay there, sometimes fighting but more often very silent, staring at each other, until the darkness came down; and there was no sign of the lake any more, no hills, no fires burning. He covered her torn deerskin smock with his coat. There was a sharp-pointed stone in his hand. He thought of putting an end to her weeping by bringing it down on her skull, and then he was ashamed. He threw the stone away and heard it streaking among the rocks below, slithering like a smooth pebble over ice, and soon her weeping ceased. The only sound came from the sagebrush waving in the wind.

Afterwards Lem remembered nothing of the journey back to the store except that it was a nightmare, stumbling against rocks, falling to his knees sometimes, and still somehow supporting the girl. He followed no pathways, though he remembered skirting the lake and passing not far from the place where he had buried Moll. The girl breathed heavily, and when he spoke to her she made no answer.

He pushed open the fence gate and went stumbling up the beaten earth path to the store. A crack of light was shining under the door. Lem kicked the door with his boot.

"It's me, Waldo. Open up!"

There was a long pause. Waldo was listening, and then Lem heard him shambling across the room.

"Where've you been, Lem?"

"You open the door, or I'll smash it down, Waldo. I ain't aimin' to wait here all night."

There was the sound of a key being turned, and then a creaking as the rusty iron bar was lifted, then another scurry of feet as Waldo retreated to a safe place back of the store. The door had stuck, and Lem had to kick at it six or seven times before it burst open; then he was half-blinded by the yellow searing light from the stove. He stood on the threshold with the girl in his arms, her head lolling back and her braids touching the floor. In places her leggings and her smock had been torn away, and one small golden breast shone in the stove light. She looked more beautiful then than Lem had ever hoped she would be. Waldo was standing at the back of the store like a great bear ready to charge. His voice came shrill, filling the store. The girl was moaning.

"You killed her! Yes, you killed her, Lem! She's dead, ain't she? Oh, for the love of God, Lem, put her away."

"She ain't dead and she ain't hurt even," Lem said, laying her gently on some sacking near the stove.

"You ain't goin' to bring her in here," Waldo screamed. "No, you ain't. What you done to her?"

"Nothing she didn't want."

Waldo looked at the girl, her doeskin smock torn and thrown up, and her leggings which had been twisted off her and were now wrapped loosely round her knees. Her belly was a soft brown, and he caught a glimpse of bruised breasts. It was as though Lem was deliberately bringing in some obscene young animal. It was an affront to Moll, and to God. Waldo's mouth fell open as though an immense trap had opened up, and he backed against the wall, screaming: "It's all filth—every bit of it!"

"Filth, is it? Well, I'm aimin' to keep it here. She's sweet and lovely as a flower, and you call it filth."

Waldo turned his face to the wall, shouted something Lem could not understand, and then fell into a fit of sobbing. The girl lifted herself up and crouched there, and Waldo took one hurried glance at the naked brown girl crouching there and screamed louder, like an animal at bay. Lem struck him. Shadows wheeled. The stove light played on the soft warm body of the girl, but against the wall Lem and Waldo were struggling in the darkness. The girl smiled and bared her teeth; life was coming back to her, and she understood that Lem was fighting for her. She saw Lem's arms rising and falling with short jabbing punches, and then Waldo fell to the floor. Lem pulled him up, and punched him again, and all the time Waldo's hands were covering his face.

"Shades of Night!" Waldo was croaking. "Shades of Night be upon you for your screamin' sins!"

V

Hootenanie

THE next day the autumn gales broke loose over the land, with high piercing winds and sheets of snow flapping against the hills. The days were cold and damp, the fog coming over the lake in the afternoons and welling up into the hills, and you could see nothing except the vapory ghosts of the mountains through the fog, and hear nothing except the crying of gulls. Afterwards there came a week of rain, and soon it was winter with long days of calm and week-long mists covering the earth, hiding the peaks. Autumn and winter came so hurriedly that the Indians had no time to prepare their annual journey to the hunting fields. They postponed the journey to November, and there were some who said they would spend the whole year in Wallowa.

In the hut the Indian girl took Moll's place and wore Moll's clothes, and shared Lem's shelter and his bed. She had dark eyes and a delicately curved jawbone; though her face was dark copper, her skin under the clothes was a warm golden brown. Moll had never really been a girl; had always behaved like a woman, with a woman's composure and sureness, slow-moving always. But this girl was quick as a bird, strong and lean, with small buttocks and the breasts of a sixteen-year-old. Lem never knew her age, and never asked about it. It was enough that she was there, filling his winter, brown against the bed sheets, free with her kisses. She would lie there, all warm and brown, spread-eagled on the bed, arms and legs outstretched, so that she looked a little like an immense golden spider, and then somehow—Lem never quite knew how it happened—she would hurl herself on him from the bed even when he was shuffling round the room. There was always a glint of defiance in her dark eyes. She was happy with him, though she sometimes scratched him with her nails. Though he had known happiness with Moll, this was something else, something more than happiness.

She was as young and impudent as a young animal with her shining teeth, her firm flesh, her long greasy braids which she would tie round his neck at night so that he could not move away from her, and her way of gazing up at him stealthily, as though about to spring.

Lem called her Shades of Night, remembering the day when he raped her and brought her into the hut.

From the beginning Shades of Night was wary of Waldo. She would sometimes turn her face away when Waldo spoke to her or else she would search deep in the eyes of the huge bearded man who knew no word of her language, and she would do this with a steadiness which made Waldo wilt.

Sometimes, when Lem was fast asleep in the bedroom, exhausted by love-making, Shades of Night would come naked into the store, brushing past Waldo, then crouching over the great yellow mouth of the stove, her young body glowing in the flames, the softest and silkiest thing Waldo had ever set eyes on. She hardly knew what she was doing. She knew she was tempting him with her beauty, and yet the knowledge meant nothing to her, for she was barely conscious of his presence and behaved exactly as though he was not there, rubbing her hands all over her body, smiling and stretching in the warmth of the flames, an unthinking animal who would grow to maturity soon and put these games away. Waldo watched, his mouth slobbering. Ah, she was fruit! Ah, he had only to touch her and— He did not know what would happen if he touched her, did not dare think of it, his nose running with tubes of bluish-grey snot, his beard awry. Then when she had warmed herself by the stove Shades of Night would go scampering back to the bed, pushing Lem aside, for inevitably in her absence he occupied the middle, and sprawled there contentedly.

During the days of Moll's illness all the life had gone from Lem's face. Now the color came surging back, the lips were ruddy, and his eyes looked as though spring water had been dropped on them. He took more care of his appearance, trimmed his nails, combed his hair, rubbed salt on his teeth, and smiled easily. He walked with loose loping strides, and he would burst out into happy laughter at the sight of Shades of Night. Even the presence of Waldo would move him to laughter. He liked taunting his brother.

"You don't like her, do you?" Lem said once when they were eating dinner and the kerosene lamp was spluttering low. "You don't like her being with me, do you? You don't like what she's doing to the shack, an' what she does in bed at night, an' the way she walks, an' all."

Saying this, Lem smiled at the girl, her doeskin tunic, her strange fawn-colored eyes and shining red lips, who smelt of fresh soap and watched every movement he made as though she was about to pounce on him.

"You don't like it, do you?" Lem shouted.

"I can't say I do."

"But you're going to take it?"

"Yes, Lem," Waldo said, and suddenly his whole face collapsed as if he was about to cry, and the eyes seemed to splinter into sharp glassy fragments. "Flesh and blood can't stand—"

"What can't they stand, Waldo? Go on. Answer me. What can't they stand?"

Waldo sat there with his face wrinkling up like the skin of a crab apple, as it always did when he was sobbing quietly to himself. He did not know how to fight them. His nose was running, and he rubbed the long tube of snot with the back of his hand and lowered his head.

"Go on, answer me, Waldo. You wouldn't say you were a purty sight, would you?"

"No."

"God knows you're not—not by a long chalk!"

"I ain't a beauty. I was born this way, Lem, and I can't help it, but it ain't outward appearances that find favor in the sight of God. I've a treasure up in Heaven waiting for me. Remember that."

"I didn't ask you to talk, did I?"

"No, Lem, you didn't."

"Then don't talk unless I ask you—"

"I'm a sick man, Lem."

"Christ, I don't remember a time when you weren't sick: sick in body and mind. I've seen you watching Shades, and there's sickness in your mind when you watch her. I reckon you're sick in mind and past curing."

Waldo shuddered. There had been many short arguments with Lem, but this was the worst. Shades of Night was smiling, but there was no comfort in her smile. The kerosene lamp was burning low. Waldo felt the hostility coming out of them in waves. He would have to go soon. He knew that. But where would he go? Craftily, hardly knowing what he was doing, he drew the small walnut crucifix from under his coat.

He thought that if he held it up to them, then they would know the power of God, the terrible and heartbreaking power of the living God imprisoned in a walnut stick. A childlike smile played on his face. He inched the cross across the table, half covering it with his hairy hands. He raised it a little, so that they could see the crosspiece protruding above his knuckles, and all the time his eyes were shining and the sweat shone blue on his cheeks. He wanted to shout: "There it is! There's God! The Indians don't believe in Him, but you will! Take Him to your heart, Lem, while there's still time!"

Shades of Night, fascinated by the slow progress of the stick of wood across the table, fascinated by the triumphant and rapturous expression of Lem's brother, who was so totally unlike Lem, fascinated above all by the way the cross quivered and jerked and rose slowly through his knuckles, turned her face sharply away. It was medicine—strong medicine. All round her the air seemed to be shaking, and sometimes the flame of the kerosene lamp was so low that there was only a small tender bubble of flame. Waldo trembled. Inch by inch the hand pushed across the table, and the little cross was quivering with a life of its own. Waldo was playing for high stakes: Lem's salvation, but not only Lem's salvation. It might happen that he would be able to put an end to the distrust surrounding him. He must act quickly, triumphantly. "Oh, come naked to the foot of the cross," Waldo whispered; and he imagined himself standing in the other world of his imagination, standing above Lem, waving the cross above him, exorcising the devils.

Lem's arm shot across the table, but Waldo was too quick for him.

"Give me that bloody stick!" Lem said.

"No, Lem. It belongs to God. You can't take it from me."

Waldo jumped up, knocking his chair over. Lem marched up to him, twisted his arm behind his back until the walnut cross fell to the floor, then he went straight to the stove and dropped the cross in. Shades of Night was laughing. They heard the cross crackling in the stove. Waldo had fallen in the corner, his great shoulders heaving.

"Poor Waldo," Lem said. "He don't know I've done the kindest thing I could for him—he just don't know."

It was November now, and the Indians were still in their lodges on the uplands. There was warm weather again, though the snow was piling up and the lake was dead white, frozen. But though the earth was white, the heavens were blue and a warm wind was springing up. Soon there was a thaw, and they heard the rustling of the waters trickling down the slopes towards the lake. As though it was high summer, the young braves went riding down to the lake, bathing in the ice-cold water, and from the shack you could hear their laughter and the hoofbeats of their ponies clear and sharp in the winter air.

Once, early in November, Lem rode down to tend Moll's grave. Snow lay heaped on the sunken rocks. The Indians had placed colored stones there, and there were sticks of pine with little bits of colored cloth waving at the corners. Seeing this grave, no more than a hundred yards away from the lake, where the ice was cracking, Lem choked with emotion. It was strange how he still loved Moll, how she returned in dreams. She slept soundly. Soft she was, and sweet-smelling as new-mown hay, but Shades was like the young grasses which come after the spring rains, strong and firm as the white roots of grasses. All afternoon Lem spent beside the grave. When he returned it was dusk, and there was a strawberry roan standing outside the fence rail. Inside the store Lieutenant Stevens was leaning over the pine counter. Lem entered silently. Stevens was talking rapidly in Indian language. Shades was laughing, showing her teeth. It was dark in the store, the kerosene lamp unlit. Shades was wearing a buttercup yellow dress belonging to Moll. She was leaning forward, her face almost touching the lieutenant's. Lem gasped. It had never happened to him before that he had seen Shades talking to some other man. Waldo wasn't a man; Waldo was a sore-tailed bear. When the Indians came to the store, Shades busied herself in the bedroom: it was as though she felt obscurely guilty for living with a white man.

"What are you doing?" Lem shouted from the doorway. "What in hell are you doing?"

The voice echoed against the timbers. The lieutenant turned round smartly.

"I'm buying tobacco, Mr. Otis."

"Buy your tobacco some other place," Lem roared. "Keep away from here."

The lieutenant smiled, caught Shades' eye and then turned smartly on his heels.

"I came for a friendly visit, Mr. Otis. I've got nothing against you and you've got nothing against me."

"That's what you say. Now get out!"

The lieutenant walked slowly out of the store. Shades was smiling still, showing her teeth, her face lifted towards the light coming through the open door. She watched the lieutenant as he mounted his roan, and she was still watching him through the door as he rode away.

"You don't have to be rude," Shades said, when Lem came up beside her.

He kissed her roughly, holding her in his arms, pressing her until he could feel her ribs bending under his weight.

"Ah, Jesus," he said. "I can't help myself. I'll kill you if you look at another man. I don't want you ever to leave my side. I found you, didn't I—that's why there's a God. Yes, there's a God, even though Waldo says it. Don't ever leave my side."

Then he lifted her in his arms and carried her into the bedroom.

That night he was more savage with her than he had ever been. Listening outside, Waldo heard him shouting, and sometimes there would be a terrified little squeal from Shades, and the straw bed creaked, and it was dark in the store. The next morning Waldo was surprised to hear them chattering away like magpies.

Because the Indians were remaining for the winter, there was more trade than usual. The braves came for necklaces and beads, rolls of calico, bolts of cotton cloth, saddles, steel chips, shagbark and kerosene; most of all they came for salt and tallow. They liked to bargain, and Lem was patient with them. He liked them more than ever, remembering the little strips of cloth and the colored stones from the uplands they had placed on Moll's grave. Now trade flourished as never before, for the tribes were rich this year: rich enough to have bought a new beef herd. They paid in gold dust, skins and coins, and they liked to remain long after they had made a purchase. Lem felt no jealousy when they talked to Shades. He knew that these handsome Indians, who rode half-naked even in the coldest weather, had no attraction for her. His stocks were running low. He decided to close the store, and make a quick journey to Lewiston. It was Shades who whispered to him that he might bring back some firewater: the braves had asked for it.

"It's against the law," Lem explained patiently. "I don't aim to go against the law."

"You could get a little," Shades said, smiling.

He did the journey to Lewiston in less than three days, and in a week he was back at the store with eight cases of whisky concealed in the false bottom of the spring-cart. Shades went with him, delighted to be sitting up there: she sang and chattered all the way, and when they passed through the villages, Lem was pleased with the approving stares.

He gave out the whisky grudgingly, always demanding a vow of secrecy. The Indians would slip into the store at night, softly closing the door after them. They sipped the small cups he offered them, squatting on the floor, and Lem enjoyed their conviviality, their bursts of song. His conscience did not weigh on him. They had asked for whisky, and he was prepared to dole it out in harmless quantities. He drank nothing himself. Then one night, four days after his return from Lewiston, a young brave called Yellow Bear taunted him for not drinking. Lem laughed, said he hated the damned stuff, he had brought it only because the Indians asked for it, and by God, he wouldn't let them have more than a few drops. It was against the law, wasn't it? Yellow Bear wore an immense yellow feather in his scalp lock. He had discarded the blanket with the crazy yellow patterns he habitually wore, and wearing only a breechclout he looked, with the sweat rippling off his smooth skin, like a young god. Yellow Bear had a habit of talking with his eyes half-closed. He had something of Shades of Night's impudence. There were about ten other young Indians. They were all chanting softly, most of them maudlin drunk, crowded round the stove. A few were leaning against the pine counter, holding their heads up with their hands, a blissful expression on their faces.

Suddenly Yellow Bear jumped up and began to dance. It was a slow dance, mostly posturing, bending the body backwards and forwards while making little shuffling steps. The flames from the stove licked the muscles of his legs. The other braves began to chant in time with the music which Yellow Bear was bellowing softly. They clapped their hands or beat against the walls. Soon they were all dancing, shouting and posturing. Lem told them to keep quiet. They paid no attention to him. Shades of Night slipped from behind the counter and began to dance and posture with them. She held her head erect. Her eyes were closed, and she kept waving her hands in a strange rhythmical way, and she bent her knees and shuffled and began singing. It was a song Lem had never heard before. She was among her own people, lost among them, dancing, wearing one of Moll's dresses—a long shapeless red garment which did nothing to conceal the vivid body beneath, for somehow you were never made aware of the dress, only of the young limbs and the belly and the way the breasts pushed through the dress, so that the shapeless dress revealed every part of her. Yellow Bear removed his yellow feather and placed it in her hair. The braves who had not slidden out of their blankets now threw them away. Soon, instead of chanting softly, they were howling like coyotes. Yellow Bear led the dance. He reached over, removed the kerosene lamp from the hook and waved it over his head, and now the chanting grew louder than ever. Shades of Night never touched any of the other Indians. There was always a wide space between them, and yet Lem was perfectly aware that an intimacy had grown between them. It was startling, how close they could be to one another. It was as though they were entering each other's spirit. Sweat streamed from them. Though their eyes were staring and unseeing, they each postured in exactly the same way. Watching them, Lem found himself lifting an abandoned cup of whisky to his lips. He drank it straight off. There was the smell of sweat and wood smoke. Waldo was sleeping in a corner. Lem drank a second cup of whisky, and prepared to pour out a third. He watched Shades of Night with his mouth open. "What has come over you?" he wanted to say, but the words stuck in his throat.

"You all go straight back!" Lem shouted hoarsely. "I've had enough."

No one paid any attention to him. The dancing went on, wilder than ever, no longer shuffling. They made great leaps in the air, twisted their bodies, bent down to pick imaginary objects from the floor, and still there was that space between them, and still there was this extraordinary intoxication of the dance, as though they had been caught up into another world.

"You come out of it!" Lem said, throwing out his arms towards Shades of Night.

Something extraordinary was happening. It seemed to him that Shades of Night was gradually being removed from him. Soon she would return to her tribe. There was a rapturous expression on her face. She was panting now, and her breasts rose and fell, and there were stains of sweat on the shapeless red gown.

"What's going on?" Lem shouted. "You've all got to go back—please go back."

He went up to Yellow Bear and stood in front of him. Yellow Bear was still dancing, one hand resting on his knee, the other holding the kerosene lamp above his head. There was a strangely secretive smile on his face, and the sweat was running down him in rivers. Yellow Bear must have thought Lem was simply a shadow standing in his way. He knocked against Lem, and continued dancing.

"It's all my fault," Lem thought. "If I hadn't given them the whisky they wouldn't be dancing like this." He shouted at the top of his voice: "You all get out of here! Get out fast! I don't want your bare faces hanging out here!"

Lem went back of the counter and carefully inserted six bullets in his Colt revolver. He did not know what he was doing. He shouted to them to stop, and waved the revolver, and because they did not stop he screamed all kinds of meaningless words at them. Once Yellow Bear nodded to him. It infuriated Lem that Yellow Bear should glance at him and pay no attention to his words. He pulled on the trigger. He saw a little red mark appear on Yellow Bear's back, then there was another, and then another, and the dancing was still going on; only Yellow Bear was slowly lowering the kerosene lamp. The lamp fell with a crash on the floor, and the oil spilled over the sawdust. Even then, for a few moments, the dancing went on. Lem kept shooting until the chambers were empty, and he had not the faintest idea what he was doing, or why he was doing it. He knew only that the dancing had to stop.

Yellow Bear lurched to the floor. He tried to rise. Blood was flowing from the small holes in his back. Then he moaned, and both his hands went to his back as though he wanted to pull the bullets out.

The young braves crowded round Yellow Bear, too drunk, too lost in the dance to realize completely what had happened. Shades of Night was leaning against the counter, covering her face with her hands. They turned the body over, saw that he was dead, and began to groan.

One by one, drawing their blankets around them, hushed and shivering, they filed out into the night. Soon the only sounds came from the roaring stove and the loud battering of the hoofbeats of the ponies as they rode towards the lodges on the uplands.

An hour later Lem wrapped the body of Yellow Bear in a buffalo robe, one of those robes which he had bought off the Indians. Early in the morning, when the first shoots of light were springing over the mountains, he carried the body to the cottonwoods and buried it; then he returned to the store and fell into a heavy sleep.

VI

The Body under the Leaves

THE news of the murder and the burial in the cottonwoods became quickly known.

In the lodges the chiefs discussed it at length, sitting in council, shaking their heads. Everyone knew Yellow Bear, the son of a Cayuse mother and a Nez Perce father. They knew he had committed no crime; it was the others who had danced and gone berserk in the little store down by the creek, for the young braves spoke at length of what had happened there and they made no excuses for themselves. The chiefs felt no particular animosity against Lem. They thought him the best of the traders, and they knew he lived with an Indian squaw. But three days after the murder, at the order of old Chief Joseph, some braves came riding up to the store. They dismounted, forced their way in, looked for whisky, and when they found a few bottles in the locker, they came out and solemnly smashed the bottles against the fence rail, while Lem looked on. Lem expected they would attack him, but instead they treated him with respect.

"I couldn't help myself," Lem muttered when they were gone. "I didn't want them drinking so much—they went clean off their heads. I shouldn't have killed Yellow Bear. I didn't want to. It's not my fault. You go crazy when you are living in someone else's territory, and that's all there is to it."

Lem was grief-stricken. He remembered little of what had happened on the night of the murder. The murder had occurred during the last days of November, and soon the Indians would be making their annual journey to the Imnaha. He wondered where to go. He couldn't stay. When Shades of Night told him that he could stay if he wanted to, the Indians would not raise a hand against him, he said shuddering: "God in Heaven, they could wipe me clean off the earth, couldn't they?"

"We'll stay," Shades of Night said quietly, pursing her lips. She had thought it out. She knew what the Indians were thinking. Waldo smiled secretively.

"So you think you're staying?" he asked.

"I reckon so. We'll see. It's another winter ahead, and I don't like for us to be winterin' here, but maybe—"

"Maybe what?"

"Maybe you can go to hell! Clear out now—that's the best!"

"You don't mean it," Waldo laughed into his beard, and then his voice took on a whining tone. "No, you don't mean it, Lem. You hold on—hold on to what you've got. We'll hold on together, eh?"

"We'll see," Lem said shortly. "We'll hold on to the devil's tail most likely."

He was glad when Waldo went lurching out, grunting. He had changed. There were long lean lines drawn over his face, and deep crescents under his eyes, and he spoke more slowly now, unsure of himself. One evening the long column began to move out of the lodges, and Lem stood on a rise watching it go. It was dusk with a blue moon, and the feathered headdresses swept past the lake like the horns of a huge herd of cattle during a midnight lightning storm; and when they had gone, he felt lonelier than ever, with an ache in his heart for what he had done.

The day after the long column set out for the Imnaha Valley, Lieutenant Stevens, riding a strawberry roan, came galloping up the slope. The lieutenant saluted and asked if he could come in for a talk. It was one of those high, bright mornings when the sweep of the sky was all chalky blue, very pure and sweet. A hawk was sailing over the lake, and sometimes a freshet of wind would come streaming across the grasses. The lieutenant tethered the roan to the gatepost, remaining outside the fence rail until Lem nodded and said: "As long as you're not looking for trouble, you c'n do what you damned well please."

"Then I can come in?"

"That's what I said, didn't I?"

Lem had been helping Shades of Night in the vegetable garden he was growing outside the store. It was a sign that they had decided to weather it out.

The lieutenant strode towards the store, taking everything in. Lem had seen him only twice before, when he had carried Waldo back from the lake and when he had come to buy tobacco and chat with Shades of Night; but that was at night. It was some time before Lem recognized that it was the same man. With the mattock in his hand, a fur cap pulled low over his forehead, his red beard jutting out, Lem waited for the man to come up close, standing in front of Shades of Night to protect her. Waldo was in the store. Nowadays Lem stayed as long as possible outside the store, for whenever his eyes took in the pine counter he would remember every detail of the strange scene on the night of the murder. Seeing the lieutenant, his heart sank. He knew there would be trouble.

"It's a fine day for planting," the lieutenant said, and Lem watched him warily, wondering whether there was any inner meaning to the remark.

"You haven't come to talk about plantin'?" Lem said, his face haggard with suspicion.

"Not exactly."

"What do you mean—not exactly?"

"Let's go into the store."

"We can talk here as well as any place," Lem said sternly. "There's nothing wrong with here."

Stevens took out his cigar case and offered Lem a cigar. Shades of Night had been standing behind Lem, and now she came out of hiding. She was wearing a yellow blouse and the long heliotrope skirt which reached to her feet. Her hair fell in long black braids; there was a beaded chaplet round her forehead. She looked worried, but her eyes glinted in defense of her man. It was strange to see her wearing a white woman's clothes, for she was not built for them. Her skirt was made for wider hips, and her blouse was fluffed out. Only her young oval face, with its pure lines, and the steady glinting dark eyes, and the brownness of her told you she was a squaw.

The store door was half-open. Stevens peered in. Lem had refused the cigar, and now all his sense of privacy was outraged by the behavior of the lieutenant whose blue coat and blue hat with a yellow cord wound round it suggested a bureaucrat paid to interfere in the lives of others.

"What do you trade in mostly?" Stevens asked pleasantly.

"Tobacco, cloth, wool blankets, steel chips, things like that," Lem said.

Stevens nodded. The store looked plain enough: there was little wealth there.

"Do you think to stay hereabouts?" Stevens asked, dead serious. He made a little gesture with his hands to show he was no longer interested in examining the store.

"I reckon there's no harm in staying. My squaw says to stay. She wouldn't say that unless she knew."

"Knew what?"

"Knew as how the Indians—well, they ain't against me. It just couldn't be helped. They were drunk. I couldn't get 'em to leave the store."

"So you shot them?"

"No, lieutenant, I don't know what happened. We don't have to go into this, do we? If I'd done anything wrong, the Indians would have killed me, wouldn't they? But they didn't. They went. Seems to me they could have killed me mighty quick if they had a mind to. So they knew they had done wrong."

Lem spoke haltingly, rubbing his hand across his face, standing there with his feet apart and his wool-lined coat flapping in the wind. There were bright red nerve-spots on his face. He looked like someone who was busily attempting to remember what had happened, but however much he tried, and however often he returned in imagination to the scene of the murder, the less he found. The lieutenant had a worried frown. He could not take his eyes from Shades of Night, who was gazing at him with a suspicion of insolence. She would walk away, and then return, swinging her hips easily and gracefully, a young animal glowing with health, attempting to attract his attention. The lieutenant deliberately turned away from her and looked in the direction of the cottonwoods.

"They say you're the best trader round here," he said after a pause.

"Who told you?"

"The Indians."

"Well, there won't be much tradin' now. Winter's settin' in. I don't cheat the Indians. I'm a fair trader. I'm glad you told me they think I'm fair. I'm stayin'. I reckon I won't ever leave Wallowa. There won't be any more trouble. I promise that. I've had my fair share of it these last days. I don't sleep nights. I've tried all my life to behave well, I've kept out of the calaboose, and so help me God, I intend to keep out of it."

"Have you got a spade?" the lieutenant asked sharply.

"What in hell do you want a spade for?" Lem exploded, and suddenly his face became bleak and cruel and his eyes, which were bloodshot, took on a crafty look.

"I'm going to dig up Yellow Bear, and I'm going to get you to help me."

Lem whistled for Silver, and when the dog came pounding out of the lumber pile, he bent low and frisked it, saying: "Good dog, lie down, that's right, you're a friend to me." His voice was low and breaking. Still bending down over the dog, Lem said: "I'm sorry you're going to do a thing like that, mister. You won't find an Indian who thinks any the worse of me for what I have done. I couldn't help it, could I?"

"Maybe not."

"Then why dig the poor fellow up? I shot him. I'm not denying it. I'd give everything I have to—"

He did not go on. Waldo had shuffled out, and he was watching the scene with a look of benign amusement, nodding his head, uncurling his lips until his teeth shone in a fixed smile. Shades of Night's mouth was wide-open. She did not understand the words they were saying, but from their expressions she understood their meaning. The lieutenant tried to put her out of his mind. He told himself he was after justice, and the girl's presence was purely incidental. When her gaze fell on him, he could not prevent himself from blushing, thinking of the brown body under the blouse and the blue skirt.

"I'm sorry, Mr. Otis," Stevens heard himself saying. "I've got my duty to perform. The Territory doesn't approve of the killing of Indians any more than it approves of the killing of white men."

"You reckonin' to arrest me?"

"I've got to see the body first, Mr. Otis. This isn't something I want to do. I want to know how he was shot, and what's at the back of it all. You'll have to show me where you buried him. Maybe I could find some Indians up at the lodges who'd be able to tell me—"

Lem had an impulse to shout: "Find him yourself," but instead he continued to ruffle the rough coat of Silver, bending his head low, talking to Silver because it took his mind from the lieutenant. Shades of Night was smiling at the young lieutenant, and Lem thought: "Curse her smiles! But she is doing it for my sake, she wants him to go and so she smiles at him." Squatting, he rocked backwards and forwards on his feet, and sometimes he would glance up at the lieutenant with an expression which said: "I'll wait my time. I don't know what you're up to." There was a spade leaning against the store wall. The lieutenant swung it up and threw it over his shoulder, and made for the fence gate. Lem bit at a greasy plug of tobacco and said: "I'll come with you."

"I'm glad you've changed your mind."

"I ain't changed my mind. I don't want you messin' about in the cottonwoods without me being there."

A strange procession began to wind its way towards the cottonwoods: the lieutenant riding on his roan with the spade over his shoulder followed by Lem, Shades of Night and Waldo on foot. When they were deep in the shadowy cottonwoods, Lem pointed to the place where he had buried the young brave. It was covered with brush. For a while no one said anything. They simply stared down at the place where, in the early morning, Lem had feverishly dug a grave single-handed. Shades of Night clung to Lem. Waldo stood a little way back, a fixed smile on his face. Stevens cleared the brush away with his boots, and when the outline of the grave was visible he began to dig cautiously at the edges. They were all silent, and the only sounds came from the scraping of the spade in the soft earth, the heavy breathing of Lem and the neighing of the roan. When the spade touched the edge of the buffalo robe, Stevens looked up sharply to observe their expressions, but their faces told him nothing: only, on Shades of Night's face, there was a fleeting expression of fear.

The buffalo robe was dark brown now, stained with earth oils, with sap and frost and snow. There had been a heavy frost during the week, and when Stevens unwrapped the robe to disclose the body of Yellow Bear, he was surprised to see how well preserved it was. Some of the skin had peeled off and turned green, but the face was recognizable. A sickly sweet smell hung over the grave, but there was no wind and Waldo, standing ten yards away, was unaware of the smell. Yellow Bear's face bore an expression of slight surprise, and he looked younger in death than he looked in life, and from loss of blood much thinner.

Stevens sketched the body hurriedly. The wounds were dark lozenges against the coppery flesh. He first sketched the body as it lay on its back, and then turned the body over gently. Then he gave a long low whistle.

"Was he shot in the back, Mr. Otis?"

"Yes."

"Then you are under arrest," Stevens said sorrowfully. He finished the second sketch and covered the body with the robe. Lem was too dazed to speak. Without a word they began to bury the brave. The wind stirred in the cottonwoods. Yellow mud was lying at the bottom of the grave; and when they had covered the body over, and stood there in silence, they could hear the sucking sound of the mud round the body; and this was strange, for when they opened the grave, it was hard with frost. Lem shivered and buttoned his coat tightly round his neck, and his hand sought for Shades of Night, but she was standing away from him, lost in thoughts of her own. Then he turned in the direction of the shack, walking slowly and dragging his heels.

The lieutenant rode beside him. There was yellow mud and some wet grasses on his boots. Lem kept looking down at his boots, and did not see the lieutenant towering above him on the roan.

"It's plain murder," the lieutenant said sadly.

"You're hard, lieutenant," Lem whispered. "If I had done what you said, wouldn't the Indians have wiped me off the earth?"

"You don't deny you shot him in the back?"

"I don't know what happened," Lem said miserably. "I just don't know. Guess I must have taken a drink or two. I don't remember shooting him. I liked him. Tell you the truth, I liked Yellow Bear best of the bunch."

"Yet you shot him—six bullets plumb in his back. Well, you'll have to tell your side of it to the judge. You'll get a fair trial, be able to choose your own lawyer, and call witnesses. They won't put you in the calaboose. They put you up in a hotel. The judge is Shillitoe. Heard of him?"

"Sure."

"He's got a reputation for being fair-minded, Mr. Otis."

Lem clutched at straws. At the name "Shillitoe" the briefest of smiles lit his face. Shades of Night had slipped up behind, and was now holding his hand. He smiled and turned to her and then looked straight up at the young lieutenant.

"What happens to my squaw?" he asked. "What happens to her? I'm not aimin' to leave her here."

"She can go with you. Maybe you won't be able to see her all the time, but you'll be allowed to talk with her. She's a material witness."

A little later Lem was piling luggage on the spring-cart. The warm wind was stirring on the grasses, which were beginning to break through the snow; and on the white landscape the lake below resembled a blue bruise. With Waldo and Shades of Night beside him, Lem headed for Lewiston. With his pistol cocked, riding a little behind them, Stevens was smiling. He smiled because the wind was in his mouth, and the yellow sun was threading through the overcast sky.

"A nice day for a ride," Lem said, turning and spitting into the road.

In all the three days of journeying it was the only time he addressed the lieutenant directly.

VII

The Trial

THE air was full of smoke because some cottonwoods had burned the previous day, and all over Lewiston there was drifting white ash. It came through the hotel windows, and settled on the tall split-seat hickory chairs and over the bar counter and on the cotton bedspreads; and Waldo, who took the bedroom next to Lem's, called it a sign and a visitation, but he wouldn't say what it was a sign of. Lem had asked Judge Josh Stamps to defend him, and promised the attorney a hundred and fifty dollars for acquittal, "and there will be more if you make it neat."

"What's neat, Mr. Otis?" Judge Stamps asked, chewing on a cigar and smiling his slow smile. He was short and fat, and looked like a small black bear. There was a bottle of whisky between them, set up on a small decorated marble table. "What's neat, eh?" Judge Stamps repeated, pouring the whisky softly into his glass.

"Neat's done quick and over with," Lem said impatiently, rubbing his red-rimmed eyes. "Curse the ash of Lewiston, I say."

"We all say the same, Mr. Otis."

"You ought to say it better'n me. You've got power of words, ain't you? Ashes everywhere—couldn't see or sleep for ashes, and Waldo's been thumbing through the good book, looking up every damn place where ashes is. Christ Almighty, there'll be ashes in the courtroom, just like there's ashes in your beard, Judge. I'm fair sick of ashes."

They had been drinking steadily all morning. In a whisky haze Lem had forgotten about the trial. He didn't feel like a prisoner. Sometimes he would remember Lieutenant Keff Stevens and curse under his breath, or else he would peer up at Waldo and wonder why they weren't back at the store in Wallowa. Josh Stamps talked as though Judge Shillitoe would release him within five minutes of the beginning of the trial, but there was no comfort in Josh Stamps. Lem drank down a tumbler of whisky: there was a thin scum of white ashes floating on the surface.

Waldo was saying: "You shouldn't drink, Lem. God's watchin' over you."

"I know He's watchin' me. I'm fair sick and tired of Him watchin' me. Don't you bring God into this, Waldo."

"God's in this right up to His neck," Waldo said, and there was a contented smirk on his face.

The sunlight poured into the bedroom; little tongues of fire were leaping from the brass bedrails.

Josh Stamps was saying: "You'll be ready at nine sharp. Remember, the court doesn't want you to have any communication with your squaw. Of course, the court won't do nothing to prevent you sleepin' with her." At the door Josh Stamps turned and said: "One more question. What church do you hold membership in?"

"What church? I don't belong to no church."

"Then I'll put you down as Episcopalian," Josh Stamps said, and then he was gone, and Lem was alone in the small bedroom with the terrible wallpaper in the Luna House Hotel, and there was an armed guard provided by the court pacing the worn carpet outside.

"Episcopalian," Lem murmured, and shook his head, dumb and miserable now that he was left alone with his sorrow. He shivered uncontrollably. He hated Josh Stamps, but he knew he would hate any other lawyer more. The only good news was the news about Judge Shillitoe, a kindly man in a nightshirt, a kerosene lamp in one hand, a shotgun in the other. Lem shook his head in the dazed way of a swimmer who has dived too deep and comes to the surface far from the place he intended.

That night he slept fitfully. Like everyone else he knew the legends of the hotel: how nearly everyone who was ever put on trial on a serious charge was put in a room on the upper floor of the hotel, and how they used to hold trials downstairs in the saloon bar, and on the way to the bar the prisoner would pass a room with a half-open door: if he peered into the room, he would see a rope hanging from a beam and a soapbox immediately underneath the rope. Prisoners had been known to scream their confessions the moment they saw the rope. Well, he had confessed already, told Stevens everything he knew, and they could do their damnedest. But though he felt strong enough to defy the whole crowd of judges, lawyers, attorneys and guards, he suffered from inexplicable shivering fits all night, and woke up early in a cold sweat.

As he walked to the courthouse, a long low log cabin overlooking the Clearwater, Lem's hands were not bound, but the guard kept pushing a pistol into the small of his back. A crowd was flocking to the courthouse, and when people pressed forward to take stock of Lem, he nodded pleasantly and jutted his chin. At one end of the courthouse there was a rostrum for the judge, a table, a few cane-bottom chairs and a jury box of plain unpolished pine with benches running all the way across. With Judge Stamps Lem took his place below the judge's rostrum. "The sheriff's a fellow called Clerkwell—ain't much of a clerk," Judge Stamps whispered. "Comes from Alabama."

"He does, does he?"

"Most of our lawyers come sure enough from the South, Mr. Otis. Seems they do better up here than down there."

"They do, do they?"

"The prosecutor's from the South, too. Tennessee. He sure talks like it. Well, keep your wits about you, feller. Think what you're saying—think carefully. Many a man's gone and hanged himself by talking too smart."

Josh Stamps made a little guffaw. He was pleased with himself, catching the eyes of the people who came into the courtroom. He enjoyed crowds, as he enjoyed drinks, always taking doubles on the plea that his character was so weakened by the first one that he was helpless under temptation. There was whisky in his breath when he rose to shake hands with the sheriff, a small man with a bottle nose and a flapping dewlap. Lem was fascinated by the appearance of the small cowlike man with the Alabama accent. Then Judge Shillitoe came sweeping in from behind a black curtain, so fat that he seemed to be bursting through the seams of his silk gown. The sheriff began pounding the table with a wooden gavel.

"Court's ready, folks," he shouted above the hubbub. "Take your places quietly. Don't want to hear no one crackin' melon seeds—judge's order."

"Where are the witnesses, Mr. Clerkwell?" the judge bent down.

The whispering between the judge and the sheriff went on. The jury filed in, lean men from the mines, an old shopkeeper with wooden teeth, the local banker with a gold chain dangling over his waist. On the chain hung his house keys. The judge spat carefully into the spittoon beside him, then wiped his mouth. There was a great deal of rattling of papers. Then: "Proceed, Mr. Clerkwell."

The sheriff cleared his throat, drew himself up to his full height, glanced at a slip of paper, frowned, lowered his head and leaned towards Lem.

"What's your name?" asked the sheriff.

"Lem Otis, sir."

"Where was yuh born?"

"Fayetteville, Oregon, sir."

"How old are yuh?"

"Twenty-eight, sir."

"And you reside at the trading post at Wallowa Creek, is that right?"

"It is, sir."

"With your brother, Waldo Otis, and the woman known as Shades of Night?"

"Yes, sir."

"No one else there?"

"No one else—just the three of us, sir."

The sheriff smiled briefly, amused by Lem's downcast gaze, the look of contrition on the rough brown face. It was a look he had not expected to see, and he wondered whether anyone else had noted the strange disparity between Lem's eyes and the rest of the face. The eyes, red-rimmed and bloodshot, had a look of hungry suffering about them, but there was strength in the jaw and the set of the lips. Having asked the preliminary questions according to the law the sheriff was preparing himself to ask a leading question when he caught a glimpse of Judge Shillitoe leaning forward and blandly examining the accused from the bench, his little owl-eyes wide-open and lit with some secret amusement. Seeing the judge smile, some cackling broke out among the rows of benches, but the judge simply set his jaw, faced the cacklers sternly and there was silence again. In the heaviness of that silence Lem knew there would be no easy winning of the case.

Taking his time, smiling his thin and incalculable smile, and spacing out the words for greater effect, the sheriff said:

"Lem Otis, did yuh or did yuh not on the night of November nineteenth last deliberately put an end to the life of an Indian known as Yellow Bear of the Nez Perce nation?"

"I did not."

"You plead not guilty before the court?"

"I do."

"You are prepared to stand trial before this court?"

"I am."

"That's all," said the sheriff, turning in the direction of Judge Shillitoe. He smiled. The smile was a signal for the audience to cheer, and the judge immediately cracked on the table with his gavel. He cracked down on the table so heavily that the gavel head broke off. There were more cheers. Judge Shillitoe frowned, and deep creases appeared in his fat cheeks: he was livid with rage, and began thumping on the table with his fist. Lem was shivering in panic. When the sheriff spoke the words "deliberately put an end to the life of," the awful enormity of the occasion had come to him like a blow. They would truss him up in words. They would make a murdering fool out of him. He had no idea how to fight against lawyers, and hated them bitterly. Why didn't they leave him alone? He couldn't help what he had done, and the law couldn't help it either. He glanced hungrily around him. Waldo was chewing melon seeds and reading the Bible, and seemed to be paying no attention to what was happening, his hamlike arms flaying as he turned the pages. There was no comfort in Waldo and none in Josh Stamps who looked, Lem thought, completely ridiculous in his high white collar and long-tailed coat buttoned too tightly round a bulging waist, so that he was more like a badly wrapped package than an attorney, an impression which was increased by the lawyer's perpetual play with the black ribbon of a monocle which he never lifted to his eyes.

The prosecutor was thundering about "this appalling and cold-blooded murder—justice for the red man—Your Honor, this case will be a landmark of justice in the Northwest." There was a great deal more of it, and Lem heard it all in a daze. Towards the end the prosecutor's voice grew shrill, and now for the first time Lem found himself listening intently.

"Well, Gentlemen of the Jury, the Territory ain't provin' nothing—the Territory don't have to prove nothing. It ain't a case of provin' that a cold-blooded, calculated murder was effected, because we've got the defendant's confession. He told Lieutenant Stevens what he done, and he told it sweetly, and I reckon he'll tell it again. The pore Indian's dead. We ain't aimin' to bring the pore Indian's body here for folks to look at. We're relyin' on the defendant's confession of guilt to a charge of cold-blooded calculated murder. Of course the Territory will, in due course of time, enquire into whether there were any extenuatin' circumstances, but it won't take a man long to come to the conclusion there weren't any."

Judge Stamps rose, waved some documents, cleared his throat and said: "I object, Your Honor."

"What do you object to now, Mr. Stamps?"

"I object to the continual damned prevaricatin' by the prosecutor. There's too much prevaricatin'. Mr. Otis is a devout Episcopalian."

"What's that got to do with it?"

"A great deal, Your Honor, as you'll see when we begin to make the defense."

"Did you say Episcopalian, Mr. Stamps?"

"Yes, Your Honor."

The judge smiled quickly, and then nodded in the direction of the prosecutor, who was shuffling through some papers. The prosecutor, aware that the judge was waiting for him to speak, said quietly: "Objection, Your Honor—a most serious objection."

"Well, what is it?"

"We object to the introduction of religious matters. Whether the defendant is an Episcopalian or a Mormon don't matter. He murdered a pore defenseless Indian in cold blood. According to the testimony here in front of me—testimony which you will all hear from the witness stand—the Indian was shot in the back. Shooting in the back ain't a religious matter." Then the prosecutor paused and waited for the hubbub to die down before concluding: "I vote we keep to the law and leave religious matters to the churches."

"Objection sustained!"

The prosecutor smiled with satisfaction, and Judge Stamps lowered his head to conceal his own quiet laughter. He had done what he intended to do, and he noted a sympathetic murmur among the jurymen. The prosecutor went on to describe the night of the murder, and how Lem lured the Indians into buying firewater, and then—"Maybe one of those Indian fellers cheated, maybe the defendant cheated, maybe they were all drunk and didn't know what they were doing, but is it likely, Gentlemen of the Jury, that a man of Lem Otis' attainments, a rich man, a cold and calculating man, would be able to shoot at an Indian as accurately as all that if he was drunk? No, Gentlemen, the way we have to look at it is this. We have evidence that the defendant don't drink much, never had a head for drinkin', but he puts temptation in the hearts of the Indians, and everyone knows that an Indian don't have a white man's resistance. You'll hear evidence that the defendant was a circumspect man and a God-fearing one, but where will you find evidence that he was a kindly man? No, you won't find it. Gentlemen of the Jury, look at him. Does he appear like a man who would go out of his way and do a kindness just for the sake of doing it? He wanted money from the Indians. He would sell them firewater against the law, and when they wouldn't pay—as we contend that Yellow Bear wouldn't pay—then this white man, in the audacity of his twenty-eight and some years—simply took out his pistol and shot the pore Indian in the back, and scared the other Indians away, and went and buried the pore feller in the cottonwoods back of his store, and he didn't aim to tell anyone what he done, he was so sure of his right to kill a defenseless man.

"Well, Gentlemen of the Jury, when you've looked at his tremblin' face and his droopin' eyelids, when you've examined in your hearts the consequences of his actions, you'll come to learn that there ain't nothin' so free and easy as a white man temptin' to sell liquor to the Indians. I want you to see the scene as it happened, and as our witnesses will show you. I want you to turn aside from all other considerations and think only of what happened on the sad night when, acceptin' the invitation of the white man, the Indians came flockin' in to the store. There he is, swaggerin' and maybe cursin' and full of peacock pride, but Hell has no terrors for such a man. There he is, a big swaggerin' trader, and by all my lights, I ought to be fightin' on his side, but the Territory is after justice, and a murder of a white man and the murder of an Indian—it's all one in the sight of the law; and so it must be, if this thing we call the law is to survive.

"So, Gentlemen, take your mind back to that windy night when the devil was walking over Wallowa Creek, and this here defendant was plannin' and plottin' after the money the Indians carry in their pouch pockets, some of it in gold dust and some of it in good minted coin, and he aims to get the mostest out of the pore ignorant Indians by all the weapons of craft and cunning—"

Lem could not recognize himself in the prosecutor's description. He listened attentively, crossed and uncrossed his legs, glared apprehensively at the judge and then at the jury, as though asking them whether they believed all this nonsense about a cold, determined man.

He wished Moll was there, to show them how little coldness there was in his heart. He wished the Indians on the bleachers were not whispering among themselves and pointing. Judge Stamps whispered: "He'll talk himself out," but Lem was not sure, and sometimes he shivered and shuddered out of the pure loneliness of being in court, the misery of wondering how every sentence would end, for all the prosecutor's sentences were enormously long, and all the time he was smiling scornfully at Lem, so that Lem wanted to rise and strike him across the face for his rudeness.

"Gentlemen, the Territory will prove that the defendant has been an unruly man, a wild man, a cruel man, a mischievous man—"

Lem wanted to cry out in grief against these accusations which tormented him only because he could not understand them. Where would it end? A rope round the neck, a sharp tug, and then the feet dangling. Continually his hands went to his damp collar. There was such vileness in the prosecutor's tone that Lem lifted a protesting hand, hoping to catch the eye of Judge Shillitoe, but the judge was listening only to the prosecutor, his fat cheeks supported in his pudgy hands and his small eyes blinking. The prosecutor's speech lasted an hour, and then he called his first witness. Lem had not counted on any witnesses besides Lieutenant Stevens, and he was surprised and shocked when a tall sandy-haired man with a stoop and a habit of sucking in his cheeks came shambling up to the stand, and the prosecutor said: "You are Jeremiah Jordan of Lewiston?"

"Yes, sir."

"Owner of the Jeremiah Jordan Liquor Store?"

"Yes, sir."

"You've met the defendant before?"

"Yes, sir, many times."

"Tell the court whether the defendant has bought a great deal of liquor from you."

"That's right. He bought eight cases off me near three weeks ago."

"Reckon you know the exact date?"

"Must have been about the sixteenth or seventeenth of November."

"Remember anything of what he said to you on that day?"

"Said he didn't want it to get about that he had bought the stuff. Said as how he was going to do some trading with the Indians. Asked me whether I could let him have eight or maybe ten cases a month."

"For the express purpose of selling to the Indians?"

"I reckon that's what he wanted."

"Did he come to you alone?"

"No, had his squaw with him."

"And he bought a pistol off you?"

"That's right. He paid eight dollars for it. I've got his receipt. He said something about wolves being in the cottonwoods behind his store."

"Now listen carefully, Mr. Jordan. You knew, didn't you, you didn't have the right to sell him the whisky in quantity? You knew he had a store at Wallowa and traded with the Indians, and only with the Indians?"

"Yes, sir."

"Then why did you do it?"

"I reckoned he might just give a few bottles away friendly-like. It wouldn't do any harm. His squaw was there. I thought if she was there, then it would be all right."

There were titters from the bleachers, and Judge Stamps smiled to himself: he hoped there would be more titters, more nudging, more laughter. He lifted his head and said quietly: "Objection, Your Honor."

"Well, what is it?"

"The squaw ain't accused. The squaw ain't party to the business. I object to the squaw being dragged in by hook or by crook."

"Objection sustained," said Judge Shillitoe, and he peered round, like an eager old owl, in the direction of Shades of Night, whose head was bent and whose hands lay folded on her lap. The judge was pleased with what he saw, and at the same time some obscure memory was troubling his brain.

"The defendant is living with the squaw at Wallowa, is that right?"

"Yes, Your Honor."

"Seems to me I remember marryin' him to Old Moll three-four years ago. Woke me up in the middle of the night to get married, and I was glad for Old Moll's sake. I recollect he came to my house and woke me up. If he's living with the squaw, then we've a right to ask what happened to poor Old Moll."

"She died of the cold," Judge Stamps said.

"Then I'm sorry for her," Judge Shillitoe said, and for the first time there was a look of genuine concern on his face. He smiled sadly at Lem, and then cocked his eyebrows at the prosecutor.

"Have you any more questions to ask of Mr. Jordan?"

"No, Your Honor."

"Then proceed with the next witness."

The next witness was Lieutenant Stevens. He stood there, looking very trim in the long blue coat with the gilt buttons, with his hair parted in the middle and slicked down, his hands behind his back and his head jutting forward as he listened intently to the questions of the prosecutor. He told how he had heard of the murder from the Indians, and ridden over to Lem's shack.

"You say you went out and dug up the body. Were you alone?"

"No, sir. Mr. Otis was with me."

"Just you and Lem Otis?"

"There was Shades of Night, too."

"And do you connect Shades of Night in any way with the murder?"

Josh Stamps rose again and shouted: "Objection!"

"I'm just tryin' to clarify the picture in my own mind," the prosecutor said. "It's in my mind that there must have been a motive. Now tell me—according to your statement you walked out to the cottonwoods and dug up the body, and you found six bullet-wounds. You're sure there were six?"

The judge was making a drawing of Shades of Night, lost in the contemplation of the young squaw. Once more Josh Stamps had risen with an objection, saying: "Why ask *him* about the wounds? He ain't no doctor. That's a question for a properly qualified surgeon, not a soldier. Another thing, judge. We ought to ask the lieutenant whether he knows a dead Indian from a live one."

The judge was puzzled. He wondered what was happening in the mind of Judge Stamps, who had deliberately spoken in this offhand way, but why? There had been a murder, Lem Otis had as much as confessed to it, and still it was mortally difficult to know exactly what had happened. He turned to Stevens and said: "I reckon you're a military man, and you know something about wounds. You've seen a lot of dead in your life, eh?"

"No, sir," Stevens said, spacing the words out to give them emphasis. "No, sir, I haven't seen a dead man before. It was the first time. I reckon I've seen a couple of men lying under blankets in saloons, but I never examined them carefully."

"So this was your first body?"

"That's right."

"And you have the audacity to proclaim yourself an expert on dead bodies?" Judge Stamps strode up to Stevens and glared at him. "You—an expert!"

"I didn't say I was an expert, sir."

"But you went ahead, and examined the body, and so far as I recall you didn't call a doctor in, didn't summon a doctor from anywhere—just went ahead."

"Yes."

"And for all you know he may have died of disease, and after he was dead someone may have pumped bullets into him. You wouldn't know the difference, would you?"

"I reckon he was killed by the bullets," Stevens said stubbornly, and the people on the bleachers did not know whether to cheer Stevens for his stubbornness or Judge Stamps for his cunning. They could see how he was deliberately attempting to confuse the witness.

"Then why didn't you call a doctor in, or have the body taken here, so that it could be examined by a properly constituted authority?" Judge Stamps said, pleased with himself because he was now in command of the situation. In a brutal voice he went on: "Well, why not?"

"I didn't think about it," Stevens said, no longer sure of himself. "I just wanted to see the body—didn't have anything in mind until I saw he was shot in the back—"

"Then you took it upon yourself to arrest the defendant, though you didn't know what in hell really happened. That's right, isn't it? You knew the defendant before, and you had a score against him, and you thought, 'I've got him this time, and by God I'll hang him.' Now didn't you?"

"I didn't think any harm of Mr. Otis," Stevens said stubbornly, and for the first time he was feeling confused and looked anxiously up at Judge Shillitoe, who was busy sketching something on a pad.

"Tell His Honor and the jury when you met the defendant before."

"Must have been a year ago—pretty nearly exactly a year ago. His brother Waldo got thrown in the lake. I was around, and brought Waldo to the store."

"And that's when you began to hate them—the whole brood of them, Waldo, Lem and Shades of Night?"

"I didn't hate them, sir. Hate didn't enter my mind. I just helped to bring Waldo to the store. Shades of Night wasn't there then. It was before Mr. Otis took her to live with him."

"But you saw Shades of Night later?"

"Yes, once or twice. Only casually. Never paid any attention to her."

"Didn't pay attention to her, eh? Take a look at her, Lieutenant Stevens. You say you didn't pay attention to her. Look at her carefully. A woman like that could raise a great deal of passion in a man, couldn't she? Fine figure, hasn't she? Your Honor, I'm goin' to call on the woman Shades of Night to stand up."

"I object, Your Honor," the prosecutor bellowed. "She ain't a material witness."

Judge Stamps smirked. He was beginning to enjoy himself. His fighting blood was up. Before Judge Shillitoe could say anything, Judge Stamps said: "I ain't aimin' to bring her into the matter as a material witness. She's the common-law squaw of the defendant, and she can't be cross-examined, but I reckon a sight of her might do a bit to change the habits of mind of the young fellow on the witness stand."

"She can stand up," Judge Shillitoe said, and he bent forward and took a long look at Shades of Night, who was being nudged into standing up. Even when she stood, she held her head down. Tears were streaming down her copper cheeks. The Indians, who crowded the back of the bleachers, craned forward again, and Lem found himself gazing at her compassionately, hating the thought that she had been brought to the courthouse and hating most of all the sheriff's order that they should be separated during the course of the trial. Shades of Night was trembling all over now, and even when she tried to lift her face, she could not. Judge Stamps strode over to her, and lifted her chin.

"Objection!" the prosecutor bellowed again.

"Objection sustained," the judge said, fanning himself with the sketch which he had absent-mindedly lifted from under the paperweights. "This court isn't goin' to examine the physical charms of witnesses, Mr. Stamps. Go on, Fortescue."

Fortescue, the prosecutor, took a deep breath, smiled and said: "The defendant's counsel has put a lot of red herrings in your path, and maybe he has his reasons. Now it's our duty to smoke all them red herrings away and utterly wipe them from the face of the earth. You're a fine upstanding man, and you saw the body, and I'm contendin' that everything must be done strictly accordin' to the law, and the law says you have a right to arrest a man when he's murderin' or thievin', and if there's an Indian or a white man shot in the back, then it's unlikely he was defendin' himself in an altercation, however the altercation arose. It's plain murder when a man's shot in the back. It's murder of the first degree, and it's a hangin' offense. And you've examined the body and told His Honor what you saw and the case for the prosecution holds you as a material witness. It's a question of your word against Lem Otis' word, isn't it? Wouldn't you say, Mr. Stevens, that that's what the position is?"

The prosecutor was floundering, and the judge was out of temper.

"Quit gallivantin' with words, Fortescue. Get down to the butter and eggs."

"I'm tryin' to show—tryin' to see in my mind the best way to tackle the problem, Your Honor. It's one man's word against another. That's how I see it."

"Have you got any more questions to ask Mr. Stevens? I hear he's a busy man."

"I've got just one more, Your Honor, and it's an important one. Mr. Stevens, would you say on the evidence before you, takin' into account what you know of the defendant's character, that this was plain murder—murder for passion or for gain or anyhow for some advantage to the accused, even if it is only the advantage of riddin' himself of the Indian's presence? Would you say it was murder, Mr. Stevens?"

Before Judge Stamps could collect his wits and shout an objection, Stevens said: "I just don't understand what happened. All I know is that the Indian was shot in the back."

There was a gasp from the audience. They saw the prosecutor had fumbled his case, and they waited breathlessly for Judge Stamps to rise to his feet and call upon the judge to dismiss Lieutenant Stevens from the stand. There was a ripple of applause as Shades of Night at last stood down, having gazed over her shoulder at the audience and smiled at them, not because she wanted to please them, but because they were all smiling back at her. Then the prosecutor said: "One more question, Mr. Stevens. My friend, Mr. Stamps, has said there might have been something between you and the woman called Shades of Night. I want you to tell His Honor and the Gentlemen of the Jury how many times you have seen this woman, and whether there was anything between you."

"I've seen her twice in my life, and there isn't anything between us," Stevens said, looking straight at Judge Shillitoe.

Then the judge said quietly: "You can stand down now, Mr. Stevens.

The court thanks you for the way in which you marshalled your evidence."

"What there was of it," Judge Stamps said in a stage whisper.

The prosecutor jumped up. "I object to these asides, Your Honor."

"Objection sustained, Fortescue. The Gentlemen of the Jury will take into account the full weight of Mr. Stevens' evidence. Have you anything further to say?"

"Yes, Your Honor," Fortescue replied, and he went on into a long repetitive account of what he called "the night of the murder," saying that he regretted there was no way of putting Shades of Night on the stand, or any of the other Indians, but the facts were clear. A peculiarly reprehensible murder had been committed, and it was the word of Mr. Stevens, a smart fellow if ever there was one, against the word of Lem Otis, a skillful trader—yes, Gentlemen, a very skillful trader indeed, and he asked permission to introduce as a witness Marcus Woodridge, another trader in the Wallowa Valley, but when Woodridge, a fat heavy man with waxed mustaches, said that he had never set eyes on Lem Otis but once, and that was on the road, the judge impatiently ordered him to stand down. Then it was lunch time, and Judge Stamps hurried back to the hotel with Lem, Waldo and Shades of Night.

"It's goin' fine," he said, blowing out a plume of bluish-green smoke from his cigar. "I'll put you on the stand and leave it up to the jury. You don't have to worry about the judge. He's sympathetic under the skin."

"You sure?"

"Sure, boy. Sure as I'm here. Sure as hens lay eggs."

Lem was exhausted. He lay back in a cane-bottom chair, all the strength leaking out of him. He had no desire to go on the stand. He hated lawyers. He hated the long courtroom and Fortescue's rasping voice, and he could no longer remember what happened on the night of the murder. It was all confused, all jumbled together, the Indians dancing with the bright feathers in their scalp locks and Shades of Night running in and dancing with them—that was it, the way she had flung herself into the dance, and suddenly she was silent, leaning against the wall with the sweat dripping from her face. If Yellow Bear had jumped off the pine counter when he was ordered to, then there would have been no murder. He liked Yellow Bear a bit more than he liked Judge Stamps, who was squinting up at Shades of Night as though he was looking at her for the first time.

"You take your eyes off my squaw," Lem muttered, but the words were spoken so low that Judge Stamps probably failed to hear them. He gave no sign that he had heard. He went on to tell Lem what to say.

"All you've got to do, boy, is to tell the jury that Yellow Bear was having a push at your squaw, and you're a free man. There isn't a jury in the world that wouldn't sympathize with a fellow defending his squaw."

"It didn't happen that way," Lem said, looking dazed.

"Now, boy, listen to me. It don't matter how it happened. Seems you don't know yourself what happened. I'm defendin' you, and I've got a right to ask your assistance, and I say that's the best thing for you to say. She's a mighty fine-looking woman, and it might have happened, mightn't it?"

"It might, but it didn't. They were all shoutin' and dancin', and I wanted them to shut up."

"A jury wouldn't believe that, boy. They wouldn't believe you killed him just because he was shouting."

"Well, that's what it was."

"Listen to me. You're going on the stand, and I'm goin' to ask you what happened in your words, and you're goin' to tell 'em something they'll believe, or you'll be flyin' at the end of a noose. You just think of that."

Lem took no lunch. Sometimes he held Shades of Night's hands, and stroked them, and he would gaze absent-mindedly out of the window. He kept saying to himself: "I just don't know," and he would shiver uncontrollably. He couldn't face those gentlemen of the jury whose faces were like red wax and whose eyes stared into him.

"You think I'll get off?" he asked at the end of the meal, pushing away the plate which he had left untouched.

"It depends on you," Judge Stamps said.

The sky had clouded over during the recess, and Judge Shillitoe ordered candles to be lit in the courthouse, for he could hardly see the people on the bleachers and even the witnesses, close at hand, looked grey in the half-light when he took his place on the rostrum. There was the smell of burning wood in the air, for more cottonwood fires had broken out. Judge Stamps noticed that the audience was peculiarly hushed and attentive. They had guessed that the trial would come to an end during the afternoon, perhaps dramatically, and they were looking forward to Lem's appearance on the stand. Most of them had eaten well: they were in a mood for excitement, and they groaned aloud when Judge Stamps rose with a little flurry of the papers he held in his hand, waving them in a circular motion, and said: "Your Honor, I vote we dismiss the whole thing. The prosecution ain't gettin' nowhere—it's plain as can be."

Judge Shillitoe, with candles on either side of him, leaned down, more like an old owl than ever, and said: "How so, Mr. Stamps? I reckon there's a case, maybe a strong case."

"Strong!" exclaimed Judge Stamps. "Why, my client was defendin' the honor of his squaw, and it's a known fact—"

"That's the line you're going to take?"

"It sure is. It's plain as can be a man has a right to defend the honor of his squaw."

"Then you'll put the woman called Shades of Night on the stand?"

"I'm hopin' I won't need to. Your Honor, I'm hopin' you'll use powers of discretion and dismiss the case—clean it right off the slate."

Shades of Night lifted her head at this moment, and everyone thought she understood what was being said, but in fact she lifted her head only because she recognized the sound of her name in English and wondered why the judge was speaking about her. In the candlelight all the gold and copper of her skin shone duskily.

Fortescue rose protesting: "It's a watertight case. You can't dismiss it, judge. Why, if you dismiss this case, every cuss will be able to murder every other cuss in the Territory."

"That's your opinion?"

"It suttinly is."

"Then Mr. Stamps will proceed with his case."

With an audible sigh Judge Stamps proclaimed that he would call only two witnesses. Before he called them the sheriff passed a note to the judge. The judge read the note, whispered to the sheriff and then announced: "We've got news that the Nez Perce ain't travellin' yet to their hunting grounds. It appears they're returnin' to Wallowa, and maybe they'll stay there the whole winter."

Judge Stamps rose to his feet, swaying. "It's not material, Your Honor. We ain't putting the Nez Perce on trial. It don't matter a goddam whether they're here or there."

"I only read this here note because I thought it would be of interest," Judge Shillitoe said, and he smiled at the prosecutor.

Lem shuddered. It occurred to him that they had returned to attend his trial. They would not, of course, attend it in person, but they would be invisibly present in the courthouse. He was still shuddering when Judge Stamps called upon him to rise and take the stand.

"I want you to tell His Honor and the Gentlemen of the Jury the circumstances of the fightin' in your store. I want it in your own words, Mr. Otis, and I'll be pleased if you tell the truth and nothing but the truth. A man charged as you are charged don't have to swear on the Bible, but I want you to tell the truth, the whole truth and nothing but the truth, so help you God."

"So help me God," Lem said, feeling a tightening of his throat.

"Now tell us what happened—"

Lem told of how he had bought the whisky, just a few bottles, because the Indians had asked for it, and he never had any intention of asking them to pay for it. He was on good terms with the Indians. He spoke their language. He did a lot of trading with them. He described the store, and for Judge Shillitoe's sake he went back over his life and talked a bit about Moll, and how he lived there happily with her, and how she always wanted him to deal fairly with the Indians. He wasn't a hot-tempered man, no more than most. But the Indians got out of hand, danced like mad, smashed things, and there wasn't any way of knowing what they would do next. He'd intended to shoot into the ceiling to frighten them. He remembered having on his mind only that one desire—to frighten them off, before they did more damage.

"And then your squaw Shades of Night came into the store, is that right?" Judge Shillitoe said, smiling a little, his lips bunched together.

"Yes, she did."

"And one of those Indians, name of Yellow Bear, went and put his arm round her."

"I guess so."

"You're not sure?"

"I'm pretty sure, Your Honor."

"Objection!" Fortescue said quickly. "Your Honor, I object to the way you're handling the witness. That's helpin' him."

"I'm just trying to find out what happened," the judge said quietly. "We want the truth, don't we?"

"That's how it happened, judge," Lem said, and he was sure now that he had discovered the explanation for all his miserable trials, his sleepless nights, his doubts and hesitancies. He smiled up at the judge, and there was no longer any tightening of the throat.

There was a long pause. The wind, rushing through the open windows (for the air had grown stale, and the judge had ordered them opened), made the candles gleam like stars; and the audience, quiet and attentive now, candles and lanterns shining on their faces, all gazed in the direction of the judge as though he was performing some mysterious rite, but in fact he was still shading in the portrait he was making of Shades of Night, and he had fallen into a kind of daydream. Without whisky, he couldn't keep awake for long. He smiled, ran his tongue over his lips, looked enquiringly at the audience as though he expected something was about to happen, and he was pleased when he saw Josh Stamps jumping to his feet, holding a lantern above his head.

"Well, what is it, Mr. Stamps?"

"I'm going to call on the squaw Shades of Night to stand up, Your Honor. I want everyone to see her."

"If that's what you want—"

Josh Stamps darted towards Shades of Night, swinging the lantern. The bronze glow passed from his face to the face of the Indian girl. Shades of Night rose unsteadily to her feet. She did not know what was happening. A cold wave of fear ran through the spectators. They knew that something sudden, outrageous and inexplicable was about to take place. Shades of Night trembled. The blood raced to her face. The lantern was blinding her. She got up unsteadily, set her jaw, smiled briefly at Josh Stamps, her skin glowing like molten metal, so that she seemed to have absorbed all the light in the courtroom; and then, still trembling, she threw out her arms towards Lem, and he ran to her.

"The defense rests its case," Josh Stamps shouted triumphantly.

"Gentlemen of the Jury," Judge Shillitoe said after a pause. "You've heard what you've heard and seen what you've seen, and I reckon you'll come to a decision on this unfortunate case without benefit of advice from me."

Then the jury filed out, and the judge disappeared behind the black curtain. Shades of Night was weeping in Lem's arms. Josh Stamps hurried furtively towards Judge Shillitoe's desk, and retrieved the pencil drawing the judge had been making. It was, as likenesses go, a good drawing. Half an hour later the jury returned. It was growing dark, and now the whole courtroom was ringed with candles.

"Gentlemen of the Jury," said the judge, "how say you, is the prisoner guilty or not guilty?"

"Sure he's guilty," said the foreman.

There was a hush, and then a strange groaning sound from the audience.

"Mr. Clerk," said the judge, "set aside that verdict and enter an order quashing that indictment and also one discharging the prisoner. Gentlemen of the Jury, you may go. It's clear as daylight Lem Otis was defending the honor of his squaw. She's a pretty squaw—the prettiest I ever set eyes upon." He paused, glared round, pulled at his beard and said: "Sheriff, adjourn the court."

"It's all right now," Josh Stamps said. "We played it straight. Now it's downhill and shady all the way."

VIII

Silver Earrings

THE trial over, everyone streamed into the street, all talking and debating the judge's strange decision. They remembered that it had happened before, many years ago, and the decision had been upheld in the *Lewiston Gazette*. Now they milled around Lem and his squaw, touching him, touching his clothes, laughing at him, congratulating or else shouting abuse, scratching him, so that he remembered them afterwards as fierce bloated creatures like dogs on holiday.

Lem caught sight of Stevens in the crowd and shouted: "They won't leave me alone. Look after Shades. She can't help herself."

Stevens forced his way through the crowd. Lem was kicking out with his elbows. A woman was tugging at his coat, and a man with a bristling red beard was saying: "Redhead, that's what you are! We all have the best of luck, don't we, and the hangman's noose round our necks?" Lem staggered, shoved out with his knees and made a path through the mob. There was no sign of Josh Stamps, and there was another crowd waiting for him at the hotel. Stevens was carrying Shades of Night as he would carry a child. She flung her arms round his neck and nestled her face against his shoulder. There were no tears. She was exhausted, and she could no more understand the trial than Lem could understand the man with the red beard.

Josh Stamps had slipped away by the back entrance of the courtroom. He was waiting for Lem in the hotel room.

"Why in hell did they want to scratch and bite me?" Lem said.

"I reckon they wanted some of your luck."

"Luck," said Lem, and fell silent, looking dazed. There was a crowd in the hotel corridor, waiting for him to come out. He looked up to see Shades of Night standing in front of him. She, too, looked dazed, as though she never expected to come out of the courthouse alive.

"Yes, luck, that's what it is," Lem said. "But what's luck? What the hell is luck?" He glared at the people who had pushed their way into his bedroom as if expecting an answer. He recognized one of the jurymen, a man with a thin chest, a tall black hat and a drooping black mustache: the man looked like an undertaker. "What's luck?" he said, going straight up to the man. "You ought to know. You've got a hell of a lot of nerve to come in here."

"I did my duty, Mr. Otis, as I saw it."

"What's duty?" Lem roared at him. "What's duty? What's luck?"

The color was coming back to his cheeks: he was fighting mad again. Stevens slipped between them.

"There's been enough trouble," Stevens said. "Take it easy now, Lem Otis."

"Now here's some good Scotch whisky," Judge Stamps said, drawing a bottle from his coat pocket.

Lem watched the whisky being poured. There was a sour taste in his mouth. He hated these people who had pursued him into the hotel. Above all, he hated Stevens, but he could not bring himself to show his hatred. He slumped down on the bed, buried his wet hair in his hands, and then, because there were people pressing round her, he pulled Shades of Night down beside him. Waldo was standing with both hands pushing down on the bedrail. "What's luck?" Lem said again, and when Judge Stamps passed him a tumbler of neat whisky, he dashed the tumbler on the floor, and there was a pleased smile on his face as he watched the whisky soaking into the carpet.

"Better take it easy, young man," Judge Stamps said. "This here bonded whisky ain't to be sniffed at."

"You're right," Lem said.

"It's the best there is, Mr. Otis. You deserve to celebrate. By Jesus, if a man doesn't deserve to celebrate on a day like this, then I've a right to ask when he does deserve to celebrate."

"I'm thinkin' of getting me some new clothes, judge. That's all I'm thinkin' about. You can swill in firewater, but I'll never touch a drop—never smell it if I can help it."

"I understand, Mr. Otis."

"Now let's get goin'. I want some new clothes, and I'd better get some too for Shades."

"It's my opinion that a pretty woman like that should have a lot of clothes, Mr. Otis," Judge Stamps said, smiling approvingly at Shades of Night. "Clothes are like the setting for jewels. The better the jewels, the better the setting, eh? You'll have to keep an eye on your lady, sir. I reckon there isn't a squaw livin' who can move a jury so much as she did. That's why they wanted to hang you—because you had the purtiest squaw in the country. It's not reasonable, but that's what it is. I'm hoping for your sake you'll keep an eye on her."

"What are you suggesting?"

"Nothing, Mr. Otis. I'm suggesting nothing. I'm talking about things which are plain under my eyes."

Once more Lem had an impulse to throw himself at Judge Stamps, but seeing the fat middle-aged man guffawing harmlessly, his eyes lit with admiration of Shades of Night, he shrugged the impulse off. He had not realized before how beautiful she was. The young face was putting on maturity. The curve of the cheekbones was tighter, and the eyes had somehow grown larger. She had a habit of holding her face a little to one side, and this gave her the appearance of someone who knew precisely where she was going, because she had pondered deeply. Also, she was filling out, her breasts no longer small and pear-shaped, but full like the moon. Lem was gazing at her with a look of perplexity when Judge Stamps said: "I'm thinkin' a case of whisky would do the job nicely."

"What job?"

"Judge Shillitoe's job. You owe him something, don't you?"

"I reckon so."

"Then you'd better have it sent over promptly—well, not promptly, tomorrow morning's soon enough. What are you planning to do tomorrow morning?"

"Ride to Wallowa with my squaw. Any reason why I shouldn't?"

"No reason, Mr. Otis. No reason at all. There may be Indians on the road, though."

"I'm not scared of Indians."

"I know you ain't, but it's my judgment a few days of waitin' here in Lewiston wouldn't do you any harm. You'll be welcome to stay here, sir. You won't have any trouble in Lewiston. The citizens of Lewiston are in agreement with Judge Shillitoe—it's only the damned jury which ain't."

Lem smiled with one side of his mouth and said: "I reckon to go to my store. That's where I belong. And I'll leave tomorrow. And if you'll get out of my way I'll go out and buy me a new suit of clothes, and a dress for Shades of Night, and maybe a jewel she can wear on her finger."

The worst was over now. These unknown people who had gathered in his hotel bedroom had begun by talking in loud voices, but now they had simmered down, and some of them were already leaving, and as darkness came down the crowds outside the hotel were moving away. With Judge Stamps in tow Lem thrust out of the room and went in search of some new clothes. That evening he bought himself a new shirt and a heavy wool-lined coat, and for Shades of Night he bought a new linen skirt of heliotrope with a blue hem and a white blouse with dimity lace and a pair of silver earrings.

IX

The Old Chief Joseph

LEM sat in the driving seat of the spring-cart, whistling away. There was a soft frost in the air, and the branches of the cottonwoods were silver with snow, but the sky was a deep blue, and he had no cares in the world. Shades of Night was sitting beside him, wearing her new blouse, her earrings flashing in the sun. He had had a good night with her, and the sap flowed through him, and he wanted to shout. Instead he sang in a deep throaty voice:

We're coming to Wallowa, Wallowa, Wallowa—
We're coming to Wallowa for to play—

It was not much of a song, but it pleased him; and even Waldo, sitting slumped up in the back of the cart, an amused blissful look on his face, joined in the song.

They had ridden twenty miles south of Lewiston when Lem heard the hoofbeats behind him. He turned and glared. When Stevens came galloping up, Lem shouted: "I don't need your protection, feller. I never did, and I don't now. I know what you're up to. You're going to accompany me the whole road."

"No, sir, I'm going my own way in my own time," Stevens said, and then added as an afterthought, smiling at Shades of Night and speaking in Nez Perce: "It happens it's the same way. We could do it together."

Lem thought of swinging his whip at Stevens, and then thought better of it. There was something in Stevens' expression which suggested he had come to stay.

"I'll give you some money if you'll only keep out of my way," Lem said.

"'I'm going to Wallowa, too," Stevens said. "I'm sorry for all the trouble I've caused you."

"You don't look sorry," Lem commented, and then drove on, pretending to ignore the presence of the lieutenant.

All the way to Wallowa Lem felt the lieutenant's eyes on him. They rarely talked, and in the evenings when Lem built a fire, Stevens built another fire further down the road. On the last evening before they reached Wallowa, Stevens strolled over. He looked grey, worn out with the journey, for the wind had been biting, but there was an amused twist to his mouth as he gazed at Shades of Night in her finery.

"Take your eyes off my squaw!" Lem shouted suddenly. "You're paying too damned much attention to her."

"Do you know why I am coming with you?" Stevens asked innocently.

"No, and I don't care. Go away. Go any damned place you please, but don't follow me around."

"I've been accompanyin' you because I think you need protection, Mr. Otis. I don't know what the Indians are thinking. I saw some of them smiling when you were acquitted, and maybe there isn't any harm in your travelling. But I'm going to make sure you don't get into any more trouble."

"You leave me be."

"Say what you like. I'm doing it for the best, and because I respect your squaw. I don't wish you any harm, but the chances are you can expect trouble from the Indians, not now, maybe, but sometime. Be careful, Mr. Otis. That's all I want."

A moment later Stevens moved away. They heard his boots clattering down the frosty road. Lem watched Shades of Night. She gave no sign of being attracted by the lieutenant, but he thought he had detected a look of approval in her face. There was a long silence. The flames were burning low, and he threw another log in. That night he slept badly, and when he woke up to find Shades sleeping beside him he grasped her roughly and pulled her to him, saying: "Jesus, stay with me! Stay with me, Shades of Night! Don't ever leave me!" He did not know what had come over him, and in the morning he looked at her a little shamefacedly.

They reached Wallowa just after sunset on the fourth day. There were low clouds, the lake was covered with mist, but there were huge fires at the lodges. Stranger than the bonfires was the low drumming sound. It was softer, more penetrating than any he had heard before. It came out of the darkness of the night, reverberating against the hills, deep and low and full of menace.

"What is it?" Lem asked.

"I don't know," Shades muttered, and she turned her face away.

He saw that she was weeping and shivering. Waldo was clambering off the cart, and holding up a lantern.

"The old chief is dying," Shades said, and then she gave a muffled scream, dropped off the driving seat and began to run in the direction of the bonfires. At first Lem wanted to laugh. There she was, running across the snow, and he had only to call her back and she would come to his arms. She was screaming as she ran. Lieutenant Stevens was still on the roan, and went galloping after her. "Jesus Christ, what's she up to?" Lem shouted. "Come back, Shades. I'll kill you if you don't come back." He jumped off the seat and went stumbling blindly through the snow, cursing her, shouting what he would do with her when he found her, and he did not know even then that Stevens had caught her up and lifted her onto the saddle and was riding hard to the lodges. All the time the drumming was growing more frenzied, louder, deeper and more terrible.

When Stevens rode among the lodges, he found the men curiously silent, but the women were screaming and beating their breasts as they huddled in the tepees. Seeing the white man riding with an Indian girl dressed in a long blue linen skirt, a white blouse and a red coat, the braves at first looked astonished, and then pointed in the direction of the largest of the lodges, which was painted over with immense hunting scenes. Stevens knew it was the lodge of Old Joseph, and he would not have gone in if it had not been that some braves were anxious that he should see their chief. Kerosene lamps were burning in the lodge. Usually, the Indians slept on the floor, but for some reason they had brought a brass bedstead into the lodge to ease the last hours of the old chieftain; and so he lay there while the lights danced on the high brass knobs, and the medicine men huddled in little groups, squatting beside the bed, and the old chief's two sons stood at either side, their eyes staring and their cheeks wet with tears. The old chief's wives were gathered in a far corner of the lodge, and there Shades of Night joined them: they were too busy with their grief to pay attention to her attire.

Bending down over the emaciated old man a young brave who might have been twenty-five, though there was the strength in his face of a man of forty, spoke in whispers, repeating some words again and again, for the old man was beyond ordinary speech, and his eyes were glazing fast. "You are here—in Wallowa," the young chief kept saying. "You are among your people."

A thin brown hand was raised among the buffalo robes, catching the light of the lamps.

"It is well," he said, and then turned his face away as though he could not bear that they should see him suffering. His mouth opened, he made an effort to rise and then fell back against the pillows. To Stevens the strangest thing of all was the appearance of the braves in their bead-embroidered buffalo robes around the brass bed. They were strange not because they seemed out of place beside a bed but because everything in the lodge, the carpets, the bundles of soft woolen blankets, the washstand, the grandfather clock, even the spittoon, all these were objects originating with the white man and they had evidently been brought in only because they comforted the old chief; and so the lodge resembled a large room in a white man's house, and yet from outside it looked exactly like any large lodge, only the designs on the skins were more handsome.

The young chief was holding the pulse of the dying man. The old walnut-wood grandfather clock began to ring the hour with a tinny sound, and afterwards the clock wheezed and groaned. One of the medicine men, with a brilliant smear of red paint on his face, began to leap up and down, perhaps believing that he was in some way helping the chief's spirit to escape lightly from the flesh. Then the old man said: "My sons, my old body is returning to the earth, and my spirit will soon join the Great Spirit Chief. Give ear to me. When I am gone, think of your country. You are the chiefs of my people, and they will look to you to guide them. Never leave them. Never leave this country. If they ask you to trade this country for another, do not trade it. A few years more, and there will be white men all around you. Take heed. Never forget my words. Never sell the bones of your father and mother."

That was all. The old man who had been blind for many years lay back against the pillows and smiled, waved his hand a little and then closed his eyes wearily.

At the moment when the pulse ceased, the young chief bent over him and seemed to be kissing him on the mouth, but in fact he was attempting to inhale into his own lungs the expiring breath of his father. For a while they had all been quiet. Now from all directions there arose the sound of wailing, and the great drum which had been beating steadily up to the moment of death suddenly grew quiet.

For three days the old chief lay in state, his face painted deep red with some yellow stripes on the forehead, his body encased in a tight deerskin robe especially sewn for him. The women wailed continually, their lips dripping spittle as they wandered aimlessly around the lodges with huge bundles of firewood supported on their shoulders: they would use the firewood later to burn down the great lodge. Dishevelled, their braids cut off at the neck, beating their breasts in unison, they looked dazed as though they did not know what had happened but guessed that some terrible calamity had befallen them. Lem and Waldo blundered into the lodges in search of Shades of Night, but no one paid any attention to them, and when they asked a question no one answered them.

Stevens had put up a tent on the far side of the valley. Now, every morning he rode over to the lodges. He did not know why he rode over. He told himself that he would observe the ceremonies and make a report of them. There were moments when he found himself searching the crowds for a sign of Shades of Night, but she was nowhere to be seen. The tribe had swallowed her. Somewhere, in one of the tepees, she was rocking backwards and forwards on her heels, uttering the death wail.

High up on a hill overlooking the lake, Lem and Waldo watched the procession moving down from the uplands. It was a bright, high morning with a few puffs of cloud in the wintry blue sky. On a horse litter the body of the old chief was taken down to the lake, and only two hundred yards from where Moll was buried, some of the braves had dug a grave, and they had piled huge rocks round it. The long procession came very slowly; there were many halts; many recitals of the old chief's prowess. At one of these halts a caged eagle, whose feathers had been painted bright red, was let out of a wicker cage, and it must have been tied by a string, for it flew in a jerky motion, very low above the horsemen. Neither Lem nor Waldo saw what was happening by the graveside. They stood there, bracing themselves against the wind, their coats flying open, their faces chapped and sore in the cold air of the mountain valley.

"I aim to stay," Lem was muttering. "They ain't goin' to push me away. I aim to get Shades of Night, too."

All around them swept the immense green valley dusted with snow, a bitter wind blowing, and from the lake there came the soft wailing chant of the women.

BOOK TWO

THE BATTLE IN THE TENT

X

The President Signs an Order

THE winter came to an end, and soon it was spring with sheets of blue camas flowers reaching up to the uplands, and then came the long summer days when the valley glowed like a green bowl and smoke was wafted down towards the lake from the lodges and the ponies gambolled in the knee-high grass. Afterwards the peaks turned steely blue with the coming of ice and the first droppings of snow, and when winter lay over the valley the hawks flew south to warmer weather.

For two years the Indians remained in the valley without wandering abroad, tending the grave of their chief. They lived quietly, wore sombre colors, docked the tails of their horses, and paid more attention to the medicine men than ever before. They watched their young chief Joseph warily. Stern, handsome, his face painted with bright red stripes, he walked among his people with a strangely indrawn look, like someone who has lost his way and believes he can only find it in himself. When he gave orders he was sometimes brusque and harsh. "He will change—he will grow better in time," they told themselves. "Everything is changing—"

There was change in the air. For a while the valley remained untouched, but there was change all over the West. The forests were being cropped, the buffaloes were being slaughtered, the Indians were being driven away. The earth was being cleaned up and squared off into pastures, lots and mining camps by men who never thought of the land as something to be owned over the years and carefully tended: they wanted quick yields and were in no mood for waiting. They fought and lived hard. They didn't understand the Indians, and because they didn't understand, they didn't care. Looking up at the sky or squatting in a trance beside the lake, the young chief could feel the changes in the air but he could not tell from which direction they were coming, just as a bird can feel the gathering of the storm but has no knowledge of the storm's direction. More and more, in his loneliness and grief, Joseph would commune with his father's grave, there, down by the green lake, where the only sound came from the rustling of the reeds. The storm was coming, but it was only a tremor in the air.

Then messengers came to Wallowa to say that the Great White Chief in Washington had pronounced that the valley of the winding waters was to remain in perpetuity in the hands of the Indians. Joseph bowed his head. Had not the Indians owned the land all their years? If the Great White Chief in Washington decided that the land belonged to them, why should they be pleased? It was theirs by right of immemorial tenure: then who would dare to take it from them? But still the air shivered when he walked down by the lake to the cairn of stones where his father lay, protected from the coyotes and the mountain bears. The air quickened, there were strange blue flashes in the sky and sometimes, when there was no wind, all the lake was set rippling. In those two years no trumpeter swans came to nest in the lake, and the starlings were late in coming, and an eagle with two heads was found dead on the mountains—all these things were taken to be signs of approaching calamity by the medicine men. Every day young Joseph went down to the lake.

"There is danger coming from the west," Joseph told his brother. "I don't know who is the maker-of-danger, but I know he will come from the west."

"Who is he?"

"Even that I don't know," Joseph answered, "but who else can it be except the white man? Is there another enemy anywhere? There were white tents here once. Now they have gone. Is that good? I ask myself whether it would be better if the white tents were still here, but I don't know. I have heard that the Great White Chief in Washington does not know what is happening here. Why do trappers come here? Why do miners come here? Have they asked our permission? I see they are crowding round us, and there is no end to it. It is strange. I stare into the lake, and see a one-armed man—"

Joseph's brother, Alokut, listened attentively. To him there was nothing astonishing in Joseph's power to see visions in the lake, for like most of the other Indians he shared this power. What astonished him was that Joseph could see no further than a one-armed man coming out of the west. Would this one-armed man destroy them? There was no answer. Would he come at the head of troops? Still there was no answer. Would he deprive them of the land which the Great White Chief had granted to them in perpetuity? There was still no answer. It was three months later before they heard for the first time that General Oliver Howard had been appointed to Vancouver and was in command of all the troops in the Territory. He had lost his right arm in the battle of Fair Oaks.

The small general with the bushy brown beard read from the Bible which lay open on his work table. Maps, scored heavily with his red pencil, were scattered over the table, but ever since he could remember he had read three chapters of the Bible a day, and even now, while the kerosene lamp swung in the wind and a storm was coming up and it was late, for he had worked all day, he read lustily, intoning the words and sometimes pausing to repeat a phrase over again. He was reading from *Isaiah*. Supporting the heavy Bible, the large veined hand, which seemed to have acquired the energy of the hand he had lost in battle, never trembled. He held the book straight in front of his eyes, and his eyes glowed as he read. When he had finished reading, he lowered his head and prayed silently. John Montieth, of the Indian Bureau, with a wax-pale face and a carefully combed black beard, with intense black eyes under a jutting forehead, had been craning forward while the general read, and now he said: "You read admirably, general. I've never heard a man read so well."

The general eyed Montieth keenly, but there was no hint of deception in Montieth's expression.

"I don't know about that," the general said. "All I know is that I put my whole heart into it. I feel God is with me when I am reading the Book."

"It's a great thing to have a fine voice," Montieth went on. "A very great thing—"

"I haven't tried to train my voice in any way, John. I wouldn't try to train it. It's something God has given me, and I am content with it as it is. I've heard Indians who have better voices—there's a richness and depth in the voices of some Indians which would make me envious if—well, if there was much envy in me. I'm not an envious man—"

"I know you are not, sir," Montieth interrupted, and for the first time that evening the general was aware of a faint wheedling tone, the slightest dissonance. He wondered why Montieth was always so pleasant to him. He was the reservation agent, a young missionary who had been selected by his church for the appointment and he had acquitted himself well. He knew that Montieth was watching him closely. The wheedling tone jarred. He said sharply: "You won't do, Montieth. You're not well enough for a long ride across the country. I'll have to send my adjutant."

"You wouldn't do that—"

"I have to. I tell you this, there's a terrible lot at stake. I can't risk accidents. Know anything about Chief Joseph?"

"I've heard he's stubborn."

"Then you think he'll fight?"

"I think he might."

"If you think that, then you're no use to me at this juncture. I want a man who can convince Joseph there's nothing to be gained by fighting."

There was a long silence. They heard the rattle of rifle stocks, a drunken trooper singing in the guardhouse, the crackling of bonfires. It was eleven o'clock, and the general knew there were two or three hours of work ahead of him. He dreaded the work he had to do. He jerked a cigar out of his cigar case and rolled it between thumb and forefinger, but did not light it, for he had already said his evening prayers. He said: "I hate force. If there's any other way I'll take it."

"There may be times when we have to use force, sir."

"I hope not."

That was all. Shortly afterwards the general dismissed Montieth. He stared into the dark spaces of the room for a few moments, and then summoned the guard. He said: "I want you to wake up Mr. Stevens." Still rolling the cigar, he began to plan in his mind what he would say to the young loping officer who had grown what the general called "a smattering of a beard" and who was the source of most of the general's knowledge of the Indians. He would have to resist the temptation to call him "Keff." He would continue to say "Mr. Stevens." He would keep the young monkey at a distance, but that too was difficult, for Stevens had the habit of smiling unself-consciously, and his mere presence could warm the general's heart. It was twenty minutes later before Stevens came striding in.

"Sit down, Keff," the general said. "I'm afraid there's bad news."

Stevens did not change his expression. The half-smile hovering on his lips when he came through the door was still there. The general was thinking of all the times when Stevens had spoken to him about Wallowa.

"Where's the bad news, sir?"

"I think you had better read it yourself," the general said, slipping a document across the table.

Printed on heavy paper in large type the document read:

Office of the President

It is hereby ordered that the order dated June 16, 1873, withdrawing from sale and settlement and setting apart the Wallowa Valley in Oregon, described in the annexe as an Indian reservation, be hereby revoked and annulled, and the same described tract of country be restored to the public domain.

U. S. Grant

When Stevens had read the document he was stunned. The words, so frigid, so commanding, swam before his eyes, and as though to blot out the words, he shaded his eyes with both hands, and his hands were trembling. For four years all his daydreams had been concerned with Wallowa, the half-naked bronze riders beside the lake, the white lodges, the mist rising among the blue mountains. He said slowly: "Is there any way out? They won't be able to live without their land. Who is at the back of it? Why do they have to go—they're doing no harm there."

The general cupped his chin on his hand, and stared gently at the young officer who was shivering with grief.

"I'll take your questions in order, Keff," he said quietly. "There's no way out because it is a presidential order. You say they won't be able to live without their land, but there is good land set apart for them at Lapwai. Who is at the back of it? I don't know, but I know the President signed the order. Why do they have to go? I don't know that either—it's a question of policy and I am not concerned with policy, I am concerned with the execution of orders. Is that clear?"

Stevens had heard not a single sentence of the general's. He sat there, hunched up on the chair, staring straight in front of him. He said: "I know one thing. They would prefer to die at Wallowa rather than ever leave it. I know that."

"You're sure?"

"Yes, it's a sentence of death."

"We're putting good land aside for them, Keff. It's not as bad as all that."

"It's worse, because there is no need for them to move away."

There was a long pause. The general had known even when he summoned Stevens into the room that the interview would be unpleasant. He had no desire to hurt his adjutant.

"Wallowa means more to them than anything they have ever known," Stevens said. "Their chiefs are buried there." He pronounced Wallowa like *Wailaway,* so that the very sound of the word was like a wail of despair.

"The President says they have to go, and they'll go," the general said. "I don't like it any more than you do, but I am here to see that presidential orders are carried out, and so are you. I thought of sending Montieth, but I thought better of it—I'm going to send you. You will have to tell them to meet me in council next month—all their chiefs—"

"They won't come."

"They will if you put the case to them properly. You must make them see that no one in this country can go against a presidential order. Will you go?"

Stevens rose unsteadily. The president's order floated onto the floor. The silence deepened. A moth, which had been beating against the kerosene lamp, went spinning across the table with a broken wing. Outside, the rain fell and they could hear the muttered curses of the guards.

"When do you want me to go?" Stevens said, still staring straight ahead.

"Can you go tomorrow? They should have three weeks to prepare for the journey. Tell the chiefs to come to a council at Lapwai by May 4th, three weeks and four days from today. They can bring fifty braves from each tribe." He pointed to the map. "There is Joseph's tribe, and White Bird's on the Snake, and they are to come together—"

"To receive orders?"

"Yes, to receive orders," the general answered, and his voice was quieter than ever. "Tell them that Old Man With One Arm has to talk with them. Take them presents. Do anything you please, as long as you make sure that they come." He paused and added quickly: "I don't want to see you until you have carried out my orders successfully."

A few minutes later Stevens stumbled from the room. In some obscure corner of his mind he was wondering what presents he would bring to young Joseph. It was Judas-like to bring presents at all, but he could not come from Walla Walla empty-handed. He thought of a rifle, necklaces, some mother-of-pearl boxes filled with snuff, but what else? What harm were they doing in the green valley with the blue peaks? Why must they go? A fit of anger froze him, but he broke himself free of it, ordered a guard to wake him an hour before dawn and then threw himself down on the bed.

In his office the general was writing in his day-book:

> *Have tonight 11.05 P.M. ordered Lieutenant Keff Stevens to proceed to the camps of Chief Joseph at Wallowa and Chief White Bird on the Snake with instructions that the chiefs meet me at Fort Lapwai on May 4th. As usual, I expect Lieutenant Stevens to carry out his orders expeditiously and rigorously.*

XI

The Young Chieftain

DELAYED by storms, Stevens reached Wallowa a week later. He came to the valley at dusk when the sky was a clear stretch of smoky blue with a sprinkling of silver stars. The wind was coming down the valley, freshened by the snows which clung to the blue crags. He was out of breath and his uniform was soaked with sweat. He rode slowly past the small cairn where Moll had been buried and the larger cairn, gay with feathers, where the old chieftain was buried; and then he watered his horse at the lake, and afterwards he changed into the new uniform he carried in his saddlebags. He was worn out with the journey, racing against time. Now as the light faded and the whole valley was drenched in the shadows of the mountains, the only light coming from the stars and the glow of the hearth-fires in the tepees far to the east, he felt as though a great burden had been lifted from his shoulders. He had arrived in time, and it pleased him to think that he had arrived on the day he had promised General Howard he would arrive; then, as he rode towards the uplands, he remembered that he carried an ultimatum, and it was no less an ultimatum by being disguised as an invitation to Lapwai.

As he rode miserably up the slope, the stillness gathered around him as it always does in the Wallowa Valley at dusk. First, there is a long silence, all dogs, birds, insects and frogs all silent as though they had disappeared from the earth. Suddenly the silence was broken by the low drumming of the Indians, and then some five minutes later all nature awoke. Instead of that heavy silence there was a deafening uproar. The birds sang, the crickets chirped, the frogs shouted "too deep! too deep!" and the coyotes began barking, and the drumming in the Indian village grew louder. In this deafening uproar Stevens made his way towards the tepees, wondering what he would say to Chief

Joseph. For the first time it occurred to him that Joseph might refuse to come to Lapwai. What then?

The lodges with their embroidered decorations shone in the light of great bonfires. The village was settling down for the evening. Inside the tepees hearth-fires were smoking, pots were simmering, there was the pleasant smell of meat and camas. Braves wandered through the village carrying eagle-poles, their faces daubed with fresh yellow paint. Stevens knew he was being watched closely, for nearly everyone had recognized him; yet the Indians did not speak to him. They went about their business. They refused to ask questions, fearing that they would only intimidate the guest. The guest must talk first. If he wanted anything, they would give it to him. So it had always been, and Stevens rode calmly towards the largest of the tepees, knowing that the chieftain and the subchiefs would be there.

When he reached the tepee, he dropped from the saddle and walked straight up to a young brave. He indicated that he wanted to talk to Chief Joseph, if it was possible, if the chief was not otherwise engaged, if— He went on in a low voice, talking in the language of the Nez Perce, filling his speech with the decorative gestures usual among the Indians. The brave nodded, slipped into the tent and returned again a moment later to say that they had known of his coming and were waiting for him. Stevens was not surprised. Scouts for a hundred miles around had probably signalled his coming.

Inside the tepee lights shone. There was the light coming from the hearth-fire, and kerosene lamps hanging along the walls. All the subchiefs were squatting round the fire: only Joseph was standing when Stevens entered. He had seen Stevens before, but never spoken to him. The young chieftain wore a bleached buckskin shirt, beaded leggings, moccasins with porcupine quills. There was a startling bright red feather in his scalp lock. Sombre, straight as an arrow, with a broad forehead, a heavy nose and a delicately carved mouth, he stood there like a majestic lion barring the path.

"I have come from Old Man With One Arm," Stevens said quietly.

The chieftain made no effort to smile; he looked straight at Stevens and answered: "We will eat and then we will talk." The voice was low, sweet and chanting, unlike Old Joseph's voice, which had been remarkably heavy and resonant.

Stevens squatted by the hearth-fire. They had begun to eat, and perhaps deliberately they paid little attention to the young lieutenant who offered gifts and smiled nervously and seemed out of his element. Women came in with the food. Stevens glanced up, hoping to see Shades of Night among them, but there was no sign of her. He recognized Alokut, Chief Joseph's brother, tall, big-boned and sinewy, with a long oval face and deep luminous eyes. Alokut was something of a dandy. His fringed buckskin shirt was soft as velvet and delicately patterned with beads; his moccasins were crowded with bright glinting beads and small brass coins. Like Joseph he wore a single painted feather in his scalp lock. Younger than Joseph, altogether more elegant, he resembled at times a strikingly good-looking boy, for there was a softness in his face unusual among the Indians. He smiled easily and well, and threw his head back when he laughed, and this too was unusual among Indians.

Beside Alokut was the old medicine man, Smohalla. A hunchback, with a broad leathery face, dark brown eyes glittering like needles, he deliberately dressed in old worn clothes spotted with candle-grease and foodstains, though he wore a beautifully mounted necklace of bear claws. He was a man to watch. He had an odd way of bending his head low, watching you through lowered lids. He, too, smiled easily, but you never knew what his smile meant. Sometimes he made a sound like a chuckle, but at such moments there was no laughter in his face. He preferred to be seen squatting, for then his hunchback was not so remarkable. All the time his eyes were on Stevens.

Chief Joseph spoke politely of the journey, asked about the health of Old Man With One Arm, and talked pleasantly of the time when Stevens had been in command of the tents. He did not mention the death of Yellow Bear or of his own father, though he remembered the night when Stevens had entered the tent where his father lay dying.

When the meal was over and the pipes were being brought out, Joseph smiled and said "You are welcome. Tell me why you have come."

"Old Man With One Arm wants you to meet him at Lapwai. He wants you to come with fifty braves for a powwow."

The subchiefs exchanged glances. Joseph drew from under the loose buffalo robes which formed a carpet in his lodge a little pile of earth, and held it in his hand. Nervously, Stevens did the same. Joseph, who was now smoking, gently pushed Stevens' hand away. The subchiefs were still exchanging their rapid glances.

"So they have planned a reservation for us?" Joseph said in a level voice, with no more emotion than if he had said "They are preparing something good for us, but no one knows what it is."

Stevens nodded. For some reason all the faces of the chiefs seemed to be shining like gold.

"You know what we will do?" Joseph asked.

"Yes, I think I know."

"What is it that you think you know?"

"There is no other way," Stevens said. "It must be done. You know on whose side I am."

"Yes, I know on which side you are, but it is a long time since you have lived here. Things have changed. For a short time we lived quietly, but it could not last. The white men found gold in the mountains around the land of the winding waters. They stole a great many horses from us, and we could not get them back because we are Indians. The white men told lies for each other. Some of them branded our cattle, and drove them off for their own. We have no friends we can plead to. There are no law councils who will listen to us. It seems to me that some of the white men are trying to incite us to war—they know we will not give up our land, and so they threaten us. Old Man With One Arm threatens us. Does he want war?"

"No."

"Then who wants war? I have heard that a man called Shillitoe wants war with us, because he wants our lands. There are others. We know who they are. What do we do? We cannot move."

The sweat was trickling down Joseph's face in golden streams. The voice was controlled, very level, very sweet.

"We must have a parcel of soil wide enough and firm enough to build our dwellings on," Joseph said, gazing down the length of his pipe, the mouthpiece an inch away from his lips. "It must be large enough for my tribe, and deep enough for our dead, and sweet and cool enough for the young to play on. And it must be our soil, here."

Saying this he dug into the rammed earth between the buffalo skins and scooped up with his fingers some flakes of earth, then he allowed them to fall on the skins. He smiled, listening to their falling, the dull throbbing sound of earth falling against dry skin, and all the while there was a slow smile playing on his face. He spoke very slowly, lost in some dream or other. There he was, bending forward a little, one hand smoking the pipe from which smoke rose in grey coils, the other hand resting on the soil he had scooped from under the buffalo skins. When Stevens leaned forward to touch some of the precious soil, Joseph quickly pushed his hand away. All the men in the tepee were watching closely, their eyes blazing in the light of the flames, their copper skins glowing. Watching them, Stevens reflected that it was pure nonsense to believe the Indians were impassive: on all those graven faces violent emotions played.

"I have not let you touch this soil because it is holy," Joseph went on. "The topsoil contains the bones and blood of my tribe. Our sweat is in it, and our bodies will form a part of it. I hold this grain of dust in my hands, and I ask: Who is it? Who lived here? Who sweated here? You smile, but the topsoil is made of man's sweat and blood. Down below you will find the soil as the Great Spirit made it, but the rest is ours, bone of our bone, blood of our blood. All that is on top belongs to us: it is our blood and our dead, and so we shall never surrender it."

The last words were spoken quietly, and there was about them a curious menace. The chieftain was saying, as clearly as possible, that he would fight for every stone of his territory.

"No, we shall never surrender it," Joseph repeated in an even quieter voice, and he glanced up at Stevens with a look of compassion for the young lieutenant's innocence, as though he could not understand why anyone should doubt his intentions, and yet he was certain that Stevens was in a doubting mood.

"The chieftain has spoken the truth," Smohalla said, gazing straight at the lieutenant, and at the same time swinging backwards and forwards as he continued to whip the fire into life with an eagle-wing fan.

Stevens had felt helpless many times in his life, but never more helpless than at this moment. He knew that General Howard would scrupulously obey the commands of Washington. He knew, too, that the troops in the Territory were no match for the aroused Indians. He could see by a single glance at Joseph's stern copper face gleaming in the light of the blazing faggots that he meant what he said. He could no longer think clearly. The fumes from the pipe, the smoke rising above the fire-bed, the heavy smell of leather and jerked beef and wild cherries being mashed in a pulp, the strange noises outside like a continual wailing interrupted only by sighs, the strange shapes of the huge shadows on the tepee wall, all these things confused and dismayed him. He had hoped to talk to Joseph face to face, without the presence of the other chiefs, and most of all he was dismayed by the peculiar mocking look on the face of Alokut, whose necklaces of brightly colored beads of glass and bone were continually rustling. Once again Stevens found his hand straying towards the little mound of earth on the buffalo skins.

"You may touch it this time," Joseph smiled. "You may even keep it all in memory of us, but you must not take our territory. Do you understand that?"

"Yes."

Once again there was a heavy silence in the tepee. Smohalla evidently desired to speak. He was already opening his mouth and jingling his bracelets a little to attract Joseph's attention, but though Joseph was aware of Smohalla's eagerness to speak, he was also aware that Smohalla would only inflame the others; wanted nothing more than to inflame the others; would have thought the day well served if the lieutenant was thrown violently out of the village. Meanwhile the pipe had left Joseph's hand, and was being passed from hand to hand, and each chieftain and brave inhaled three times and then lifted his head, allowing the smoke to curl from mouth and nostrils. It was as though they were all performing very slowly a kind of dance—a dance of smoke. And seeing the smoke rising, the lieutenant made a little gesture of clutching the smoke and said: "See, it is insubstantial —it passes through the fingers—"

"Everyone knows that smoke passes through the fingers," Joseph replied with a troubled look, "but smoke is not the same as earth. Listen, the smoke is carried away by the wind, but the earth remains—nothing carries it away. I know what you are thinking. You think we shall vanish like smoke before your troops. We shall not vanish."

There was something terrible in the way Joseph could read his mind. The dark eyes of the chieftain gazed unflinchingly into his own. One moment they were warm, the next moment cold, but whether they were cold or warm they saw through him. They were relentless and determined, and they never left him.

"I was not thinking about our troops," the lieutenant said, blushing. "I was thinking that between friends all quarrels vanish like smoke. I have told you that we want peace. Do you believe that we want war?"

By this time the pipe had reached Smohalla. He, too, had been gazing at Stevens, unable to take his eyes away, those eyes that had more smouldering flame in them than any Stevens had ever seen. He was dressed raggedly in coarse rumpled brown deerskin and he wore the kind of loose moccasins that old women wore with not a trace of decoration on them. Apparently he did this to show that he was not to be counted among the braves or the war chiefs; and in his tattered clothes he was the complete opposite of Alokut and Joseph, who wore bleached buckskin shirts as soft as velvet and decorated their moccasins with porcupine quills and every kind of bead. Smohalla lifted his pipe, inhaled twice deeply and then pretended to choke. It was a calculated insult to Stevens, and by the pleased expressions of the braves in the tepee Stevens knew exactly how calculated it was. Smohalla smiled. His coarse weather-beaten face, as broad as a pumpkin, shone with pleasure, and he was about to say all the things which he had been wanting to say during the past hour when Joseph once more lifted his hand and said "It is the young man's turn to speak. When the young speaks of peace, shall the old refuse to listen? What has come over us that we refuse to listen to the young one's words?" Then he leaned over and placed something hard and cold in Stevens' hand, saying "Look, here is an arrowhead. This is a sign between us." Stevens thought the placing of the arrowhead in his hand was some kind of demonstration of hostility, but the chieftain then put his own hand over it. "What is man but an arrowhead clothed in skin?" he asked gently. "What is he? Surely he is an arrowhead on which the Great Spirit has breathed life. Because he is an arrowhead, he must fight for what he has."

"Then you intend to fight the white men?" Stevens asked, breathing hard, fearing that Joseph was bringing the discussion to a head and falling under the influence of the others.

"No, there must be no fighting," Joseph answered. "The word between us must be strength. This is why I have placed the arrowhead in your hand."

All the time Joseph was leaning forward, cupping one hand over the hand which contained the arrowhead. At first Stevens could not understand the gesture, which seemed so meaningless and so arbitrary. The chiefs were whispering together, not in the least put out by Joseph's behavior. Stevens' eyes were smarting from the fumes of the fire, and his head was reeling. How could one talk to the Indians? There were always barriers of understanding: why the arrowhead?

"We trust you," Joseph went on slowly. "You have known us. You know the valley of the winding waters well. You have come to us. This is enough."

"What will you have me do?" Stevens asked, smiling a little, for there was warmth in the young chieftain's hand, and he knew all these words were only an introduction to a demand of some kind. Then he said softly: "Because man is an arrowhead, he must fight for what he has. Is that what you want to say?"

"Yes, that is true," Joseph said eagerly. "I see you have your ears open to me. Listen, I cannot leave Wallowa of my own will. I cannot leave it. I belong here, and my strength is here. This is the power I have within me, given me by the fowls of the air and by the creatures who leap and creep about along the earth. Who is the White Chief of Washington who dares give me orders? Who is he? Ask him why he orders me to desert the earth who is our mother. You tell me to leave Wallowa, but you forget I dare not leave Wallowa—I dare not!"

"It is not I who ask," Stevens said.

"I know it is not you. I know there are people who do not understand. They are using you—"

"No, they are not using me. I obey orders."

"Who gives the orders? Does God give the orders? Who gives them?"

Silence again, while they fenced for position, and waited, and did not know where to turn.

"Old Man With One Arm wants the best," Stevens said. "The best for you. The best for all of us."

It was lame, but the message went through. A faint smile played on the corners of the chieftain's lips, and the eyes glowed with the radiance of understanding.

"We are friends," the chieftain said. "We have a sign between friends." He raised his hand, separating the fingers: the shadow of the raised hand on the wall resembled an eagle alighting.

"This is the sign. No war! No war! No war! I have spoken three times, therefore I speak the truth. Between you and me there is no war forever."

Then Stevens raised his hand, and there were two eagles alighting on the wall of the tepee.

They smiled at one another.

"It is better that there should be no war between us," Joseph said. "I am very powerful. I am thunder."

Stevens wondered whether he had understood aright. What did Joseph mean when he said he was thunder? Suddenly the tepee was quiet. They were all listening. Far away they heard the thunder, and through the open flap Stevens saw blue lightning streaking across the hills. Joseph was smiling again. It was strange how suddenly the thunder came, and he remembered that as he rode to Wallowa in the evening the sky had been unusually clear for this time of year, with depth upon depth of blueness.

What did it prove, this sudden appearance of the thunder? That Joseph spoke to the elements? That he held the thunder at his command? What age was he living in? Did he expect Stevens to report to General Howard: "Chief Joseph has strange powers. Do not touch him." There was a great heaviness in Joseph's face. He said: "You look frightened. I have these powers. Truly I summoned the thunder. Why not? When I was young I was sent to the mountains. I was ten year old. I was made to fast, for all of us at this age are made to fast. In this way we receive our names from the Great Spirit. I fasted, and waited beside the lake for the name to be given me, and it was in winter, and I was naked, for this is our custom. I waited, and did not sleep. Then one night I heard my name. My name was Thunder-echoing-in-the-mountains. All this was long ago. The Great Spirit spoke and gave me a name. Can you hear the thunder?"

Stevens shivered. The thunder growled. It seemed a cold wind was moving through the tepee and under the buffalo robes, for the smooth skins were billowing in the wind like waves. Joseph leaned forward and plucked at Stevens' sleeve.

"You think we do not know," he said. "You are wrong—we know too much. I have known for two years that danger would come out of the west. I went down to the lake, fasting. Then I saw a man with one arm. You do not understand this, but it is so. Do you know there are great birds in the sky? When they flash their eyes, it is lightning. When they beat their wings, it is thunder. I saw the man with one arm rising out of the lake. Yes, I saw him, and now I fear for my people. Why should I meet the man I last saw in the lake?"

"He is a good man."

"You say so, but how do I know? Do you want me to come to him?"

"It is the best way," Stevens said miserably.

The thunder was still playing over the blue crags. Some women came with food. The chiefs were silent, staring straight ahead, lost in the strange impassivity of the Indians which is like the impassivity of the earth itself. A little later Joseph rose, beckoned to Stevens and walked slowly out of the tent. Stevens followed. He did not know what to expect. Chief Joseph walked to a place on the edge of the lodges, overlooking the lake. The lightning crackled on the mountains, and sometimes you would see the wavy blue reflections of lightning on the lake. Chief Joseph turned and went up close to Stevens, so close that they were almost touching, and for a long while they stared deeply into one another's eyes, as though their eyes were mouths and they were drinking one another.

"I will come to Lapwai," Chief Joseph said, "but only out of my love for you."

Early the next morning Stevens rode to the Snake River and the camp of Chief White Bird.

XII

Cavalcade

IT was May now, the snows melting on the slopes and the green valleys smoking in the sun. A few silver-bellied clouds were reflected in the lake, but mostly the sky was a clear blue, almost violet. The clouds moved swiftly, for in the days before summer a stiff wind came from the north, and sometimes there would be inexplicable patches of silver in the grass where the wind came in fury; then once more there were only the gentle green slopes with their sheets of blue flowers.

Riding on their speckled cayuse horses the Indians looked like conquerors. Mostly they rode naked to the waist, their bronze bodies gleaming in the sun, and their painted horses moved to the measured music of the bird-pipes. Their feathers nodded and trembled and glittered in the sun; it was as though an immense and brightly colored ribbon hung on the level of their heads.

Joseph, wearing the longest tail of feathers, one that sprang backwards in the wind for six or seven yards, rode ahead. His face was painted with red hatchings; there were ribbons of blue otter fur in the long braids; he wore a coat of bleached doeskin ornamented with small white sea shells. His doeskin moccasins were delicately painted and sewn with porcupine quills. Behind him rode Alokut, taller and more handsome, but his feathers reached only half as far. He wore a necklace of deer hooves and leggings sewn with colored glass, and his face was painted like Joseph's.

Behind the two chieftains of the Wallowa tribe came a small bodyguard naked except for breechclouts, and a little behind these came the braves, usually in small groups, so that there would be four or five together pressing forward on their painted horses, and then there would be a little space, and behind the braves came the women and children. The women rode on high pommeled saddles and wore their best blankets, with little caps of painted basketwork on their heads. They wore bright skirts which reached to their ankles and top moccasins, and there were ribbons and strips of colored fur in their braids. The men were mostly silent, but the women sang as they rode. None of these Indians carried rifles, but some of them had concealed knives under their garments and all the men carried carved tomahawk pipes: they could be smoked peacefully, and the ax-blade inserted at one end was sharpened to a razor edge. When at last, late in the morning, they came riding down the valley towards the fort at Lapwai, they began to gallop at full pelt, their hair flew out and they broke out into chanting cries. The braves remembered that Joseph had been born in the Lapwai Valley at a time when there were only a handful of white men in all that territory, and it was their way of saying that they were returning to one of their own hunting grounds.

The fort lay at the western end of an immense ravine, with rolling foothills behind and still further behind lay the immense stretch of Blue Ridge gleaming blue and silver in the bright sunshine. There were barracks and guardhouses and officers' quarters and offices around the parade ground: there were stables about a hundred yards away, and still further away lay the trading post and the laundry. Near the barracks a large hospital tent had been erected, with the sides looped up and the fly extended, so that if any danger arose the soldiers in the garrison could sweep out of their barracks and rush the Indians in the tent. When he saw how the tent was placed outside the fort, and there was no one coming forward to receive them, Joseph drew up and extended his right arm, a sign for the braves to halt, then he swung the horse round and began to ride slowly down the line, and though he remained silent he gave the impression of talking. Simply by reversing his direction he was saying he did not trust the white men. There was no sign of activity around the tent, no soldiers were marching, no honor guards were preparing to receive him. The green valley was silent except for the singing of the meadow larks. What did the white men expect? Did they expect he would enter this silent fort? He would not go there until they came out and assured him once again that he was coming to treat with equals. The braves watched him closely, muttering among themselves, and all their beads and sea shells and porcupine quills and daubs of paint glittered in the noon sun.

As usual Keff Stevens had spent the morning working in General Howard's office. He had drawn up a list of the matters to be discussed with Joseph, gone through the general's correspondence when it arrived by courier and then for a while he had read the Homer he kept buried underneath the papers on his desk, but Homer had unaccountably wearied him and soon he went searching for a copy of Vergil's *Aeneid* which he had left somewhere in the office—he was not sure where he had left it. It was a warm mellow day, and occasionally he would find himself standing by the window, looking down the green valley with a haunting sense that something was missing. Afterwards he returned to the Homer, and he was still reading when the general came in, out of temper, the frayed ends of his mustache uncombed and the beard wild and straggling as it always was when the general's tranquillity was disturbed.

"There's no sign of the fellow," the general said, standing squarely at the window of his office which was two stories high and gave a clear view of the whole valley.

"He'll come," Stevens answered, and there was a note of defiance in his tone.

"How do you know he will come, Keff?" the general asked, turning sharply on his heels. "It's an article of faith with you, isn't it? It's all very well to say he will come, but will he? Are you reading your Homer again?"

"Yes, sir."

"I always said Homer was a heathen," the general muttered, and then he lifted the book off the table and held it to the light, staring with a puzzled frown at the delicately printed Greek letters: the page was upside down. After trying to make sense of the words he flung the book down and went to stare moodily out of the window again. Little puffs of yellowish smoke were rising from the laundry.

"I'm sure he is coming, sir," Stevens said when he saw that the general's impatience was mounting. "I could swear he will be here by noon, with all his subchiefs and the women."

"That's the trouble," the general said, still staring moodily at the empty valley. "If he brings the subchiefs, who shall we deal with? According to their way of thinking, every subchief considers himself as important as the chief. How do you talk to these people? As for you, I would feel more confident in your ability if you stuck your nose in a Bible occasionally. What do you find in Homer?"

"A lot, sir. The Greeks are like the Indians. You learn a lot about the Indians from studying the Greeks. I'm sure they will be here by noon, sir."

The general looked at his watch. It was two minutes of noon. Suddenly he cocked his head towards the window, and there came from him a long low whistle.

"You win," he said, watching the Indians as they came out of the blue mist at the end of the valley.

Ten minutes later he was still watching them, but the smile had gone. The Indians had not ridden straight up to the fort, as he expected. Instead, they were setting up their camp a mile and a half or two miles away. The tepees were coming up. You could see them running along the shores of the creek, blankets and beads and painted feathers all glittering in the sun. Half an hour later they were still there, smoke rising from their cooking-fires, and some of the young braves were racing on horseback across the valley.

"Beats me," the general said. "I've told you before I don't understand them. Have a look out of the window and tell me what they're up to."

"Resting, sir."

"Maybe they are; maybe not. Maybe they're cooking up something. They haven't sent anyone to me. It's high time they did. Do they think I'll sit here, sucking my thumbs till Doomsday?"

"I think they're just resting, sir. May I go out and tell them to come to the fort?"

"You certainly may."

As he rode to the lodges, Stevens reflected that everything was happening as he expected it would. He had said that Joseph would come, and he had come. They were coming peacefully. He was sure of that. He remembered how they had spoken solemnly in the tent. He found the chieftain at the edge of the encampment, riding a black stallion. He waved; there was no answering wave, only a steady stare. Joseph's eyes flashed as he turned very slightly to follow the movements of the man riding towards him.

When Stevens rode up to Joseph and saluted, he was asked: "Where is Old Man With One Arm?" Joseph's tone was that of a man asking a servant for something which had been mislaid.

"He is at the fort and waiting for you," Stevens answered, blushing.

"Why is he in the fort?"

"Because that is his place," Stevens said patiently. It occurred to him that Joseph might be exhausted after the long journey, and his exhaustion was taking the form of anger.

"And my place is at Wallowa," Joseph said bitterly. "Listen, and give me your ear. This is important. We have come a long way with our squaws and papooses. Then why do you insult us? We know Old Man With One Arm has two troops of cavalry at the fort. He should come out at the head of his cavalry instead of hiding behind the walls of the fort. Should we trust a man who hides?"

"He wishes you well," Stevens said. "You mustn't think he wishes you evil, or that he hides. It is our custom to send a young officer to greet guests. Later he will come to greet you."

"Tell him to greet us here, where we are," Joseph said proudly. "Tell him this at once!"

Stevens saw that a real anger had overtaken the chieftain, whose lips were trembling. Then, like lightning, the anger vanished; and instead of the stern face with the blazing eyes, there was a wonderfully sweet smile of affection and understanding.

"Is it your custom—is it really your custom?" Joseph asked. "Then I shall think about it. Go now. He sends you to me, and we are friends. Are we friends?"

"Yes, we shall always be friends," Stevens answered, and once more he remembered the night when they stood together under the stars.

The braves who had watched the two horsemen no longer looked menacing. They smiled and exchanged glances, and there was about all their movements an ease and assurance which had been absent before. Stevens saluted the chieftain, and then began to ride slowly in the direction of the fort. The sun was directly overhead, and the whole valley shone now like an immense yellow cup, and the only sounds came from the trotting of his horse, the humming of the bees and the distant whistling of bird-pipes.

When he reached the fort Stevens was as puzzled as ever, for it occurred to him that nothing had been settled, he had received no promises and there was still no assurance that Joseph would come to the fort. He had no idea what to tell the general, who would demand a neat answer to the question: "What is Joseph going to do?"

"Well, he's still out there," the general barked, when Stevens returned to the office. "What's he up to?"

"He'll come soon, sir."

"And what's soon?"

"He wants to talk with his braves a little longer."

The general looked out of the window. The braves were racing up and down the plain, and there was no sign of a powwow. He could see through glasses the figure of Joseph on horseback at the very edge of the encampment, and he thought he detected on Joseph's face a smile of derision.

"Soon! Soon! They always say soon!" the general exclaimed, his cheeks flaming red, while anger made him shoot out the words as though there were bullets in his mouth. Montieth stalked into the room. The general turned towards the agent and said: "They're coming—if they come at all—in their own time. They're determined to make us kick our heels. I sent my adjutant to Joseph an hour ago, and he tells me the chief wants to have a long talk with his braves before coming here. The triumph of audacity over inexperience! There will come a time when he will make us kick up our heels once too often!"

"He may have his own reasons," Montieth suggested. "I hear that White Bird and his followers won't arrive till tomorrow."

"Reasons be damned! He makes his reasons as he goes along. What has White Bird got to do with it? Joseph is here, and he should come and treat with me according to instructions. I can see White Bird separately, if necessary."

Then the general turned to Stevens and said: "Did he say what he was going to discuss with the braves?"

"No, sir."

"There you are! If I am sure of anything at all, it is that Joseph is eternally untrustworthy."

"We have always been able to trust him in the past," Montieth said, hoping that his voice sounded casual enough. He was already frightened by the bright flame of fury on the general's face. Everyone knew that the general detested being kept waiting, and would go to great lengths of subterfuge and cunning to prevent any of his visitors from being more than a split-second late. He would terrify men into punctuality, and drive the weapon home. Now, drumming his heels on the floor as he sat beside the plain wooden desk where the papers were kept in orderly piles, he looked like a man at the end of his tether.

"I can't trust an unpunctual man," the general observed. "I have found that a man who is punctual is generally an honest and temperate man, with a head on his shoulders—"

"And you would regard a man who is unpunctual as dishonest and intemperate?"

"I would have grave suspicions of his honesty and his ability, Mr. Montieth. I believe Joseph is pulling wool over my eyes. He is inclined to be mischievous. He will stay out there until he knows I am mightily annoyed. He will take pleasure in my annoyance. To be able to annoy me will be a sign of his superiority over me. He will come in his own time when I am least expecting him, and in a manner which is least in keeping with the dignity of the government which I have the honor to represent."

"Come now—" Montieth began, but seeing some slight movement in the Indian camp he reached for the glasses and for a long minute he gazed out across the plain. Without glasses all you could see was the sparkling of blankets and jewelry. With glasses you could see the features of the braves and squaws, the patterns of their blankets, whether they were smiling or glum, and you could almost see the shapes of the shells and beads they had sewn on their clothes. All Montieth could see was that some of the women were threading ribbons in their hair and some of the braves were chalking their buckskin clothes, and they were all in a great hurry, and some of them were already mounting their horses and forming in line. Suddenly there was a coyote-howl, and the hurry became greater than ever. Evidently Joseph had given orders for the advance, and the coyote-howl was the signal.

"You won't have to wait much longer," Montieth said, handing the glasses to the general.

Stevens breathed again. For some reason he had expected that Joseph would delay his approach to the fort until the evening, or even perhaps until the next day when he would have joined with White Bird. He was relieved when he saw them coming. The general turned to him and said: "See that the cavalry is on the square," and then he strode outside towards the immense white calico tent now fluttering and creaking in the wind which came up the valley almost at the instant when Joseph's column began to advance. It occurred to the general that perhaps Joseph had been waiting until the wind rose, though he could think of no reason why Joseph should wait for anything at all. With Montieth by his side, a small group of officers behind him, and the interpreter James Reuben standing some paces away to the left, the general waited for Joseph to come riding up to the tent. There was a pleased smile on his face. All his weariness and impatience had vanished. He told himself he would greet Joseph kindly and ceremoniously, as befitted the chieftain of a powerful tribe. He was going on to recite to himself some of the observations he would make during the meeting when he observed that the Indians had quickened their pace and their hair was flying out and they were breaking out into strange cries and chants. They were waving their arms and at the same time crouching low over their saddles and making straight for the tent.

"They're going to charge the fort," the general shouted, when they were fifty yards away and the thunder of their hooves on the gravelly earth could be heard above the weird chanting, the sudden explosive cries and war whoops.

The general's shout was drowned by the noise of the charge, by the flapping of the calico and by the sudden scream of James Reuben, who really believed that his last moments had come.

As the Indians came closer to the fort the wild shouting gave place suddenly to a shrill and plaintive song, and though the song was melancholy there was something defiant in it, but the note of defiance may have come from the shrill whistling on hollow eagle bones.

The general stepped back into the tent.

"What the devil are they up to?" he said, and he knew they could come straight through the tent and trample everyone underfoot. His hand went to the place where he kept a pistol strapped to his waist, but there was no holster, no pistol. He had trusted Joseph sufficiently to believe that the Indians would come unarmed. He cursed himself for a fool, and wondered how he could have left himself open to a trap. At the same time it occurred to him that the Indians with their red faces and feathers bent back in the wind looked magnificently virile, and he thought that the children of Israel hurling themselves against the walls of Jericho must have looked a little like these painted Indians. He did not know why the thought occurred to him. He looked round quickly, and saw no sign of Stevens. He felt absurdly helpless, and went running through the tent towards the fence gate and the transverse hall, followed by the officers and by James Reuben, and he was pleased when he saw the cavalry in line in the square. Twenty yards away from the tent the Indians wheeled and went riding at full pelt along the length of the fence. He knew now what they were up to. They would make a huge circle round the fort, and then attack. But no, they were riding more slowly now, and from inside the square he could see the riders whenever they appeared between the buildings, and these buildings somehow broke the weird chanting into irregular bubblings of sound as they made the entire circuit. It was strange to be standing in a hollow square and feel oneself at the mercy of the Indians.

"Do you think they mean to fight?" James Reuben asked in trepidation. His eyes were wide-open, and even when the Indians had reduced their pace to a slow ambling trot, and were singing in slow soft cadences, there was the look of shivering terror on his face.

"It's not a war song," the general replied. "No, I don't think they are going to fight."

The scare was over. The general, alarmed because he had been unreasonably apprehensive, glared all around him and saw that his cavalry had behaved with perfect decorum, never once betraying a sense of panic. They were drawn up in eight columns across the square, standing there exactly as though they were on parade. He was sure the Indians were careful to observe the behavior of the cavalry. He was pleased with them, and told himself he would congratulate them later. Stevens was hurrying across the square from the direction of the transverse hall which led to the tent.

"Well, what have they got to say for themselves, Mr. Stevens?"

"They say they have come and they are prepared to talk."

The general thought for a moment, cupping his chin with his closed fist, his thumb and little finger pressing up into his beard.

"They've had their fun," he said. "Now we'll make 'em talk turkey."

XIII

The First Encounter

THE blue canvas billowed in the wind, and the Indians also seemed to billow like waves, for the wind caught their feathers as they craned forward in the tent, never taking their eyes off the general and the small staff that sat behind the pine table. The general could not see at long distances; he saw only a sea of bright feathers lit by the sun coming through the tent, and the faces of the chieftains nearest to him.

There they were, all scarlet and red and indigo, their beaded clothes rustling a little. Sitting on benches, the chieftains sat there, looking as though they were graven from stone. Joseph sat with Tuhulhulsote and Hushhushkute on his left, Smohalla and Looking Glass on his right. Alokut lay at his brother's feet, his right arm lying along his side, his head turned upwards towards his brother. Behind the chiefs were fifty braves and their womenfolk. In a reedy voice the general was delivering his speech of welcome. The interpreter translated after every second sentence.

"He welcomes you in his own name and in the name of the White Chief in Washington and in the name of the Army and in the name of the Territory–"

The Indians listened patiently, absorbed in the patient process of listening to things they would never be able to understand.

"He says you may speak your minds openly and always say what is right——"

When the general's speech was murmured by the translator, who spoke in a sweet penetrating voice, Joseph rose quietly and allowed the blanket to fall from his shoulders. His gaze was directed at the general, as he said: "The general wants to know *now* what we have on our minds. Tell him we have many things on our minds. We cannot speak of them all now. What is 'now'? There are others who should be allowed to speak. White Bird should be heard—he is also a chieftain of our nation. He will be here tomorrow. So let us wait until tomorrow, and then let us talk."

As Joseph's words were translated, the general, who had been gazing down at the table, began to look at the Indians with unconcealed annoyance, and deliberately he refused to meet Stevens' eyes. He knew it would be difficult to convince the Indians that they would have to move to Lapwai, but their insolence could only be interpreted as hostility.

"It's no use, Chief Joseph," he said, when the chief's speech was translated. "We have received orders from Washington. If you decide to comply with the orders, then you shall have the first pick of the land. If you insist upon it, we shall wait for Chief White Bird, but the government's orders to him are the same as the orders I am giving you. The only difference is that he is coming late, and will have to await his turn."

These words, translated by James Reuben, were not understood by the Indians. They could not believe that the general would speak to them in this way. Old Chief Tuhulhulsote, grey-haired and barrel-chested, with a rugged face of dark leather and smouldering eyes set in deep sockets rose and began shouting at the interpreter: "Take care that you translate correctly! We are not alone here! Remember that our children and our children's children are also present. That is why you must translate correctly."

Immediately after Tuhulhulsote's outburst Smohalla interrupted: "Tell the general we are not here to receive orders! Tell him we are here to talk. We may have to spend many days talking—tell him that!"

The Indians, exasperated by the sudden turn of events, were now craning forward eagerly, their faces taut and shining with sweat. Joseph swung up his arm in a gesture commanding silence, and then he said: "We have heard the word 'orders.' I hear there are orders given by a White Chief in Washington. What are these orders?"

"They are very simple," the general answered. "You must take your horses and beef herds and come to the reservation at Lapwai. This is true for White Bird as well."

"Is that an order?"

"I said it was an order. I did not make the order. I am merely here to execute it."

Alokut rose gracefully and said: "It is not enough to speak words. We must think carefully. The Indians respect the white men, even when they are treated like dogs. I say there should be one law for all. Is that true? If I murder, then I am hanged! It is true if I am an Indian, but it is not true of white men. It is not always true. There must be one law or no law. Is this true?"

"I cannot argue with you," the general said. "We must obey the government. What it commands us to do, we must do. You must not think of disobeying the government. I see by their bearing that Joseph and Alokut are friends to the white men, but there are others—"

Smohalla was slobbering at the mouth and shaking his fists. Strange squeaky sounds came from him, high-pitched. They sounded more like incantations than any recognizable speech. Everyone was shouting at once. Even Alokut sprang up, his feathers trembling, and he was about to march up to the general when Joseph placed a restraining hand on his shoulder. The general gazed at the rippling stretch of blue-white canvas overhead. He pretended that the uproar among the Indians had no existence, and simply because he stood his ground and behaved in this way, they respected him. The shouting died down; then the muttering died away. The general said quietly: "This behavior is not worthy of you. You must listen in peace."

Smohalla began babbling again.

"You must not talk, Smohalla. You have talked enough. It is time others talked."

"Let us talk about the murders," Smohalla exclaimed. "This going to Lapwai is one thing; the murders are another thing. We have suffered too much from white men. Now let us talk of all the harm they have done to us."

"I told you to keep silent," the general said patiently, and then he turned towards Joseph with a strange look of innocence on his face and said: "What is all this talk about murders?"

"The murder of Yellow Bear and all the others," Smohalla said triumphantly.

"I know nothing about Yellow Bear. Who is he? There have been murders on both sides. The government, as you know, is always trying to stamp out murder."

"Yellow Bear is dead; no one has been punished," Smohalla cackled.

Without moving an inch, without altering the impassive expression of his face, simply by being still, Joseph dominated the Indians.

"He is strong beyond words," Stevens told himself. "If there was only Joseph and the general, then they would come to an amicable agreement—"

Joseph still said nothing at all. He was like someone lost in a dream of hunting: you could always tell when an Indian was dreaming of a buffalo hunt. The general was saying something about justice —there had been trials—some Indians had been found guilty, and so had some white men. There were more shouts from Smohalla, whose broad and ragged face was continually bobbing up. He would bob up halfway through the interpreter's translation, saying he did not want to listen any more, he must answer at once, the general was saying inexcusable and unheard-of things. Once Joseph motioned to Smohalla to sit down. On the benches the Indians were leaning forward, their faces urgent, and often their mouths were wide-open. Whenever Smohalla spoke there was a burst of excited shouting.

"It's no use," the general said. "We are getting nowhere. You must compose yourselves, or else we will have to adjourn the meeting."

Joseph rose, smiling. It was the signal to the others. The smile showed that he had no animosity towards the general: they would have to wait until tempers calmed. He strode up to the general and grasped his hand, and the sense of menace which had hung over the tent vanished.

"I don't understand what they're up to," Montieth was saying. "Delays. Delays. You'd think they wanted to delay a decision till Doomsday."

"Perhaps they do," Stevens said quietly.

"As you can see, the general has them well in hand," Montieth smiled.

There was no cynicism in his smile. It was true. The general was laughing, and twenty Indians were crowding round him, all eager to shake his hand or touch the empty sleeve. Their anger had vanished as suddenly as it had risen. There was no sign of Smohalla.

Soon, at another signal from Joseph, they left the tent. They were unusually quiet. They mounted their ponies, rode round the fort and shouted their coyote-shouts, but this time there was little excitement in their shouting. Then they rode through the dust towards their encampment on the creek.

"They're like children, aren't they?" Montieth was saying. "One moment weeping, the next laughing."

"No, you're wrong. They're not in the least like children."

"Then what are they like?"

"Homeric heroes, but you wouldn't understand that," Stevens said, and he was glad when he was outside the tent, seeing the valley in the sun with its bright patches of silver haze.

XIV

A Mysterious Visitor

"WELL, what do you make of the scoundrels?" the general said, laughing. "I reckon we've got them by the short hairs. I'm not being unsympathetic, but it seems to me that fellows like Smohalla are going to make my work easier."

It was late in the evening, the time when the general's mind worked at its best. There was no more kerosene oil: the general's office was lit by candles. They could hear the guards pacing restlessly below.

"What do you think, eh?"

"I believe Joseph is trying to hold them back."

"Of course he is, but when you come down to brass tacks, who is more important—Joseph or Old Smokeholer? I'm sure of one thing: Old Smokeholer wants to send the Indians out on a rampage, and he won't be happy until they do. Joseph—well, I admire Joseph, but I can't take any risks. I've come to the conclusion that we'll have to make a show of force. I'm ordering Captain Trimble's company from Walla Walla to Lewiston, and I'm sending some cavalry over to the Wallowa Valley. It's the only way."

The general said the last words sadly. There had been a gleam of defiance in his eyes. He had been testing his adjutant. He knew, or thought he knew, exactly what was going through Stevens' mind. But what else could he do, faced with these recalcitrant Indians? His huge shadow raced along the wall, resembling a portrait of Moses, so dark and bearded and vigorous, the high forehead and the hooked nose grotesquely exaggerated. Stevens felt the blood pounding in his ears. The general was pacing backwards and forwards across the room. All the time his large crafty eyes were on Stevens.

"You don't think it's the proper thing to do?" he said at last.

"No, sir, I think it will cause trouble. They distrust us now, and they'll distrust us all the more if we send troops to cut their lines of communication and to occupy the Wallowa Valley. They'll hate our guts."

"Yes, they'll hate our guts," the general said, and there was a note of regret in his voice, as though he desired nothing more than peace with the Indians but knew it was impossible.

The nights in the log buildings of the fort were often hotter than the days. The long valley was like a cup in which all the heat of the day seemed to trickle down. Sweat ran over the general's forehead and down his cheeks. He lifted the glass over a carafe and poured himself a drink of water, and while he drank he listened to the noises of the guards as they paced along the fence rail, their unruly whisperings and grunts, and sometimes a horse neighed, and from a long way away there came the soft chanting of the Indians. The chanting was getting on his nerves. His mouth open, his face turned scarlet from the heat, his one hand moving restlessly over the map, the general sat at the table, seeing the map as though he was a hawk hovering high up above the rumpled mountains and ridged valleys and canyon walls of the territory he commanded and would have to shield from the depredations of the Indians. Eastward lay the mountains. Closer at hand were the deep gorges of the Snake River and the rough uplands and the sheer valleys, the landscape a maze of winding streams and roaring rivers, where a small army could disappear and never be hunted down. There were creeks along the whole length of the Snake; the river was a thousand miles long, as long as the Hudson, Delaware and Susquehanna combined. That was where the trouble lay. The traders expected the Army to clear the country of Indians, but only the Indians knew the trails. They could be forced into a reservation only by an overwhelming act of authority. "God help us," the general murmured. "We're at their mercy, if the truth be told. We'll have to use the power of our authority over them—nothing else serves."

"You mean the Army?" Stevens asked helplessly.

"Of course I don't mean the Army. Something greater than the Army. Authority, the power that lies at the heart of government. Government is a powerful thing, Stevens. It may be strange to you, but it is so. Tell me, you don't agree to sending troops to Wallowa?"

"No, sir."

"But they've got to go on the reservation. How else can we manage it? We must get troops where we can, ring them round, force them to it. I tell you, unless we're damned careful there's going to be war between the Nez Perce and the United States Army."

The general's shadow wheeled across the wall. All the general's power, his stubbornness, his sense of duty, his astonishing pride and real humility, all these were evident in the furious wheeling shadow, which tore across the wall. When Stevens turned from the shadow to the faintly smiling face of the general, he was aware of a startling inconsistency: there was more of the general in the shadow than in the man himself.

The general was saying: "You're a good adjutant, and you're in my confidence, but I'll be damned if I'll have you falling in love with the Indians. Is that clear?"

"Yes, sir."

"Remember, we have to take the usual precautions. I'll admit that, in the present case, the Indians may only be exuberant—I wasn't particularly happy with their display this afternoon, and someone ought to tell them that there's nothing to be gained by war whooping round the fort."

"May I tell them, sir?"

"You may indeed."

"May I go out and talk to them now?"

"Now—at this hour of the night?"

"Yes, sir."

"Your life wouldn't be safe, Mr. Stevens. There's no moon. They'd cut you down."

"I'm prepared to take the risk, sir."

"No, I won't have you going on secret expeditions to their lodges at night. You've got better things to do. Have a good night's sleep and prepare for whatever exhibition they are going to put on tomorrow."

"It wouldn't do any harm, sir. I'm perfectly sure I would be received by Chief Joseph."

"I've told you not to go."

"Yes, sir."

There was a short pause. Most of the time while the general was speaking Stevens had been eyeing the grotesque shadow on the wall. The general was sucking at his teeth, and this had the effect of making his upper lip jerk upwards and downwards very quickly and rhythmically. He sighed, poured himself another glass of water and said in the clipped voice he employed whenever he had other things on his mind: "Well, good night."

"Good night, sir."

Stevens had reached the door when he was called back.

"You're leaving your blessed Homer behind. You'll want it, won't you? I wouldn't be surprised if you put it under your pillow each night and dreamed about the heroic exploits of the Greek heroes. Myself, I'm content with the exploits of the great Napoleon."

With that Stevens was dismissed, and he walked slowly across the parade ground to his own sleeping quarters behind the barracks and the blacksmith's shed. As the general's adjutant he had acquired sleeping quarters remote from anyone else, and this pleased him: it was a small hut once used to store commissary supplies, now empty of everything except a bed, a chair and an apple-box full of books. Groping in the dark, he lit the kerosene lamp and then lay down on the bed, staring up at the ceiling, where the cobwebs were festooned like hanging veils. He had written out for the general a complete report of the discussions during the afternoon, but nothing in the report pleased him: it lacked color and fire, the cold statements of General Howard and Montieth were followed by the bristling responses of the Indians, and no one reading the report could have been aware of the splendor of the scene under the tent. The report itself would never reach Washington, for the general would simply make an abstract of it, and keep even the abstract among his own papers, and no one would ever know how desperately the Indians had fought for their rights.

"Shadows everywhere," he said aloud, and lifted his hand, so that its shadow wheeled across the wall.

For a while he read Homer, drawing the lamp nearer, but after a few pages he could no longer bear the brazen heroism of those god-like characters who were always saved at the last moment by the intervention of the gods. He put the Homer aside, and drew out from the apple-box a volume of Byron, but Byron was no better. "There's no end to the shadows," he murmured, snapping the book shut and flinging it across the room. "What's the use? They'll destroy Joseph and turn his men into shopkeepers!" The kerosene lamp was going out already, and when he turned up the wick there was a bright silver explosion of flame and then darkness. He lay down at full length on the bed while ghosts haunted him—the ghost of Yellow Bear, the ghost of

Lem Otis. Was Lem alive? He did not know, but it would not have surprised him if Lem had become a ghost, nor would it have surprised him to discover that Lem had remained at Wallowa and was overjoyed when the valley of the winding waters was filled with surveyors and tradesmen. Summer lightning was playing on the hills, and the Indians were still chanting, but their voices came like the dying echoes of the wind in the cottonwoods.

Stevens had been asleep an hour when he was awakened by the sound of someone moving in the room.

"Who is it?" he said sharply.

There was no reply.

"Who is there?" he said, his voice dropping to a whisper, and he was not surprised when he heard someone speaking in the Nez Perce tongue: "Make no sound. I am here. Do you not recognize me?"

"How can I recognize you in the dark?"

"It is I—Bird-with-one-eye."

The voice seemed to come from the direction of the apple-box. The window was open, and suddenly a dark shape moved across the window, hiding the stars. For some reason he could not believe Bird-with-one-eye had come there. All this—the black shape against the sky, the whispering, the sound of a foot moving across the floor boards and the faint shine of light on dark flesh which lasted for a moment, but only for a moment—all this, it seemed to him, was only the continuation of his nightmares. Then, as his eyes grew accustomed to the darkness and the shapes in the room, he saw that a brave was standing above his head, naked except for buckskin leggings and a single eagle feather in his scalp lock.

"So it is you, Bird-with-one-eye," he said, peering up and smiling, and all the time he imagined that the Indian would vanish like a puff of wind. "How did you come?"

"An Indian can go anywhere," Bird-with-one-eye replied, kneeling at the head of the bed.

"You go through walls?"

"No, I go over them with a tepee-pole. It was easy. There are only four men guarding the fort."

"You vaulted over the palisade?"

"Yes."

There was a sound like a chuckle. Feeling safe, Bird-with-one-eye made his way from the head of the bed until he was crouching halfway down its length. The only light came from the gleam of his teeth and the curve, like a sickle moon, of his shoulders. He said slowly: "Chief Joseph sent me. He offers you this."

Something was being pressed into Stevens' hands, but he could not see what it was, or recognize the nature of the gift by its shape. It was dark, furry and pointed, and about the size of the hollow of a man's palm, and it nestled like something living in his hand. At first he thought it was some very small animal, or perhaps the paw of a small animal, but when he pressed it, it was hard as stone beneath the fur.

"What is it?" he asked.

"Can't you guess?" Bird-with-one-eye answered. "Surely you can guess?"

Bird-with-one-eye was speaking close to Stevens' face. Unaccountably Stevens felt afraid. He remembered Joseph saying: "What is man but an arrowhead clothed in skin?—He must fight for what he has." So it was an arrowhead clothed in fur, but still there was something left unsaid, some message undelivered. He held the arrowhead between thumb and forefinger.

"It's a sign," said Bird-with-one-eye. "He comes with peace. His power is in the arrowhead, but he hides it. Tell me, what are they going to do with us? Are they going to take us away from the valley of the winding waters? Will they send soldiers?"

"No, not by force," Stevens said, lying, and he knew his voice was unconvincing. "They will talk first."

"Have they sent soldiers already?"

"Yes—five years ago they sent soldiers."

"But now?"

"They will be sent, but it means nothing," Stevens said slowly, and he wondered how convincing he was, there, in the darkness, when only the tone of the voice spoke and the words meant nothing at all. A child would have known he was lying.

"Then they have sent soldiers to go behind us?" Bird-with-one-eye said slowly, weighing each word carefully.

"No, the soldiers are being called for tonight or tomorrow, but they won't disturb anyone. The soldiers are nothing."

Then there was silence, a long silence. Somewhere outside a guard scratched a match to light a cheroot, and somewhere the thunder creaked, and there was always the chanting of the Indians in their encampment. They would chant all night.

Stevens leaned forward and whispered: "Another thing. Don't ride round the fort. It does no good to alarm the general."

"You say we mustn't?"

"I say it's better not to."

Silence again.

"What is going to happen to us?" the Indian asked. "They'll take everything away, and give us nothing in return. Chief Joseph wants to know."

"Everything will be all right."

"You say that, but do you know? What does the general say? Are you and the general of the same mind?"

"Yes."

"This is not what we think."

"Nevertheless it is true. We must all work together, Bird-with-one-eye. Do not threaten. Listen, and be cautious, and everything will be for the best. Tell Chief Joseph that."

There was a gleam of teeth, a smile, and Bird-with-one-eye was gone. For a long while Stevens could not sleep. He listened for faint sounds, but there was only the eternal pacing of the guards. He tossed restlessly, brooding, wondering what the general was up to, and then he wondered what the general would say if he learned that he, Stevens, had told the Indians the soldiers were coming to Wallowa.

He groaned, pulled the blanket over his head, and still he could not sleep.

XV

Shadows in the Tent

THROWING off his clothes and splashing himself with soapy water, Stevens drank in the sunlight from the open door. A milky haze hung over the fort. The sun glittered. The meadow larks were singing, and there was the pleasant rumbling sound of the horses at exercise on the meadows back of the fort. He was rubbing himself down when he remembered the visit of the Indian during the night. He remembered only disconnected fragments of their conversation. Then there was the arrowhead. Where the devil was it? He found it lying on the bed: an arrowhead of green obsidian in a fur sachet. It was beautifully carved and veined, with a razor edge, as he learned when he drew his finger along it. But why an arrowhead? Was it a warning? He remembered dimly that Chief Joseph had spoken of an arrowhead, but when? He dressed quickly, marched to the mess hall, and tried to throw off the nightmare. He found himself sitting opposite Captain Perry. The captain was tall, red-faced, with a boyish manner which the heavy mustache could not conceal. The captain's eyebrows were perpetually raised, so that you always felt he was about to ask a question. Stevens was annoyed. He wanted no questions. He wanted to have his breakfast of coffee and hard tack without interruption.

"I hear you know a devil of a lot about these Indians," the captain began. "Clever as a bunch of kittens, aren't they?" There was no reply. The captain went on: "The noise they make when they come to the fort. It's disrespectful to the general—most disrespectful. I wonder the general stands for it."

Again there was silence. The captain leaned forward.

"Did you hear about the Indian who slipped into the fort last night?"

"No."

"I'm surprised at you. How do you sleep? I'm told you sleep on your stomach and suffocate yourself in the pillow. You wouldn't hear anything if the whole bunch of Indians came over the wall—"

"What happened?"

"You really didn't hear the shooting?"

"What shooting? What's all this about, captain?"

"Well, I'll tell you. The guards reported this morning a buck came over the wall, looking for rifles probably. Didn't find anything. They think he prowled around for a while. Anyway one of the guards saw him climbing over the wall and opened fire. We found bloodstains—not far from your hut. You're sure you didn't hear anything?"

"I'm quite sure."

Stevens' face reddened, as it always did when he lied.

"Two guards reported they saw something—may have been the buck—prowling by your hut. They think he could have slipped through the window."

"Could be," Stevens said, pretending it was a possibility which he thought in the highest degree unlikely. "Could be."

"You're sure you didn't hear the shooting?"

"I've told you I didn't. What time was it?"

"Just before dawn."

Stevens smiled with relief. He was not sure why he was relieved. Bird-with-one-eye must have stayed within the fort for three or four hours after seeing him. Why? He told himself he would learn later. Meanwhile he avoided Captain Perry's enquiring glances, and got down to the hard tack.

Stevens sipped his coffee carefully, and then went out into the sunlight. The sun was fierce and strong on his face, and the air was blue and spinning. Only the fort looked barren, no more than a shoddy collection of unpainted timber buildings with a pathetic stockade of upright wooden logs. The small bastions at each corner of the fort, from where the armed sentries looked out on a flowering valley, seemed as though they were about to fall. Some men were drilling, but they too looked ragged. "The Indians could take the place if they wanted to," Stevens thought. "There's nothing to prevent them."

The general was already at work when Stevens climbed into the office: even the wooden stairs were crumbling. The general was writing on a sheet of folio paper held down at the corners by pellets. The empty sleeve flapped in the wind coming from the open window.

"Good morning, sir."

"Hello, Keff. You're missing the fun."

The general smiled. He was evidently in an astonishingly good temper.

"Look out of the window," he said. "Chief White Bird arrived half an hour ago. I can't understand these poor devils. What do you think they are doing?"

"Running races with Joseph's men," Stevens said, and went to the window.

Yellow horses were streaking across the green plain; there were war whoops, and sudden excited cries, and smoke rose from the tepees. The general was still smiling. He had slept well, and the look of contentment on his face showed that he was no longer in any fear of the Indians. He rose from the desk, strode to the window, and began to swing backwards and forwards on his toes.

"I can't make them out," he said delightedly. "Wonderful people! D'you know where Chief White Bird comes from? He drove his ponies over Craig's Mountain. Think of that! It's three feet deep in snow, and he drove everything over—lodges and squaws and papooses, and the moment he arrives here, he engages in racing. I dare say that except for the storms around November this is the worst time of the year to cross the mountains! I sent word to Chief Joseph that I planned to hold the meeting this morning at ten sharp. I think they're coming round. It shows you what authority can do."

There was silence. Some blue butterflies were roaming across the parade. Troopers were rubbing down their horses. A bugler was practicing somewhere in the hills, and the thin notes of the bugle were pleasant on their ears.

"You seem dubious, Mr. Stevens."

"No, sir. I just don't know. There must be nearly a hundred braves now. I keep thinking they could attack the fort, and kill every one of us."

"They won't dare," the general said, shaking his head from side to side.

Stevens obtained no clue to the general's satisfaction. It was perfectly clear that the general was afraid, but at the same time he was in a mood of buoyancy. He half admired the Indians and half hated them. He was afraid of their numbers, their gaudy feathers, thei brilliant blankets, their cunning as sharpshooters, their ability to trav in all weathers. The truth was, he admired courage, and he thought Chief White Bird's arrival after crossing the Craig's Mountain was a remarkable accomplishment. He had thought Chief White Bird would be a week late. Now he smiled at the valley filled with painted horses.

"We'll have to wait and see," he said gruffly, and went back to writing his long letter on army note paper.

They did not have to wait long. At ten o'clock the procession was formed, and all you could see from a distance was the great waving of headdresses and the speckled cayuse horses. The sky was a deep summery blue with no hint of cloud; a gentle wind came coursing through the valley and over the smooth hills, and the thick grass waved and rippled in great noiseless swells, and indeed the whole plain looked like the sea and the Indians in procession resembled a long painted boat coming to shore. The sound of their chanting came with the following wind.

"Well, they've come," the general said, throwing his pen on the table, and then walked down the wooden steps with his head bent and his lips moving as he prepared the speech he would deliver in the tent.

This time the general had taken precautions. He feared a ruse. It had occurred to him that Joseph might be attempting to lull him into a false sense of security. Yesterday, they came galloping wildly up to the fort, but they had been peaceful enough, and not a shot had been fired. What of today? So he had given orders that the troops should fire at the first sign of hostile intent on the part of the Indians. Stevens, too, hoped they would come riding calmly, for had he not warned Bird-with-one-eye against the display of horsemanship and singing around the fort? But when he walked across the parade a little behind the general, as they made their way to the tent, he knew that the warning had been in vain. Once again the thunder of the horses' hooves came clear in the scented air, and the shouts of the Indians were wilder than ever. They were more numerous now, and more sure of themselves. They galloped straight up to the tent and then wheeled, throwing up a huge cloud of dust in which feathers gleamed like banners.

The day before Chief Joseph was calm, brooding, sunk in himself. Now his eyes flashed, and there was a tight expression on his lean face, but the strangest thing of all was his fantastic uniform. Evidently, he had dressed up to receive Chief White Bird. His headdress was the skin of a wolf-head, the pointed ears standing erect. He wore immense chains of bears' claws round his neck. The ruff of feathers floated eight or nine feet in the air, and every feather was a different color. He wore a bright blue coat of buffalo hide, and a scarlet blanket fell from his shoulders, and his leggings were adorned with little brass bells and splinters of glass. Chief White Bird, a head shorter, gruff and surly, followed, and he too was dressed to the hilt, with smears of yellow along his nose and gashes of red along his cheeks. Afterwards came the bodyguard of the most handsome of the young braves, and as though they were deliberately setting off the splendor of the chiefs, they were nearly naked, their bodies rubbed with oil and shining in the sun.

The great procession roared towards the fort, everyone shouting and singing at the top of their lungs, exactly as they had done the day before. Then, having ridden round the fort twice, they calmly dismounted and unhurriedly made their way to the tent.

Joseph explained to the general that they were only celebrating the arrival of the chief.

"Here he is. I spoke to him of you. I want him to understand what you have been saying to me."

The general smiled and thrust out his hand. Chief White Bird seized it and would not let it go, all the while gazing deep in the general's eyes. High above them the bluish-white canvas rippled in the morning wind.

When the Indians were all settled on the benches, the general rose quietly to address them.

The general began hesitantly, with one eye on Montieth, for he was convinced now that the Indians would simply repeat their behavior of the previous day. Stevens wrote in his notebook: "Achilles sulks in his tent. Will he break out when the fit of sulking is over? There are orders from Washington. Perhaps in the Grecian wars it was the same—orders from Athens or some faraway place." The general was coming to the end of his peroration. "You must trust us," he was saying. "We are here to help you. You must obey orders, though."

On the face of Joseph there was the contemplative sadness you see often on the faces of Indians at dusk but rarely on bright mornings.

"What are orders?" Joseph whispered, but the general was looking in another direction, and in any event he would not have understood what Joseph was saying.

It was Tuhulhulsote who rose and shouted: "So you set yourself above us? You invite us here, saying there are matters to be discussed, but how can we discuss when there are only orders? We are in the right. The land belongs to us. Who will take it away?"

Tuhulhulsote, small and leathery and thickset, spread out the fingers of both hands. The fingers looked like black twigs. It was some kind of sign, but there was only silence among the Indians. Alokut ostentatiously yawned.

"The earth is our mother," Tuhulhulsote screamed. "How can you take our mother away from us?"

"What is all this about the earth being our mother?" the general said impatiently. "We must obey Washington—that's all."

Tuhulhulsote glared. He was like a bird dashing against a window. He said: "Can a man before Heaven say when he stands on the earth: Underfoot is mine, and above my head is mine. Who says that?"

"The President in Washington says that."

"Who is he, then? Does he possess power over all? Does he possess power over the earth, and everything that is in the earth?"

"Certainly he does—he possesses power over the territorial extent of the United States."

"He does? Then remember the coyote who bled from the giant's mouth—"

"What is all this about the coyote? We are talking about instructions received from Washington."

The general was angry. He thought he had begun well. Now he was on the defensive, faced with the strange relentless and irrelevant questioning of the Indians.

"The coyote is important. Listen. The coyote is our beginning. He bled in the giant's mouth. Ha! Do you know how our nation came into being? Let me tell you. A giant came—the giant who was going to swallow the whole earth. But the coyote took fire into his mouth, and when the giant attempted to swallow him, the giant's mouth was scorched, and the coyote also was scorched, and from the blood of the giant and the coyote arose our nation. The blood fell on Wallowa. Do you understand that?"

"I understand nothing, Chief Tuhulhulsote, except that you are impertinent. These are all fairy stories."

"Do you believe there was a giant?"

"No."

"Then what do you believe? A man must believe. The coyote is true. I know the place where the blood fell. What is man? The earth is his mother. Do you believe that? Our mother does not sit in Washington. She is everywhere. All may rest on her. All must rest on her. When a man is born he rests on her, and when he dies he rests on her. I am Tuhulhulsote, and I have spoken the truth!"

The debate went on. The general was always attempting to bring the subject back to the Lapwai Reservation: the minds of the Indians, in fear and fascination, were fixed upon Wallowa, the land they could never leave. They could not understand why the general had called them for a discussion, and then brazenly given them orders. What kind of a discussion was that? With his dark leathery face, twiglike hands and eyes blazing like diamonds, Tuhulhulsote returned continually to the attack. "Poor devil, he babbles," the general said, and when Tuhulhulsote was screaming, the general ostentatiously read his Bible, shaping his lips though he read silently; then he would put the book down to listen to the translation. Suddenly Joseph was standing, a brilliant scarlet and white blanket now falling from his shoulders.

"There is too much talking to vain purpose," he said. "Let us think all these matters over for a few days."

"Very well," the general smiled, "let us meet on Monday. We shall have three days to think. You—" He indicated Joseph with a nod. "You will talk it over with your men; and if there are problems, then come to me here at the fort, and we can discuss them man to man. Remember we are here to help. We are not your enemies. We are friends."

Once more the Indians surged out of the tent. Montieth rose and collected his papers together. Stevens shut the little notebook filled with drawings of the chiefs. James Reuben buried his face in his hands. The general brushed the ends of his mustache with his knuckle and then glared benignly at Chief Tuhulhulsote, like a father glaring upon a recalcitrant child.

The Indians were beginning to file out of the tent when a trooper rode up, dismounted and came hurrying towards the general with a letter. The general opened the letter without glancing at the envelope, thinking it was a report sent by courier from Walla Walla: he had been expecting such a report, had indeed expected it nearly every minute of the past three days and was afraid that something had happened to the courier—either he had been attacked by Indians or had met with misadventure. The thought of the message had preyed on his mind throughout the discussion with the Indians.

When he had read the letter right through, the general whistled.

"A lot of damned nonsense!" he exclaimed. "Does he think I have time to see all the riffraff who come to the valley? Judge Shillitoe! I suppose he wants something of me. He wouldn't come otherwise, would he?"

The questions were addressed to himself, for he would often find himself murmuring aloud when his strength was exhausted. Stevens was pricking up his ears.

"Did you say Judge Shillitoe, sir?"

"I did."

"And he has written to you?"

"Worse, he has written that he is staying at the agency. He expects me to give him a few moments of my valuable time, and he has brought Mr. Lem Otis with him, and he ends the letter: 'Please reply at your earliest convenience and oblige.' Well, I have no liking for Mr. Shillitoe. If I had my way he would stew in his own juice, but he's a civilian and a judge, and I suppose I shall have to see him. I'll make him kick his heels a bit. I'll see him late this afternoon. I don't mind telling you I'm not happy with his coming. I think you told me something about him once, Mr. Stevens?"

"I did, sir."

"Then I'll have to get you to refresh my memory. He's a troublemaker, isn't he? Well, you can tell me about him later. I'm surprised that either of them should have ventured through territory where the Indians could have attacked them with impunity. I suppose he will want an escort back to Lewiston. I won't give it to him."

At that moment Stevens caught sight of Bird-with-one-eye hovering behind at the other end of the tent. All morning he had been hoping to set eyes on the brave, but without success. Suddenly, while the general was talking, Bird-with-one-eye had detached himself from a group of Indians and swung round to face the nearly empty tent. There was no expression on his face. He simply stood there, wearing an eagle feather in his scalp lock, a short buffalo-skin coat, leggings and moccasins, but from his right arm there hung a long rope of white fur, and some more of the white fur had been twisted round the arm in a bandage. Though Bird-with-one-eye was nearly twenty yards away, Stevens was aware of an accusing gleam in the brave's eyes. The general was still pondering the note he had received from Judge Shillitoe.

"He shouldn't have come, and he shouldn't have brought Mr. Otis, and I don't mind saying he's a damned nuisance. You're not listening to me, Mr. Stevens."

"Yes, sir."

"I'll want you to write out everything you know about these two gentlemen to refresh my memory. I'll want it by four o'clock. And I'll see Judge Shillitoe alone—I'm going to keep you out of this."

"Yes, sir."

"Remember, I don't want you to have any dealings with the Indians—don't speak to them—don't go among them unless you have my express permission."

"Yes, sir."

At the further end of the tent Bird-with-one-eye was making urgent signs. There was a bright mocking expression on his young handsome face as he pointed to the bandage round his arm. He was waiting for Stevens to come up. The general was watching. He seemed to know what was happening. He seemed to be at once amused and crafty, deliberately keeping Stevens by his side, asking about documents and whether the record was being properly kept, and what Stevens thought of his manner of dealing with the Indians. At last Bird-with-one-eye slipped away. Later, when Stevens went to the end of the tent, he saw only a solitary horseman streaking across the grass to join the main procession of the Indians. Soon the horseman disappeared in the thick haze of dust, and then there was only the long plain of grass smoking in the sun. High above, the meadow larks were singing.

XVI

A Meeting with the Judge

"COME in, gentlemen, you are very welcome," the general said, standing at the head of the wooden stairs.

Judge Shillitoe climbed the stairs slowly, supporting his immense weight with difficulty. Lem Otis walked gravely behind him, as though hiding from sight.

"Come in, gentlemen," the general said again, when they had reached the small platform at the head of the wooden stairs. "I think I know what you've come for. I've heard of you by report."

Judge Shillitoe settled comfortably in a wicker chair. He looked down at his fingernails, and then smiled sharply at the general.

"You're kind to welcome us," he said. "We've come a long way for this interview. We appreciate it. You're thought highly of in the Army, general, and I'm thought highly of in Lewiston."

"That makes us equals," the general said with a ghost of a smile.

"I think we both put the interests of the people first, general," the judge went on. "I put God first, then the people. You'll forgive me for bringing Mr. Otis. I did it apurpose, general. He's the one man who knows the Wallowa Valley. I told myself, there's one man who knows the valley, and I'll bring him along."

The general sighed. It was clear that the judge was having difficulty broaching the subject of his interview. His eyes were quick and darting, much quicker than you would expect from a man so heavily built. The general was wary. He was prepared to believe that Judge Shillitoe was a fool, but if he was he was a calculating fool. He could make nothing of Lem Otis: the beetling red eyebrows and the fierce red beard, and a face red from the sun. There was no warmth in Lem's face, nor gentleness of any kind, but this may have been the result of the long journey through troubled territory. The sunlight coming through the open window lit the two visitors, while the general remained in shadow.

"I'm at your service," the general said coldly.

"Well, that's good of you, general. I'm pleased to hear a soldier talk like that. Yes, sir, I'm pleased to hear it. We've come to talk on a very serious matter. I represent the best interests of Lewiston—"

"They sent you?"

"A representative committee of the best citizens sent me, general. I've come with a mandate from the city on a matter I feel strongly about. Let me get down to brass tacks. I'm not going to take much of your time. The people of Lewiston are scared of the Indians. They're plumb scared. They want to know what you're going to do about them."

"Go on."

"We don't want our womenfolk placed at the mercy of the Indians, general. We want to be sure that law and order will be extended over the Territory. We know the Nez Perce. We know they're the fightingest Indians in the Northwest, and if there's any fighting we want assurances. I reckon we have a right to assurances. The truth is, we want the Indians cleared out. We don't care where they go as long as they are cleared out."

"You said cleared out?"

"I did, sir. We want to have done with the Indians once and for all. We want to get it over with. The people of Lewiston have asked me to tell you this in no uncertain terms. Get rid of them, general, and the people of Lewiston—"

"Who are these people of Lewiston?"

"The inhabitants, sir," Judge Shillitoe replied with a look of surprise. "When I say the people I mean the inhabitants."

"All of them?"

"Well, no, but the important ones and most of the others. There's hardly a man in Lewiston who hasn't got my friendship, general. Name anyone of any importance in Lewiston, and I'll swear I've known him as well as one man ever knows another. The people through me wish you to know that they are willing to help you get rid of the Indians, any way you choose."

"You'd like to kill 'em all?"

"Yes, sir, I would."

"Fair means or foul?"

"By fair means if possible—"

"It isn't possible, Mr. Shillitoe, to kill a whole nation by fair means. It just isn't possible. What have you got against the Indians?"

"They're a dagger pointed at our hearts, general. They're a-meetin' and assemblin' and a-makin' for war. They're buying up weapons, tradin' horses for rifles. Every day now Indians are swaggerin' into Lewiston and tradin' for rifles."

"And they get 'em?"

"Yes, sir, they get them. I'm sorry to say there are a few white men and half-bloods who sell to the Indians."

"What kind of rifles?"

"Magazine rifles, repeating Winchesters, everything. They've got 'em cached pretty near all over the place. Get 'em to give up their rifles and then banish 'em, that's what I say."

"Where would you banish them to?"

"Canada."

"You think the British would have 'em?"

"I don't know whether the British would have them or not, general. All I know is they are no use to us here. There isn't an Indian born yet who has done an honest day's work. I'll tell you frankly we're scared of them in Lewiston. We're a God-fearing town, but we're scared of the Indians."

"I don't believe Mr. Otis is scared of the Indians," the general said with a thin smile, turning towards Lem. "I think, Mr. Shillitoe, you overestimate the dangers. I suppose you brought Mr. Otis as your bodyguard."

"I did, sir. A man of my substance has need of a bodyguard. I don't mind telling you the sight of Indians—we saw a good number of Indians on the journey here—did no good to me. I have faith in God, sir, and my strong right arm, and I have faith in the Army. I'm hoping you'll rid us of the Indians, general, and we in Lewiston don't care how it's done!"

"I reckon you've already said that. I take it you want us to go down to their lodges and murder every last man."

"Well, sir, I think the people of Lewiston would be mighty pleased if some such arrangement could be made. We are prepared to offer a large sum of money—a very large sum of money—if we could be rid of the Indians."

"Are you offering me money?"

"No, general," Judge Shillitoe drew back in his chair, for he had seen the narrowing in the general's eyes. "We have not come to bribe you or anything of the sort. The money could be placed in the name of some charity. You might say it is a free gift on the part of the people of Lewiston for services rendered, and if you would name a charity, then we would be obliged to you and keep it in mind."

Judge Shillitoe was puffing with the exertion of talking with the general. Sweat streamed down his face, and from time to time he mopped the sweat away with a red bandanna handkerchief. The general turned from the judge to Lem, and shook his head sadly from side to side.

"You want the Indians cleared off the slate, is that it?"

"That's one way of putting it, general."

The general rose and went to the window, partly to breathe the fresher air. He reached for his binoculars and for some moments stared silently through them at the Indians. Fires were burning in the lodges. Naked braves ran races. Others were running beside their ponies, and a few were practicing for the buffalo hunt, riding at immense speed and at the same time hanging by one hand on the pony's mane, their young bronze bodies completely hidden until the ponies veered round. Some young women with gay blankets over their shoulders were polishing deerskins with pumice. They seemed to be a calm friendly people going about their business.

In silence the general handed the glasses to the judge. The judge looked blankly at the spectacle of the Indians amusing themselves on a hot summer day, and then, at a nod from the general, handed the glasses to Lem.

"What did you see, judge?" the general said, and there was a hint of scorn in his pronunciation of "judge."

"Indians."

"They're the people you want to rid us of?"

"That's right. I'd get rid of the half-breeds too, if I had a chance."

Lem stared moodily at the women and the riders. There was no sign of Shades of Night. The horsemen were riding furiously all over the valley.

"I've seen them at their game for five years now," he said in a thick voice. "Know what they're doing? That racing—it's training for war, general."

It was the first time Lem had spoken since he entered the general's office. The general was so astonished that he returned to his desk, settled himself and said sternly: "I wonder you have the courage to come here, Mr. Otis, after all the trouble you have caused. I know your record."

"I'm proud of it," Lem said, looking straight at the general and jutting his jaw. "I've never done anything against the law, general."

"You've sailed close to the wind, and you've caused a great deal of disturbance among the Indians."

"I've defended myself against one Indian, and I'd do it again, general."

"You would?"

"A man has to defend himself. It isn't in human nature not to defend himself."

"All right, we won't discuss human nature. It's an inexhaustible subject, Mr. Otis."

The general sighed. He remembered all that Stevens had told him about Otis, and it was almost more than he could bear to see the man standing there with his feet wide-apart, his arms akimbo, his lips pursed into a thin line, damp hair falling over his forehead, a strange look of disdain in the widely spaced eyes. Turning to the judge, he said: "I've heard what you have to say, and as I understand it, you invite me to kill off every mortal Indian I set my eyes upon, and in return for this action on my part, your friends in Lewiston are prepared to put a sum of money at my disposal. Do I understand you correctly?"

"That's the rough and the short of it," the judge replied. "We don't ask you to kill them, general, if there's some other way we c'n get rid of them."

"You want the land for yourselves, is that it?"

"I'm not denying that. We want it, and by God, we're going to have it. It's rich dairy land, most of it, and there's gold at the grass roots, and we're for turning a profit from the land. You can't do it with the Indians around. You can't even begin to do it. We're asking for what's ours by right of conquest, and when I say 'we,' I mean all the people. You can't resist the clamor of the people, general, and you know it."

"Yes, I know it," the general said softly, and then turned his dark eyes towards Lem, who for some time had showed signs that he wanted to speak. "Well, Mr. Otis?"

"I'm thinkin' you're goin' to be in a lot of trouble soon, general. I've been a trader now for gettin' on eight years, and I know trouble when I see it. Believe me or believe me not, you can't gentle the Indians. I reckon they're going to fight and nothin's goin' to stop them. I'm offerin' my services as a volunteer."

The general leaned forward and said abruptly: "I can't prevent you."

"Then you'll have me?"

"I said I couldn't prevent you, Mr. Otis. I understand there is a volunteer company forming in Lewiston. I'm hoping we won't need volunteers."

"But if you do?"

"If we do, we'll need every man we can get."

The general smiled. It was intended as one of those cold smiles he employed to put an end to an interview: there was something deliberately final about it.

"I reckon you'll need me," Lem said. "I reckon you'll need a lot more like me before you're done. Why don't you take me now, general? I talk their language. I could find a bunch of Cheyennes who would fight with me."

"I'll think about it," the general answered, but he was not looking at Lem.

"Then you won't have me?"

"I'm not saying that. I said I'd think about it. The truth is, I believe the differences between Chief Joseph and the government may be settled to the advantage of both."

"Are you quite sure, general?"

"I'm not here to be cross-examined. I'm telling you what I think. I think you are overestimating the dangers—gratuitously overestimating them, if I may say so, and perhaps you have reason to overestimate them. Is there anything further I can do for you, gentlemen?"

Shortly afterwards the general was standing at the head of the platform, looking down at the judge and Lem Otis as they walked across the parade. They were oddly pathetic as they blundered about, looking for the gate. The general smiled, stroked his beard with his heavily veined hand and turned to contemplate the Indians. Standing there, above the level of the palisade, he could see them clearly, though they looked very small in the distance. He saw the sun gleaming on the painted ponies and the smoke rising in blue coils from the cooking-fires.

"What the devil did he bring Lem Otis for?" the general said, and then he shrugged his shoulders and returned to the table littered with maps and the drafts of the letters he was writing to Washington.

XVII

A Circlet of Diamonds

IT was evening again, and the mist was coming down the valley. The snow was melting in the Blue Mountains, and they could hear the distant roaring. The Indian ponies were grazing on the plump grass, all gold with sunset, and there were still some Indian women gathering camas bulbs. They seemed to have settled in the Lapwai Valley. Smoke rose from the baking pits, and the tepees shone in the fading light.

The general was restless, still pacing up and down the small office. He could make nothing of the visit. He had never trusted civilians: the best friends the Indians ever had were the military. This was true, and you could break your head against it, and it would still be true.

"They want us to rid 'em of the Indians—make a clean sweep. Well, they're not going to. I'm not going to give anyone an excuse for making a clean sweep of the Indians. If the truth was known, we'd probably find those ruffians have an interest in the Wallowa Valley."

The general looked like an animal at bay; he kept glancing out of the window.

"We're getting nowhere with the Indians and nowhere with the civilians," he said.

"Could I go and talk with Chief Joseph?" Stevens asked.

"If you must—go and be damned to you!"

Half an hour later Stevens rode across the parade. Gusts of evening wind were flying; the clouds resembled huge tattered birds. A sentry said: "Think they're coming tonight, Mr. Stevens?" He was pale, about eighteen. "They could come, couldn't they? Heard say they were coming. Maybe they'll come," the boy said reflectively.

"Maybe they won't," Stevens announced, laughing.

"You really think they won't?" the boy asked eagerly. "I don't want them to come. Of course, sir, we would put up a good fight."

"I'm sure we would—that's what we're paid to do."

"Yes, sir, I didn't think about it that way."

Stevens guessed the boy had never been in battle, never heard a gun fired in anger, never known the danger he was in now. Stevens nodded to him, and then went to the stables, saddled the roan and then cantered down the valley towards the lodges. He was determined to see Joseph, and he hoped he would be able to see Bird-with-one-eye. The wind turned the grass to dusky silver. Smoke rose from the Indian cooking-fires, hiding the lodges. Seeing some braves, he asked them whether Joseph was in his lodge, for there had been rumors during the day that Joseph had made a journey down the valley; they said he was in his lodge, but no one had seen him; evidently there had been continual discussions between the chiefs. When Stevens came close to Joseph's lodge, Bird-with-one-eye darted out of a crowd of young braves who were busily chanting around a horsehide drum.

"You have come at last," Bird-with-one-eye said, and there was a hint of impudence in his tone. It was as though he was saying: "You have taken a long time to summon up enough courage to come here."

"I came because I must," Stevens answered, and dropped down from his horse.

"You want to spy on us?" Bird-with-one-eye said bitterly. "What else?"

"I want to help."

Stevens had said these words so seriously and with a smile of such quiet understanding that Bird-with-one-eye looked astonished. He tugged at the lieutenant's coat, smiled sheepishly and said: "Come to my tepee. We can rest there, and talk."

Bird-with-one-eye was strangely excited. He walked with a swift loping stride. It was a small tepee, with the usual hearth-fire burning. All the way Stevens had observed the brave making signs to the other Indians he passed. The signs were enough: there was no need for words: but what did they say? Stevens had the feeling that he was being led into a trap. But once inside the lodge, seeing the village through the flap, listening to the singsong voices of the children, the knock of an ax or the soft leathery sound of a pony being rubbed down, he was contented. In the dark dusk the village was preparing for the night.

"What have you come for? To see Chief Joseph?"
"Yes, if they'll let me see him."
Bird-with-one-eye put out a hand and laid it on Stevens' knee. His features remained tranquil, but a half-suppressed movement of the lips and a hasty glance towards the flap betrayed his emotion. Suddenly Bird-with-one-eye craned forward and blew on the hearth-fire, raising a cloud of bitter ashes in the air. Stevens watched him closely. He said: "I shall keep the arrowhead always." Bird-with-one-eye nodded. He was smiling broadly. Something had happened while he craned over the hearth-fire. He had done it deliberately to distract Stevens' attention. Stevens glanced up. Coming from the dark shadows of the tent someone was moving gracefully toward him; and all he could see in the darkness was a circlet of diamonds about the head.
"Do you remember me?" Shades of Night, a red blanket thrown over her shoulder, came in the circle of the hearth-fire. She walked with the mysterious assurance of a grown woman who knows exactly where she is going.
"Yes, I remember you."
"Is that all you can say to me?"
"You have grown—grown so much."
Stevens did not know why he had become suddenly so nervous. She smiled, squatting beside him, and her smile was very slow, a blossoming, a wonderful lifting of curtains. The face had filled out, and though there was still the eagerness of a child, there was understanding in the dark, flashing eyes.
"Are you happier now?" he said.
"I don't know. I never ask."
He held her hand. He saw that the circlet of diamonds was only glass beads mingled with the colored beads she normally wore around her head. She leaned forward, and with her dark face glowing in the light of the coals, she pressed her cheek against his, so softly that it was like the brush of a bird's wing against his face.
Stevens shivered. He had not expected this. He had lived without women, never thought of them, put them out of his mind. The glass coronet glowed, sparkled, sent up shoots of blue and yellow light. It was blinding, that radiance around her. She stared into the fire, and when he drew her closer, she was unresisting, and Bird-with-one-eye has slipped from the tepee.
He kissed her, and for a long while gazed at her face. A single drop

of sweat moved down her cheeks, and thinking it was a tear he brushed it away.

"We must be together," he said. "Somehow, somewhere—"

"You don't hate me?" she asked, holding her head to one side, gazing at him.

"Why should I hate you?"

"Because of Lem."

There was only silence and love between them; only the darkness of the shadows, and the blazing of the coronet of beads, and the flames from the hearth-fire shining on her uplifted face. They were there for ten minutes, their bodies touching, holding hands, when Shades of Night suddenly started to her feet. She looked frightened. Stevens followed the direction of her eyes. Chief Joseph was standing at the opening of the tepee. Evidently Bird-with-one-eye had gone in search of the chieftain, who stood there alone, smiling, wearing a blanket embroidered in great star-shaped patterns of red and yellow.

The chieftain lifted a bare arm in salutation. He towered there, looking like one of those immense figures in dreams, an extraordinary tranquillity attending him: motionless like a stone. Then on that heavy graven face with the high beaked nose and the deep-cut lips there appeared a smile of such friendliness that Stevens gasped.

Some braves, riding down the lanes between the tepee, saw the chieftain and pulled up their horses, to gather round the tepee.

"Tonight there will be dancing among us," Joseph said. "You will stay for the dancing? Have you brought messages?"

"Old Man With One Arm would like to see you."

"I shall not see him alone, only with the other chiefs—"

"Have you a message for him?"

"Yes, I have kept my faith. Let the white men keep theirs."

For a few more moments they gazed at one another, then Joseph turned abruptly, nodded to the horsemen and strode rapidly toward his own lodge.

The dancing that evening took place in front of Joseph's lodge. A huge fire of pinewood was burning. Around the fire old men chanted and beat drums and assumed strange animal-like attitudes, and sometimes they would recite their memories of the old chieftain, the father of Joseph, or of battles which occurred long ago. Smohalla was there, and Tuhulhulsote; and Alokut, as usual, took his place close to Joseph. Joseph sat on a buffalo robe just outside the lodge, his face bright yellow in the light of the roaring flames. The old men, their bodies painted over with strange drawings, mostly in bright yellow paint, postured and sang and crooned and jerked into little scuffling dances, and sometimes they would make terrifying lunges, or shake their fists at the sky, or else they capered round the fire or leapt over the flames, their old withered bodies streaming with sweat. The braves meanwhile stood in shadow, their blankets round them; usually there was a girl with them under the blanket.

"You must have a blanket, otherwise you will distract everyone," Bird-with-one-eye explained to Stevens, and when Bird-with-one-eye threw a blanket over Stevens' shoulder, Shades of Night slipped under it. With a single blanket over them both, they stood just outside the range of the roaring flames.

"It is well. We are together," Shades of Night said, and so they remained, holding hands, warm under the embroidered blanket, until the dancing abruptly ceased.

"Will you come to me again?" Shades of Night asked.

"I will come whenever you want me to come," Stevens said, and in a softer voice: "I have found you at last. We must never go far from each other."

She smiled and watched him swing up on to his horse, then he bent down and kissed her lightly on the mouth. A moment later he was cantering out of the village in the direction of the fort.

The stars hung low in the sky; the wind rustled the grass. It was one of those nights when the clouds resting on the hills glow russet with the flicker of lightning. After the brightness of the pine-log fire, after the warmth of the blanket, the night seemed dark and cold, with a freezing chill on the air. No lights shone from the fort. Sometimes he came upon swathes of grass sparkling with dew, and thinking he had come to the edge of the creek he would pull up his horse, and then, by the red glow from the hills, he would discover where he was and press his heels into the horse and speed on, but his mind was filled with Shades of Night, the warmth, the sweetness of her as they stood together under the blanket and watched the painted dancers. And suddenly he found he was passing out of the dark valley in which he had lived for a time into a bright pine-scented world of braves, the old and the young, their bodies burnt to brown silk or coppery leather in the sun, their feathers shining, their faces filled with glowing health: the faces of men and women who lived for the companionship of their warm tepees and cared nothing for governments or presidential orders or indeed anything except their families, their lodges and their earth. By what stars am I being driven? he asked, and brought the horse to a walking pace. Is Shades of Night waiting for me, or am I waiting for her? Is it war or peace? He did not know the answers to these questions. He knew he was walking his horse now towards a clump of cottonwoods far from the lodges, and a man was swinging a lantern on the dirt road, and now at last, standing not far from the creek and on a rise he could see that there were lights burning at the fort and more lights nearer at hand, and then he recognized the squat outbuildings of the agency.

The man with the lantern came running up the dirt road. Behind him came another man. Black puffs of smoke were coming out of the high chimney of the agency.

"I'm glad to meet you," the man said. "Sure enough, it is Mr. Stevens."

"How did you know it was me?" Stevens asked, recognizing Lem, whose face shone like a narrow sliver of red glass in the lantern light.

"I knew you would come by," Lem said. "I've waited and hoped you would, and sure enough you have come."

"I didn't intend to come," Stevens said ungraciously. "I had other things on my mind."

Judge Shillitoe was peering over Lem's shoulder, his small eyes twinkling.

"It's a pleasure to see you, young man," the judge said. "A great pleasure. You can be a great help to us if you have a mind for it. You would be doing me a favor, Mr. Stevens, if you would give us some advice."

"About what?"

"About Wallowa. A lovely valley. When I think of the place I truly believe God has produced a wonderful fruit for the human man. They say the Indians are going to leave it. They say a mint of things. Well, are they?"

"You want to know whether they are going to leave, is that it?"

"Correct."

"I don't see why they should," Stevens said, smiling in the darkness, for he had pushed Lem's lantern down and turned his face away.

There was a long silence. He could hear the judge's heavy breathing, Lem's lighter breathing. He could smell the bread being baked in the bakery. He knew there were Indians prowling along the road. For all he knew they may have been waiting even then among the clumps of cottonwood, waiting to pounce on the judge and the red-bearded trader.

"It's no use," Stevens said. "You'd better not ask me questions. You know the army rule."

"I'm not asking for anything secret—just a hint or two will be enough."

"And what's a hint?"

There was no answer. The lieutenant was silent, brooding. Somewhere on the retina of his eyes the gleaming coronet was still glowing. The judge was studying the lieutenant's face, trying to read the limits of his strength. Suddenly Lem was clutching the bridle. The face, red in lantern light, turned suddenly to gold as he lowered the lantern a little.

"Where's Shades of Night, lieutenant? Where the hell is she? I've got a right to know, haven't I?"

There was nothing whining in Lem's voice, but the voice was shrill. He was simply asking a question. His blue eyes blazed in the light, and the crust of orange beard looked like golden wires, and his mouth was wide-open, the teeth shining. Stevens could stand it no more. He drew his riding whip above his head and then brought it down on Lem's bare head. The lantern crashed to the ground, and there was the thin sound of glass breaking into splinters. The judge was shouting curses, and Lem was whimpering.

Stevens rode straight to the fort. The moonlight turned the walls silvery-white, and in the distance the lodges glowed like tents of marble.

XVIII

Uproar

STEVENS reported his short conversation with Joseph. The general growled into his beard, rammed some tobacco into his pipe, paced the wooden floor and said: "He won't see me alone, and he talks poppycock about white men keeping faith. Faith is a big subject, and I'm doing the best with what I have. What do you think they're up to?"

"They want the best terms they can get. They hope there's some way they can stay in Wallowa."

"Well, the Lord have them in His mercy," the general said, and after some discussion about the papers and reports on his desk he dismissed Stevens.

That night the general slept badly. There had been a cutting edge to the single phrase which Stevens had brought from Joseph. Let the white men keep faith! Well, it was a question of the meaning of faith. Those poor devils were not Christians; they hardly knew what faith was. The general stared up at the ceiling. He felt confused. He did not understand the workings of God's plan. That there was a plan he was certain. God was everywhere and watched all things, and His instrument—you might almost say His chief instrument—was the United States Army, the host of the Lord, the right arm of His justice. But why had God deprived the Indians of His grace? They were like beings of bronze, beautiful in their feathers and necklaces of eagles' claws: how strange that they had been deprived of His mercy!

"All very strange," the general murmured the next morning as he crossed the parade in the heavy sunlight, shaking his head, "and perhaps there is no explanation for what I am trying to tell myself this side of the grave. In the end I shall know, but not now. Here we are, millions of mortal men whose lives hang by a thread, and we fight one another and threaten one another, and to what end? That God's mercy should be justified? Then I must be more merciful and understanding of the Indians, but how shall I ever prevail upon them to understand that orders from Washington must be obeyed?"

It occurred to him, then, that the meetings in the tent were in the nature of an armed truce and "the conversation" in the tent represented the ultimate in war, the challenge of wills, the modern equivalent of the ancient spearmen or wrestlers who fought together while the opposing armies watched, secure in the knowledge that the champions could decide the issue. In this sense the conversation in the tent represented the ultimate in war, for within the tent the will, and only the will, prevailed; and weapons were a needless complication, to be avoided wherever possible. The bloodshed, the sorties, the night marches, the planned campaigns, all these were incidentals: in the naked contest of wills the war could be fought to a conclusion without anyone being physically hurt.

All this was simple and easy to be understood, and as the general entered the tent, he was aware that it was no longer possible or desirable to bring the Indians to the reservation by force: he would employ instead the authority of his will. Inside the tent he stood bareheaded, praying silently. The Indians were expectant, and the great bronze face of Joseph was turned towards the small pale general. "Not my will, but Thine," he prayed. There was no sound, no ripple of canvas. The Indians, seeing him, thought he was in a trance. He seemed to be standing there while his spirit wandered away towards the Great Spirit Chief.

For nearly a minute the general stood there, and then Montieth gently took him by the elbow and led him to the table. Suddenly the general lifted up his head and smiled towards Joseph, and then towards Alokut and the other chiefs. On this calm morning, the sunlight dancing on the tent and the yellow butterflies flying among the feathers of the Indians, everyone seemed to be relieved of the weight of a great responsibility, and yet the responsibilities had not changed in the least, and the decisions were still to be made.

"We must talk together as friends," the general said. "I hope you have all come to a conclusion on the matter."

Joseph rose, inclined his head slightly and said: "What matter? Are you still demanding that we go on a reservation?"

"I think it is best," the general answered, and there was such assurance in his smile that the Indians who failed to hear the translation thought he was talking about the weather.

"We—we do not think it is best," Joseph said. "We have talked and talked, and we come to the same conclusion. Today, I am ready to talk. This is the third of our meetings, but I am no wiser. We—white men and red men—are all sprung from women, although we are unlike in many things. We cannot be made over again. You are as you are: as you are fashioned by the Great Spirit so you remain. We are as we were made by the Great Spirit, and you cannot change us. Then why should children of one father and one mother quarrel? Why should one try to cheat the other? I do not believe that the Great Spirit gave one kind of men the right to tell another kind of men what they must do."

The general closed his eyes and murmured: "Patience! The prize belongs to the most patient." Aloud he said: "Do you deny my authority? I have listened patiently to all this talk of how we are born of one father and one mother. How long will it go on?"

There was no answer from Joseph. Tuhulhulsote rose, and asked whether he could say a few words. He promised they would be to the point.

"Then you must be short," the general said. "Last time you spoke about things which had nothing to do with the matter."

"I will be short if you will let me speak. May I speak?"

"I would like you to speak."

"Then I have this to say. You want us to go on a reservation. Why? Why? This is the question. What good does it do?"

"You must obey orders."

"Why?"

"Because they are made to be obeyed."

"Who made them?—that's what we want to know."

Yellow and blue butterflies were swarming into the tent, alighting on the feathers. The general watched the butterflies: he had no more patience with the Indians. He said: "If you do not understand that I have orders from Washington, then you are all fools!"

Tuhulhulsote raised a protesting finger. There was a mocking smile on his face.

"You lose your temper like a child," he said. "First you say one thing, then another. We are not fools. We are good Indians. We know what is best for us. You—what do you know? Are you the Great Spirit? Did you make the sun? Did you make the grass?"

The veins were standing out like iron from Tuhulhulsote's temples, as he shouted: "You know nothing—nothing at all!"

"You must not be impudent. I represent the President. There is the plain fact, and you know it. My orders are clear, and will be executed. I hope the Indians have sense enough to make me their friend and not their enemy."

White Bird, from behind his eagle wing, said in a curiously mild voice: "If I had been taught from early life to be governed by the white man I would be governed by the white man; but the earth governs me."

The general was now completely out of patience. He said: "So you refuse to obey the orders of the government?"

"I want to be left alone—that's all," White Bird answered. "What is government? I think as the stars think, and as the winds, and as the waving grass. What is this thing called government?"

"You are simply avoiding the issue," the general said in a hot, explosive voice. "You don't seem to understand that the question is very simple: Will the Indians come peacefully to the reservation, or do they want me, in compliance with my orders, to put them there by force?"

Tuhulhulsote drew himself to his full height, pointed at the general, advanced three paces and said in ringing words: "We shall not go! We refuse to go! Is that clear? I say it three times. We shall not go!"

In a stern voice the general answered: "You are giving the Indians bad advice. Because of this, I shall have to send you to Indian Territory. Do you understand that? You are asking the Indians to fight, and that means losing all their horses and beef herd. Joseph and Alokut are more sensible. They do not shout and point at me."

"We will not go!" Tuhulhulsote screamed again, and came three paces nearer.

The ropes were snapping which tied the general's temper together. He called a guard and said: "Old man, listen to me. You have talked enough. Now there must be an end to talk. Your body must be taken to the guardhouse."

"Do you want to frighten me with this talk of my body?"

"I am not frightening you. I am simply ordering your arrest."

"Ha! You order my arrest! That is all you can do! You can arrest me, but you cannot change my words."

The old chieftain was crowing with joy. He had found the general's weak spot. He had triumphed, because the general had admitted defeat by arresting the man who had spoken against him. A trooper forced his way through the crowd of Indians and placed a heavy hand on Tuhulhulsote's shoulder. The shock was so sudden that Tuhulhulsote reeled, and at the moment of falling he had hoped to strike a knife into the trooper. As he fell, he stumbled over Alokut, and then lay sprawling in the grass in the space which separated the general's table from the Indians. By falling, he lost face. He knew this. A rage mounted in him. He pulled at the grass and buried his face in it. He wanted to be alone, far away from the clamoring Indians and the spiteful white men, and when he half-rose to his knees his face was contorted with pain. Joseph whispered: "Go quietly. They will do no harm to you." Tuhulhulsote rose unsteadily, glared at the general, wiped the mud from his face, and then stumbling a little, throwing fierce little glances in the direction of the general, he allowed the trooper to lead him away.

All the Indians except the chieftains were now murmuring and shouting. They wanted vengeance. Had not the general shown that he had no friendship for them? The meeting was a fiasco, a trick, a deliberate trap.

The general was startled by his own words. He was sorry for Tuhulhulsote, an old man who spoke the truth as he knew it. He knew the chieftain's fall to the ground might have grave consequences. Yet he could do nothing else. He was afraid of showing weakness. The general had a trick of opening his eyes wide to express surprise or emphasis, and now as he watched Tuhulhulsote being led away, his eyes were enormous, and they seemed to grow even larger when Captain Perry entered the tent, looked the assembled chiefs up and down, and then seeing an old Indian stumbling across the grass with a trooper supporting him, he ran up and took Tuhulhulsote's other arm, thinking that the old chief had perhaps fallen ill; but when the general shouted: "I am putting the old fellow under arrest for disobeying my orders," Captain Perry still showed respect and kindliness towards Tuhulhulsote, but everyone could see that he was gripping the man's arm more firmly.

The Indians were completely confused by what was happening inside the tent. When Tuhulhulsote had passed out of sight, they stared at one another, and on their lips you could see the question: "How can such things be?"

"You see what happens to those who disobey me," the general said. "Bear what I say in mind. The government has offered you a magnificent reservation here in Lapwai. You will have fair grazing ground for your animals, and plenty of wood for the winter months. If you don't want to accept the government's offer, that is your affair."

He paused until the translator had finished, then he said: "Who will come to see the new lands? I am asking you. Who will come?"

There was no answer from the Indians. They were all looking at Joseph, whose head was bent low, hidden by an eagle fan.

"What is your answer, Chief Joseph?" the general asked.

"I will see these lands you talk about," Joseph answered. "I will see them, and then I will report to my people."

"That is as it must be," the general said, and then he turned smartly and made his way into the fort.

XIX

A Summer Journey

WITH the arrest of Chief Tuhulhulsote the heart went out of the Indian resistance. One morning, three days later, Joseph sent a message that he would see General Howard. Soon, Howard rode out to the Indian encampment. In a tepee set apart from the rest they talked about the Lapwai Valley, and when the discussion was over the general invited the chieftains to ride with him down the length of the valley. The interpreter was an Indian called Black Feet Bent in the Middle, and Stevens had been left outside the tepee to watch the Indians racing along the grass valley. None of them knew that the decision had already been made in the tepee.

The sun shone high and bright as they rode in the direction of the Clearwater. Joseph wore a scarlet blanket. Alokut's was multicolored. All the chiefs rode in their splendor. They had talked briefly with Joseph, and though Joseph had only hinted of the surrender, they knew in their hearts that this would be their valley. They could not fight against the white men. And there was the wide valley, the grass sparkling like emeralds, little puffs of smoke rising from the sunlit dew.

"It's good growing land," the general was saying, as he rode at the head of the small column. "Good for raising animals, good for corn. It's your land—all yours as far as eye can reach."

A deep sorrow was welling in Joseph. Had he not dreamed during the night of the high blue crags of Wallowa? Can a man leave his land, and remain unchanged?

"They say Lapwai means 'flutter of a butterfly's wings.' Is that right?" the general turned to Joseph.

Then with his white-gloved hand he made the gesture of a butterfly flapping wings, smiled and then pointed to the yellow butterflies hovering in the knee-deep grass. Wrapped in a gay scarlet blanket painted with designs of white birds Joseph bent his head and smiled.

"Yes, butterflies," he said, and he turned over his shoulder to see the small procession of young braves following him. "All land is good. I have nothing against this land."

"Then you will come to live here?"

"If I have to—"

The words, when they were translated, infuriated the general, but he kept his temper in check. The sun was burning his face. He rode bareheaded. Stevens was riding a little way away, with Looking Glass by his side. Looking Glass looked majestic, with his immense painted eagle feathers, the bronzed leathery face expressionless as a mask, the blanket falling loosely from his shoulders so that his coat with all its embroidery of porcupine quills and little slabs of colored glass glittered in the sun, and flashed like rubies. "I'm here with a bunch of savages," the general told himself. "Handsome devils, but savages nevertheless." From time to time he looked admiringly at their swinging sidelocks and braids in which strips of otter fur had been intertwined, but while he admired their costumes, he admired their set and expressionless faces more. Even now, though they had spent three days together in the tent, he did not know what was passing through Joseph's mind. Pointing to a small white frame house with a green fence, he said roughly: "What's the good of living in a tepee? A frame house—there's more comfort in it, it lasts longer, you can go out and work in your garden, and when there's a rainstorm, why, there's a good sound roof over your head. Have you ever thought of living in a frame house, Joseph?"

"Yes, I have thought of it."

The general thought Joseph was speaking ironically.

"And I suppose you are dead set against living in one, eh? You would hate it?"

"No. If I come to Lapwai, I must have a frame house. I have thought of it many times. I shall be like the white men. Will you give us houses?"

"Yes."

"And schools?"

"Yes, you will have schools."

"And teachers for the schools?"

"Yes, you'll have teachers for the schools, and we'll build you a church, and maybe a park."

"What is a park?"

"Some meadows to rest in."

"Churches I understand, but I cannot understand a meadow to rest in. We rest in all meadows. There are not some which we rest in and others we work in. You will give us schools, teachers, parks, meadows, churches and gardens. We don't want them. The earth is our mother. We must not break the earth by planting. No, we want to hunt buffalo and fish for salmon. We want to harvest the grain and berries which our mother grants us. Will you give us buffalo and salmon?"

"There are salmon in the Clearwater," the general said impatiently. "What is the matter with you? You came to me this morning and said you would come to the reservation, and now— Must we have arguments again?"

"No arguments."

"Then what are you trying to tell me?"

"I am not arguing. I want to know what is ours."

"Then I shall tell you—yours is all the land to the Clearwater. I shall show you a map."

Joseph smiled. The general thought he was smiling approvingly at the land: in fact he was smiling at his brother Alokut, from whose bare shoulders a rainbow-colored blanket flew in the wind. As Alokut rode he was juggling with five colored balls, and all his attention was concentrated upon keeping these red, green and yellow balls in the air. When the general turned slightly in the direction of Alokut the young chief simply gathered the balls together and pretended he was in deep conversation with Lieutenant Stevens.

"I should like to see one of the houses," Joseph said, when they had ridden a little further, past the creek and the willows. Once again the general was conscious of a note of irony. The heat of the day was beginning to dampen his spirits, but the sun shone, the chiefs were laughing, and occasionally they would come across an Indian boy who had strayed from the lodges to hunt jack rabbits. All along the grass there were summery fumes, blue-grey and glistening white, and all the scents of summer were in their nostrils.

"Then you shall see one," the general said quickly. "I don't suppose you would know the difference between a good one and a bad one, but I shall show you a good one. You are a chief. You deserve a good one."

"Of course," said Joseph quietly, and rode on in silence, dreaming of Wallowa again.

Halfway up a rise a large frame house with a rubblestone chimney and a painted fence looked over the valley. A small creek ran beside the house. There was a wooden water mill, but the mill itself hung above the trickling stream: and the wind, catching the wooden buckets, turned the mill slightly. Blue smoke came from the chimney. The house was hardly more than a cottage, and was owned by two women whose husbands were gold miners. The women were pleasant and red-faced. They were not frightened when they saw the general riding up at the head of a column of feathered braves. Leaning on their hoes, they smiled and waved, thinking that the general had come, as he often did, to wish them a good morning.

"It's a fine morning, general," they called across the fence, and they waved their handkerchiefs.

"Fine, fine," the general shouted. "Are the beans doing well, Mrs. Caldwell?"

"Fine, general."

"Everything fine?"

"Fine!"

The Indians thought this word "fine" must have some special magic power, and they began to shout "fine" at the top of their voices, vying with one another in shouting loudest. The general was not sure he approved of their shouting. They were like noisy children. Even Joseph, usually so reserved and staid, had bellowed "fine" and tossed back his head. Looking Glass, his leather cheeks wet with tears of laughter, rode up to the general and said: "General, I feel like laughing this morning. Why is this?" He could hardly speak from laughter, and he waved a knobkerrie made out of a great thonged lump of yellow quartz.

"Well, Looking Glass, there are three kinds of laughter—one arises from fun, another from deceit, another from real joy. Which is yours?"

"I am laughing from real joy," Looking Glass said, and his grizzled face exploded again with laughter.

Mary Caldwell was opening the gate with the idea of inviting them in to examine her vegetable garden. They all crowded into the garden. Looking Glass, observing the general's good humor, said: "Chief Tuhulhulsote must be miserable in the guardhouse. You should let him free, so that he can come with us into the garden." The general smiled, and put his hand on Looking Glass's shoulder. The gesture was enough: he knew that Looking Glass had understood, and there was no need to say: "I will free him soon. You mustn't worry about him any more. You are all good Indians, and now at last I am coming to recognize it."

Occasionally stroking his beard with his thickly veined hand, the general watched the Indians in the garden with approval. They were kneeling down to smell the flowers, scampering over the beds, shaking the fruit trees, and they would go up to the two ladies and examine their dresses, and they did this with such grace that no one took offense.

"General, Mrs. Caldwell asks whether they would like to share a meal with her," Stevens said.

"Nonsense, she can't possibly feed so many."

"She says she can, and she would be delighted—"

The gesture pleased the general, who reflected that the Indians rarely had an opportunity to share the civilizing influence of a home. They crowded inside, shouted "fine! fine!," sat on the chairs, opened cupboards, carefully examined each pan in the kitchen, and even stretched themselves on the beds. They were served with beef soup and cuts of lamb. All this was prepared by the two ladies with remarkable speed. It amused the Indians that the ladies went about their work singing hymns, and in an effort to please the ladies, the Indians began to sing sounds which approximated these hymns. Stevens explained with his tongue in his cheek that hymns were always sung during the preparation of food, though in fact Mary Caldwell was singing to hide her nervousness and Elizabeth Cornvallis sung because she possessed a fine voice and liked to demonstrate it. There were not enough chairs to seat all the Indians, and some of them simply sat cross-legged on the floor. The general sat at the head of the table, with Joseph on one side of him and Looking Glass on the other.

"You will give me a house like this?" Joseph said, smiling. Into his glass Mary Caldwell poured some cider which, on the general's instructions, she had plentifully diluted with water.

"Of course. If you want a house, then one will be provided for you. Do you want to live in a house or a tepee?"

"If I come here, I shall have to live in a house like the others, and my people will also have to live in houses."

The general nodded, lifted his glass, smiled, and said: "If you come here, there will be no difficulties between us. We want to help you. You shall all have houses."

Joseph repeated the general's words to the others, and drained his glass of cider.

"We shall all have houses—the general says so," Looking Glass said, gazing benevolently at a square of embroidery nailed to the wall above his head. The embroidery showed a field of poppies, and a hill on which a shepherd was wandering with his sheep, and above the shepherd were the words: "God is Love." Mary Caldwell, seeing that Looking Glass was gazing at the embroidery, carefully removed it from the wall and presented it to him.

The Indians gave presents to the two ladies: eagle-feather fans, knives, war clubs, blankets, necklaces, until there was a heap of these things in the dining room. Sometimes in their excitement the Indians uttered war whoops, and the general would gaze at them with the disapproving stare of a headmaster gazing at refractory pupils.

They spent the afternoon riding down the valley. A kind of grotesque and happy humor had descended on the Indians. You could see how they would suddenly ride ahead, spurring their horses into a mad mile-long dash; then they would return, while the foam came from the horses' mouths. They were accustomed to the valley now, and wanted it, but they wanted Wallowa more.

When they returned to their encampment beside the creek, it was already late, and the summer mist was floating down the mountains. Long shadows lay on the grass. There were more and more of these strange excited war whoops; then, when they rode into their camp, they were sullen, sheepish, talking in soft voices together, while the women and children came racing up, to seize Joseph and the general by the hand. They did not know why they did this except that it pleased them in their misery to hold hands which were strong.

"Fine! Fine!" Joseph murmured, gazing above the heads of the women at the green valley.

"Fine! Fine!" the women answered, and soon everyone in the encampment was shouting: "Hurrah! Fine! Fine!"

"They'll be going back to Wallowa in a day or two," the general said to Stevens as they rode to the fort. "When they come back to the reservation, I think you'll find them a hard-working and peaceful people. Do you know, Keff, I think God's grace is working on them."

BOOK THREE

THE STORM BREAKS

XX

Thunder on the Snake

WHEN Joseph returned to the valley of the winding waters at the head of fifty braves, their women and their children, he knew what he would have to say to his people. He would tell them exactly what had happened. They were good people; they would understand. They would know what had to be done; and so, when he rode silently among the lodges, he told them simply that they would have to leave immediately for the reservation at Lapwai, and they must hurry, for there was little time for the journey.

Drums beat mournfully. The hawks flew high in the sky. The white tents of troopers had appeared mysteriously on the other side of the lake. The women went out to gather camas bulbs, the young braves combed the ravines and brushy bottom land for their thousands of ponies and cattle. Orders were given for some of the most precious objects to be burned; others were cast into the lake. On the evening when Joseph went down to the lake, carrying the blanket which his father, Old Joseph, had died in, a sudden storm rose. He had intended to go into a trance, ask the lake for a sign and then throw the blanket, weighted with stones, in the water. But there was only the white boiling lake in the moonlight, and out of it there came white clouds like the spirits of the ancestors, huge men in white blankets, with white eyeballs, white outstretched arms. "Lords of the lake, have pity on us," Joseph murmured. From the screaming winds and gusts of smoke there came no answer to his questions.

The work of dismantling the lodges went on. The women cut tepee-poles, loaded the travois, pounded the camas. The general had announced an ultimatum: they must be in Lapwai by the middle of the following month. Already ten days had been spent in the journey back from Lapwai and the dismantling of the lodges. They would have to hurry.

On the day before Joseph was determined to leave, Alokut said: "The braves want to talk. They say they will not leave unless they can talk."

Joseph looked up sharply.

"What is there to talk about?"

"Many things."

"Then tell them to come this evening," Joseph said hopelessly.

He had observed for some days that Alokut was strangely nervous. He had been talking with Tuhulhulsote, and he had sent messages to Chief White Bird, who had returned to the Snake River.

That evening, when the braves assembled outside Joseph's tent, there was rebellion in the air. The young men kept whispering; and their bronze faces, usually impassive, were quick with excitement.

"Who wishes to speak?" Joseph asked.

Tuhulhulsote rose slowly and made a display of carefully arranging his blanket around him.

"I am old, and have not long to live," he said. "Why should I go to Lapwai? I have spoken with Old Man With One Arm, who has one arm only, and therefore is only half a man. He knows nothing. Foolish and ignorant, he thinks he knows everything. Does he know our strength? We have many good braves. Some, like Yellow Bear, are dead. Is it our fault? The white men rape our women, and cheat us with false weights in their shops. Listen, my heart is on fire with sorrow. I hoped the young braves would fight!"

Some braves urged Tuhulhulsote to go on, but this was all he wanted to say.

Alokut stepped forward, glanced at his brother and then shouted in ringing tones: "All that Tuhulhulsote says is true. We can fight the white men. They are weak. They do not use scalping knives. They use firewater to poison our hearts, and promises to poison our minds. If any one of us was as bad as the white men, he would not be allowed to live in our nation: he would be eaten to death by the wolves. Yellow Bear was killed. This is true. We have not killed the murderer, because we are peaceful, because the spirits have told us no good will come from killing white men, because we hate killing and kill only when we have to defend ourselves. Is this the truth?"

Standing there, his feathers streaming down his back, his chest bare,

Alokut glared in the direction of the braves who had been urging Tuhulhulsote to speak, and though his eyes were fierce, a smile was playing on his lips.

"Do you want war with the long knives?" he shouted. "They are many, and we are few. What is the use of war? They offer us peace, because they are powerful. They say: Leave the valley of the winding waters, and we shall see that you have good lands. They say this. They have done bad things, but it is a good thing that they do not kill us. We cannot fight them. They have heavy guns which run on wheels. How shall we fight their guns? No, it is best to go to Lapwai and be alive than to remain in Wallowa and be dead."

"Let Tuhulhulsote speak!" one of the braves shouted, and Alokut recognized the voice of Bird-with-one-eye.

"He will tell you to fight the white men, Bird-with-one-eye. What is the good of fighting? Listen. We are small rabbits, and they are eagles!"

A groan ran among the braves who were all squatting together, bunched and crowded together, their faces alight with a fierce solemnity. They looked cruel now. They wanted someone's blood; they wanted a sacrifice; they wanted an end to the doubts in their minds.

Bird-with-one-eye knew the moment to strike. He rose, arched his shoulders, glanced at the assembled braves with a look of amazement, as though it surprised him to find such animals there. Then he shouted in a high-pitched reedy voice: "Am I afraid? Have I ever been afraid? You know me—I am the man who slipped into the stockade at night and talked with the lieutenant. No walls kept me back. They shot at me, but they did not hurt me. They are weak. Bah! why be frightened of them? Red Moccasin Top is not frightened by them, nor is Melting Icefloes. Let the soldiers come! We are strong!"

If at that moment Bird-with-one-eye had shouted: "Let us go to the white tents on the other side of the lake and kill everyone there," half the braves would have followed. Joseph knew they were reaching a point of danger. Taller than Bird-with-one-eye he rose and pointed at the brave.

"Do you know how many white men there are in the world?" he asked. "Bird-with-one-eye, Melting Icefloes, Red Moccasin Top, they are all brave warriors, but they have not counted the number of white men. There are millions of them, that is why they are powerful. They will come and fight us with their guns on wheels, and they will hang us all by the necks if we resist. We have no chance against them. There is good land in Lapwai. This I know."

Then they knew it was the end: there were no more arguments. So they looked at one another as they had never looked at one another before, seeing the black outline of the hills against the sky, and on their faces there was an expression of desperate affection, as though they thought that in losing Wallowa they would lose one another. The strangest thing of all was that Tuhulhulsote was silent.

Suddenly, speaking in a voice so low that it was some seconds before they realized that he was speaking, Joseph began to say the words which for a long time had been biting into his mind. He said: "The hawks and the mountain eagles and the salmon know their homes, but we—what do we know? We know we must go away from here, but no one has told us why we must go. Nevertheless we cannot escape. So let us go proudly, and everyone must go about in the valleys and the meadows, in the deep brush and by the shores of the lakes, in search of what is ours. Our beef herd and our ponies, and every stick of our tepee-poles, whether pierced or not, we shall take with us; and let us go in good heart. First of all let us go down to the lake and talk to the ancestors—"

Usually, when the Indians went down to the lake at night, they went by starlight, without lamps, but this evening everyone took a candle or a kerosene lamp or a lantern with him. Mostly they rode on horseback, but some walked, and all the time they were singing. A few were muttering against Joseph, but even Tuhulhulsote, though he muttered to himself, took part in the long winding procession. They would go to the lake and beseech the spirits of the ancestors to forgive them, and later some would go to the mountains and lay scented grass near the hawks' nests, and others would strew scented grass on the river and in the pastures where the cattle dwelt. But there were no ceremonies appropriate to leaving their home: perhaps this is why they took their lamps with them. Only now at last did they realize this terrible thing that had happened to them, and on all their faces there were graven deep lines of misery: it was as though the sharp edges of battle-axes had been pressed against their faces. The women sang piercingly, and the men in low, soft voices:

We are coming to the lake:
The lake is ours:

The lake sheds its blessing on us:
Let us go to the lake and ask the lake's favors:
Let the ancestors speak to us.

This song they had sung many times before, but now every word had acquired a new meaning, and when they reached the lake they instinctively held out their lamps towards the cool waters and knelt in silence for a long time. They seemed to be offering their lives, everything they lived for, to the lake which had seen the beginning of their nation.

Then Joseph lifted his lamp and hurled it into the water, and immediately afterwards everyone was throwing a lamp into the water. The lamps going out made a sound like branches crackling in a high wind or the spitting noise of a serpent. For a few more minutes Joseph stood there, gazing into the darkness in the hope of hearing a voice, but there were no voices except the whispering of the wind among the reeds.

Drawing his blanket over his shoulders, he jumped onto the saddle and led the long silent procession back to the lodges on the uplands.

The long, heavily burdened procession made its way to the Snake River. The braves were in the saddle before sunrise, and they were still in the saddle after sunset. Behind them came the pony herds, nearly three thousand ponies, and the slow, dragging beef herds. Joseph had calculated on reaching the Snake in four days, but the herds kept straying: he heard the roaring of the river on the evening of the fifth day, and then he knew he would have to hurry mightily if he was to reach Lapwai in time.

That evening the air was all flame in a fierce sunset, and the herds, plunging through the scented dust of the valley, were colored red in the sun. Joseph was looking for a sign. All day he had been weighed down with a strange melancholy. Darkness was coming on, and he could hear the faint roaring of the river in the distance. He sent Alokut with a handful of braves ahead to scout the approaches to the river. When Alokut returned, it was dark and the Indians were bedding down for the night.

"The river is high," Alokut said.

"How high?"

"Higher than three snows ago—much higher."

Three summers before there had been a famous flood. Joseph felt his heart was breaking. The river was fighting against him. How could he cross? He looked at the dark camp, the people sleeping, the braves attending the small fires built to keep wolves and mountain tigers away. All along the valley there were these hot red flames shining in the dark, that darkness which seemed to come from the earth itself, for there were no stars, and no moon. The roaring of the river seemed to grow louder.

"We must cross the river," Joseph said quietly, and then he lay down to catnap beside his horse.

In the morning, an hour before dawn, Joseph was in the saddle, watching in the ghostly darkness the young braves as they rounded up the strays, combing the ravines and the bush by the light of branches dipped in oil. When the sun rose, everyone was ready for the journey. Already it had been whispered that they would have to try to cross the river in the morning.

From the valley they came to a region of box canyons where the creeks are walled in with sheer cliffs. The north faces of the canyon walls were tangles of jack pine; above the jack pine lay cool pools of snow. They pushed their way through, but it was nearly nine in the morning before they reached the raging river. There it was, an ice-cold flood, made bright yellow by the spring rains and the melting snows. They had never seen the river in such a violent mood. It roared like thunder, tossed up huge yellow silky manes, flung vast curtains of sleet-cold spray at the rocky shore, and the middle of the river rose in a great white frothy hump. When they saw the river, the Indians drew back. Deafening, resembling a huge implacable animal in a mad rush to escape some other huge animal tagging at its heels, the river looked as though it could destroy them all with a single flick of its watery paws.

"There is nothing else to be done—we must go on," Joseph said.

He could feel the horror and the hatred of the young braves as he spoke. It was far worse than the ice-cold spray on his face.

The Indians went to work. They knew what had to be done. They had brought thousands of tightly rolled buffalo skins; these they rolled and stretched, and then sewed willow stems round them: each skin then formed a coracle to carry three people and their possessions across, while young braves on horseback rode at the corners of the coracle and guided it. The Indians had no use for paddles. It was enough to thrust the coracle into the stream and swing it across the river with the help of the horses. If the current was particularly strong they would simply lash the tightly rolled skins together, and then there would be no need for a wooden ring. But now the river was raging so violently, with the great white frothing hump in midstream, and so they used both methods, hoping that the very lightness of the coracles would allow them to survive.

An hour later the first coracle entered the water, and four naked boys on ponies raced down to the river and hooked their arms in buffalo-hide thongs. In the coracle were placed some of the sacred objects of the tribe: relics of the ancestors, a jug of water from Wallowa Lake, some strange blue stones found in the mountains above Wallowa and buffalo robes worn by chieftains whose names were forgotten. From the stony bank the whole tribe watched breathlessly except the braves who were ordered to guard the herds. Joseph dared not speak. He knew that the whole fate of the tribe depended upon the crossing, and if the relics were lost, then perhaps the whole tribe would be lost. The youths were swimming as well as riding: they were employing all their strength; they thrust against the water, and sometimes they disappeared under the waves, and then there would be the gleam of their copper-colored bodies in the sunlight. Everything on the coracle had been roped down. Two of the youths attempted to work their ponies against the stream; two others employed all their energies to prevent the coracle from breaking away. A half-mile of turbulent water separated the banks, and the rocks on the other side were so steep that it would be difficult to clamber on them. Yet it had to be done, and if possible it had to be done in full sight of the Indians on the banks, for if they were swept downstream and landed on the other side without being seen, this too would have been considered an ill omen. The first coracle was lifted ashore successfully. It had disappeared in the white froth in midstream, that hump two feet high which resembled a huge waving spine to the river's progress, but the young braves were seen again, and they were even attempting to lift the coracle out of the water. As they clambered up the rocks, their horses slipped, and one of them, a cream-colored pony with strawberry-colored markings, was washed down-river, but the riders were unhurt. Very small on the opposite bank the braves lifted the coracle in full sight of the Indians clustered along the shore; and a sound like an immense sigh sprung from the throats of the tribe.

"Now we must see if the old men and women and the youngest children can be taken across," Joseph said, and looked up at the sky, bright blue now, though there were occasional dark stains which suggested that a storm was on its way.

Some old men on coracles and others on rolled buffalo skins were next sent across. A few were lost from sight, either disappearing in the white hump or being carried quickly downstream, but though they were lost for a while they reappeared later, stumbling along the rocks on the opposite bank, stripped to the skin, and weakened by the journey, but still whole. So it went on all morning, with the naked boys riding their ponies to the water, then casting off, each one holding to the raft, each solemn and intense, naked except for the threads of otter fur they wore in their braids, riding without saddles, digging their heels in, so that the horse and the rider seemed to be one animal gleaming in the yellow fume of the river.

At midday most of the old men, the women and the children had been ferried across; none were lost. About thirty ponies had been drowned, but they could afford the loss of ponies. It was time now to see whether they could get the beef herd across. Protesting, the herd was led down to the water. Alokut had the idea of thrusting the whole herd across in one tremendous crossing, but Joseph was against it. He decided that about twenty cows and bulls should be roped together, and that young braves riding horses should ride ahead with loose ropes joined to the herd, so that if the herd was washed away, at least the ponies would be saved. Joseph's face darkened. At all costs he wanted the beef herd across the river; and if he failed in this he knew that the tribe would be reduced to poverty. "The herd, the herd," he kept muttering. He was praying with all his strength that they should swim over safely. They were in the water, only their heads visible, when the sky suddenly clouded over, and all the white rocks along the sandy shore turned grey and dark. Was this an omen? Joseph did not know. He wanted to give orders for the twenty beeves to return, but it was too late; and the young braves would not have been able to hear him above the roar of the river. They struggled on, and then there was a clap of thunder followed by a flash of lightning, and then the rain fell in torrents. The twenty beeves struggled on, moving further and further downstream until they were lost to sight, and you saw only the braves who seemed to be leaping up and down in the water, and sometimes very faintly you heard their shouts. The storm lasted half an hour. In blue and purple curtains the rain fell, hiding the bank. It was an hour later before they saw the braves riding upstream, making signs that all the beeves were lost. After resting, some of them swam back and when they were still in the water flowers were thrown at them.

In the afternoon there were more attempts to get the beeves across; nearly a hundred were lost before Joseph decided that it would be better to wait until the river had fallen. There would still be time to reach Lapwai. By nightfall half the Indians were across, and about four hundred ponies had made the journey, but there were only twenty beeves on the other side. He left Alokut in charge of the remaining half of the tribe, and after swimming the river and spending the night on the other side, he pressed forward towards Rocky Canyon, some twenty miles away. On the journey he received a message from Alokut. It said: "Where is Red Moccasin Top? Where is Bird-with-one-eye? Where is Melting Icefloes?"

XXI

The Sheriff

THE evening when Lem watched the last of the Indians disappearing round the shore of the lake, he was sick as a dog. He spewed over the rail fence. He did not know what it was that had shaken him. He wanted vengeance, because Shades had run away, and now that he had been avenged, it meant nothing to him. There was only the emptiness of the valley, and the great path cut in the grass by the Indians and the scented grass they had piled on Yellow Bear's grave—nothing else. He kept peering into the dark, as though he thought the Indians would return. Afterwards he kept whispering "Shades of Night" over and over again, as though he could summon her presence.

"You'll get over it," Judge Shillitoe said kindly. "They're doing what's proper—leaving the valley for civilization. What's the matter with you? Thinking of your squaw? You'll find another whenever you want one."

The judge had ridden back with him through Lewiston. Waldo was still there, slumped beside the stove.

"I'll play a game of cards with you," the judge said, leading him back to the store.

"I don't play cards—never have."

"It's never too late to learn."

"I'm not playing, judge."

Lem rubbed the place in his cheek where the lieutenant had whipped him. He felt no hatred toward the lieutenant, only an obscure sense of loss. The judge sat down to play solitaire, his large head directly below the swinging kerosene lamp. While he was dealing the cards, and without looking up, the judge said: "We've known each other quite some while now, Mr. Otis. I reckon there's a reasonable feeling of trust between us. There should be. I've always thought there was a good deal in you which never came out in the open. You're a man of sensitive perceptions, and you're something of a dark horse, and I flatter myself I know the core of you, and I'm telling you I think well of you, always have—"

Lem could not understand where the judge's speech was leading him. It was as though the judge was talking to himself, lost in his own words as Lem himself was lost in his own dreams.

"Are you listening, Mr. Otis?" the judge went on, smiling his secretive smile.

"Of course, judge."

"Well, I wanted to tell you I think I can see my way of appointing you the first mayor of Wallowa."

"I wasn't thinking of running for mayor."

"You don't have to run, Mr. Otis. It's there for you to take. I'd be pleased to recommend you to the position."

The wind was blowing the muslin curtains, and through the window Lem could see the valley all silver now, sparkling in the moonlight. In this valley there were perhaps fifteen white men, no more.

"I'll just build me a house and be a farmer," Lem said. "I ain't aimin' to run for anything, least of all for mayor. What's a mayor do?"

"He runs the place. Legally, you could say he's in charge. He can do what he damned well pleases while he's in office. I've had my eye on you. Remember the night you came to my house in Lewiston with poor Moll? I've had my eye fixed on you since that day. I knew you would get into trouble, but it wouldn't be bad trouble. When trouble came, I helped you out, didn't I?"

"You did, judge."

"Then why don't you listen to me? I've told you you are going to be mayor. You are, aren't you? You don't have to look at me like that. You're a twice-damned fool if you don't take it. It's wealth, Mr. Otis, real wealth. There's more wealth in being a mayor than in being a judge. I'm giving it to you for friendship's sake. Call yourself mayor or sheriff, it's the same to me. Well, are you going to take it?"

"What do I have to pay for it?"

"I wasn't thinking you would have to pay anything. Maybe you could see your way to paying me some of your fees, but I'm not insisting on that. You could do me a favor or two once in a while. I'll need someone here while I'm at Lewiston. You're a good fellow right down to the roots of you."

"I wasn't thinking of asking for favors, judge. I've got that eight hundred acres, remember, and more if I want it. Good farming land, the best bottom soil. I don't ask for more. No, judge, I reckon life's dealt me some hard blows, but there's nothing a good farm wouldn't set to right."

"Then sleep on it, Mr. Otis. I'll keep the offer open until the morning."

The judge, displeased with the progress of his game of solitaire, shuffled the cards and returned them to his pocket. For a few moments longer he sat at the table, gazing out of the window. Waldo was still mumbling, but his voice was softer now, no more than a whisper. Abruptly, the judge rose, lit a candle and went to the bedroom. Lem heard the door closing, and then there was the faint click of the bolt. Lem knew the bolt well enough to know that if there was only a faint click, it was being very deftly slid along the groove.

"Time for sleep," Lem said to Waldo.

Waldo closed the Bible and looked up at Lem with a smile. There was something boyish in that sweet approving smile.

"I reckon you're lord of Wallowa now, like I said you would be, Lem. I reckon God has you in His mercy. I reckon all this land and the lordship thereof has been given into your hands. You ought to thank God, Lem."

"I'll thank Him in my own way," Lem said, and blew out the kerosene lamp.

He slept fitfully. Sometimes there were wild dreams. He dreamed of Moll and Shades of Night. He dreamed that the lake had disappeared, and all the bottom of it had turned into pasture land. When he woke up he heard Waldo snoring, and willed himself to sleep again simply to avoid listening to those terrible grunting sounds. Early in the morning he heard something stirring outside: it was like a knife striking against flint. Lem's dog, Silver, was chained to the woodpile, but remained quiet. It was still dark. Lem was sure someone was wandering outside, but after listening intently for a while he paid no more attention to those strange sounds. When dawn came, he was fast asleep, sprawling over the matting near the stove.

The blue light of dawn pushed through the muslin curtains which were all soiled now, hanging loose and thick with dust, untouched since the day when Lem went to stand trial in Lewiston. The light formed a blue puddle on the floor around Lem's sleeping head, and then advanced stealthily towards Waldo who was sprawled out on his back, breathing so heavily that he resembled a volcano in eruption. No one had washed the plates. In the early mornings especially the storeroom looked bleak, empty, raw. The noise was repeated: a thin scraping accompanied by a faint whistling. Waldo got up, walked once round the table, pushed his fist into the cracker barrel, and began to settle down with the crackers over his Bible. By this time the thin fluted noise had awakened the judge. It was a curiously penetrating noise, no longer like a knife striking against flint but more like the sound made when you scratch a coin on enamel. Waldo listened to the judge walking about in the small bedroom. It was a strange morning. He knew in his bones it was unlike any morning he had ever known: then he remembered that the tribes had left Wallowa and there was no longer the usual early morning procession to the lake accompanied by distant drumming. "Something's wrong," he muttered. "I don't make it out." He knew that the Indians had gone, but he still could not understand why the morning was so different from all other mornings. It was as though the air in the little store was slowly being sucked out. He shook Lem by the shoulder and said: "Better wake up. I don't know what they are up to." The door of the bedroom burst open. Haggard, having slept little, Judge Shillitoe stood in the doorway wearing a cotton nightgown. Lem rubbed his eyes, yawned, peered up at the man in the white cotton cap and the long white wrinkled nightgown, and then smiled pleasantly. It pleased him that the judge was staying in the store, and he was surprised that the judge should look so pale.

"Hear that whistling, Mr. Otis?" the judge asked, trembling.

"It's not whistling—too low. Maybe a bird—trumpeter swan—anything."

"You're not scared then?"

"God Christ, no! Why should I be scared? You think the Indians are coming back? Is that it?"

"I don't know what I think, Mr. Otis. I reckon I'm not used to living much in the country—it's the strangest damned whistling I ever heard."

They were all silent. The sound had stopped. When he saw the slow smile dawning on Lem's face, the judge retreated to the bedroom and dressed. When he came out into the store, the water was boiling and there was the smell of coffee grounds. The blue pools of light from the window were turning yellow.

"You'll take coffee, judge?" Lem asked, and still there was a faint dazed smile on his face.

"I certainly will."

"The rest is hard tack, judge, but it's the best we have."

"I'm used to that," the judge said affably, "and mighty obliged to you for your welcome."

"Sleep well?"

"Not too badly, Mr. Otis, not too badly."

The judge sat down by the table, and from an inner pocket he drew a roll of paper, which he pushed across the table.

"It's your appointment as sheriff of Wallowa. I thought about it. Sheriff's better than mayor. Sheriff Otis. How do you like that?"

"When did you make it out, judge?"

"Last night."

Lem smiled, brushed his fingers lightly over the paper as though to make sure it was there, and then poured the boiling coffee down his throat, and afterwards he smacked his lips. It would be a warm day and sometime in the morning they would go out to meet another surveyor's party. For some reason none of them had left the store, and from time to time they would glance up at the windows and the door with a curious look of distaste: it was from there that the whistling came, and now it was louder.

Lem slid the heavy wooden battens off the door after peering through the window slits. Mist swirled in the valley, but the sky was a pure watery blue. There was no one on the plot of land reaching to the fence rail. Judge Shillitoe wandered out and stood there in the sunlight, the sun full on his face, breathing deeply, and then excused himself for some business behind the woodpile. Waldo came lumbering along the path with the heavy morocco-bound Bible pressed tight beneath his arm. The faint sound of whistling was still going on.

"I don't like it," Waldo said, his thick lips trembling.

"What don't you like?" Lem shouted, and because there was no answer he went on: "God Almighty, I won't have you be afraid. It's the best morning of your life, Waldo. I'm sheriff. Did you ever think I'd be sheriff of Wallowa?"

"Be humble, Lem."

"Fine morning," Lem shouted when the judge came from behind the woodpile.

"Yes, indeed," the judge said, while the color came back to his cheeks and he stood there with an enchanted look on his face. "It's a fine morning. You might even say a historic morning."

Lem had pushed the fence gate open and was standing just outside the fence rail when the first shot cracked out in the still morning air.

"It's the damned Indians," Lem shouted, and threw himself on the earth, crawling along the shadow of the fence.

Waldo did not hear his brother. He was surprised by the shot, and he felt sure that someone was hunting nearby, but he did not know he was being hunted. A rifle bullet drove straight through his forehead. As he fell, he was still conscious. He waved his right hand limply, and then fell down heavily with his head leaning against the gatepost. Some braves were running up the path. They were naked except for breechclouts, and there were stripes of red paint on their legs and they were grasping their war clubs. He heard Judge Shillitoe calling out for mercy. The sun was blinding. Waldo was gripping the Bible with all his strength and his heavy lips were attempting to frame words: *Yea, though I walk through the valley of death, I shall fear no evil. The Lord is my shepherd, I shall not want. He preparest a table before me in the presence of mine enemies.* He could not go on. "Poor Lem," he murmured, and then his head fell forward because something was driving deep into his skull, and it needed all his strength to lift his head up again.

"God have mercy," he said to all the green valley of Wallowa, the blue lake and the high hills, and his eyes were weary and they would hardly open to see the immense pasture land stretching before him, the mist curling away towards the sun.

As his eyes closed for the last time, Waldo saw a young Indian leaning against the fence rail and smiling down at him. The Indian was painted all over, and he was playing on a bird-pipe.

XXII

News from Camas Prairie

ALL that day Lem lay hidden in the cottonwoods. Once or twice the Indians came near him as they prowled through the woods, but they never saw him, never came close enough to where he lay in the bush. The Indians spent the morning searching for him and drinking whatever spirits they could find in the store. At noon they set fire to the store, and then threw the bodies of Waldo and Judge Shillitoe into the flames. Afterwards they rode round the fence rail, singing and shouting. They were still there, drinking and watching the small flames late in the afternoon.

When Lem emerged from the cottonwoods, he thought the Indians were still there. It was after midnight when he dared himself to approach the store. The roof had fallen in, the embers were smoking, the store was a black shamble. Treading carefully, he pushed against a charred log. He thought it was a log, but when he pushed harder some yellow intestines came out of it, and then he recognized Waldo, an inch-deep black crust over his body, the head broken open with the meat-ax which lay close by. Judge Shillitoe lay sprawled in a corner, face downwards. The moon shone, and there were still a few red flames licking the ruins of the store. The hawks were coming out of the sky, and he was too weak with hunger and misery to shoo them away. He went down to the lake to wash himself, and there he saw one of his own horses and decided to ride to Lapwai, even if it killed him.

"God Christ," he said, "they're on a rampage. I've got to tell the general before they tear the whole Territory to pieces!"

He rode by night and rested during the day. Five days later, when he reached the fort at Lapwai, he was a lean wolf on a trail.

When Lem arrived at Lapwai, he rode straight to the fort. It was dark, and only the lanterns at the corner bastions were shining: it would be another hour before the sun was up. He hammered at the stockade gate, shouting at the top of his voice. The guards, thinking he was drunk, fired a couple of rounds around him, and set some dogs at him. He was covered with blood and frothing at the mouth when he was eventually allowed inside the fort.

"Where's the general?" he shouted, and began to curse, and someone suggested the best thing would be to throw him in the guardhouse.

"You can't wake the general, and he ain't here," the guard said. He was a thin bony youth six foot two, and Lem stared at him as he would stare at some incomprehensible idol. There was nothing human about the guard. He was the kind of man who would set dogs on strangers and fire warning shots for the pleasure of it.

"Then where is he?"

"Likely at Walla Walla. Likely at Portland. Likely at the Dalles."

"Then who is in command?"

"Bed down, brother."

"I've got a message for the general—"

"Sure, brother, but bed down and maybe we'll give you a bite of bread in the morning."

Lem was crazed by the death of his brother, the long journey, the blather of the guard. He leaned up and struck the guard across the face, shouting: "The Indians are out to kill—they're killing everyone—they killed my brother!" The guard, who thought Lem had either gone insane or was deliberately asking for punishment, let go of his Winchester and went into Lem with all his strength. Lem did not know why he struck the trooper. He remembered only two long thin arms striking like pistons. There was blood on his beard now, fresh blood, and a huge cut across the eye, and his mouth seemed to have dropped to one side. He breathed great lumps of breath, rolled away from the trooper's hobnailed boots, tried to rise and then crashed to the floor, and when he reached a corner he sat up, burying his face in his hands and whimpering.

"You had it coming to you," the guard said. "You strike a trooper, and that's what you get."

"What do I get?" Lem asked, with a last little whimper of insolence. "I'm telling you the Indians are on the rampage, and all you do is kick a friend in the teeth. I tell you the Indians are killing all the white men in Wallowa, and raping their women—"

"You're drunk!" the trooper shouted.

"I'm not drunk. They killed my brother. Killed him right in front of my eyes—"

"Sleep it off, brother."

In the guardhouse there was only this guard, a beaten earth floor, four wooden cells. Two of the cells were occupied, and Lem was glad when he heard from the sounds within the cells that he had disturbed the occupants.

"Who's in command?" Lem said in an unnaturally high-pitched voice. He wanted his words to carry, and somehow they came out like shrill screams.

"Captain Perry is in command, and he's sleeping. Maybe he'll see you in the morning. Maybe he won't."

"He'll see me now if you wake him."

"Oh, brother, do you think I'd wake the captain?" the guard laughed quietly to himself. "I'd just as soon wake the general as wake Mr. Perry."

"Then the general is here?"

"Likely he is."

"Then for God's sake tell him I'm here. He knows me. Tell him Lem Otis is here. Tell him the Indians are—"

"Raping our women and killing our children," the guard said with a mocking laugh. "I've heard it all before, brother. Save your breath."

There was nothing Lem could do until morning. He was too sick, too exhausted to argue further with the guard. He bedded down on the straw, and waited. For some reason the guard did not throw him into one of the cells, but let him lie where he lay. Lem slept fitfully, and was awake with the dawn. A new guard took over. He was short and fat, wearing a uniform too tight for him. Like most fat men, he smiled easily.

"I've come from Wallowa," Lem said tearfully, when the new guard brought him a mug of coffee and half a loaf of bread. "The Indians are on the rampage."

The guard, who had been smiling, let the smile freeze on his face.

"Are you sure?" he asked, and there was a little quiver in his voice. "What makes you think so?"

"I've seen it with my own eyes. I'm dead sure. They murdered my brother."

It was like a refrain, repeated so often that it had almost lost meaning. Lem was not sure whether the Indians were on a rampage. He knew only that they had attacked him and set fire to the store and killed poor Waldo with a meat-ax. It might have been revenge, but he remembered Bird-with-one-eye and Melting Icefloes, and how they had shouted at him. "God in Heaven," he exclaimed, "they are on the warpath, and you don't do a damned thing about it."

"I'll see the general," the squat guard said, and Lem said quickly: "You'd better."

It was less than ten minutes before the guard returned, out of breath.

"I'll have to wash myself before I see the general," Lem said, his voice breaking again.

"No, you don't. You'll go straight as you are."

Dazed, Lem walked across the sunlit courtyard. It was less than ten days since his visit to the general with Judge Shillitoe. The stockade had not changed. There were the same troopers going casually about their occupations, the same horses were being rubbed down, the same vegetable gardens, the same armed watchmen on the bastions. Lem was full of an ungovernable fury against the general: it was the general's fault that all this had happened. He did not know why the general was responsible, but in some obscure way he was convinced that the general had behaved too generously towards the Indians; and if it was not the fault of the general, it was the fault of that young adjutant of his. Stevens had created trouble in the past, and he could be expected to create trouble again.

When Lem climbed the wooden stairs which led to the general's office he found a deputation waiting for him. There was not only the general and the adjutant, but there were two captains and three or four lieutenants. There was caked blood over Lem's beard; his eyes were red with broken veins; his clothes were mud-splattered.

"I see you have been in the wars," the general said, but there was a surprising gentleness in his voice. "Rough stuff in the guardhouse, eh?"

"I don't answer for your troopers, general. I didn't ask for rough stuff. They gave it to me—thought I was drunk. I wasn't drunk."

"Well, what's your story?"

"The Indians are on a rampage, sir. They killed my brother, and mighty near killed me. They set fire to my store. I know the fellow who did it—Bird-with-one-eye. Melting Icefloes was there, too. Couple of others. I reckon Joseph sent them."

"What makes you think that?"

"They were acting queer, general. Bonfires, processions down by the lake, chanting all day and all night, more chanting than I ever heard before. They're up to harm. I know that. I'm cold sober, general. Your trooper tried to kick my teeth in, and he wouldn't let me see you last night, but I'm cold sober."

Lem felt dizzy, at the end of his strength. The general poured out a tumbler of water and pushed it across the table.

"I see you're sober, Mr. Otis," he said. "You have my sympathy."

"I don't want your sympathy, general. I want you to do something about the Indians."

"I'll do what I can. Yours is the first report we have had of any trouble."

Lem's face fell. He had hoped there were more reports, to corroborate his story. It might be, it probably was, a simple act of vengeance. He remembered how Stevens had stiffened when he mentioned Bird-with-one-eye. He glared round, uncertain of himself. The general was toying with a rolled-up map, gazing up at him through bushy eyebrows, the eyes almost invisible.

"You killed an Indian once, didn't you?"

"Yes, sir."

"And you went on trial for it?"

"That's right."

"Before Judge Shillitoe in Lewiston?"

"Yes, sir. Judge Shillitoe was killed at my store."

"What was he doing there?"

"He came to visit, sir."

"So he's killed, and your brother's killed, is that it? What did your brother do?"

"He kept store for me, read the Bible—he was a religious man, general, but he wasn't bright in the head. He's dead. So is the judge. I didn't bury them, didn't have time. They're all dead, general."

"All right, we'll do what we can."

"Thank you, general. I hope and pray you'll kill every man jack of those Indians. There wasn't anything wrong with my brother except that he was weak in the head. There wasn't anything wrong with the judge. You didn't do the right thing. You should have made sure there wouldn't be any trouble. Now they'll be murdering everywhere—rampaging everywhere—maybe there won't be a single white alive by the time they're done!"

"That's enough, Mr. Otis. Mr. Stevens will look after you—"

During the morning no further news came through. When Stevens lunched with the general, they exchanged significant glances when Lem's name was mentioned. In the afternoon it was the same. The valley lay peaceful under the sun. The general rode along the creek, passing the place where the Indians had encamped. He observed that they had left no sign of their coming, everything clean. "They have some godliness in them," he observed to Stevens, and then looked up to see an Indian riding towards them. He was caked with dust and sweat. He had ridden hard and was at the end of his strength. He belonged to a friendly branch of the Nez Perce, who lived in houses and cultivated small farms. The Indian rode up to the general. He spoke English, but very slowly and distinctly, stressing every word.

"I've come from Camas Prairie, sir. Mr. Brown sent me—"

"I've met him, haven't I? Keeps the hotel at Mount Idaho?"

"Yes, sir. He speaks truth."

He handed the general a letter. The letter said:

There are about sixty lodges of Joseph's Indians on the prairie. They are behaving insolently. I have seen over a hundred well-mounted and well-armed, and they are out for trouble. They behave insolently. A good many were in town today and were trying to obtain powder and other ammunition. Mr. Scott told me today that they offered him two dollars and a half for a can of powder. One Indian came here and asked when the general was coming up. They are insolent. I believe it will be well for you to send up, as soon as you can, a sufficient force to handle them without gloves, should they be disposed to resist. Sharp and prompt action will bring them to understand that they must comply with the orders of the government. I write this for your own information and at the suggestion of many settlers who are living in exposed localities.

Very respectfully yours,

L. P. Brown

The general read the letter carefully twice, and then turned it upside down so that he could read the writing on the upper margin. These words, written in a small crabbed handwriting, said: *"Send your men soon, general, or they will massacre us all."*

"What do you think of it?" the general asked, turning to Stevens. "Do you think the damned Indians are up to their tricks?"

"I don't know. Mr. Brown doesn't say so. He only says he is frightened by their behavior. Well, I daresay Mr. Brown has never seen a hundred Indians marching together."

"They're buying powder."

"They are always buying powder, sir. They need it for hunting."

"There are no buffaloes in Lapwai, Mr. Stevens. What would they need to hunt when they come here?"

"It isn't a crime for them to buy powder," Stevens said stubbornly, looking straight at the general whose face shone strawberry-red in the sun. "The only testimony we have comes from Mr. Otis, and I would say that was doubtful."

With the Indian they rode back leisurely towards the fort. Once more the general settled himself in his office. He called Captain Perry in, and together they studied the maps. At half past four another messenger arrived from the prairie. The message was short:

> *General Howard*
> *Dear Sir,*
> *The Indians are on a rampage. They have killed two of our people. Send your men, or there will be none of us left.*

This letter was unsigned, but it was in the same handwriting as the letter from L. P. Brown. As soon as he read the message, the general said: "They've asked for it, and they'll get it. Captain Perry, I shall want you to take all the men you can spare to the prairie tonight."

XXIII

Night March

DAYLIGHT was no more than a thin glow in the western hills when the trumpets blew "Boots and Saddles"; and now the small cavalry column rode along Lapwai Creek under the shadow of the hills, the horses blowing and the saddles creaking, and the whole valley dark underfoot. Captain Perry, riding at the head of the column, pointed to the faint outlines of houses on the slopes: "Mary Caldwell over there, sleeping, I hope." He smiled to himself. Stevens, riding beside him, could not get out of his mind that only a few days ago he had ridden along the same valley with the Indians, and they had called at the Caldwell house, and taken lunch there.

In the darkness the men rode stiff in the saddles, their thoughts lost in the immensity of the dark. No lights shone from the agency; nothing stirred in the houses they passed; only the signal lamps shone at the fort; and soon the night mist gathered, and when they were a mile away from the fort, the fort itself vanished. The mule train, with the soft packsaddles loaded with ammunition and supplies, shuffled behind the column of about a hundred men. Soon a soft rain came down, and the muttered voices ceased, except for the whispered conversations at the head of the column.

"Do you know this country well?" Captain Perry turned to the dark shape riding by his side.

"Yes, I know it, but I wouldn't say I know it well," Stevens said. "I know Wallowa better."

"Wallowa–" Captain Perry said, and then paused, trying to summon up some picture of this valley which Stevens sometimes attempted to describe. "Is Wallowa worth a battle?" he asked.

"Yes, it's worth a battle," Stevens said grimly, and all the time he was thinking of Shades of Night and the blazing coronet of diamonds, as she knelt beside him in the warmth of the tepee.

It was no more than a wretched little column wandering into the dark: five pack mules, rations for three days, forty rounds of ammunition to a man. There were some farmers from Lapwai at the tail end of the column, and Lem Otis rode with them only because Stevens had not summoned enough energy to have him turned out. The mules plodded slowly along the slippery road; the horses, unaccustomed to the dark, plunged and reared. There was no moon, no stars. If there were any Indians about on the Lapwai Hills, they would have seen the column long ago.

As they climbed towards Camas Prairie they found the ground breaking into deep ravines. There was heavy timber ahead. Every one of the men in the advancing column was certain he was being watched. Captain Perry gave orders that pipes should be knocked out.

"You can smell them," he said. "Every damned hill has one of them on it somewhere."

"Indians don't smell," Stevens laughed quietly in the dark.

"That's what you say! I can smell 'em anywhere."

They both laughed. Rain was coming down. Faintly in the dark they saw the soft white packsaddles on the mules. They were climbing higher, skirting the ravines. Sometimes Captain Perry would drop to the ground, and there, shielded by Stevens, he would light a match and take a quick glance at the map. He whistled nervously under his breath. Past midnight, the horses, unaccustomed to climbing, began to flag, and he ordered a ten-minute rest to group his men together.

"We are not doing too badly, and we're not doing too well either," he told his officers. "The packers are having trouble with their trains. There's too much noise, and too much talking. We're not as well mounted, nor as well armed as the Indians. I reckon they know where we are more or less, so keep the men quiet. That's one thing the Indians have got, a sense of quiet. Now we'll go on to Grangeville without stop."

"One question, sir."

It was young Lieutenant Theller, lank-muscled and beardless, and in the starlight he looked ridiculously young, about seventeen. He was twenty-one, and his mouth was set in a firm line, but his eyes glistened like a boy's, and he held himself like a boy.

"Well, what is it?"

"If they attack, we group around you, is that right?"

"If we attack, I'll lead the attack. If they attack, God knows what we'll do. It depends where they attack from, Mr. Theller. You'll get your orders from the trumpeter. Where's the trumpeter?"

"We haven't got one."

Captain Perry, who could still hear the long-drawn notes of "Boots and Saddles" echoing across the fort at Lapwai, looked surprised, and stared from one officer to another. They were all silent, each one weighing in his own mind this new and dreadful knowledge. To go without a trumpeter meant they had no way of making commands to a straggling column. They had left the trumpeter behind at Lapwai, perhaps because General Howard needed him, perhaps because an oversight had been committed, perhaps because no one realized the importance of a trumpeter. The long faces, glistening with sweat, grew longer. The look of blank astonishment on Perry's face gave way to a puzzled smile.

"I suppose we shall get on perfectly well without one," he said, and everyone knew it was not so, and simply because they knew this they smiled reassuringly. He smiled back at them, at young Theller, at Stevens with his yellow beard which shone like fine white hairs in the starlight, at Parnell who resembled a grizzled warrior at twenty-seven, at Trimble who wore his new uniform as though he was still unaccustomed to it, and seeing them there, Perry wondered how long he could bear this terrible responsibility—the lives of these young officers and all their men depended upon a single command or a sweep of an arm. "Good luck," he said, and stared moodily towards the west, where the stars were brighter, and then he swung into the saddle and led the advance. Stevens, riding beside him, was aware that Perry was praying silently, praying as he had never prayed before, and there was a strange unfathomable quietness about him.

"We'll go on to the end," Perry said once, and though the words were simple Stevens knew he was attempting to say something profound and mysterious, something that had come to him after long pondering.

"No, there's no escape from it," Stevens answered. "I've thought and thought, and I believe that if they are out for war they will give us the best fighting there has ever been in the Territory."

Perry nodded, sucked at his unlit pipe, said: "We'll give them more than they bargained for," and until the morning came he remained silent, lost in himself as in a dream.

When the first light rose, the mules began to feed on the wayside grass, holding the column back. There was no sign of any Indians, only the immense plateau stretching away into the morning mists, the air cool and the skies filled with drifting low-lying clouds. Mud-splattered after the journey up from the valley, the men looked weary already, though they had covered barely thirty miles during the night. It was nine o'clock before they reached Cottonwood House, a small settlement of frame houses lying beside a creek. "We camp here for a bit," Perry said, and smiled his mysterious smile at the men, and then waved at the farmers who came running out of the houses. They looked scared and excited, but they had little news to offer. Farmers with leather faces, pistols rammed in their belts, some trailing Winchesters, stood gawkily around, watching the men as they fed and rested their horses or went back to help the mule train which had bogged down in the mud.

"It's war, isn't it?" said Amos Grainger, the oldest of the farmers, a lean man with two bright red spots on his cheekbones.

"We don't know—we just don't know," Captain Perry answered, and went on to ask what news there was of the Indians, but there was little enough; a small group of Indian horsemen had been reported in the east, and all night they had heard coyote-howls, but whether the sound came from coyotes or Indians, no one knew.

Stripped to their undershirts the officers went to the creek to wash; then they set about eating their own hard tack and salt bacon, refusing the food the farmers offered because they felt they were in no position to take it from them. The men were exhausted by the long ride at night. Some slept in the fields; others curled up on the farmers' beds, and were waited upon by the farmers' daughters. It was noon before they set out again across rolling country for Grangeville, and it was already dark with a lowering sky when they reached the place, where there was no more than a mill or two, and three or four houses. Grangeville was sixteen miles from Cottonwood House, and it had taken them more than six hours to cover the easy trail because the mule train was always lagging behind. On the way they saw three huge columns of smoke from burning straw stacks, but soon the smoke disappeared into the clouds. The smoke was something you could smell, and when they came in sight of Grangeville they were surprised to see the houses still standing. Perry and Stevens rode on ahead to meet the huddled group of farmers waiting at the crossroads.

"You're a tidy bit late," one of the farmers said, as they rode up. "Indians crossed the prairie this morning, making for the river."

"What time?" Perry asked, gazing steadily and sadly at the farmer with a long bony jaw and wide-open frightened eyes.

"Around eleven, maybe eleven thirty. Oh, we could have fought them if we had the weapons. They're cowardly wretches. They go up to a house tucked away somewhere on the prairie, and burn and burn! Man, you'll have to hurry."

"I'd hurry fast enough if I knew where they were. What's your name?"

"George Shearer, former major of the Confederate Army, sir. They're down in White Bird Canyon now. That's the last we heard of them."

"You're sure of that?"

"Dead sure. We've got a couple of friendly Indians, Cheyennes, who came in an hour ago. Man, you'll have to hurry. It's difficult country. Sixteen-eighteen miles away. Did you see the stacks burning? Well, Indians burned them when they saw you coming. It's their way of telling how many there are of you, and which way you're driving up, and where you're posted for. They know. I reckon they know everything there is to know. And you'll have to get at them quick, before they cross the Salmon and take the buffalo trail east. I tell you, captain, if you don't hurry after them this minute, they'll slip out of your hands."

The former major's voice rose into a singsong wail. Fear was written on his face, on the trembling of the long bony chin, on the deep quivering lines of his cheeks. He kept staring in the direction the Indians had gone.

"Well, will you do it?" he asked, and there was defiance in his tone. "I've got ten men here who will help you."

"I've got to rest my men," the captain said miserably, looking into the major's eyes in the fast-fading light. He turned to Stevens and young Trimble, who had ridden up quietly, and he could see Lem Otis leaning on his horse not far from where the major was standing. "Seems they are in White Bird Canyon and might escape over the river tomorrow. What do you think?" He whistled under his breath, for it had only just occurred to him that the major was demanding another night march, and his men had had no sleep for more than thirty hours. "I'll put the question another way. When can we leave?"

"Might as well leave in an hour," Trimble said, and though he tried to disguise it, his voice was cracked with weariness.

"How about two hours, major?" Captain Perry turned to the farmer. "I can promise we'll be in shape to leave in two hours. We'll need guides, every man you can spare, and every rifle. How many Indians were crossing the prairie this morning?"

"Maybe a hundred."

"Maybe more?"

"Sure. You can never tell with Indians. Maybe they have a hundred scouts. God knows how many there are. The Cheyennes don't know. Ask a Cheyenne how many men they were, and they're all for saying there's a thousand because it sounds better. I've had experience of Cheyennes. All I know is there's a hell of a lot of Indians down at White Bird Canyon, and they'll be taking the trail east in the morning."

"You're sure they haven't crossed the river already?"

"I don't know, captain. I reckon they might have crossed this afternoon, but the Cheyennes say they didn't. That's all we've got to go on."

"What's it like at White Bird Canyon?"

"Rough and rocky, captain. Damned rough and damned rocky, if you'll excuse the expression."

"Then it will be a pleasure to have your men join us," Captain Perry said quietly, and he began to ride slowly, with the major walking on foot beside him, towards the frame houses on the slope, which were ghostly white in the darkness. Then he ordered that no fires should be lit and the men should take what shelter they could in the houses.

It was nine o'clock before they were ready to set out again. There was no moon; the stars were clear and thick, lighting the tussocky land with frosty silver. The delay had been caused by the difficulty of finding Major Shearer's promised volunteers and because someone had lost the coffee sacks and one of the mules had wandered away. Lieutenant Theller went in advance with eight troopers and one of the Cheyennes, and after him came a group of Grangeville farmers; then came the long straggling column; then the mule train. They rode in dead silence save for the crunching of the horses' hooves on the earth. Little rain had fallen here, and the sound of the horses' hooves was like incessant drumbeats on the stretched earth, and though the night was cool to freezing, there was promise of a roaring hot day ahead.

An hour before dawn they reached the top of the canyon and thought they could see the river shining below, and all the interval was dark jagged rock and a long descent to the canyon bottom. Captain Perry told the men to sleep if they could, after posting guards, but he knew they had no taste for sleep now, with the Indians so near. He did not know whether the Indians were still in the canyon, but he was sure they were not far off; and when he heard the Cheyennes muttering among themselves, and called them over, they pointed towards a patch of intense darkness below and said: "They were down there during the afternoon." Far away, some snowy peaks glittered. The Salmon in its raging flood lay cool and silver beneath the stars, no more than a thin stretch of winding ribbon. "For God's sake tell no one to strike a match," Perry said to Lieutenant Theller, and a moment later he saw a red glow shining against the rock, and immediately afterwards there was a long piercing coyote-howl from somewhere quite near. The howl ended with a high whistling note. Perry shivered, and he prayed that the sound had not reached the encampment below.

When small threads of reddish light came over the eastern hills, Perry ordered the men to descend into the canyon in single file. It was a few minutes past three o'clock. Quietly, gathering together in little knots, the men loaded their rifles and whispered together, swallowed ration coffee, bacon and hard tack, then swung into the saddle. The slopes were naked basalt, with rough-ridged defiles leading down to the valley. The White Bird was a straggling stream which cut deep, with a few willows along the banks, though there were no trees along the Salmon itself. High bluffs and buttes hemmed the valley in, and the defiles were treacherous, broken by gullies, with steep-walled rocks on one side and there was a sheer drop of nearly three thousand feet on the other. Willows clung to the rock, so that sometimes you would see high above you a twisted willow clinging to the rock face, and white-winged birds nesting in them. Mostly, it was ground that no horseman in his senses would think of treading, but there was only this winding and broken path to the canyon bottom.

They had been riding for ten minutes when Stevens and Theller in the advance saw something they never expected to see, and both gave a little cry of shocked surprise at the same time. There in front of the[m] stood a white woman with a child by her side, leaning against on[e] those willows which somehow clung to the side of the rock. Her hair fell over her face. There was a bloodstained bundle in her hands. Her mouth kept opening, but no sounds came from her. She looked like a sturdy, well-made woman, but her skirt had been torn by the underbrush, and at one time she must have been caught in the rain. Stevens, who had been dreaming of Shades of Night and praying that the Indians had already crossed the Salmon, dropped from the saddle and walked towards her cautiously. He could make no sense of it. It occurred to him that she might be a squaw in disguise, or even a brave who was determined to delay their advance. He remembered the unnatural high-pitched coyote-howl which had broken not far from where he had been standing. The summer mist was writhing among the mountains, and there were deep pools of mist over the canyon, and here was a woman trying to walk towards them. He was completely unable to understand what she was doing there, and as he walked towards her he drew his revolver.

"You soldiers?" the woman said, when he was a pace or two away from her.

"Yes, we're soldiers. You ought to rest. You shouldn't be here."

"There isn't anywhere else," the woman said, looking down at the bloodstained bundle. "They killed my husband. They tried to kill me. This is Mary." She pushed the bundle into Stevens' hands, and he saw that there was something moving inside it, something wrapped in what was once a white woolen shawl. There was fresh blood on the shawl. A white-faced girl of twelve was clinging to the woman's torn skirt, and the girl tried to say something, but no sound came from her lips.

"What is it?" Stevens said, lifting the top of the shawl. He knew it was a stupid question, but there was nothing else he could say. Lieutenant Theller had dismounted beside them.

When he lifted the shawl, he gasped. Carefully wrapped up there was a two-year-old child with long flaxen hair, and it resembled every other flaxen-haired two-year-old except for one thing: the face had been smashed in, and bubbles of blood were coming out of the terrible gap which was once a mouth. The baby still breathed.

"Why did they do this?" Stevens asked, showing the baby to Theller. It was a cry of despair.

"I don't know why they did it," the woman said. "Maybe they don't know themselves why they do these things. We've been here for two days, me and Mary and Emily. We haven't eaten. We're scared. We don't know where to go."

Stevens looked into his haversack after getting Theller to hold the baby; then he put all the food he had on the ground beside her. Afterwards Theller did the same, and so did twenty other troopers, until there was a small mountain of food there. The twelve-year-old girl, Emily, began to eat ravenously, but the mother only looked on. Sometimes, on her drawn white face, there would appear a momentary smile, like those quick flashing smiles which appear on the faces of mad people.

"What's going to happen to me?" the woman asked, as the soldiers began to push their way further down the slope.

"We can't help you otherwise than by giving you food, ma'am," Stevens said. "You'll have to get back to Camas Prairie and make your way to Mount Idaho—that's the nearest place for you."

There was almost nothing more he could do. He rested his hand on her shoulder to comfort her, and then jumped into the saddle to join the advance.

The mist was melting. Eastward lay the snow-capped mountains, the immense cliffs and jutting bluffs along the shores of the Salmon; beyond the peaks, beyond the winding river below, beyond the canyons filled with morning shadow, ghostly-blue and black and indigo, lay the sunlit plateaus where the Indians hunted buffalo; but here, along this stretch of river, there were only the jagged slopes. There was something eerie in the way the mist melted, as though the deep valley below them was deliberately being concealed, and then revealed by the mist, and through this mist the white birds travelled soundlessly. The sunlight inched along the swollen river, turning it to gold. Then at the mouth of the canyon, not far from the Salmon, among the small buttes which lay along the shore, they saw blue smoke rising in slow columns.

"We don't have to hurry," Lieutenant Theller said over his shoulder. "They're waiting for us down below."

XXIV

White Bird Canyon

IN a quiet lodge set away from the main huddle of lodges near the river, Joseph had spent a part of the night comforting a girl who lay in childbed. She was his second wife, and as she lay on the buffalo robes with blankets heaped round and over her to keep her warm during the chilly night, he knew that the birth would be hard, for she groaned a little and locked her teeth and sometimes very suddenly her face would gleam with sweat in the light of the hearth-fire.

"Little one, it will be hard—harder than you know," he kept muttering, and then he would turn his head away and gaze at the glowing fire where the squaws were heaping scented sweet-grass.

All night the messengers came. Scouts rode into the encampment from the plateau above; they all told the same story of a long column of weary horses and heavy-eyed troopers making their way to the canyon. He knew their numbers, what weapons they carried, how long they had rested at Cottonwood House and Grangeville, and he even knew the names of their officers. He knew that Lieutenant Stevens was among them, and that someone resembling Lem Otis was also there; and he knew they were being sent out to arrest him and his braves. As he knelt beside his wife, wiping the sweat from her face, he sometimes groaned, thinking of the battle ahead, for he had decided that he would never allow himself to be arrested. He had not wanted war. The blame lay with Melting Icefloes and Bird-with-one-eye. They had brought this on him, and they had done it in such a way that he could not refuse battle. Now, wearing only a shirt and a leather breech-clout under his striped blanket, he listened for the coyote-howls of the scouts on the plateau, those thin frail voices which sometimes carried three or four miles, so penetrating they were, and when the dawn touched the tepee, he slipped away to join Chief White Bird.

White Bird was in his own tepee in the center of the encampment, and from there, looking through the open flap he could see the creek and the canyon wall glowing in the dawn, the cliffs red, and purple shadows below. White Bird's tent had become the war station. Alokut and Tuhulhulsote were both there, staring through the wandering veils of sun mist, craning forward eagerly, restlessly debating with themselves the meaning of the coyote-howls, the black shapes coming down the cliff, the way they could best oppose the people whom they called, from long experience, the Bostons.

"What are they after?" White Bird said, sucking at his pipe. "Our herds, our weapons, our lives?"

Joseph said nothing. Then he whispered hurriedly to Alokut: "Get the glasses." Alokut ran down the slope with long springy strides, tall and sinewy, bronze in the growing sun. When he brought the glasses back, Joseph focussed them without a word on the cliffs, and then silently passed them to White Bird.

"They are weak, worn out. We could fight them," White Bird said grimly. "We can stop them here, or anywhere. We can go across the river and wait. Let them follow us. Then we shall make them so weary they will die."

"Where shall we fight them?" Joseph asked.

"What does it matter?"

He turned to Tuhulhulsote, whose heavy face was beautiful now, lit with excitement.

"We go where we have to go," Tuhulhulsote said gravely. "They have brought this on themselves."

"Then do we cross the river?" Joseph said, deliberately phrasing the question in such a way that he knew Alokut would reply: "No, we must fight them here." But Alokut said nothing: he simply smiled, and in the flashing of his teeth Joseph knew that his brother accepted battle now; then he turned towards Tuhulhulsote and White Bird, both leather-faced, both old, both calm and curiously remote, as though their thoughts were elsewhere, as though they were both dreaming of Wallowa, and he said: "Let them fire first. If they wish to fight, we shall fight. They are weak, and will scatter at the sound of our firearms. Let the women and children take the pony herd nearer the river, and let them bring ponies up for us if our own are shot down; and as for you, White Bird, since you are the oldest and wisest, take your men and turn the Bostons when they reach the canyon floor and make your hiding place beside the butte, and I will stay here with my men behind these rocks. And let my brother stay with me."

All this was said in whispers, while the sun glazed the rock and they crouched like animals ready to spring, for every moment the thin column was approaching nearer. Like fumes the sun veils fell now across the canyon. Tuhulhulsote hurried away towards some rocks which Joseph pointed out for him; as he ran, doubling up his wrinkled body, he played on an eagle-bone flute, summoning his warriors to him. White Bird did the same. Joseph's men did not need to be summoned by flute: they simply watched him as he crouched there, high up on the rock, and he made a few gestures with his arm, while looking straight ahead, and they knew exactly what each gesture meant. There was the gesture which ordered them to take down their lodges, the gesture to come close to the rock, a short jabbing gesture which told them to see that their firearms were loaded, finally the gesture—a single slow sweep of the arm—which told them in which direction the troopers were coming.

The sun was beginning to burn on the rocks when the advance under Lieutenant Theller came down the last slopes of the broken pathway. He could see no Indians, for they were all hidden by the buttes. An ominous silence, broken only by the whinnying of the Indian ponies, hung over the canyon, and sometimes they heard the dry crackling of the range grass underfoot. He turned to Stevens and said, smiling: "I suppose they are waiting for us," and he bent forward to see whether the saddle girth was tight. Smoke rose from the Indian cooking-fires, and this smoke, drifting into the sun veils, looked wonderfully beautiful, changing color as soap bubbles change color. Very faintly they heard the roaring of the river. Neither Stevens nor Lieutenant Theller had any feeling that the battle was almost joined. They suspected an ambush, and were looking across the canyon floor towards the low ridges which were like protecting arms and through which they would have to pass to reach the river, and though they were certain there were Indians behind these ridges, they could not make themselves believe that the Indians were armed, and were crouching there, and would fire into the column, and were even now waiting for the moment when the first horsemen came into the line of their sights. They could see the Indian village, the painted buffalo skins, a few men pulling the tepees down, but the men seemed to be in no hurry.

"We should send a man ahead with a white flag," Lieutenant Theller said, and then he ordered a halt, to let Captain Perry come up.

Five minutes later, when Captain Perry hurried up to join Theller's men, there was the same ominous quiet.

"Do we send a man ahead?" Theller asked, pointing to the rocks which were now the color of bronze.

"Why not? We had better send someone who knows them—someone they can recognize. We could send Chapman."

Chapman was a squaw man. Tall and dark-skinned from the sun, he looked like an Indian and spoke the Nez Perce language. Captain Perry sent a messenger to find him. Another five minutes was wasted in looking for him, and all the time, by faint murmurs, by the faint changes in the color of the air above the rocks, by the soft padding sounds of moccasins, they knew that the Indians were moving behind the bluffs. There were about two hundred of these warriors, armed with bows and arrows and muzzle-loaders, and though Captain Perry did not know how many there were, he guessed he was outnumbered. When Chapman came up, he said: "I want you to go ahead with a white flag. Talk to Joseph. Tell him there is no sense in fighting, and he must come here, unarmed, and we can talk."

Chapman nodded, and rode out alone down the length of the creek, sometimes disappearing in the shade of the willows, then coming out into the sunlight again. There was a Winchester lying across his saddle. He was laughing to himself, because the silence oppressed him, and once he turned round to wave at Perry who was standing on a square yellow rock beside the path. From the direction of the tepees five Indian horsemen were coming to meet him, and Chapman felt sure by their behavior that they were unarmed. He had gone about two hundred yards down the path when a shot rang out, and suddenly all over the rocks the heads of Indians bobbed up. Chapman paused. The five Indian horsemen had disappeared as though swallowed up in the earth. Immediately Chapman waved his arm, and Perry said: "We'll have to save him," and gave orders to the volunteers to hold the high rocks on the left while the main column pushed through the gap between the buttes. He was still not sure whether there would be fighting, but the strange appearance of the Indians who had suddenly bobbed up from behind boulders and bush, and every clump of willows, alarmed him. They were straggling up the rocks and all moving towards him, and they were doing this very stealthily and silently. He had the feeling that there were Indians, too, behind him, climbing towards the path which led down from the tableland above. He was not sure, but he thought he was being encircled, and the most obvious strategy would be to cut straight through the opening between the buttes and occupy the lodges: he thought there might be a short, sharp skirmish, and then the Indians would come to talk. Now the whole column was moving down towards the buttes, and they could see the smoke rising from the campfires and Indians lying stretched out at full length on all the rocks, waiting. When Perry came up to Chapman, he said: "Tell them we have to talk." Chapman began to shout at the top of his voice. With one arm he was still waving the white flag, but some of the troopers were already riding past him and the white flag was probably invisible to the Indians. Suddenly, from all the rocks, all the gulches and ravines and clumps of willows, shots rang out. Perry's men returned the fire, shooting over their horses' heads. The air was full of smoke and noise. The Indians began pressing forward, and now they were no longer lying stretched out on the rocks but on ponyback, and they were riding from the flanks against the long column. Some of these flankers had Winchesters, others were firing with bows and arrows: those strange thin whistling arrows painted with bright colors and with obsidian heads.

"Close your ranks, men," Perry shouted, and now for the first time he regretted deeply that they had come out without a trumpeter. Already some of his riders were racing out of the column against the Indians, and there was no way to prevent them. "We'll push straight through to the river."

"We can't do it," Lieutenant Theller said. "They're all there behind the rocks—it's annihilation to go further."

"Annihilation be damned," Perry replied, but the Indian fire was growing stronger, all the surrounding bluffs were being held by them and the whole valley seemed to be full of angry painted warriors racing up and down the slopes, waving war clubs, or else on ponyback they were swarming over the rocks. They were swarming in front and on both flanks. Already some of his men had fallen. The volunteers on the left were falling back. It was now nearly six o'clock, and the sun was hot on their faces, but mostly the Indians were in shadow.

"We'll have to turn back!" Perry shouted, and rode at a canter along his center line, shouting to his men, repeating the same words over and over again. Sometimes he said: "We'll have to get on the second ridge." There were two ridges below the horse trail leading down the canyon wall, and the second was close to the foot of the wall. When he found Lieutenant Theller he said: "The volunteers are falling away. I want you to get up on the rocks and draw their fire. It's the only way we can save the column." Theller saluted smartly, and began to lead about eighteen men, all there were close to him, up on the craggy slopes from which the volunteers had withdrawn. At the same moment, bright and painted and flashing in the sun, a herd of bronze ponies was let loose by the Indians behind the two big bluffs which separated the hollow where Perry's column was retreating and the approaches to the river. There were Indians hidden among the pony herd. The ponies swung to the right and then charged through the column, breaking it in two. Perry was caught in the struggling mass of horsemen who were trying to beat the ponies off. Another group of Indians, nearly naked, with their bodies freshly painted, came charging up along the west canyon wall, hanging on the sides of their horses and at the same time firing into the huddle of Lieutenant Parnell's column, for Parnell had immediately taken charge of the troopers in the rear when he saw that Perry was having trouble with the ponies. Arrows, looking like little colored flames, spurted among them, and some of the warriors from higher ground were throwing sharp-pointed stones. "Stones and arrows!" Perry shouted, and thrust the gleaming Winchester against his shoulder and took aim at an Indian standing casually on a rock. He missed, and fired again, and the Indian was still there. Unlike most of the braves this Indian wore a shirt and there was a red sash falling from his shoulders: evidently he was one of the chiefs, perhaps Joseph, but the strange thing was that he stood against the skyline and not by a word or a gesture did he show that he was in command.

"It's no use: we'll have to turn back," Perry said, turning to Stevens. "I mean right back, up the cliff."

The ponies had been beaten off. Some had raced back to the gap, others were charging across the valley floor, to lose themselves in a small ravine thick with thornbushes; but they had done their work, the Indians were in good heart, and though Perry was able to join Parnell, he did not know how long he would be able to hold off the Indians who were coming in small scattered groups, hopping from rock to rock, naked and glistening, and the few who were armed with Winchesters aimed with incredible accuracy. With his hand on the bright lock of his rifle, Perry hardly knew where to shoot. He saw that Theller's small column was being surrounded. He shouted and waved his arms: "Come back! Join us here!" Theller was too busy fighting off the Indians to hear. "Ride over—get close to him—tell him to join us," Perry shouted to Stevens, and he began to push his way, with the rest of the column trailing behind him, up the first ridge with its grey thornbushes smeared with the dust of the canyon. Some of his men were already panic-stricken. Perry was out of breath. He had seen eight or nine men killed, slumping off their horses with bullet wounds in their foreheads, and then their horses panicked, and the noise was unbearable: the crack of rifles, the whistling of arrows, the whinnying of the horses and the high-pitched yelling of the Indians, and louder than any other sound, reverberating against the cliff walls, were the screams of the wounded and dying. "Can't stay here! Get back from here! Take ridge farther back!" Perry was shouting hoarsely, and when a bullet clipped off some of his horse's mane, he was sick, and the violence of his retching made him pull up short, so that he was left behind for a few minutes with only a handful of men round him. Worst of all, the Indians were now beginning to maneuver and deploy in fine order, with long columns of Indians on speckled ponies coming out of the line of willows, preparing to charge up the slope. One column was heading off Theller's detachment; another was about to break against Parnell's flank; a third was racing towards Parnell's rear. A small group of troopers from Company H under Captain Trimble had been broken through, and the men were running frantically in all directions. Mastering his sickness, Perry began to race towards the remnants of Trimble's troopers. All he could do was to hold the Indians in check from knoll to knoll, until they had gained the ridge; behind the ridge there was a ravine which might offer shelter, but for all he knew it was swarming with Indians. There was a rocky outcrop to the ridge shaped like a lion's head with a great sweeping mane, and he remembered that on the further side there was a gentle slope down to the ravine. He shouted to one of Trimble's sergeants: "Hold that ridge if you can!" A moment later he was thrown from his horse. The horse had been shot in four places almost simultaneously, and suddenly hurled itself in the air. Bright yellow guts were streaming out of the belly. The horse began to go round like a windmill, frothing and bleeding, kicking wildly with its forelegs; then it crumpled up. Perry's rifle had disappeared in the creek, and there was no time to search for it. He had lost his column, his rifle and his horse, and the Indians were riding hard towards him, screaming and waving their arms, and at the head of them, wearing a long yellow shirt and a red sash falling from his shoulders was someone who could only be Chief Joseph.

Perry thought it was all over. He waited to be shot down, for he could only wait. Suddenly the column of Indians veered to the left, towards the box canyon where Theller was fighting a rear-guard action. They were riding hard on the heels of Stevens. When they caught up with Stevens, Perry closed his eyes. When he opened them again, the column had passed beyond Stevens, and firing was breaking out again in the horseshoe-shaped hollow in the bluffs. Stevens was coming slowly across the canyon floor. His rifle must have been taken from him by the Indians as they passed, for he jumped down and retrieved a rifle he found lying on the floor. Perry waved to him, and at the same moment he saw a riderless horse making for the canyon wall. He raced after it, and then met Stevens in the shadow of the lion-headed rock. Parnell was covering the slopes above. There was a great scrambling of men riding through the thornbushes, eager to escape. Stevens was saying: "They went past and made the eagle-sign. Do you know what that means?"

"I don't care. Get up on the rocks. Thank God it will be sundown soon."

Perry pulled out his watch, but it had been smashed during his fall.

"What time is it?"

"Eight o'clock in the morning, and we've been fighting for two hours. It's going to be a long time before the sun goes down."

In a small horseshoe-shaped hollow among the bluffs Joseph on his red horse surveyed the dead. In their blue uniforms, with the bright yellow cartridge cases scattered around them, and the wind waving on their hair, they looked as though they were sleeping. They were all surprisingly young, and they were all facing the direction by which the Indians had advanced. Dropping from his horse he walked among them slowly, and he counted nineteen: not one of them could have been over twenty-five. The Indians were standing on the rocks some distance away. A messenger from White Bird's Indians came riding up, but seeing Joseph walking among the dead the messenger kept silent.

"You may take their uniforms and their weapons, but you must not harm them in any way," Joseph said at last. "Let them rest where they are, until the dust covers them."

Then, very slowly, the chieftain walked to his horse, and began to ride down to the canyon floor, his long shirt fluttering in the wind. The messenger told him that Alokut and White Bird were throwing their men against the cliff and expected within an hour to kill every one of the enemy.

"Then it must be," Joseph said quietly, and a moment later he was spurring his horse into a gallop, riding alone beside the stream in the direction of the tepees.

When he reached his own lodge he found that his wife had given birth to a daughter. His wife was sleeping, her pale face turned towards the lodge wall. The women who had been present at the birth said it took place more than two hours before, almost at the moment when the first volley was fired by the Indians streaming over the rocks. Now the little wrinkled baby, naked and howling, lay on a shawl. Joseph gathered it up in his arms, walked outside the lodge, held up the baby so that its face was turned toward the canyon wall, and said in a low chanting voice: "O little one, you shall be known as Little Wrinkled Wolf of Red Canyon Wall—"

From far away there came the faint crackling of rifle shots.

XXV

The Smell of Corruption

SIXTY men were working their way up the trail. Breathless, exhausted, their faces grimy with sweat and powder stains, their clothes tattered, less than half of them on horses, they clambered up the trail without knowing where they were going. The Indians were all round them. There were Indians at the top of the trail, waiting for them. There were more scurrying up behind them, yelling. The yells drowned the thin screams of the dying in the canyon below. Stevens rode slowly, keeping to the cliff wall, all the blood drained from his face. Lem was cursing, groping for cover, firing from behind the willows and the boulders, and always missing, because his hands would no longer obey the commands of his brain. Of all the stragglers up the cliff face only Perry was completely calm.

"Hold on, men, hold on—it's the only way," he said grimly, and sometimes he would shout an encouraging lie to some wounded soldier on horseback. "Come on, men, we'll be all right when we get to the top."

The strange thing was the terrible smell they met halfway up the cliff.

"It may be the tule swamp up above—the wind's changed," Perry explained, but the smell frightened him. It was as though the smell was somehow mocking their defeat, rubbing it in.

It was noon when they reached the plateau. Parnell's men had gone on ahead, and were now out of sight. The smell was stronger here. He counted the survivors, twenty-seven of his own, and another thirty under Parnell, three lost on the journey up the wall, and there were eight horses and fifteen Winchesters among them. The Indians had vanished now. He laughed. All he had in the world, all he would ever have, was those fifteen Winchesters with which to hold off whatever force the Indians threw against him. In front of him there was only waving grass, thornbushes, clumps of willows and the blue hills in the distance. There were no trails here, for they had taken a shorter route up the cliff than the one they had taken when they set out; and he knew only the general direction of Mount Idaho.

They marched on for an hour, at intervals calling out to Parnell's men, but there was no answer, and sometimes they rested. Whenever the grass waved in the wind, they thought Indians were waiting for them. They had almost no ammunition, and Perry gave orders that they were to shoot only when they saw an Indian. Further along the plateau there was a heavy growth of brush and willows, and there for the first time they felt safe; but beyond the willows they found their way barred by a deep ravine. They would have to clamber down and then up again, or else skirt the ravine for more than a mile. Perry decided to drop down into the ravine. They were halfway up the other side, slithering among boulders topped with thorngrass, when the Indians found them. There was a sudden yell, and then the Indian rifles cracked among the boulders, and once again there was panic with the horses losing their foothold.

"Keep down, men, keep down—don't show your heads," Perry shouted. "There are only three or four of them," he went on, shouting so hoarsely that sometimes the men heard his shrill cry, but more often they heard only a long-drawn choking whisper. Perry thought he had heard only three or four men yelling, but soon he discovered there were more than twenty of them. More horses were killed, for they provided larger targets and the troopers were no longer riding them. Lem was shot through the hand. Perry received a glancing wound in the forehead, the blood pouring into his eyes, so that he was momentarily blinded. Buzzards wheeled overhead, and he thought the end had come: they would perish in the ravine, just as Theller had perished in a small box canyon from which there was no escape. But at the moment when the Indians were beginning to gain on him, he heard firing from the canyon rim. It came from Parnell's men who had hurried round the edge of the canyon just in time. The Indians fled.

"I've sent my scouts ahead," Parnell said a little later, "and the shortest way to Grangeville leads through a tule swamp."

"Then we'll go through the swamp," Perry said, and for the first time since he left White Bird Canyon he smiled weakly.

They rested for five minutes. Lem was attempting to bandage his wounded hand with a bandanna. He was sweating as though he had a fever. Stevens, surprised that Lem could stand, for he had lost his horse and looked exhausted to the point of fainting, offered to help with the bandage.

"I don't want no help," Lem said. "Not from you."

"Well, will you let someone else help? I don't know what you've got against me."

"I've got a heap against you, Mr. Stevens. I watched you from that knoll below. I saw you circled by Indians, Mr. Stevens, and you came out of it fresh as a daisy. I reckon they must have been Indians you know."

Stevens blushed. The sun was glaring down at him. He felt helpless, and at the same time he wanted to smash his fist into Lem's face. There was a knowing look in Lem's eyes, but he was gritting his teeth with the pain of the wound.

"Will you let someone else help with the bandage?"

"No, I'll do it my own way, thank you."

Afterwards, when they were up to their knees in the tule swamp, suffocating in the smell of rotten vegetation, with Indians springing up on the higher ground all round them, Lem edged close to Stevens and said, "You didn't believe me when I said they were on a rampage. Do you believe it now?" Lem laughed the long-drawn cackling laugh of a man at the end of his strength, and he would have fallen at full length into the swamp if Stevens had not helped him. Stevens heard himself saying: "I wouldn't be surprised if you had brought this war on us, you and your like." There was no answer from Lem. Gritting his teeth, swaying from side to side, holding a rifle above his head with one arm, he made his way through the swamp, and he kept looking straight ahead even when some Indians hidden in the high grass fired at the column.

All that afternoon and halfway through the night the column was attacked by Indian skirmishers. Perry had hoped that with nightfall the attacks would be called off, but even when they were marching in the dark, and there was almost no light because the moon was clouded over, there would be sudden spurts of flame, yells, the soft padding sounds of Indians moving through the grass.

"Where are we? Are we near Grangeville?" Stevens asked once, peering into the darkness ahead in the hope of seeing a light.

"I don't know where we are," Perry answered. "All I know for sure is that we are reeling to Hell and Grangeville in the dark."

BOOK FOUR

THE LONG WAY HOME

XXVI

The Snow Falls

DOWN below, where the Snake flowed in yellow flood with its rippling white spine in midstream, the naked Indian boys were bringing a buffalo-robe raft ashore. It was evening, with all the cliffs shining a dull red on the further side of the river, but where the boys were, purple shadows swirled; and only the hawks, catching the sun with the tips of their wings, shone gold in the shadows.

Lying on a blanket with Alokut beside him, Joseph watched the boys through glasses and wondered whether Howard's scouts had seen them. He had deliberately sent them across the river early in the morning to spy out Howard's strength and to collect information from the Indians near Howard's camp at Grangeville. Now they were returning, as others would return during the night and for many nights to come. Boys were best: they could hide in the grass and flatten themselves against rock and steal noiselessly among the enemy at night. From them he had learned every detail of Howard's movements. He knew now that Howard was bewildered. On the night of the battle at White Bird Canyon, Joseph had sent the whole tribe across the river; then five days later he swung across the river again, and sent a party of skirmishers against Cottonwood, and then once again he retreated to his hiding place beside the Snake, where the beeves were cached and the women were busy jerking the meat. From now on he would keep his herds of ponies, but the beef herds would have to be sacrificed to the war. Here among the snowy peaks, high up where the hawks had their nests, he was safe. If Howard pursued him among the cliffs, he could turn him. If he decided to march south, he could turn Howard's left. He could march to the meeting of the Snake and the Salmon, and cross wherever he wanted to, always out of reach, and from the Salmon he could swing left towards Wallowa.

When Alokut slipped away, Joseph was left alone to watch the river sweeping through the granite cliffs below. He liked being alone. He liked waiting for the youngsters who were sent out to spy, those twelve-year-olds who were quick as deer and almost as beautiful. When they reached him they were smiling and pretending not to be out of breath. Where was Howard? They said he was camped still on the canyon rim above White Bird, and was bringing up more guns. Another column was on its way from Lapwai. The soldiers looked dispirited; they had been burying the bodies in the box canyon, but the bodies had turned black and fell apart when they lifted them up. The boys laughed, showing their teeth. Then Joseph clapped them on the shoulder, and raced with them back to the village in the cliffs.

During his absence Looking Glass had arrived with a story of how the troopers had fired on his braves. He had been peacefully making his way towards the reservation when he was surrounded, and then someone had come forward with a white flag. Joseph heard the tail end of the story. "They came with their white flag and their guns," Looking Glass was saying, his hands shaking nervously. "I looked at the guns and then at the white flag, and told them I was making my way to the reservation. They told me to give up my guns. I promised to do so, and just at that moment they fired. We fired, and then we ran, and we have come here for protection."

The old man laughed derisively. The little glass mirror he wore on his forehead shone with the light of the fire. Looking Glass puffed at his pipe, passed it to Joseph and said: "I have done what had to be done. Now do we fight?"

"What is the use of fighting?" Joseph asked helplessly. "We have fought, and we are still far away from Wallowa, and you, Looking Glass, are far from your hunting grounds. We must think carefully."

Looking Glass shook his head slowly, exhausted by the long climb. Rage shook him, but he concealed his rage. Joseph held his hand and said: "I am thinking of my people and your people. I say we must avoid fighting. At White Bird Canyon they forced a war on us, and perhaps it is in their hearts to force more wars on us. All I know is this: We must be prepared for war and hope for peace, and we must stay close to our hunting grounds, and we must never think of moving far from here. If we fight well, we shall be allowed to return to our hunting grounds."

"How is this?" Tuhulhulsote asked, and there was bitterness in his tone. "They want to humble us, they want to kill us, they will never stop making war on us. They are like snakes. They go quietly through the grass, but when you are not looking, they will fall upon you."

"Tuhulhulsote says the truth," Looking Glass exclaimed helplessly, and he turned from one to the other of the chieftains in the lodge until his glance fell on Alokut. "Is it war or peace?" he asked.

"It is neither peace nor war," Joseph said.

"I was asking Alokut," Looking Glass interrupted. "Alokut knows they are treacherous. Tell me, Alokut, what shall we do?"

It was the first time Looking Glass had asked Alokut's advice. Everyone knew why Looking Glass had turned to Joseph's brother. He was a man who liked to weigh the opinions of others; when he thought he had discovered the opinions of the majority, then he would loudly proclaim that he had thought this from the very beginning. Alokut was saying, smiling towards his brother: "Joseph is our war chief. Why should you ask my advice?"

After this, they all turned towards Joseph expectantly. They trusted him because there was no one else to trust. He was grave, and could not be moved easily, and there was about all his gestures an extraordinary solemnity.

"What does Chief Joseph say?" Looking Glass said.

"I say this. It is neither peace nor war. We do not want war. We know the enemy, what kind of man he is. He is a soldier and thinks like a soldier, while we are people who live in the uplands and we think like people who live in the uplands. He knows we are not responsible for the murders, but he is determined upon war. So we must fight him, but in our own way. We must worry him, as a dog worries a wounded deer. We must make him so mad that he will not dare to fight us any longer. Then he will say: 'You, White Bird, return to your hunting grounds on the Salmon,' and he will say to Looking Glass: 'Go where you please, Looking Glass, for you are a worthy man,' and he will say to me: 'Joseph, return to Wallowa.' If he is a man, he will do this. So I say we must fight well, and then we will be able to go to our own homes. This we must remember: whether we fight for a short time or a long time, we must return to our own homes."

He said these words very slowly, lost in dreams. He was sorry for the general, and sorry for his own braves. There was only fighting now. When it would end he did not know. Beside the fires of heaped pine branches and fir cones the young braves were dancing in time with drums. The snow fell. Whenever the fire was in danger of going out, someone threw more pines branches in the flames. Half the night the braves danced in the snow. The chiefs watched, never showing what was on their minds.

XXVII

The Heat of the Day

ALL evening the column made its way across Camas Prairie, losing itself sometimes among the tamaracks, the pines and the brush, but always finding itself again. The air was sweet with the coming of summer, and a low mist lay on the fields; and when the stars came out they were still marching. They had come over the foothills of the Blue Mountains and then circled towards the Clearwater, and then for some reason retreated on their own tracks—"You would think he was mad," Stevens said softly, "if you did not know there was some purpose in his madness."

"I'll swear that he's mad, and there's no purpose in it," Captain Perry answered, and peered through the gathering dusk at a solitary thorn tree which somehow resembled an Indian standing alone in the middle of the prairie. "Well then, there's no hope for it, is there?"

"No hope for what?"

"An end to the madness," Perry laughed, and then turned his head towards a small stream running at the bottom of a gulch. It was very dark in the gulch, and he thought he had seen something moving there, but there were only some rocks and stunted trees; and soon they came to a small river where they watered their horses and filled their canteens; then they rode on. Soon, when it was dark and the whole column lumbering behind them was no more than an indistinct smear across the plain, the general gave the order to encamp; the guns were trundled up; guards were stationed; and the general set up his tent with the pack teams not far away. His men were tired after the long journey, and glad to get to the safety of the tents.

All afternoon and all evening, as they came through the forests and then across the plateau, Stevens had the curious feeling that he was being watched: he had known exactly the same feeling when they were riding through White Bird Canyon. The whole column seemed to be possessed with the same apprehensive feeling. Once, during the morning, when they were skirting a field of tall rye grass, they had seen black shapes moving. Immediately, fearing an ambush, they had galloped across the field, yelling at the tops of their voices, shooting at those black wriggling things in the grass which resembled Indians, and when they discovered they were riding through a herd of black hogs, it occurred to them that perhaps the Indians had deliberately thrown the hogs against them to confuse them, and they kept on firing. It was half an hour before the column could be re-formed. All day scouts had reported "signs"; caches of buffalo robes were found; friendly Indians reported that Joseph or Looking Glass or White Bird had been seen riding across the prairie, but some of these reports were false, and it was impossible to tell which were true; worse still, there were occasional brush fires, usually on the horizon, but whether they were the brush fires that occurred every summer or were deliberately set by the Indians no one knew. All they knew for certain was that the Indians had come down from their hiding place high up in the mountains and were somewhere in the region of the Clearwater.

When Stevens and Perry went to the general's tent, they found him out of temper, his beard uncombed and his eyes bloodshot. Maps were spread out on the little folding table in front of him. The general cocked one eyebrow and said: "Your friend is leading us a merry dance, Mr. Stevens." Through the tent flap they could see the stars shining in a cloudless sky. From somewhere there came the sound of men digging rifle pits.

"I'll tell you the truth," the general went on, a stubby finger moving across the map. "I don't know where they are. I reckon nobody knows. They've crossed the Snake and the Salmon four times in the last two weeks—maybe more. I'm ready to give battle, but I don't know what the red devils are up to. Maybe they don't know themselves what they are up to. Have you any opinions, Captain Perry?"

"I think we're doing well, sir."

At first the general thought Perry was being ironical; his eyes blazed, and he thrust out his chin, so that his beard seemed to leap forward.

"I want sensible opinions, captain," the general said. "I don't want claptrap. As far as I can see, there is no evidence that we are doing well at all."

"We are letting them know where we are, sir. They can't avoid seeing us. They'll give battle when they think they have the advantage. They did it at White Bird Canyon, and they'll do it again."

"You're sure they want battle?"

"I'm sure of it."

"And you, Mr. Stevens?"

"I don't know, sir. I don't believe they will give battle unless they are sure of the outcome. I reckon they just want to tire us out. The important thing to remember is that they want to go back to Wallowa. I don't believe Joseph wanted war—he may have been forced into it by White Bird or Looking Glass. I reckon he'll stay in the neighborhood as long as there's a ghost of a chance that we'll talk with him."

The general sighed. The small mess-fires were throwing up small packets of bright flame, and sometimes these flames would lick the silken quarters of a horse with a flash of gold or crimson: then the horse would pass out of sight, and there would be only the campfire and the inky darkness beyond. The calm bustle of an army bedding down for the night always pleased the general. He had time now to think out his problems, talk with officers, write a letter to his wife and prepare himself for sleep with two chapters of the Bible; but now for a whole week he knew he had been marching blind, with nothing to show for his labors but a gnawing hunger for a battle which might never be fought. From the high mountain peaks Joseph had descended, but where was he? There were signs that the Indians were running to his banners. Soon—for no man could be certain about these things—there might be a blaze of revolt from the crest of the Cascades to the banks of the Mississippi. And it was all quietness now, the quietness before the storm.

The general's stubby finger continued to move across the maps. Sometimes the finger would pause, as though it was establishing some kind of communication with a name, a valley, a mountain outpost. As always, even when he seemed to be gazing vacantly across the tent, his mind was occupied with problems of war: this hill could be taken by assault, that valley could be blocked by enfilading fire. He could no longer see a hill as a hill: it was something to be gained, fought over, pocked with rifle pits, defended, encircled with the strength of his will. "We're marching like blind bats," he said. "Is there anything to be gained by it? By God, I've never known a man as elusive as Joseph. I remember at Antietam—"

It was always like that when he was weary. Memories of the Civil War crowded upon him at night, and sometimes, as he related the events of the war, his voice would quaver, and it was as though his memories were more pressing than the world he saw everyday. Suddenly, while he was gazing miserably across the tent flap, he saw a bright silver light flashing up on the horizon, then two more behind it. These bright lights resembled meteors, curving up and then falling to earth again. He knew what the lights meant. He knew that the Indians were signalling to one another. They took pitch from the pine trees and smeared the pitch on balls of dry grass, and then set fire to them and hurled them high in the air. The light lasted only a few seconds, but the general knew that from hill to hill the news that his column was approaching the Clearwater was being taken to Joseph's camp.

"They've just sent up some more of their light-balls," the general said. "Damn them to hell, they're on our tracks wherever we are. Well, gentlemen, I wish you a good night's sleep. I'll want the guards reinforced, and that will be all."

With a nod and a salute Perry and Stevens went out. Neither had seen the lights directly, but they had seen a faint quiver of light shining for a fraction of a second on the general's face: and this was enough. They rolled up in their blankets not far from where they had picketed their horses, and went to sleep.

In the morning there was only the plain with the dew sparkling, the blue curve of Craig's Mountain dipping northward to the Clearwater, the long rye grass, the rich black soil underfoot, that soil which could produce immense crops of wheat, barley, oats and fruit if any man turned his hand to it. The level field stretched for miles with only an occasional farmstead, white-timbered and gaunt against the sky line. These small farms of ten or twenty acres produced great crops of hay in peace time, but now most of the hay had been burned by marauding Indians, and some of the farms were no more than black shells. High on the hills, grouse and deer and not a few black bear wandered at leisure; and sometimes they heard the howls of mountain wolves. Now all the plain was peaceful and sparkling in the sun, and there was no sign of any animals, no black hogs or mountain cougar or Indians anywhere in sight. Under the clear pearly blue sky of dawn the long column with its baggage trains and mule packs made its way to the south fork of the Clearwater.

At midday with the sun overhead, Perry and Stevens marching with the advance decided to rest their horses. The grass was parched, but there was a spring nearby and some tamaracks growing on the banks of the stream which disappeared in the parched grass. They were nearly abreast of the spring when for the first time they heard voices —Indian voices. It was a sound like a long low pleasant chanting. As they listened more intently, they realized that it was simply a work song sung by some Indian women. Then they realized that they were much closer to the river than they thought, for the river was flowing between high canyon walls, beyond the timber and the bluffs, and somewhere on the canyon slopes or on the canyon bottom these women were working. The timber and the warm wind coming directly towards them must have prevented the Indians from knowing they were there.

Pushing forward cautiously, taking only three men with him, leaving their horses behind, Perry and his men made their way to the edge of the timber. A stone rattled. Suddenly the singing ceased. They saw two Indian herders driving a small beef herd over the bluffs down to the river, which was very blue and half as wide as the Snake. Beyond the river, calm in the midsummer sun, smoke pouring from the cooking-fires, was Joseph's camp, the painted lodges set out exactly as they were set out at Wallowa, with the huge red-embroidered lodge of the chieftain set a little apart from the rest. You could not see them from the plateau unless you were right up close. On this side of the river below the timber there were only gullies, craggy bluffs and boulders in shadow.

"They're all so damned peaceful," Perry said. "It seems a pity to disturb them."

Then he thought of White Bird Canyon, and he would have fired straight across the river if some braves had not come stealthily out of the woods and fired at him instead.

He dropped to the ground, cursed, and saw that the woods were full of naked, painted braves, and they were all coming stealthily towards him. He aimed at the nearest Indian with his Colt. To the left some scouts, seeing the Indians approaching, opened fire. Perry promised himself he would find out who these scouts were. They had saved his life. He began to race across the field, his body bent, keeping close to the waving grass. The Indians who had swarmed out of the woods had vanished again.

"Some of them are already across," Perry reported to Howard. "The whole encampment is on the other side, and they're swarming over."

It was partly a guess. He heard their cries, and he knew what they would do, but he had not guessed at the full daring of their plan. The general was looking for his mule train. There was no sign of it until he heard firing on the flank, and then he realized that the Indians were creeping through the grass towards the mule train as it came behind some rocks. He shouted: "Cavalry to the left, infantry and artillery to the right. We must hold, men!"

The column began to form in a half-circle, facing the bluffs and the timber and the hidden river. If the general had been afraid of a repetition of the White Bird Canyon disaster, he need not have worried. The Indians had swum the river and climbed the gullies in a surprisingly short time, and soon the timber was thick with them. They were there, barring the path to the river, naked and shining in the hot sun, and they kept making sorties across the grass and then retiring to the shelter of the pines and tamaracks. Some were on horseback, and these streaked across the grass, fired into the soldiers who were hastily preparing rifle pits and then streaked away again. Swarming out of the river bottom they now occupied the whole rim of the plateau as far as the eye could see, occupying the rocks and timbered heights of the ravines which sloped down to the river, throwing themselves flat on the sunburned grass, yelling from all directions, and already some of the Indians were maneuvering towards the rear of the semi-circle which Howard had thrown out and seemed in no haste to close. It looked as though someone was organizing every maneuver. They would attack and then fall away, and a moment later there would be another attack from an unexpected quarter beautifully concerted with the first. A column of dismounted cavalry leading the pack train was caught in a cross fire. They heard the packers whipping up the mules, and then the sudden crackle of rifle fire from the head of a ravine, and then a long silence. From another quarter the general heard a sound he had never expected to hear in a war with Indians—the sound of Indians throwing up stones to make stone barricades. Both sides were now digging themselves in. The advantage should have been with the whites, for they were on higher ground, but the

Indian fire was so fierce and so accurate that the advance rifle pits had to be abandoned, and this happened at the same time that the remaining mules and gun carriages were being led into the great semicircle.

"Is this Joseph's work?" Perry said, glancing at Stevens as they made their way through the yellow grass towards the forward positions on the left which were still holding out.

He had hardly spoken when he heard someone calling fiercely from the edge of the tamaracks. It was a superb sound, as though ten deep-voiced coyotes were howling at once. It was Joseph's voice. They heard him loudly ordering a charge, and then a little while later the voice resounded faintly from the distant rocks. Once, peering up through the grass, Stevens caught sight of Joseph riding from one clump of pines to another, his shirt flapping behind him, a crown of feathers on his head. Joseph was everywhere: so were his Indians. Among the rocks and scrubby pines you would see their brown naked bodies flying from shelter to shelter, and their yells were incessant, deafening the men who were attempting to bring their guns up into position so that they rarely obeyed the frontier injunction: "When an Indian yells, yell back at him." And all the time, while the grass crackled and the wounded screamed and the semi-circle grew gradually smaller, the hot sun blinded the defenders.

The general's face, caked with sweat and dust, showed the terrible excitement playing upon him. There were moments when he altogether lost hope. When the Indians charged his rear or cut through his line, he grew very quiet and his mind worked with mathematical precision, but in his heart he did not know how Joseph thought of the art of war. It was a game which Joseph played magnificently, according to his own rules. He could not understand why the Indians had chosen to fight along the rim instead of waiting for his army to climb down the slopes of the ravines and then attempt to make their way across the river. Presumably, they were determined to keep the village out of range of the Gatling guns and the howitzer. His scouts told him that the Indians were ferrying their own wounded across the river: they had a ferry service which acted with perfect mechanical efficiency, the wounded being lifted down the gullies on ropes and then swung onto the waiting buffalo-skin rafts. Meanwhile the sight of naked Indians painted all over with war paint was beginning to sicken him, and he was worried because the Indians held the only spring: the packers were saying they could not be responsible for the mules if they were not watered.

Lem Otis was in the advance rifle pits with the volunteers. There were only twenty of these volunteers, for many, seeing that the general's forces were now well equipped, had decided to return home. As the afternoon went on, Lem's mouth became so dry that he thought of pricking his skin and drinking blood. Everything was parched and yellow, even the sky. He wondered how long he could hold his rifle, and how long his ammunition would last. Horses were going crazy. Clouds of dust blotted the Indians from sight, and when you saw them again they were charging straight for your lines, and they would race up to the bayonets before falling back. There were few things which pleased Lem more than the sight of an Indian stumbling towards the shelter of the pines and the low walls of stone on the edge of the plateau. Sweat was straggling down the thick dust of his face, and he kept coughing: he had not coughed since the winter, and this frightened him almost as much as the sight of the Indians. When he aimed, his hands shook; and he held them from shaking at the moment of firing only by an immense effort of the will.

When Stevens came across him late in the afternoon, he was lying on his side and panting.

"You all right?" Stevens asked with an unexpected kindness in his tone. For some reason he often came across Lem, but usually they averted their faces when they passed one another.

"I can bear it," Lem said, and then waving a hand in the direction of a dead Indian fifty feet in front of him, an Indian who was not lying on the grass but kneeling with his eyes fixed on the white lines, he said: "Dead Indians stink worse than turkey buzzard." He laughed silently, his parched worn face all crinkled. "They'll wait for the night, Mr. Stevens. Then it's all up with us. I reckon the general just doesn't know how to fight 'em."

"He is doing the best he can."

"No, he's not. He's just holding them. We ought to swing them off the ravines and push 'em in the river."

"We can't do it—not with the forces we have."

"We ought to try," Lem muttered, and wiped his hand across his mouth. "Goddammit, we ought to try."

Later in the afternoon the general came to the same conclusion. He ordered one of his officers to bring up the Gatling guns and force a way to the head of the ravine and attempt to take the Indians in the rear. It was the favorite tactic of the Indians to work around the flanks and get in the rear. Well, he would do the same in the inhospitable country of crags, boulders, gulches and ravines which they offered him. His own ragged semi-circular line was still holding. He knew the Indians had posted sharpshooters in the ravines, but if he could bring his guns to the head of the ravine, he would be able to shell the village. Doing this, he would kill women and children, but there was no other way to dislodge the Indians. He detached all his cavalry including the horse-holders and the orderlies for the assault. "Take your time—take your time, but get there!" he shouted, and now more than ever he resembled an Old Testament prophet, his long beard streaked with dust so that it seemed to be white, and his eyes red-veined and swollen looked as though they had feasted on flames.

The line of the advance rose, ragged and yellow with dust, making for the ravine which jutted closest to his semi-circle. The cavalry guns squeaked as they raced forward. A sweeping fire from the tamaracks delayed the advance and put an end to the men's cheering, but the line went on until it reached the canyon rim, and there it stayed for ten minutes, the guns firing down into the hollows, until the pressure of the sharpshooters at both sides made them retreat. Then once more there were the forays and alarms, the hot rides of the Indians along the edge of the woods, and the semi-circle stiffening, waiting for an attack. When night came, they were still there, and there was still no water until some officers led a party of skirmishers to the spring: they returned with a few drops of water for each man.

The clouds hurried over the sky, and in the darkness there was only the faint ring of men, mostly in rifle pits, and in a semi-circle facing them were the Indians behind low walls of stones. Sometimes they would see the Indians moving behind rocks and scrub pines, and sometimes there would come, surprisingly loud in the cold summer air, the sound of shrieking and yelling from six hundred yards away. Down below, in the ravines and on the other side of the river, the women were chanting the death wail and the medicine men were beating on drums. The song of the women would rise plaintively and slowly gather strength; at the end there would be a quick scream. Some minutes later the death wail began again. The drumming and the singing tried the nerves of the defenders, but still more trying was the sudden roar which would come occasionally from the chieftains. It was a sound of blood-curdling proportions, and seemed to come out of the low hurrying clouds.

The night was bitterly cold, with a chilling dew on the grass: when dawn came the dew smoked away, and the hot sun struck against the faces of men who had enjoyed little sleep. Deliberately the Indians had attempted to keep them awake. The general wrestled with his conscience. Everything depended upon having more supplies: he expected a pack train from Lapwai: what if the pack train had been encircled elsewhere? and how do you dislodge the Indians from their prepared positions on the rim?

With dawn there came skirmishes. Once more the Indians rose from cover, drew close to the white lines and then sped into shelter again. Afraid of another long day without water, the general ordered twenty men to make a charge in the direction of the spring. This time they returned with enough water to last the rest of the day. There were more brisk skirmishes, but there was no plan and there were signs that the Indians were wearying. As always, the general was waiting for his opportunity, refusing to make up his mind, digging his toes in. He wanted to sweep the Indians out of the Clearwater Valley with a single blow, but until the pack train came up he did not know where the blow would fall and even refused to think in terms of attack: he would hold them off, and if he could do it successfully, this was enough. "I have to think about ambushes—ambushes everywhere," he told Perry, and at that moment he heard a hoarse cry from his own men and knew instinctively they were cheering the pack train; but a moment later, winging on the cheers of the white men there came the yelling of the Indians who had sent out skirmishers to cut off the pack train almost at the moment when it gained the rifle pits. The fighting grew fierce. It was at close quarters now, with the Indians riding through the grass, converging on the train, leaving their own flanks open. When they were thrown back, the men thought they had deserved a rest, but the general ordered a sweeping attack to the left, against the stone walls at the head of the canyon, an attack at an angle which would slice through the Indian positions. It meant flanking the flankers, but it was the only way out, and it gave him the hope that he would be able to form some of his men on the riverbank behind the Indians on the rim. It was sultry weather, and though the morning was hot, the afternoon was hotter. The attack began quietly. Soon a hundred men were scrambling over boulders, shouting at the top of their voices, then breaking through the woods and so down the steep canyon paths, over rocks and precipices and along trails too steep for horses. The general had guessed rightly that there would be no repetition of White Bird

Canyon: most of the Indians were on the rim, and now they were forced to fall back. There was a wild stampede down the canyon. You would see Indians jumping immense distances, flashing red in the sun.

"May I throw the cavalry in?" Perry asked, having raced back from the trees. "They're in full flight, sir. You know the Indians. Once they run, they never stop."

"Can you get the cavalry over the river?"

"I reckon so. If they can do it, we can."

The general thought for a moment. He was an infantryman, and distrusted cavalry.

"I can't afford to lose my cavalry," the general said quietly. "We'll keep them in reserve."

Perry wanted to argue, but the general was in no mood for argument.

"We'll lose all if we don't follow, sir. Will you come to the rim and see for yourself?"

"My place is here, Captain Perry," the general said, and dismissed the idea of a cavalry pursuit from his mind.

By sunset all the Indians had left the rim they had defended for two days. In good order they crossed the river, helped the women load the horses and travois, and soon they were racing into the woods beyond their village. The voice of Joseph was no longer heard summoning his men. It was as though very quietly, with one accord, the Indians had decided to offer no further resistance: they would wait, establish a foothold somewhere else, or simply vanish in the mountains.

When Lem Otis rode his horse into the river an hour after nightfall, he found Stevens riding by his side. They did not speak to one another until they reached the village, where a few tepees were still standing and some cooking-fires were still burning. Some saddles and buffalo robes lay about; axes were lying on the earth where they had fallen; an old squaw wandered about the village jabbering to herself. In a sinister quiet the village remained in its desolation.

"The general orders us to hold the village in case they return," Perry said, riding up.

"What in hell does he want us to hold the village for?" Lem whispered. "They don't care about their village. They only care about their men. They won't defend their village." His voice rose as he drew courage from the silence around him. "You soldiers—you don't know what you're doing! Give the heavy guns to the volunteers! God in heaven, the whole place is a sucked lemon unless we get at their men!"

XXVIII

The Lo Lo Trail

GAUNT and lean, Joseph stared out from the branches of a high tree across the river. Far in the distances he thought he could see the white tents of the army. It was late afternoon, and the air was sweet in the forest, and through the leaves he saw the small fires burning. Here, on the slopes of Kamiah, twenty miles from Howard, the braves rested among wild-strawberry beds and clear rushing streams.

Resting against the branch, shading his eyes from the sun, Joseph reflected that the battle at Clearwater had been fought vigorously and well. They had retreated because there was no further advantage in fighting for the rim. He had saved half the beef herds, and nearly all the ponies. He had shown Howard the power of his people. As he whittled on a stick, absent-mindedly carving the general's head with his scalping knife, and sometimes gazing down at the braves who rested in the shelter of stretched buffalo skins, he waited patiently for the messenger to return. The messenger had been sent that morning under a white flag to ask for terms. It was evening when he saw the messenger coming through the encampment. He climbed down the tree, clapped a hand on the shoulder of the messenger, who was called Wolf With Grey Pocks, and said: "Did you see the praying one?"

"I saw him."

"What were the terms?"

"Surrender of all our arms, all our ponies and beeves. He says the chiefs must be brought to trial before his officers."

"That means they will hang us?"

"Yes."

Joseph groaned. He knew there was no alternative to fighting now. He was trapped; he knew that. He had altogether four hundred warriors. How long would it be before they too were exhausted? On how many more battlefields must they fight off Howard's implacable army, and all this because three braves had gone murdering through the Wallowa and the Salmon? The streams came singing down the hills and the strawberry blossoms glimmered in the darkness, and there was no answer to these questions.

"Tell the chiefs we must talk," Joseph said, and went to lie down at full length on a spread buffalo robe. Clenched in his hand was the little wooden carving he had made of the general. Later, when he had time, he would paint it with bright smears of sky-blue paint over the eyes and savage brown paint over the beard.

When the chiefs came together they were in ill-humor. They had each heard rumors. They knew a messenger had been sent to Howard, and the messenger had returned, and simply because Joseph confided the message to no one, they knew there was bad news. Looking Glass, his leather face shining blood-red in the light of the fire, quivered with anger, and old Tuhulhulsote could not contain himself. Only White Bird, waving his eagle-feather fan, smiled continually to himself, remembering how he had led an early morning attack on the Clearwater. When Joseph spoke of the message from the general, Tuhulhulsote's voice rose shrilly: "He thinks he can hang everyone who displeases him. Why? Then he must hang everyone on earth. What kind of a man is this?"

The other chiefs paid no attention to Tuhulhulsote's outburst. There were graver matters to discuss. Ever since they escaped from the Clearwater, they had rested: now it was time to gather their strength and decide. Looking Glass was all for fighting. Howard's men were in camp, waiting for reinforcements less than thirty miles to the south. Then why not attack at night? Why not put an end to all their doubts and troubles by destroying him completely? White Bird spoke of a meeting with the Crows beyond the Rockies and reminded them of the great feasts they had shared with the Crow chieftains; but all this had happened a long time ago, so long before the battles that it seemed to have happened to different people, and soon White Bird forgot to talk of feasts, and spoke of trails instead, the long trail up the Lo Lo Pass, and all the other trails. He wanted to move now, at once, before Howard could bring reinforcements up. Tuhulhulsote agreed. His old and breaking mind went wandering back among recollections of the ancient buffalo *illahees* which had occurred before Joseph was born; and he spoke as though Joseph's father was still alive, and he smiled at his own recollections. "We go to the Crow country. Who follows me?" he cried, and they were all strangely silent. "Is there no power left among our people? Then follow me, for I have the power. The eagle beats its wings within my heart. Come, it is time to go!" Alokut said softly: "The eagles may beat their wings, but the eyes must seek for the trail."

"What trail?" Tuhulhulsote asked sharply. "We have no need for trails. We go like lightning."

"Ah, but what if the lightning strikes us instead of giving us its power?" Alokut asked, and then they were silent again until Joseph began to speak.

Joseph had been brooding through all the speeches of the chieftains. Trapped, he thought of the long trail which would lead him to the country of the Old Woman in the North; then of the Crow country; then of the country of the Shoshones on the Salmon; then of the Snake River Mountains where they had hidden among the cold crags. But none of these offered safety: the real safety lay in Wallowa. Always there was Wallowa like a light bursting at the end of a trail. They were not fighting for themselves: they were fighting for their lands, and once this was understood, the rest followed. So he said calmly, in a voice which seemed to come with the rustling tamaracks and grasses on this windy night: "What are we fighting for? Is it for our lives? No. It is for the fair lands where the bones of our fathers are buried. I do not want to take my women among strangers. I do not want to die in a strange land. Some of you tried to say once that I was afraid of the whites, but I am not afraid. Stay here with me and you shall have plenty of fighting. We will put our women behind us in these mountains and die in our own land fighting for them. I would rather do that than run I know not where."

"Then we stay here?" Looking Glass asked.

"Here or elsewhere, what difference does it make as long as we return to our own lands? It may be a long way home or a short way, but our homes call to us. We must keep our braves alive if we can—"

"If we stay here 'the praying one' will attack tomorrow."

"Let him attack."

"You are the war chief, and you say 'let him attack,' but we are also chiefs, and we say 'let us rest from fighting for a little while, let us be stronger before we fight, let us think about this matter a little longer.' We lost thirty men at the Clearwater. 'The praying one' lost fifty. He can afford to lose fifty, but we cannot afford to lose thirty. I say we should join the Crows. Where is Smohalla? He also said we should join the Crows. Then let us go over the Lo Lo trail, as far away from 'the praying one' as we can."

Looking Glass was speaking, but Joseph thought he detected in the voice a sense of identity with the others. It was as though all the people were speaking.

Joseph nodded. He knew now that they were right. The only solution was to join the Crows. Instead of swinging down against Howard they would have to march over the Lo Lo trail, and he knew there would be no joy in it. It was a terrible trail, rarely used, all jagged rock and fallen timber and steep climbs through a jungle growth. His face had turned scarlet at the thought of making his braves and their women follow the broken trail, yet it had to be done. He let them rest till midnight, then in the dark, with a low moon and the wind blowing in their faces, they set out. At dawn they could go no further, for the wind was strong, buffeting them. The beef herd had to be abandoned, but they kept their small army of fifteen hundred ponies, dragging them up the steep slopes. It was strange how silent they were as they grappled with the trail in the dark.

After dawn, they rested in the fir bush. White Bird slept for an hour. When he awoke, he said: "I have seen the shape of my death. I see darkness ahead. We must hurry."

Joseph was half-asleep, and hardly understood what White Bird was saying.

"We are hurrying as fast as we can," he said.

"This is true, but we must go faster still. Old Man With One Arm is following us. He has tricks. While I slept, the dream came to me: unless we hurry we are lost. We must go like lightning."

A storm was blowing in the valley. All below them was thick with mist. Joseph turned to Alokut. Branches, whipping in the wind, had cut a gash in Alokut's handsome face. Nearby there were braves fast asleep, sprawled out on the rocks, as motionless as the dead.

"Did you dream?" Joseph asked his brother.

"No."

"There have been many dreams. Melting Icefloes says he has dreamed of his own death. He says we shall all die. The soldiers will kill us, and nothing will be left."

"He dreamed that during the night?"

"Yes, and there are others who have dreamed the same."

At that moment the sun came out, shining through the rain. Joseph laughed, for the rain glittered like golden veils.

"What is all this about dreams?" he asked. "We all have dreams. White Bird says we will lose everything unless we hurry. This, too, he dreamed. But the rain shines, and soon there will be a rainbow."

Alokut stared at the sky. The soft pat-pat of rain falling came to an end, and suddenly a rainbow, all fiery red and blue and gold, could be seen arching through the trees. Joseph was pale. He had prayed with all his might that a rainbow should appear, and when it came he was even more surprised than his brother, whose blanket was now steaming in the sun.

"Then we go on, whatever men dream?" he asked, and Joseph nodded.

The steep and ragged trail was like fire. It scorched them, burned into their souls, made a mark on every man, woman and child who marched and slid and scrambled over the sharp rocks and the thick underbrush. The trees hemmed them in. Sometimes there were small clearings of wire grass where the ponies could graze, but mostly it was a steep ascent over rock slides, among fallen timber, so that they were forever having to haul the ponies over tree trunks. Sometimes the ponies would go crashing in the undergrowth, and then you would hear them disappearing over a ravine; sometimes, too, they came to dark mountain pools where the braves speared salmon, but these pools were rare, and for the most part they lived on the roots the squaws dug in the swamps. The windfalls gave Joseph an idea. He ordered some of the strongest braves to saw through the trunks of the trees on both sides of the trail. They must hide the sawdust, and then cover the cuts with moss and bark. When the general's scouts rode up, the braves would be waiting close to the trees, waiting until the scouts passed before hurling the trees down and then firing among them; these trees, cut four feet from the ground, would prevent them from returning, and in the panic the scouts would become easy victims of the Indian sharpshooters. So it happened sometimes, but not as often as Joseph would have liked; and as the days passed and the scouts grew wary of the trail, Joseph came to the conclusion that they must have seen some of the sawdust left by the cutters, and too often the scouts escaped the fire of the sharpshooters.

At night the rain fell in torrents, but during the mornings it was often clear. Granite boulders were in their way. They had to slither up the boulders, dragging their ponies with them; and more ponies were lost, and others had huge strips of skin peeled off them by spiky branches, and some had to be killed because their legs were broken. The braves chopped their way through the forest with axes, but often they left blood on the trail. They had no time to sleep. They had to push on. Occasionally they would fall into a kind of waking sleep for a few hours, and then they would hear the bird-bone pipe urging them to hurry on, even in the dark. Sometimes, too, at night they lit fires which they protected with buffalo robes, and they would squat beside the choking little gusts of flame, warming those bodies which were sore and scratched and ribbed with scars, telling each other how they had jammed their ponies through, up and under the windfalls.

"Neither the rocks nor the trees show mercy to us," Joseph said, standing on a granite boulder and looking down to where he could see, among the huge carpet of branches, the shaking twigs which spoke of his people climbing below.

Towards the top the trail grew even worse: rougher and steeper, so that sometimes they seemed to be climbing up the sheer walls of a mountain, and now the only advantage was that the trees were stunted, and they could see further. The rains had made the earth like quicksilver. Spruce, hemlock and white pine grew in abandon, and though the trees were small and slender enough, yet they held up the progress of the army on the march; and at the very top they found traces that white men had been there only a few hours before.

While they were climbing the trail, they had no time for fear. Now fear gripped them. Everyone saw the traces, and everyone knew that the white men possessed a method of communicating over long distances. Howard was behind them, but Howard could order men to the east of the Lo Lo path to stand in their way. Looking Glass examined the traces carefully. There were footprints of hobnailed boots, marks left by cantinas, fresh fur from ponies on the barks of the trees, and hoofmarks everywhere.

"Fourteen men," Looking Glass said, and smiled. "Should we be afraid of fourteen men?"

So they pushed their way down the eastern slope of the mountain while the sun shone and the thick forests hid them. Ahead lay the Bitter Root Valley and the Ross Hole country and the headwaters of the Jefferson and the tepees of the Crows, who were their allies.

XXIX

The Cheyennes

"SEEMS the bird's flown," Lem said tauntingly, glaring at Stevens. "Seems the bird's flown and don't want to have salt put on his tail. Seems the army ain't got no salt. Seems—"

Stevens was rarely angry. He could usually keep his temper under control, even when everything went wrong. In his own way he had a curious liking for Lem. But Lem had shouldered his way into the tent, his face bright with vindictiveness, his beard and mustache ragged with sleeplessness, and there were blue hollows under his eyes.

"Where's Joseph? Where's Shades of Night?" Lem went on, savagely striking the table. "Tell me what the hell you're doing about it? The truth is, the Army don't care. The Indians can get away with murder, but the Army don't care! You'd like them to get to Canada, wouldn't you? Like to kiss them sweet good-by—wipe them off the slate! Did you know they've left Kamiah? They're going up the Lo Lo trail. The Cheyennes told me. Did you know that?"

Like everyone else, Stevens had heard the rumor, but there was no confirmation yet. He looked calmly at Lem and said: "Get out of here! I've had enough!" Lem saw the awakened strength in Stevens, and flung a curse behind him as he wandered out of the tent, remembering all the things he had wanted to say, though it was too late to say them now, while Stevens returned to contemplate the papers listing supplies and ammunition, and the maps which showed the columns of troopers converging towards Howard's headquarters from Portland, Vancouver, San Francisco and as far as Atlanta. It was not true that the Army had forgotten Joseph. Lem wanted some blazing violent action. The Army, more cautious, was bringing up reserves. Lem was merciless. If the Indians had a single neck, he would have swung an ax against it. "Poor devil," Stevens said, and with an effort he began to concentrate once again on his work.

Later in the afternoon Stevens was summoned to the general's tent. The general was in good humor. The clouds were clearing. He had waited for five days, and now at last he thought he had a sufficient reserve of men to make the journey up the Lo Lo Pass.

"We'll leave tomorrow," the general said, smiling faintly. "I've promised I'll go after Joseph, and by God I'll get him. In this weather there isn't much likelihood he will have gone far."

"Well, sir, I think the Indians can go farther on a horse than any man."

"That's your opinion, Mr. Stevens. We'll see whether a white man is as good as an Indian. I've had a talk with Lem Otis. He wants to join our scouts. I've told him he has my blessing. He can take some of the Cheyennes with him. I think I can spare him six or seven. He proved to me he was a man with a mighty hatred of the Indians who killed his poor brother. I reckon he used the word 'hatred' sixty times in the quarter of an hour I gave him."

"A man hates only those he has injured," Stevens said quietly, and he was a little surprised when the general said: "I hated the Secesh, but God knows they never injured me until I lost my arm to them. No, a man hates for a million reasons. If we could see into the darkness of the human heart we would find there were reasons for hatred we never thought of."

That night, with six Cheyennes, Lem rode out from Kamiah to the mouth of the Lo Lo Pass, four miles to the east. He did not know what he would find. He knew only that he wanted to be close to them and wanted to kill them. To be alone with the Cheyennes filled him with a wild sense of liberation. He would track them through the mountains and the valleys, and never lose sight of them. In the five days they crawled and hacked their way up the Lo Lo Pass his hatred for Joseph went beyond anything he had known before, and he would shiver with an excruciating feeling of horror and happiness whenever he reminded himself that he was on their trail.

He drove the Cheyennes hard, and this pleased them. By day they hacked their way through a jungle of brush and fallen timber, climbed over rocks, slithered through swamps, but at night they rested. The rain had ceased. Everywhere they went they saw the tracks the Indians had left behind: the dead ponies, the spilt blood, the discarded buffalo robes and tepee-poles, the little burnt-out fires, the little heaps of pony dung. The path was unmistakable. The Cheyennes were all tall, over six foot, and they rode bareback or with a blanket which only covered the horse's withers. They made twenty miles a day, and they knew that Joseph had made a bare sixteen. Usually the white men found the Cheyennes difficult to command, but Lem's harsh stringy voice, his leanness, his long red beard, the way he continually muttered to himself and the way his eyes glittered gave them the feeling that he was endowed with great powers, and after the second day they were blindly obedient to him, pushing on even when they were utterly exhausted. The oldest of the Cheyennes was Grey Wolf, a man about forty with the lean body of a young brave and white scars on his red cheeks. Grey Wolf spoke enough English to be understood, and it was through him that Lem gave orders.

For weeks afterwards the nightmare of the journey plagued Lem. He remembered the green shadows, the hot sun pouring through the hemlock, the blaze of the western sky at night and the chilly dawns when a mist shrouded the hills. He remembered the traps the Indians had set, the sawdust on the trail, the trees which came crashing to the ground when you passed them, and the sudden silences which followed every time you shot into the dense undergrowth, but most of all he remembered the thorny branches which cut into his flesh until he was a mass of red welts, the swinging of a branch against his cheeks, and how he had slithered twenty feet down the sharp side of a granite boulder, and felt there was no use in going onward, till he discovered that he had fallen on a dead Indian squaw, who could not have died more than forty-eight hours before. Two of his Cheyennes were dead. He did not look at their bodies, did not feel that their deaths meant anything, never talked about them. It was all a nightmare, but soon the nightmare would come to an end. Soon, very soon, he would pounce on them unawares, somewhere in the Bitter Root Valley.

At the head of the pass Grey Wolf saw signs that white men had thrown up barricades, and then deserted them. He growled under his breath. All the way down into the valley there were signs that Joseph had progressed unhindered.

On the afternoon when they reached Missoula at the foot of the pass, the blue mists were swirling. They raced joyfully towards the small town set among cottonwoods. They rode through the darkening streets like conquerors. The wheat was green in the ear, and the wind was singing in the trees. Saloon doors swung open. There was life in the town, but there was a strange air of emptiness about the place.

"Could be the place is just plain dead," Lem laughed, watching some old drunks quarrelling on the sidewalk. No sign of fighting; no sign of Joseph. Outside a saloon he slipped off the saddle, and shouldered his way in, past drunken farmers and miners. At the bar he asked for five brandies, thinking of the Cheyennes.

"In this saloon you'll take your brandies one at a time," the barman answered. "That's the law, and you'll keep to it."

"I've got four friends outside."

"Indians?"

"Yes, sir. Cheyennes. It may be against the law, but by God they deserve a brandy. We've come over the Lo Lo trail. I've come from General Howard, and I've authority to get remounts, and I'm told there are some horses here, and I'll be glad if you'll let me know where the devil I can find Captain Rawn. They say he's in command here."

Immediately Lem mentioned the captain's name there was a burst of laughter.

"What's funny about it?" Lem said, banging the bar with his fist.

"Take it easy, stranger," a man with sideburns replied. "If you're after Joseph you won't get any help from us. We've had a talk with Joseph. Most of the citizens of our town have had a good look at him, and we wouldn't quarrel with him. We don't aim to cause any trouble."

"You mean he came through here, and you let him be?"

"That's right. We don't aim to cause any trouble. He paid for what he bought in good coin and greenbacks. We sold 'em a good amount of meat and vegetables, and I reckon it's a good thing to trade with a man like that. The citizens of this town have a mighty high opinion of Joseph."

"God Jesus!" Lem said, and bent his head in white-faced fury, not trusting himself to speak. He shivered a little, and the hand lying on the counter trembled uncontrollably. It was some moments before he realized that the people in the saloon were crowding round him, all anxious to look at the sweating red-bearded man whose clothes were torn and whose face was streaked with welts. On the polished counter there was a solitary glass of brandy in front of him.

"I asked for five," Lem shouted, glaring at the barman.

"Now you take it easy, stranger," the man with the sideburns repeated. "We've got our own ways of doing things here. If you don't like our ways, you know what you can do."

There was another gust of laughter. Lem lifted the brandy glass to his lips, and drained it, and then glared at the barman again as though he hoped to frighten the man into revealing the reasons that lay behind the extraordinary behavior of the citizens of Missoula, but the barman simply smiled pityingly. The brandy gave Lem strength. He pushed the glass towards the barman, but the barman paid no attention to the gesture. The man with the sideburns was saying: "Money's mighty scarce in Missoula. We all like to see a bit of money, stranger."

"What in hell has money got to do with it?"

"I'll tell you. We've got a trading store here. I reckon most folks go to the trading store. It's good for the town, and when a man like Joseph comes along with seven or eight hundred mouths to feed, well, that's trade and trade's money. I reckon if the devil came to Missoula, we'd trade with him. They say General Howard's on his way. They say he has got fifteen hundred soldiers. We'll trade with him, too. Why? Because trade's the lifeblood of this nation, stranger. It took us three days to hammer the facts of life into Captain Rawn's skull, but he came round to our way of thinking."

"You mean Captain Rawn wanted to fight the Indians and you wouldn't let him?"

"That's exactly what I mean. Captain Rawn is a mighty fine man in some particulars, but he was stubborn as a mule. Said he had received orders. Wanted to turn the town into a battlefield. Wanted to blow the Indians all to hell. Well, sir, we were sorry for those poor Indians. We've traded with them before, and we hope to trade with them again. Politest Indians you ever saw, and Joseph—he's an all-right man if ever there was one. Do you follow me?"

"Maybe I do, maybe I don't."

"You're speaking like a man, stranger. If we have any trouble with you, we'll do what we did with Captain Rawn. It isn't nice to think about."

"I reckon I see what you mean. Where's Captain Rawn now?"

"We've let him loose. General Gibbon came here two days ago, and we let Captain Rawn go with him. They think they're going to trail Joseph. About two hundred of them all told. They won't get near enough to Joseph. I know that. I told you he was an all-right man, didn't I?"

"You did."

"Now you can get out of our town, and make it fast, stranger."

There was more laughter. The lights in the saloon were going out. Lem knew the reason for that: the saloonkeeper was expecting trouble. The brandy made his head reel, and the empty glass was still there in front of him. Lem wanted to shout: "You let the murderers through, so you are murderers yourselves." He wanted to fight them, but he was hopelessly outnumbered. He edged his way to the swing doors with his head down, glad because the lights were being turned off. Someone slapped him across the face, but it was impossible to recognize which of the fifty or sixty men in the saloon had done it, and he was in no mood for fighting.

In the street the air was pure, no longer filled with fumes of alcohol, there was no smell of damp sawdust, only the pure air and the shadowy forms of the Cheyennes, but the Cheyennes were no longer opposite the saloon; they had moved further down the street to avoid trouble with the men in the saloon. As Lem came through the swing doors there was a long low whistle, and he saw that his horse was still there but the others were two hundred yards down the road. He climbed stiffly on the saddle. As he rode slowly to meet the Cheyennes a shot whistled past his head. He expected another, but there was none, and except for the Cheyennes the street was empty.

"Where do we go?" Grey Wolf asked.

"We follow Joseph," Lem muttered. "Captain Rawn and General Gibbon are following him, and we must join them."

"No," said Grey Wolf. "We go to the fort."

"What fort?"

"The fort at Missoula. It's four miles away."

In their own mysterious way the Cheyennes had been making enquiries while Lem was in the saloon. They, too, knew that Gibbon and Rawn were trailing Joseph, but they never told Lem how they discovered these things. They rode across the fields with the evening wind blowing against their faces, their horses exhausted now, their legs bruised and bleeding, wet with foam, and sometimes the staggering animals were within an ace of stumbling and falling.

"At the fort we will rest," Grey Wolf announced, but Lem shook his head vigorously and said: "No, we'll get new horses. There isn't any time to rest in."

The fort lay dark and silent at the edge of the fields, and for a while Lem thought the fort had been abandoned, so silent it was.

After twenty minutes of shouting in a hoarse voice, a man came to the gate with a lantern.

"Open up!" Lem shouted hoarsely. "We want remounts—there's five of us here, and we have authority from General Howard—"

"How do I know who you are?" the man asked suspiciously, standing behind the gate.

"Jesus Christ, how does anyone know who anyone is?" Lem said, and there was a scream of despair underlying the thin voice. "We've come over the Lo Lo Pass. We've been to Missoula. They're rats—nothing but rats! For God's sake give us remounts! They say General Gibbon and Captain Rawn are following Joseph's trail, and we aim to join them."

The gate squeaked open. The man at the gate was a thin lieutenant suffering from fever, and behind him stood two troopers with Winchesters. Lem guessed they were the only inhabitants of the fort.

"Thought you were townsmen," the lieutenant said. "We've had trouble with townsmen."

Lem nodded. He could hardly sit on the saddle, hardly keep his eyes open, and he was swaying from side to side. The lieutenant steadied him while the troopers kept their rifles pointed at the Cheyennes. Suddenly Lem reeled off his horse and fell with a crash to the ground, his arms flailing wildly. When he woke up, he was in a small bare room and the lieutenant was bending over with a whisky flask. A candle was burning on a table near the straw bed.

"You're all right," the lieutenant said. "You ain't broken no bones. You rest."

"How long have I been here?"

"A couple of hours."

"God Jesus, I've got to get goin'. Where am I?"

Lem was lifting himself off the bed, struggling to get up.

"Stay where you are. I'm not going to let you get up till you're in fair shape. I don't believe anything you tell me. All right, you want to have a crack at Joseph. Did he ever do anything to you? No, you just want to have a crack at him because he's an Indian, and you're sick of seeing their faces around. Well, I've seen him. I ain't sick of him. Now you rest, feller, or I'll have to throw you into the guardhouse."

Lem remembered another day when he had fought his way into a guardhouse. He whined: "Just give me remounts, and I won't trouble you again."

"Rest, feller, just rest," the lieutenant said, and blew out the candle.

Lem heard the sound of a door being locked and he knew he did not have strength enough to force the lock. He fell asleep, and dreamed of Joseph, a huge feathered man with a face the color of the sunset riding at the head of his people. Then, instead of Joseph, he saw Shades of Night, and after Shades there was Moll, and then other women, and then once again he saw Joseph. The strange and terrible thing was that all these faces were calm. Shillitoe came out of the dark, and General Howard stared at him with the same calm and accusing stare. It was a nightmare of calm faces, and he wanted to rise up and tear his claws through the calm flesh. When he awoke he was sweating and there were crusts of blood on his forehead and deep purple rings under his eyes. Because the room was small and the door was shut he could hardly breathe, and his heart was pounding.

The door opened, and a shaft of bright yellow light suddenly flooded the room.

"I've got horses for you," the lieutenant was saying. "You'll find General Gibbon three-four days' march away. Now get out of here quick."

"Have you got something for us to eat?" Lem whined.

"Sure. You can fill your cantinas. Now get out of here."

"I reckon you could show a bit of respect to one of General Howard's scouts," Lem muttered. "Do you know who I am?" He went rambling on about Wallowa and the ride across the pass. He was sheriff of Wallowa, wasn't he? He was in the general's confidence, wasn't he? He would have a thing or two to say to the general about the impudent lieutenant. "God damn all lieutenants!" Lem shouted hoarsely, rising from the bed, his head aching and his tongue dry, and the smell of whisky was everywhere.

"What's that you said?" the lieutenant asked, coming forward with fists clenched.

"I said, thank God for you, lieutenant. Three-four days' march. Well, we'll do it in two. Have you talked to my Cheyennes? They're wonderful men."

The lieutenant nodded. Over breakfast he produced a map. He showed the road down the Bitter Root Valley which Rawn and Gibbon were following, and then abruptly he left the table.

"You'd better go, Mr. Otis, before I change my mind. Go double-quick."

Lem rode out of the gate with a curse on the town of Missoula and another on the lieutenant. In honor of the occasion the Cheyennes had painted thick ribs of red paint on their faces, and each of them had somehow stolen a Colt revolver. As they rode south along the edges of the fields, they found in the dust the ruts made by the supply carts. Howard was making his way over the pass and Gibbon was pursuing Joseph down the valley. What more could a man want? "We'll be in at the kill," Lem said, and for the first time in many days there was a pleased expression on his face.

XXX

The Haunted Forests

THE sun was already hot in the clear sky. Swarms of lazy yellow butterflies were hovering on the bronze rocks where they had taken shelter against the noon heat. Beyond them lay the forests of pine and tamarack, and beyond the forests lay the snow mountains with their blue crags. Silence brooded, the silence of a blazing hot day which would grow hotter.

Joseph was resting beside the road, shading his eyes. Deer flitted through the glade, and high on the snow mountains he could see the herds of bighorn. He looked at the bedraggled braves crowding round him, and beyond the braves were the squaws and the waggons they had bought on the journey, all piled with pemmican and buffalo robes. The journey up the trail had drained their strength. They must rest soon: it was as simple as that. He glanced at Looking Glass, well knowing what the gnarled old warrior was thinking.

"We must rest," he said. "Then we will be stronger. It is a small risk."

"There can be no rest for us," Looking Glass answered. "Take my advice. Hurry. I am telling you this for the good of all."

"No, we must rest," Joseph said, smiling sadly. He told the braves to stay where they were, then rode past the rocks towards the forest. Half an hour later he returned to say that he had found a secluded camping site at the place where the Big Hole River turns back on itself, a place surrounded by sloping hills and tamarack. There they could sharpen their arrows, clean their rifles, collect tepee-poles and take the rest they needed. Soon, in the valley of the Big Hole the weary braves were stretching out naked on the grass, waiting for the sun to heal the deep scratches made by the thorny branches during their long journey over the Lo Lo trail. Shades of Night lay in the lodge beside the white frothing stream, talking to one of Joseph's two wives. A great flare of golden sunlight came through the flap, and she heard, as though from far away, the sound of wood touching against wood as the Indian boys played stick games.

"It is beautiful to rest after long travelling," she said, and smiled at the young woman on the bed of buffalo robes.

In honor of the birth of a child at White Bird Canyon Joseph had given his wife a necklace made of eight strands of green beads. Now, though she was naked to the waist because she was feeding her child, the green beads sparkled on her brown throat. Joseph's wife, called Blue-breasted Bird Rising from the Waters, was surrendering to an abandon of joy as she played with the baby.

"The men work too hard," Blue-breasted Bird said. "They are always fighting. They should know that rest is the best thing. They will learn."

"When will they learn?" Shades of Night asked helplessly. "Men are made like that. Their hands are restless. Their finger tips are lightning; they must strike. And we—we are the calm mountains struck by them."

"It is pleasant to be a mountain and to receive the lightning," Blue-breasted Bird said, smiling to herself, hugging the child to her breast.

Shortly afterwards Shades of Night joined the women collecting tepee-poles on the hillside, wading up to her hips in the cool stream. All the time she was singing to herself and dreaming of the child which had Joseph's square chin and his wife's enormous eyes. All afternoon there came the clear, ringing tones of axes as the women cut the tepee-poles, while the braves rested, for Joseph had ordered them not to exert themselves: they would have enough to do the next day. A few were allowed to fish, and others were allowed to hunt the deer and antelope in the forests. In the evening when the fires were lit the braves danced and sang, while the women made the beds and cut the venison into strips for the next day's journey. The braves leaped through the flames, chanted the war song, told stories about the battles they had fought, while the fires glowed redly on their painted bodies. The crickets chirped, and sometimes they heard the coyote-howls of their scouts far away.

While the Indians were resting in the small meadow shaded by thickets, Lem was pushing towards them. Two days after reaching Missoula he found General Gibbon's column, two hundred men resting by the side of a dusty road, drinking coffee, eating hard tack and cursing under their breaths. General Gibbon, younger than Howard, rode a dappled mare, and though he looked immaculate enough at a distance, his eyes were sore from the dust of the valley and there was a look of hopelessness about him. He had received Howard's telegraphic order to close in on Joseph, marched down from Fort Shaw, joined Captain Rawn at Missoula and now he was in a fever of fright at the thought of ambushes. His scouts, mostly half-breeds, he thought inexperienced. He distrusted some of his own officers, and he knew that Joseph's braves outnumbered his own men. When Lem came riding up in the slanting evening light, a bandage round his head, his face crusted with scars, his red beard flattened by the wind, the general waved a white-gloved hand and said: "I want men like that. Where have you come from, feller?"

"From General Howard, sir. Name is Lem Otis. Come from Wallowa. Fought at White Bird Canyon and the Clearwater. I'm aimin' to be in at the kill. Reckon it won't be long now."

"Then you're mighty welcome," the general said. "Did you come over the trail?"

"Yes, sir."

"With those Cheyennes of yours?"

"Yes, sir."

"Then I'll be pleased to have you with us, Mr. Otis. We're underhanded. We need some good men, and can profit by your experience."

"I don't reckon to join your column, sir. I've been on my own, and I aim to keep on my own. You could use us best as scouts—"

Three hours later, after a swill of coffee and a meal of salted pork, Lem and the Cheyennes were already riding ahead. He had catnapped for two hours and spent ten minutes in the general's tent, poring over maps. Now on his own, he was elated at the knowledge that the Indians were only two days' march ahead. He would race his horses. He would do in six or seven hours what an army on the march could do in two days. There was a fever in the air. The Cheyennes were grinning. They knew they would be rewarded if they captured Joseph. At dusk Grey Wolf pulled up his horse. "Smoke," he said, lifting a finger towards the curving tamarack-covered hills in the distance.

"Where's the smoke?" Lem asked.

"See it, over there," Grey Wolf said. "Smoke at the Big Hole."

Lem could see no smoke, but he knew the Cheyennes could see better than white men. He gave a wild shout, threw an arm over Grey Wolf's shoulder, and soon they were cantering down the slope, digging their spurs into their horses' flanks, afraid that Joseph's scouts may have seen them; and already the sun was setting. Once they were in the valley they sheltered among the jack pines. Now low stunted hills and a winding watercourse separated them from the lodges ten-twelve miles away. Grey Wolf dropped from his horse and with a stick he began to draw a map of the Big Hole Valley, the river curving to a fork, with steep pine-clad hills above the place where the lodges were and long meadows reaching towards the foothills. Grey Wolf's eyes were very bright. His nostrils quivered with the intolerable excitement of the chase. He showed where he thought the lodges would be, in a sheltered hollow of the valley, where the river curls round. He made crisscross marks where he thought the pony herd would be, and little circles at the places where he thought they would post sentinels. All the time a grim smile hovered at the corners of his lips. The map was clear enough. They had only to act carefully, and all Joseph's braves would fall into the trap. Now they must hurry, get as close to their quarry as possible and send their reports back. General Gibbon's column was thirty miles behind, and Howard perhaps a hundred and fifty miles away.

"Two of you must go back to the general: the rest must stay with me," Lem said, breathing heavily, wondering how he would stay awake during the night which was coming down on them.

Grey Wolf nodded. Hungry for the chase, he quickly selected the two youngest Cheyennes and sent them back with a scribbled letter from Lem. Then in the gathering dark, bearing to the southwest, with Grey Wolf beside him and a brave called Red Elk leading the way, Lem rode towards the Indian camp.

In the forest of brush, alder and jack pine no breath stirred. The earth was mossy underfoot. They made their way in silence, and sometimes the Cheyennes paused, cocked their heads to one side and listened for sounds too faint for Lem's ears. In the weird light of the forest lit by the stars, Lem felt hemmed in. He thirsted for a fight. He wanted to race among the Indian lodges while everyone was sleeping: he would set fire to the tepees and shoot down everyone who tried to escape. They rode forward in silence, wading through trickling streams, the coolness of the forest on their faces; and sometimes Lem would turn towards Grey Wolf and in the half-darkness he would nod, and it pleased him that Grey Wolf nodded in return. Once he paused in fear, for a deer came running through the trees and he thought at first it was one of Joseph's scouts. Mile after mile they rode in the dark, seeing the stars through a lace of branches, keeping to the lea of the wind, Grey Wolf going a little ahead, and always they followed the great curve which would bring them to the north of the encampment on the Big Hole River.

When they were within two miles of the lodges, and even Lem could see the faint smoke drifting across the sky, Grey Wolf paused and explained the exact path to be followed.

"I'll take that path," Lem whispered.

"No, we'll all take it," Grey Wolf replied.

But there was no further argument. Lem had decided to go on alone. He would be the first to see Joseph's camp on the river. His red beard was damp with sweat, his hands trembled, and even in the starlight you could see his eyes blazing like diamonds.

"If we are separated, who knows where we shall meet?" Grey Wolf complained.

"Keep fifty lengths behind me," Lem replied, and he roped his horse to an alder tree, making signs to the others to do the same.

As he walked forward, he lost all fear. The bright sap had been rising in him, and now, with the Winchester under his arm, he made his way to the lodges as though he was walking in sunlight. Very faintly behind him he heard the moccasins of the Cheyennes on the hard-baked earth with its coating of summer dew. Far off, the wind picked up the sound of the Indians beside their campfires, singing and dancing, and though the sound sent a pleasant chill through his veins, sometimes he paused with a look of perplexity on his face, wondering at his own good fortune, and sometimes too a raw branch whipped against his face, yet he felt no sting, no sense of hurt: he was like a moth making mechanically for the campfires, the naked savages, the face of Shades of Night coming out of the dark.

A little later the hunter emerged over the breast of a hill to see the whole camp lying in the hollow beside the winding river, which shone like dusky silver in the starlight. Smoke from the fires hung over the meadow. Speckled ponies lay on the hill facing him. There must have been more than eighty tepees there, formed in a V on the high banks, but there were only eight or nine fires burning. The braves were shouting, clapping their hands, dancing over the flames, and sometimes for long periods they squatted silently beside the fires. Some women came out of the tepees and joined the braves. Through glasses Lem saw that the women wore beaded blankets but the braves were naked except for breechclouts, and he could even see the shapes of the painted marks on their bodies which shone gold in the light of the flames.

He had been quiet within himself until he surveyed the scene. Now he rejoiced so much that he shook and trembled like a tree in an earthquake. He wanted to shout. He wanted to run up to the camp and tell them that General Gibbon was on his way. Before dawn perhaps, or by noon, General Gibbon would have brought his column up. Keeping in shadow, moving quietly, he inched closer to the camp. He could no longer see the Cheyennes, but this did not disturb him. Looking down towards the river and the tepees, he saw a girl chopping wood beside a tepee with red designs embroidered on it. She wore green stripes across her blanket, and instead of the usual beads which young Indian girls wear across their forehead, she wore one made of squares of glass. The light from the blazing fire shone on her forehead. She had finished chopping wood. She was standing there and stretching herself in the glare of the flames, like a contented animal. He whispered: "I'll shoot her, and then it will be over with. It's better to shoot her than let anyone else have her." He aimed for the glass beads. His hands trembled. His heart went out across the dark spaces of the valley towards her, and almost at the moment when he squeezed the trigger, a brown hand fell against his Winchester and it went clattering to the ground.

Lem wheeled round. At first he thought it was one of the Cheyennes, then he saw the mocking face of Bird-with-one-eye with its thick yellow crusts of paint. He was in war paint, and naked. "Come," said Bird-with-one-eye, and he swung Lem round, lifted his knee against the hollow of Lem's back, and then watched Lem crashing to the earth.

Lem never knew why he was not killed as he lay there with earth in his mouth, one eye pierced by a sharp twig, blood streaming down his face. Fear paralyzed him. He remembered Bird-with-one-eye's soft triumphant laughter, then he remembered the cord being fitted round his neck. Then he was stumbling, covered with dirt, down towards the encampment; drums beating, braves dancing, the roaring of the fires and the sweet, high-pitched sound of the bird-pipes.

Outside Joseph's tepee all the chiefs were gathered to watch the dancing of the braves. They squatted on the grass. Bird-with-one-eye thrust Lem forward without a word. Old Smohalla, with his medicine bag and a deerskin drum beside him, leaned forward and peered at Lem, wondering what kind of man it was who dared to penetrate the village; and his dark smouldering eyes, his leather cheeks and pursed lips, all these somehow suggested that he was deep in a trance, attempting to discover by the help of the spirits the true motives of the stranger.

"Who are you?" Joseph said, and there was no eagerness in his voice: only a terrible weariness. He had worked so long and so hard to keep his people together, and was this man attempting to stand in their way? Was he evil? Was he sent by Old Man With One Arm? Where did he come from? "Who are you?" Joseph repeated, and was surprised to hear Lem answer in the Nez Perce language: "I am the trader at Wallowa. Everyone knows me."

"I do not know you, and yet you speak our language," Joseph said, while the light from the hearth-fire gleamed on his high cheekbones and a smile softened the contours of the lips.

Bird-with-one-eye whispered something. Lem was sure he was not talking about the raid on the store. The chief shook his head. It was evident that he no longer trusted Bird-with-one-eye, and instead he gazed sorrowfully at Lem, his eyes steady, lit with a deep penetrating light. For the first time Lem felt that all his secrets were being revealed one by one. He thought he would be killed. He did not care. The chiefs were whispering together. It was strange how peaceful the camp was, the dancers still dancing, and the singing was never stilled. Fishbones were scattered in the grass, all glinting. There was the smell of pemmican meat. He saw some girls in beaded blankets watching him from a distance, and sighed. Joseph was still examining him, looking carefully at the left eyeball which resembled a blood-red marble. All one side of Lem's face was shining with blood, and blood was spattered over his blue coat and over his leggings. He still breathed with difficulty, and kept swaying.

While the chiefs whispered, Lem saw that they were rapidly coming to a decision. He no longer cared what decision they made. He said simply: "I came for my squaw. She is here. I know that. You have been hiding her from me." He did not know why he said this. He thought he wanted to see Shades of Night again before he died. Suddenly, edging her way behind Joseph, her head bent and the fall of her braids obscuring her face, Shades of Night came closer. She looked healthier than when she was at the store, her face ruddy, her bare arms golden brown, health streaming out of her. She was looking squarely at him now, a faint smile playing on her lips. He thought: It would be much better if she died with me. Joseph was looking him up and down, observing every detail from the riding boots to the soft matting of red and sweaty hair which fell down over his forehead.

"You have followed us for the sake of the squaw?" Joseph asked, and his face looked drawn, as though he was debating with himself. "Did you come alone?"

"I came alone."

Bird-with-one-eye told the story of how he had found Lem with a rifle on the edge of the woods.

"Where is the rifle?" Joseph asked. "Is it here? What has been done to it?"

"I knocked it out of his hands."

"And you left it there?"

"Yes."

A look of fierce anger crossed Joseph's face.

"Then find it," he said sharply. "We must have rifles. We must have them."

Shades of Night was kneeling beside Joseph with her hands clasped against her breasts.

"Let him go," she whispered.

"Dear one, if I let him go, who will benefit?" Joseph said. "Look, he is ill. If he goes, who will look after him? Better to give him to Smohalla. Better to heal his wounds. We are not fighting the white people, only the Bostons. We must care for him."

"Let him go," Shades of Night repeated in a voice so low and urgent that Joseph reached out for her hands and pulled her a little nearer.

"Do you wish to go or stay?" Joseph said, and once more his eyes travelled the whole length of Lem's body.

"Give me my squaw," Lem answered sternly. It was as though he was accusing his accusers. Bird-with-one-eye had already hurried away.

"She belongs to us. She will never join with a white man," Joseph said. For the first time his voice was high-pitched and angry.

"Let him go," Shades of Night said quietly. She was horrified by the hunger written on his wounded face. How could a man follow her so far? The blood was still drooling from the wounded eye, and Lem was still swaying. The warmth from the fire was making him weaker, and one of the braves was supporting him.

"If I cannot have her, what is my life worth?" Lem asked, marching a step closer to Joseph so that he was almost standing over the chieftain. "Kill me. Do what you please. I have come for her."

He was acting as he had never acted before, and at the same time he was not acting in the least. He wanted her now. By Indian law he had a right to her. What was more natural than that he should pursue her? She looked very soft and warm, hiding within her beaded blanket. Joseph thought for a while. He said calmly: "Then you must go, if that is what you want. You can rest for the night, and then in the morning you can go."

"You can do what you like to me," Lem said stubbornly. "I have thought of her—only of her."

The flames were crackling and spitting sparks. A muscle was working at the corner of Joseph's lips, where the flesh was tight-drawn.

"Why did you come?" Joseph asked sharply, seeing that Lem was swaying again, and perhaps as consciousness faded from Lem's mind, the truth might be extracted from him.

"I say this three times. I came for her. I came for her. I came for her."

Then, with the cord still dangling from his neck, Lem fainted, and he would have fallen to the ground if the brave had not supported him.

When he woke up he was in a tepee. Smohalla and Shades of Night were bending over him. The old drummer smelt of rancid oil, and his face was wet with grease. There were pots of medicinal grease on the buffalo robes all round him. He was dipping tamarack leaves in the grease and making a plaster of them; these he wrapped with a bandage over Lem's broken eye after first gently pushing the eye back in the socket. It was the pain of the operation which awakened Lem. The pain was so extreme that he burst out in a loud sobbing, but Shades of Night held his hands tight. Outside, the singing was still going on, and now there were twenty drums echoing among the pines.

"You must sleep now," Shades of Night was saying, her face so close that he could have kissed her if he wanted to. The drumming kept him awake. The singing was very loud. Bird-with-one-eye came into the tepee, and then wandered away. It was still early in the evening, and the singing and dancing would go on, and all the time Lem's head was splitting open and the pain made him scream. "Threw me down—that's all he did, and there was a sharp-pointed twig there, that's all there was." He could remember that, but he remembered nothing else of the strange moment in the haunted forest of jack pines when he had lifted the Winchester. Where was the Winchester now? Why had no one spoken about it? Then he remembered Joseph had ordered Bird-with-one-eye to fetch it, and now Joseph was in the tepee, his face more gaunt and sombre than ever as he bent down and said: "Why did you come? Was she the only reason?"

Lem said nothing. He was almost beyond speech, beyond putting two syllables together.

"Let me go," he said plaintively, and even when he spoke in the Indian tongue there was a whine in his voice.

"If I let you go, will you promise on oath not to let the Bostons know where we are?"

"Yes, I promise it," Lem said, struggling to get to his feet.

"You promise three times?"

"Yes, I promise. I promise. I promise."

His voice was shaking, but with his one good eye he looked squarely at Joseph, while Smohalla with a trembling hand lifted a candle to his face. It was a strange face: a terrible, prominent blue eye, one eye covered with a matting of leaves, and a wild red beard, a face which had grown thin with exhaustion. The lips trembled convulsively. The bandage on his forehead was thick with little leaves and straws from the place where he had fallen, and from under the bandage there escaped matted strands of bright red sweaty hair. His beard was damp and seemed to be coated to his flesh. And when he stood up, leaning on the tepee-poles for support, he shuddered at the immensity of the task in front of him: how could he walk at all when every nerve in his face was singing with pain? Once he lifted his finger and pressed it against the bandage over his eye as though he wanted to tear his eye out; then he dropped the finger, smiled weakly at Shades of Night, touched her lightly on the shoulder and made his way out of the tent. The braves were still dancing. No one paid any attention to him as he walked quickly past the campfires into the night.

For half an hour he walked stiffly along the banks of the winding river and then sat down to rest. His senses were alert, for the pain sharpened them. He heard the river sighing between its banks, and the soft sound of the river mingled with the drumming from the lodges. A water bird, splashing white across the river, startled him when he was on the verge of falling asleep. He got up, and making a wide circle round the meadow along the edge of the forest, he made for the place where he had left the Cheyennes earlier in the evening.

XXXI

The Big Hole

THERE was no moon, but the sky was clear, and sometimes the wind rustled the dry midsummer grasses. The men moved across the edge of the forest, cursing under their breaths, and too weary to speak to one another even if they had been allowed to. General Gibbon had ordered silence. An hour after Lem had left, he decided to push forward. There were rumors that Joseph was at the Big Hole, and the more the general thought of it, the more likely it seemed. There was just a chance—a ghost of a chance—that Joseph would be resting up. So they made their way in the dark, fording the ice-cold streams, wading up to their armpits in the places where the stream bottoms suddenly dipped, and after the streams there were marshes. Farm waggons lumbered behind, their axles heavily greased.

The thought of being able to throw his forces against Joseph made the general breathless with joy. He did not hate Joseph; it was simply that he wanted to measure his strength against the Indians. He kept singing shanty songs under his breath, and his eyes glowed as he ordered the men to take a late supper of hard tack and cold salted pork. He lay down at full length beneath a pine. From there he gave orders that no fires should be lit, and no one must wrap himself in a blanket. He thought blankets on cold nights made men soft. He asked his officers to make sure that every man had ninety rounds.

"I've got a feeling that luck's on our side tonight," he told one of his lieutenants. "We'll get Joseph before Howard has a smell of him."

The lieutenant said something about Joseph's scouts. The general laughed. There were no scouts. He said good night, and then fell asleep. When he awoke an hour later the men were already getting into ranks. The wind was more violent now, whipping the sagebrush and the pines, cold against their raw faces, and they were glad when the trail led down to the bottom of a washout, and then into more open country with a few willow thickets and the earth spongy underfoot. They marched hard, fearful of the black shapes which rose before them, the bristling crests of the low hills, the sudden apparition of trees where they had expected no trees. They walked almost at a running pace, drained of energy, going forward only because they were ordered to go forward, with no excitement for the chase. The knowledge that the Indians were camped in a hollow meadow at the Big Hole left on their minds no more than a faint scoring. It seemed to them that they had not rested for more than an hour since they left Fort Shaw in the north, and already their clothes were scratched and torn, and there was about them an air of extraordinary weariness. Why had not the general let them ride on their horses? Why not sleep? Why hope to catch the Indians by surprise when everyone knew you could never catch the Indians by surprise?

They were within three miles of the lodges when two Cheyennes came riding silently up to them. The horses' hooves were padded with cloth, and the Indians in their grey blankets looked like ghosts. Grey Wolf asked to be taken to the general, and when he reached the general's side he peered through the dark and touched the general's uniform before he was satisfied that Gibbon was standing in front of him.

"Mr. Otis—he dead," Grey Wolf said, his voice trembling. He was shivering as though with a fever.

"I reckon he died fighting," the general said, and wondered whether the Indians were now alerted, and cursed again under his breath. "Are the Indians still in the camp?"

"They sleep peacefully," Grey Wolf said, and smiled: there was a flashing of brilliant teeth.

"I'm sorry that Mr. Otis is dead—very sorry," the general said slowly. "I suppose the scouts got him."

Grey Wolf nodded, and shortly afterwards went to join the other Cheyennes at the head of the column. The men were marching at ease now, to avoid the drumming sound of military steps. There were still no sentinels, no coyote-howls, though very faintly in the distance they heard the barking of dogs. They had gone another four hundred yards when the Cheyennes stumbled over someone lying in the pathway. At first they thought it was an Indian scout, but it was Lem Otis. He had staggered back through the pine forest, stumbling and falling, unable to see clearly because his one good eye was covered with a mist of watery vapor. For a few minutes he had slept, but the scuttling sound of some animal had awakened him, and he went on with his arms flaying, afraid to butt trees head-on. Grey Wolf lowered the rifle he had been pointing at the man huddled on the trail. "You come back from dead?" he said. He could hardly recognize Lem with the great plaster bandage over one eye, and the ragged bandage over his forehead.

"Where are the troopers?" Lem asked, staring at the shapes of darkness which were now gathering all round him.

The general came up five minutes later.

"You have been a great service to us," he said, and even though the pain was coming back again, Lem squeezed his lips into a smile. "What happened, Mr. Otis?"

"Oh Christ, what happened?" Lem repeated. "I don't know what happened. They were all over me."

"Better go back with the baggage train, Mr. Otis, and have yourself seen to."

"Why?"

"You're in bad shape."

"God Jesus, I can fight, can't I? I've fought 'em this evening, and I'll fight 'em again. They're sleeping now. I've been watching them. They're sleeping like pigs."

"Don't raise your voice."

"I've got a right to raise my voice. They took my rifle away, didn't they? You have to be careful of them. They'll take your rifle away, and tell you sweet nothings."

The general gazed at Lem with a frown of perplexity. Once again he wondered whether everything told him was true. Lem Otis was rambling. He was ill, and there was a strange bandage over his eye, and something in his behavior suggested he was lying. Well, they would have to go on. There was always the possibility of an ambush; and he was about to order one of the troopers to carry Lem away when a half-breed came running up with news that the Indians were asleep, and their smouldering campfires could be seen in the valley beyond and their ponies were tethered peacefully somewhere to the northeast of the great meadow.

The wind had died down, and for this the general was grateful, standing there under a large spraying alder tree with a set smile on his face, a smile of pity for Lem and pride for his own men. The half-breed was saying: "Keep the command together, general. We're not fighting the Sioux now."

"I know damned well we're not fighting the Sioux. Are you sure they have prepared no ambush?"

"They don't know we are here. If you come a little way forward, general, you'll see some fires being built up by the squaws." The general followed, creeping through the brush, till he reached the top of the hill. He gasped when he saw the quiet lodges in the cold starlight, the fires burning redly, no scouts or sentinels in sight, and the great meadow stretching for a mile along the banks of the white river below. In the starlight the smooth backs of the tethered ponies flickered like moths in summer around oak trees. He said: "We could drive the ponies away."

"Why?"

"It would break their backs, not having them."

"No, general," the half-breed said. "There are warriors guarding the ponies. It is always like that. Even when they do not guard themselves, they guard the ponies."

The general crept back to a command post in the hollow. The troopers who had spent the last eight hours crawling along the bottoms of ravines and washouts were now spread over the bank, hiding in the sagebrush, looking straight down on the Indian camp. They lay there shivering, their rifles beside them. It seemed incredible that the Indians had failed to notice their coming. Occasionally a dog barked or a pony neighed, and once or twice a woman came quickly out of a tepee and gazed at the quiet meadow under the hills as though some noise had perturbed her, but after a few moments she would return, huddled in her blanket, to the warmth and comfort of the tepee, the bear robes, the husband waiting for her.

At dawn, when the first grey light came sloping across the meadow, a thin and watery light which threw no shadows, the troops began to climb down the slope, treading carefully, groping stealthily through willow brush until they reached the marshy banks; then very slowly and patiently, keeping in line and holding their rifles above their heads, the water reaching their armpits, they forded the icy river. The tepee openings faced the meadow, and none of the Indians saw them coming. Now thin ribbons of smoke were drifting over the dark pines, and the ponies tethered to stakes and willows or simply roped together were becoming restless. Suddenly an old Indian huddled in a blanket crept out of his tepee, jumped on his horse and rode across the meadow towards the pony herd. The troopers had been moving towards a position halfway between the tepees and the herd; and some of them were already advancing through the wet grass when the rider appeared. He saw them, swung his horse round, and then there was a loud echoing shot, and a moment later the old Indian had fallen and the horse was careering wildly across the meadow, and soft blue smoke hung on the air.

The general had hoped the troopers would be able to creep up to the lodges and take them by assault. He wanted the men to keep under cover until the last moment, and as far as possible in the rear of the lodges. He had given the strictest orders about how the attack should be delivered; and now, as he stood on the crest of the hill looking down on the lodges, he saw that all his orders were being disobeyed, for the men, startled by the appearance of the Indian, began to shoot in the direction of the tepees. Immediately there came a long wailing yell from the Indians who a moment before had been sleeping peacefully. Naked warriors ran out of tepees, only to fall before they had caught a glimpse of the sun rising over the hills. Women screamed. Dogs were barking. The ponies, startled by the firing, set up a chorus of neighing, and pulled and pushed at the ropes which bound them to their stakes. The loud, terrified cries of children could be heard on the crest as though they were crying only a few feet away. The general saw some Indian braves slithering naked through the grass, resembling bronze snakes. Nearly all the troopers were now across the river, and most of them were moving through the clouds of smoke which hung lightly over the meadow. The Indians, quick to see in which direction the white men were coming, calling loudly to one another, yelling and screaming, hiding behind the tepees or crawling from underneath the tepees, began to make their way to the riverbank. There were twenty naked braves lying beside the fires, and small children lay beside them.

"It has to be," the general said, pulling at his beard. "We have to have law and justice. It's as simple as that." Lem was standing beside him, shivering in the cold morning air, his face more ravaged than ever, for the cold wind had mottled his flesh and there was a bright pink spot on his cheek. "You're dead right," Lem said, and then smiled softly to himself, telling himself that Joseph must have been killed in the heavy fire on the tepees, and perhaps Shades of Night was dead, and it was all for the best. He clenched and unclenched his fists, and he would have gone running down the hill if someone had given him a rifle. When he asked for a rifle, the general said: "You're more useful here, Mr. Otis. The department owes you a great debt, and we'll remember it."

The barking of the rifles echoed on the hills, and already the blue-coated troopers were making their way among the tepees. Some of the braves had reached the riverbank, taking cover in the thickets or in the shallows of marshy loam dipping beside the riverbed, and you could see the bronze bodies moving in the half-light, swift and graceful as young deer. Some squaws were standing knee-deep in the river, holding their papooses to their breasts, shivering in the icy water. Some were shot at. There were small groups of braves and troopers fighting among the tepees. A handful of braves had slipped through the line of troopers, and was busy rounding up the pony herd, driving it deeper among the willows. The screaming of the women, the yelling of the braves, the strange hissing sound made by the women thrashing in the water when they were shot down and the high-pitched cries of the children, all these became deafening; and listening to these sounds the general concluded that the Indians were baffled and frightened, with no more strength left in them, and so he ordered an orderly to ride down the hill and tell the troopers to set fire to the lodges.

"They'll know then there isn't anything can save them," he said, thrusting out his chin. "They'll be coming in and crawling for mercy in a shake of a dog's tail," he added, turning to Lem.

"I ain't ever seen an Indian crawling for mercy," Lem said, "but maybe you're right, general."

Five minutes later the first torches were being set to the tepees, but there were no large fires. The skins forming the tepees were wet with dew. Some grass burned while the sunlight came thick over the meadow. The braves were beginning to fight back. They were in two groups: one group held the willows beside the riverbank, the other was racing round the great arc of the meadow to join the pony herd. Most of the troopers were among the tepees where the only Indians were either dead, or else too old, or young, or weak to fight.

A naked girl standing up to her knees in the white river suddenly fell over, while a long boat-shaped stain of blood shone on the water. Beneath the water she seemed to be swimming.

The Indians had grown strangely quiet, and all the meadow was lit with sun veils. From the willow clumps their marksmen were picking off the troopers one by one; and as they emerged from the tepees the troopers saw that they were caught in the cross fire. It was an untenable position. They could only hide among the tents they had hoped to burn, or make for the hills down-river. A corporal was shouting: "To the top of the hill! To the top of the hill, or we are lost!" Down by the willows a great humming voice, louder than the sound of weeping among the women, was urging the braves to attack the troopers among the tepees. It was White Bird's voice, and perhaps spoken through a deerhorn, for it was unaccountably loud and inhuman and frightening.

"What's he saying?" the general asked, turning away from the battle with relief, for he could see no way now of getting his orders across the river.

"He's saying that since the world was made, good braves fight for their women and children. He's telling the braves to shoot down the white dogs—says we are no braver than we were at White Bird Canyon or the Clearwater. General, I'd be pleased if you could give me a rifle."

"You're in no shape for fighting, Mr. Otis. I've told you before we're grateful enough for what you have done."

With a sigh, the general turned to face the battle. Nothing was happening as he expected it to happen. The troopers were shooting wild: they would soon exhaust their ninety rounds. The sun was already hot on their faces, and they had marched continually for thirty-six hours with only short rests. The braves were gradually gaining on the tepees, pushing the troopers out. The fighting on the edge of the tepees was confused, and there were moments when the general wondered whether he had behaved correctly in giving orders to set fire to the lodges. By escaping to the narrow gullies beside the river and the thick clumps of willows, the Indians were able to re-form. Also, seeing the women who had escaped to the river holding up their babies to him, standing there in the water, some of them naked, the general was ashamed of having attacked an unprotected village without warning. "Poor women! Poor children!" he murmured, and then turned away to follow the movements of the Indians across the meadow.

The strange thing was that they seemed to be coming from all directions towards the tepees. They seemed to spring out of the ground.

They were everywhere, and the troopers were being forced back across the river. When the Indians reached the tepees and peered into them and saw the dead women and children lying on their buffalo robes, some clubbed to death, others shot through the eyes, others mangled with bayonet wounds, there arose a wail of mingled grief, rage and horror, a terrible deep-throated sound which ended in a kind of long-drawn sobbing. At the end Joseph's great trumpet voice could be heard shouting: "It is better to die than to live against these people who kill women and children. Come, Melting Icefloes. Come, Red Moccasin Top. Come, Bird-with-one-eye. You are the cause of the trouble! You killed the white men! Now is the time to show your courage! Kill, or be killed!"

Melting Icefloes began to run across the grass, while his young wife followed him. At the edge of the river he threw himself down, his wife behind him, behind some thin logs, and from there he began to fire up the slope and into the river at the retreating white men, shouting at the top of his voice, crazed with the smell of death from the tepees. His wife was shouting too, the two voices rising clear. When Melting Icefloes was shot, the girl took his rifle and went on shooting up the slope, until Lem shot her between the eyes, for the general had relented and given him a rifle. Seeing her lying there naked against her husband, Lem shivered. The general also shivered, for his keen ears had heard in the distance, coming from the north, and perhaps from four miles away, the sound of a shell fired by the howitzer which he had left behind during the night march with orders that it should be brought up as soon as possible. The firing could only mean that the howitzer under its small escort had been attacked, and perhaps put out of use. He listened for the sound of another shot, but there was none.

Down in the meadow the women and children were pulling down the tepees. They worked feverishly. One of the tepees was burning. The torch flung inside had set fire to some wooden boxes, but the women paid no attention to the smoke. One by one the women were picked off by the soldiers crouching on the slope. "O Christ, leave the women alone," the general said, but the wind was coming up the hill, and the firing went on. He counted eight women wounded and three killed before they fled down the valley.

During the long afternoon the edges of the woods, the banks of the river, the little clusters of tepee-poles, every rock and cranny beside the river were occupied by the Indians. It was August now, and the sun came strong against the hill, leaving the Indians in the shade. Troopers cried out for water, but dared not go near the stream. There was little firing. Both sides were trying to conserve ammunition; and when the Indians shot, they shot accurately, at the moment of bringing their rifles up, and when the troopers shot they often fired wild. Occasionally, making a strange humming noise, there would come a shaft of arrows from the forests or from a brave hidden behind a small rampart of rocks beside the stream.

When night came the Indians were silent. There was not a breath, not a murmur. There were moments when the general had it on the tip of his tongue to order a night attack, but always there was the consciousness of that silence so deep that it seemed to be deliberate. The Indians wore silence as they wore their robes: once there came a muffled scream, and then a long choking sob, and the general knew that one of his troopers, somewhere down at the foot of the hill, had been killed with a knife—the flash of the knife in the starlight was seen by half the troopers on the hill, and all of them cursed and muttered and prayed under their breaths. All night, as they shivered with cold, they thought the Indians were moving silently among them.

Pinned down on the dry slopes of a gulch, their clothes still sticking to their skins because they had waded twice through the river, without food, without blankets, with no hope of sleep, they waited through the longest night they had ever known. Occasionally out of nervousness they would fire into the darkness ahead at a leaf trembling in the starlight, at any black shadow on the river. The general had despatched messengers to Howard's column which was advancing slowly down the Bitter Root Valley, but everyone knew that Howard was a good thirty-six hours away. When dawn came, pale and blue, most of the troopers wondered how it was that they were still alive.

At dawn, the general half-expected that the Indians would have vanished, but it was not so. Deep in the forest they had held a war council. Looking Glass had urged a night attack; Tuhulhulsote had spoken of a march which would lead them to the general's rear; Joseph, whose wife lay dead in the one tepee which no one had dared to remove, said bitterly: "Let us sleep during the night, and send our best braves to keep them awake. Let them rot during the night." An hour before dawn Joseph was awakened. With the other chiefs he rode to the edge of the forest, and long before the dawn appeared he was able to make out the positions of the enemy. "They are well placed," he said, shaking his head. "Let us keep a few braves behind, and go on our way to the buffalo country."

All that morning, while the women and children rode south, the general thought the whole fighting force was lurking beside the stream or on the edge of the forest, but in fact there were no more than thirty braves left behind. They fired from the forest up the slope, and then ran and fired again from some other place entirely, and were so quiet in their movements, and they kept so closely to the long morning shadows, that none of the soldiers saw them. It was like fighting an invisible enemy. When the general saw that some of his soldiers were sleeping the morning away, he ordered two large tins to be banged together to keep them awake; the Indians thought there was magic in the banging of the tins, and they began to beat on a deerskin drum; and the drumming drove the soldiers almost to madness.

Lem slept the morning away. The pain in his left eye had increased and the whole of the left side of his face was inflamed. His teeth chattered with the pain. It seemed to him that the pain grew like a flare, sweeping up from some place in his neck until it burst within the eye socket; and there were times when the pain became so great that it drove him into unconsciousness. It was during one of these moments of intense pain that he fell asleep as he crouched beside the general. When he awoke it was late afternoon, and thick black clouds were billowing up from the river. He jumped up and shouted: "They've poured oil on the river and set it alight."

"I don't believe it," the general said, and shouted to one of the troopers nearby. "Well, what is it, Mr. Mathis? What the devil are they up to?"

"They've set fire to the grass, sir."

"They have, have they? Well then, if the worst comes, we'll charge through the flames when they reach us, and meet the redskins on open ground. I hope we'll be able to send them to a hotter place than they have prepared for us."

The wind was now blowing the great flame directly uphill. Smoke was everywhere, blinding them and suffocating them. Sparks exploded out of the sagebrush which was dry tinder, and they could no longer see the river, the meadow or the forest: there was only the black wall of billowing smoke and the great leaping flames. They coughed and choked, and the men down the bottom of the hill came running up, panting, their faces blackened, staggering and cursing, and their voices were faint and hoarse. It was impossible to tell how many Indians were coming up behind the wall of flame. The crackle of the flames sounded like chattering Indians; and when some alder trees began to burn on the left, they were sure that the Indians had crossed the river and were climbing the rocks on the left flank and so, with the flames directly in front of them, they began to fire at the blazing alders. Worse than the black choking cloud was the hot wind on their parched faces. Suddenly, when the flames were almost on top of them, the wind turned about and blew the flames back so that while the grass was still burning underneath another flame, bent backward, was racing down the hill, and then when it reached the water's edge, it went out. The smell of burned bunch grass was everywhere, and all the hill was black. The men cheered; it was a very hoarse trembling cheer. The general turned to his men and said: "Your mothers wouldn't recognize you," and once again there was a hoarse ripple of cheers. Beyond the smoking grass there was not an Indian to be seen. Half an hour later, when the general decided to lead his men down the hill, and the first men were already on their way, a fusillade of shots from the forest and the riverbank stopped them on their tracks. "Better dig in, men," the general said hopelessly, and gazed up at the evening sky where a black cloud hovered ominously overhead.

For three more hours, while powdery black ash filled the air, the men waited for the dark. The sultry air turned cold; the stars came out; and still the Indians waited below. Mysteriously, they crossed the river, invisible to the troopers on the hill; mysteriously, they fell back to the safety of the forest. Twice they charged the entrenchments, and though there were only twenty of them in the charge they seemed like a hundred, yelling at the top of their lungs, their painted bodies gleaming dully in starlight. Lem was still next to the general. There was no other place he could go. He felt that the soldiers were whispering against him, as they whispered against the Cheyennes, for leading them into this trap. He was crouching there on the rock, staring into the starlit darkness below, when the general suddenly jumped up in the air, as a lizard will sometimes give a little leap from the rock, and then rolled on his side, clutching his thigh and screaming with pain. A bullet fired from somewhere to the left, among the alder trees, had gone through the flesh of his thigh; a tendon seemed to be broken; the leg made quick spasmodic movements; and when the doctor came bounding among the rocks, having heard the scream and recognized that it came from the general, he fell against Lem; and then it was all confusion as Lem, the doctor and the general rolled on top of one another. In the dark the trouser leg was cut off and the wound bound. Soon afterwards they heard a last fusillade from the Indians, and then there was silence.

That night they fed on one of their horses, and the raw meat was passed from hand to hand. They dared not light a fire. Just as on the previous night there were long intervals when they thought all the Indians had fled, so now there were long intervals when they could almost feel the breaths of the Indians on their necks; so they fired at random into the dark, and two troopers were killed by these stray shots. Lem slept through the night. The pain in his eye was less now. He made a shelter of pine branches and lay within it, and he did not care any more whether the Indians attacked. Close to him in another shelter the general rested through the night.

The next morning there was no sign of the Indians except the dead who were strewn over the meadow, their bodies already turning black. One brave lay spread-eagled on a rock which jutted into the stream. The sun shone hot upon the rifle pits, and on the troopers who lay along the hill with rough bandages round their heads or with their arms in splints: there was hardly a man who was not wounded. Relief shone on their faces; at the same time there was the dawning fear that the Indians were preparing an attack in secret, from some direction unknown.

"I sent four despatch riders," the general muttered. "Howard should be on his way by now. If he isn't, then he's a damned slow rider, or else—"

The general said no more. He knew it was perfectly possible that not a single messenger had reached Howard. In his little tent of pine branches he lay restlessly nursing his wound; and when one of the troopers slithered down to the river and brought him some water in a tin can, his blue eyes opened wide and he said: "I didn't know I would ever be so grateful." Then he ordered a huge fire to be lit, in the hope that Howard would see the smoke and recognize his need and hurry on.

At ten o'clock in the morning, during one of those curious intervals when the men shuddered in panic at the thought of a renewed Indian attack, they saw a cloud of dust rising on the further edge of the forest. A few minutes later a cheer went up, for they heard Howard's buglers playing; and when at last Howard came down into the meadow at the head of his troops, the fresh troops gleaming in sunlight, their horses fresh, their pennants and guidons blowing in the wind, looking as though they had come out of barracks only a few moments before, for they had rested after crossing the Lo Lo trail, the cheers gave place to open-mouthed scorn, and there was a strange silence from the troopers on the hill as Howard ordered his men to ford the river and ride up the slope.

When the general reached the top of the hill, Lem was standing just outside Gibbon's tent of pine branches. Gaunt and red-faced, with his fiery red beard all tangled with twigs and leaves, with the plaster bandage slipping down and the bandage over his forehead pushed to the back of his head, with a great hollow under the one open eye, Lem stood there with his feet apart.

"You're late, general," he said accusingly, and lifted up his hands as though he would refuse entrance to Gibbon's tent. "You're late and sorry, and there ain't no excuse for you, general. You didn't want to fight the Indians, did you? I've seen it in your eyes. You've wormed and twisted and squirmed like a dog with a flea in his hide, damn you, and by God, this is what we've had to pay for your slowness!" Saying this, Lem made a sweep with his arms which embraced the blackened hill and the green meadow in the sunlight.

"I'll deal with you later," the general said grimly, and then went into the tent. Open-mouthed, Lem listened to Howard and Gibbon exchanging greetings. They were talking as though they had met only the day before.

"Hello, Howard, I'm glad to see you!"

"Well, Gibbon, how do you do? Are you hurt?"

"Oh, not much hurt—just a flesh wound in the thigh."

"Where are the Indians?"

"They drew off last night round eleven o'clock. Will you dine with me?"

"How can you ask me to dine? You haven't any supplies."

"Oh, we'll find some—"

Lem was at the end of his temper.

"God damn them," he shouted. "What kind of animals are these soldiers? We've suffered and bled and fought and where have we come to? A black hill in a black valley. Go after Joseph—that's what you're paid to do!"

Then he made his way slowly towards the river, stamping heavily in the black ash, and half the time he was looking over his shoulder. On the crest of the hill, with the blue mountains behind, the two generals were sitting and quietly puffing at their pipes.

XXXII

The Lava Beds

LEM'S rage with the generals vanished when he was with the Cheyennes. He knew now that all his life he had wanted to rule over men. When he wanted food or water the Cheyennes brought it to him. When he slept they guarded over him. He had no doubt that if he wanted a woman the Cheyennes would have found one for him. So he was happy as he rode in the advance, though his head throbbed with the pain of the broken eye and his hands shook and the rage against Joseph mounted in him, a never-ending rage which made him break out with sweat whenever the image of Joseph came to his mind.

"We'll get him yet," he kept telling himself, and then he would stare at the wide trail Joseph left behind him, a width of a hundred and fifty feet of smashed grasses and bushes, the hoofmarks of ponies, the scraping marks of the travois in the dust, and sometimes a dead pony, or else a trinket thrown off by one of the Indian women.

Joseph was always a day or two's march ahead. The trail led over bare hills, dropped into canyons, and then across rivers; and nearly always it was straight. It was as though Joseph refused to accept the obstacles nature set before him: he would cut straight through them. They lost the trail for four days, and then found it again at Horse Prairie Valley. Two days later Bannock scouts reported he was preparing an ambush at the pass leading to Yellowstone Park. The army turned about, and raced for the pass.

"They're damned will-o'-the-wisps," General Howard said. "You can't touch 'em. They're south, north, east, west. What's the matter with our scouts?"

Stevens said nothing. There was nothing helpful he could say because the general was now continually out of temper.

Two nights later they encamped on Camas Meadows. They had picked up the trail of the Indians, and then lost it again, but scouts reported that they were some thirty miles away, heading for the pass. The troopers were tired. It was Sunday. There were broad grassy meadows and the spurs of blue mountains and there were even a few haystacks, each a hundred yards wide, the strangest and most beautiful things they had seen in a month of wild wandering. There were two streams of white water, and beyond the rolling meadows towards the north, shining blue in the evening light, were lava beds with curious rounded knolls and bubbles stretching away for ten miles towards the foothills, like blue bald heads. There were cottonwoods in full leaf and slender willows. It was so peaceful a place, and his men were so worn out, that the general decided to rest the night there and push on early the next morning. He ordered outposts to be set at all the approaches, and the mule train together with the cavalry horses were picketed in a wide circle. Forty miles to the east lay the pass leading to the Yellowstone Park; behind him was the long trail down the Bitter Root Valley and the Rocky Mountains.

The camp slept. There was no moon, but the stars shone brightly. In the silence there was only the soft tread of a sentinel, the neighing of an occasional horse, the braying of the mules. Once or twice a dog barked. There was no wind. The willows and cottonwoods stood stiffly against the silver-flooded sky. Some of the troopers slept in shelter tents, but many slept under the waggons, and most slept under the stars.

"You'll have a good night's sleep, I promise you that," the general said, stroking his beard, lying down next to Stevens. Lem had already fallen asleep under a waggon twenty yards away. The general wrapped himself in blankets, said his prayers, and then sat up for a short while, staring into the darkness at the huddled men all round him. He said: "I remember once, at Antietam, I found myself sleeping among some soldiers. Their heads were covered, and I thought they were sleeping soundly, and the next morning I found they were dead men laid out by their comrades." He shivered, and looked across at Stevens, but the lieutenant gave no sign that he had heard. "Sleep well," the general murmured, and then he drew the blanket over his head.

He slept dreamlessly, as he always did when he was exhausted. It seemed to him that only a few moments after he had fallen asleep he was awakened by the familiar terrible shrill yelling of Indians. Horses were neighing; musketry was rattling; there was no end to the confused sounds which had suddenly invaded the camp. The wild sounds seemed to be echoing against the distant lava beds. Shots rang out, not singly but in volleys, and they seemed to be coming from all sides.

"Here they are!" he exclaimed, and sat up in his blanket.

"For God's sake lie close or a stray bullet will hit you," Stevens shouted.

"I won't lie close. I'm going to get up and see what the devil they are up to. I hope they'll stay and give us battle—that's the best!"

There was a note of triumph in the general's voice. It was still dark, and the stars had misted over. In the camp there was confusion everywhere. Troopers jumped up and picked up guns belonging to others; percussion caps were being dropped; the cavalry horses were stampeding and converging in the darkness towards the mule herd. He could see now that the Indians had come from the direction of the lava beds, and had led their attack against the horses and mules, presumably in the hope of driving them away with their own herds. It flashed through the general's mind that he had ordered horses and mules to be picketed. Well, they were still there. The Indians, having failed to panic the horses, were charging through the camp, which was in fact no camp at all: the camp was three hundred men, a third of them volunteers, sleeping on the hard and dusty earth. The mules were trying to break loose. A bugle sounded piercingly. A soldier with bare legs and his military coat flapping loose over his bare chest was wheeling his horse among the wagon trains, and suddenly out of nowhere twenty Indians on ponyback rode him down. From the rear another group of Indians fired into the camp. It was still cold, and the men's breath came in silver plumes, and the mules were being driven away in the direction of the lava beds, and the Indians were still yelling—they were yelling on the left and on the right, and they came yelling out of the river bed, and they were still yelling when they were riding over the dusty plain towards the lava beds. Because the air was still and windless, the sound of their yelling was more blood-curdling than ever before, and it seemed to hang in the air. Lem fired blindly into the dark. Stevens had to run twenty yards under fire to reach his horse, and when he jumped in the saddle all he could see was a great black shadow moving across the plain: this was the mule herd which the Indians had somehow unroped and were driving swiftly towards their own encampment. The general was shouting hoarsely: "Where's my bugler?" The bugler was found, and ordered to blow "Boots and Saddles." The cavalry was forming into line four abreast, preparing to race after the herd.

"May I join them, sir?" Stevens asked.

"No, I shall want you here. I want them to get our mules back, every last one of them."

The cavalry rode off after the mule herd. Someone came running up to say that the Indians had panicked the mules by waving buffalo robes in front of them.

"I don't believe it," the general said. "I reckon they cut the hobbles of the bell mares and took off the bells. It's not panic. They knew exactly what they wanted to do with the mules. The Indians yelled, didn't they? It was pitched for the mules."

The earth was like a drum. They could hear the hoofbeats of the cavalry riding the mules down. Company after company of cavalry was moving off into the darkness. In the end there were about fifty infantrymen, two pieces of artillery and two companies of cavalry remaining in the camp.

"I'll tell you this," the general said. "There isn't a thing we can do until we get our mules back."

"Mules?" Lem said, with a sad smile. "We don't fight Indians with mules, do we?"

"I didn't ask for your advice, Mr. Otis. I didn't ask for it now, and I don't remember asking for it before, but the truth is—we fight Indians with mules, with supplies, with everything we can get."

Dawn came up like a streak of blood on the horizon. Some orderlies prepared the general's breakfast: the bread was hard, but the coffee was steaming pleasantly. A black horse came swinging out of the shadows. A soldier dismounted, out of breath, his forage cap askew, and his coat wet with fresh blood.

"The compliments, sir, of Major Sandford," the soldier said, "The mules have been overtaken, and some fifty or seventy-five are on their way back."

"Tell the major, all right. I do hope he will get them all."

Sitting on folding stools, with the dawn breaking cold and watery, the red dawn turning to saffron, all the shadows of sage and willows on the plain turning dark purple, and the wind coming from the direction of the lava knolls, the general and Stevens exchanged glances. From far away there came the thin notes of a bugle, but the drumbeats of the horses on the plain could no longer be heard. Half an hour after sunrise a thin bluish mist drifted over the plain, and now there were only a few restless horses remaining in the camp. Before the general had finished breakfast another messenger came riding through the mist.

"Well, what is it?" the general asked sharply. There were deep lines in his forehead. From the look of the messenger it occurred to the general that the cavalry was in difficulties, and perhaps the inevitable had happened—an ambush somewhere in the region of the lava knolls, which had looked bright blue the previous evening, but now, as he saw them at intervals through the drifting mist, they had turned rust-red.

The messenger was still on horseback, and the pinto was sweating and foaming at the mouth.

"I reckon there was a sort of ambush, general. The Indians began to get round Norwood's left, and then around Jackson on the right."

"Where's Norwood now?"

"We don't rightly know. I left him over yonder, fighting hard in the sagebrush."

"Then he isn't in the lava beds?"

"No, to the right of them."

The general studied the map stretched on his knees. The mist was drifting away. He could make no sense of the messenger's words. Five minutes later he ordered the remaining cavalry to ride towards the lava beds. He heard shooting. He had a curious feeling that Joseph's fate would be determined among those rust-red beehives of lava, but when he reached the skirts of the lava there were only a few cavalry rounding up some scattered mules, cursing because the mules were stampeding again, and some were making for the Indian herd. It was afternoon before he found Norwood's company, which he had thought lost. The dead were lying among the cottonwoods, and the heat was coming out of a cloudless sky.

"Where are the Indians?" the general asked.

"Ahead eight or ten miles."

"Then why in deuce name don't you follow them?"

There was no answer. The troops looked ragged with heat. They had fought hard. They stood about, aimless and white with shock, taking shelter under the cottonwoods, saying little. There was a strange reserve about them, and when the general asked questions, they would look away. They had fought so hard that they had little strength left, and in their eyes there was an accusing glance. They needed help, and the general had sent none. On this scarred plain, with the mountains blue and shimmering beyond, they had fought through the long dusty morning without water and with barely enough ammunition, and now they were in no mood for argument, and it was only with difficulty that the general could make them talk about the engagement. Suddenly, out of nowhere, the Indians had sprung upon them.

In the evening, when the general was sitting beside the campfire, a strange figure came riding up to him. The scented sagebrush crackled and gave out sparks; and the general's face, weather-beaten and covered with small freckles of sun-blisters, was expressionless as he read his Bible. His lips moved, and sometimes a small trickle of sweat ran down his drawn face. The man who came towards the fire was naked to the waist, his trousers were torn and frayed, and you could see his bony knees, and he wore a terrible plaster over one eye. The plaster had turned bright purple. There were powder burns on the man's shoulders, and when he dropped off his horse he walked with difficulty. The general, peering through the darkness, smiled coldly.

"So it is you, Mr. Otis," he said sadly. "I expected you to come."

There was something black in Lem's hand. Now he threw it at the general's feet, on the edge of the sagebrush fire. It was a long hank of hair with some blood and flesh still attached to it. The scalp did not look like human hair, and when the general first glanced down at this strange thing which was thrown at his feet, he thought it was a horse's tail. Beyond Lem, still on their horses, were four Cheyennes. For a while no one spoke. The general was afraid of another outburst, and Lem seemed to be withdrawn into himself, his eyes closed as he tottered there beside the fire.

"I know what you're thinking," the general said at last. "It's not an easy campaign. It never was. They're clever as cats. We're dead beat. The men's blankets are falling to pieces, and their clothes, too, and we haven't got enough supplies to pursue the campaign. I'm thinking we'll move north to Virginia City, and get the men into shape."

He went on, talking to the blazing branches of sagebrush, conscious of Lem's presence but paying no attention to Lem, his voice thick and his heavily veined hand lying listless on the open book on his knees.

"Then you're giving up?" Lem said, and there was no savagery in his tone. It was as though the general's sadness had infected him also.

"No, I'm not giving up. I'm going to push on after them, but my men will have to rest for a day or two. I know what the Indians are up to now. They'll go through the Yellowstone Park, and then maybe turn north to Canada, and we have to stop them. We'll stop them all right."

"You won't stop them that way, not by resting up," Lem commented. "I've fought them singlehanded and with one eye. I reckon I've got a right to talk, and I'll tell you this. We've got to head them off every which way. We've got to go without rest or sleep or canteens or anything. We've got to be so we haven't got any thought except how to head them off. We've got to dream and sleep and think of nothing but murderin' them."

There was a long silence. The wind from the fire turned the pages of the book. A crowd of ragged soldiers was gathering round, and sometimes a horse neighed in the silence of the night. Lem was gazing down at the hank of blood-clotted hair on the ground. Some sparks fell on it, but did not set light to it.

"I'll tell you this," the general said. "We just haven't got the supplies we need, and we're worn out. Look at the men. They're not like you, Mr. Otis. I won't lead worn-out men to battle."

"You've got to."

"But I'm not going to. It's time there were fresh forces in the field. Do you know Fort Keogh?"

"I've heard of it."

"Then ride there, follow the Indians as far as you can, and then report to Colonel Miles. I'll telegraph him from Virginia City. I'll tell him you're on your way with those Cheyennes of yours. I reckon I'll be four days behind you, maybe more, but you can send your Cheyennes back with reports. You'll find Colonel Miles ready to listen to you."

"Is that all, general?"

"Yes, that's all."

For a few more moments Lem stood by the fire, then he stooped down, picked up the black scalp and thrust it into his belt; then he drew himself to his full height, saluted, wiped the back of his hand across his red beard and then walked towards the Cheyennes. A moment later the general heard the clip-clop of a horse's hooves in the dark. The general said: "He'll hang on to the Indians' tail and they'll never be able to shake him off. He'll be there, even if they get to Canada."

"Think they'll reach Canada?"

"I'm beginning to think so," the general answered, and then he closed the book and stuffed it in his pocket.

XXXIII

Towards Canada

LONG ago Joseph had discarded his Indian dress. As he rode at the head of his Indians he wore a black broad-rimmed hat, a black alpaca coat and a pair of grey trousers. He tended his braids carefully, and sometimes wore a red kerchief round his neck, but otherwise he resembled a sturdy farmer. He did not know why he had exchanged his Indian dress for the dress of a white man except that it seemed appropriate. Soon, very soon, he would be in Lapwai or Wallowa, or else he would be in Canada. He hoped he had tired Howard out. If not, he would slip over the border into Canada.

The long dusty procession of Indians, driving their pony herd with them, had pushed their way uneventfully through the Yellowstone Park. True, they had arrested some visitors to the park, but later these were released. Looking Glass had wanted them shot. "They are all spies," he said. "Every white is a spy." Joseph had laughed, saying: "We are not the enemies of the whites—only Old Man With One Arm is the enemy."

"And Lem Otis?"

Joseph shrugged. He knew a great deal about Lem Otis. He knew from the scouts he had left behind that Lem Otis was ill. His scouts had crept up close when Lem was asleep, and they heard him muttering and raving in his nightmares. He was a broken man, too ill to fight. He had to be helped onto his horse by his Cheyennes, and the Cheyennes were continually debating with themselves whether to kill him. No, he did not share Looking Glass's fears: there were more important problems. Food and ammunition were running out; there were not enough horses; they needed a doctor for their wounded, and for the squaws who had fallen sick, and for the papooses who were bleeding at the nose: they needed medicines, maps, even a compass, and they needed guides. They marched by the stars and by instinct, thankful enough when they knew for certain that Old Man With One Arm was many sleeps behind. "Why should we be afraid of a man with one eye?" Joseph asked.

"The Cheyennes have two eyes apiece," Looking Glass murmured. "They are his eyes."

Joseph stood on the rise, watching the procession pass in the hollow below. Sorrow welled up in him. Why were they wandering? Was there never to be a day of rest? He had fought off the enemy in every battle, and still they pursued him and his people. Why? He smiled briefly at Alokut, but it was noticed that he smiled only for his brother now. On the cleanly chiselled face men sometimes saw a terrible look of despair.

So the days passed, while the leaves turned red with the coming of the frost. August gave way to September. The Indians had become wanderers in the land, dropping into deep canyons, then racing across mountains in case anyone should see them in the valleys, playing their desperate game of hide-and-seek to the end. They drove north to the Musselshell and then through the gap between the Snow and Judith Mountains, and then swept into the deep buffalo country south of the Missouri. Until they reached the Missouri they were attacked only once, but the skirmish was soon over and the troopers ran before the Indian marksmen, more desperate than ever now because they knew the end could not be much longer delayed. Joseph was glad they ran. He wanted the braves and their squaws to preserve their strength. For himself, he rode at the head of the procession, confident and carefree, showing everyone who watched him that he knew where he was going. The high passes, the steaming geysers, the forests and the deep canyons and the lava beds: all this belonged to the past. In front of him there were only the long plains leading directly north. They had passed the snowy mountains and the muddy Missouri with their swarming pony herds, and they had lost no more than a handful of people, mostly by disease, and they had shaken off "the red-bearded one" somewhere in the region of the Yellowstone and Howard was still five or six sleeps behind. It was late October now, with snow falling on the slopes of the Little Rockies and Canada no more than a day's march away.

"We'll rest here," Joseph said, looking up at the grey drifts of cloud. "It is fat country, with many buffaloes. Rest, my braves. We have left a clean trail and won our freedom. Tomorrow we shall send runners to Sitting Bull and tell him that another band of red men have run from the soldiers of the Great Father in Washington."

He stood there, beside Alokut, Tuhulhulsote and Looking Glass, under the high bluffs, while the snow dusted his face and all round him the squaws were setting up the tepees.

XXXIV

The Blinding Snows

WHEN Lem rode into Colonel Miles' parade ground at Fort Keogh, he resembled a scarecrow. He was hollow-cheeked, feverish, with dust and mud splattered all over him, and his clothes were in ribbons, his bare knees showing through the rents in his trousers and one sleeve had been cut away. When he spoke there was a kind of dark muttering coming from deep inside him. Two days before Lem's arrival, the spruce young colonel had already received the substance of Howard's message by telegraph. He had gone about collecting his provisions for the march to the Northwest cautiously and thoroughly: the column was still not ready to leave. Lem glared at the colonel and said: "You've got to leave now, provisions or no provisions. It's our only chance."

All the way it was the same. As they rode through the mist and sleet, there was always Lem at Colonel Miles' side, saying: "We can't delay. It's more than our life is worth, colonel." Miles with his thick mustache and jutting chin and needle-bright blue eyes would turn and stare at Lem, and pity him, and wonder why he brought the man with him at all. "Mr. Otis, we are doing our best. You'll have to learn that it takes time to assemble two battalions of cavalry and one of infantry. You go at the speed of your guns and your baggage train, remember that." Then he would look approvingly at the vast baggage train extending behind him.

All that day, and for many days, the ghostly army had been marching through the snow towards the Little Rockies. Then two of Lem's Cheyennes found Joseph's trail, a fifty-yard-wide black slash cutting across the snow, and the bodies of dead ponies still warm. Miles talked of setting up camp for the night. Lem screamed at him: "Would you give it all up now? Don't you believe the Cheyennes?"

"I believe them, Mr. Otis, because they are your men, but my men must rest. It's eight o'clock now. We'll only blunder if we follow in the dark."

"My Cheyennes can see in the dark, colonel. Follow them. We'll fall upon them at night, when they're sleeping. We did it before. By God, if we don't take this opportunity—"

At that moment some of Miles' scouts returned. They, too, had seen the trail, but they said the ponies were three or four days old, and the main body of the Indians may have passed five or six days before.

"Well, which is true?" the colonel asked. "For all we know they are in Canada now."

"We have to make sure, colonel. God in Heaven, would you take this cup from my lips?"

The colonel smiled, stroked his mustache, said something about the danger of quoting the Bible and then, with an appealing look at Captain Hale in command of one of the cavalry battalions, he turned his back on Lem and entered his tent, and it was only when he reached the folding bed which his orderly had prepared for him that he turned and said: "We'll leave at two in the morning and skirt the trail till we find them." Lem went away, muttering to himself.

In the dark, after six hours' sleep, the army formed into column and prepared for a dash to the border, a last and almost hopeless effort to head off the Indians. They skirted the trail, always keeping two or three miles to the east of it. Before dawn scouts reported that the Indians were sheltering in a hollow less than twenty miles ahead, sleeping the night away, and Miles ordered the men to move at an easy trot. When the sun rose and he saw the smoke rising from the Indian fires, he ordered a charge.

Above, the bluff rose steeply to twenty or thirty feet, with narrow ravines scoring the high brown wall. Below lay a kidney-shaped stretch of bottom land, and on the edge lay the tepees brightly painted in stripes and crowding under the bluffs, and there was sagebrush dusted with snow and winding coulees where the Indians were entrenched, waiting with their Winchesters, invisible to the men galloping across the plain. To westward lay the winding creek, all dried up now, and beyond this lay more plains rolling to the blue mountains dotted with sage and withered gorse. They saw Indians on the heights and others around the tepees, and still more were gathered on the plain. A soft powdery snow was falling from the ash-white sky, and on the frozen earth the thudding of the horses' hooves sounded like gongs, but there was no answering sound from the enemy: only quietness, men moving on the bluffs in flurries of snow, the plain rolling and dipping and rising, so that sometimes the blue-coated horsemen disappeared entirely from the sight of the small group surrounding Colonel Miles.

"We'll cut through them like paper," Miles said, and a slow smile of expectancy and pride lit his face, and with the knuckles of one hand he stroked his mustache. His eyes, burned deep with fatigue, for he had slept only two hours the previous night and three the night before, stared across the wastes of brush and snow, the gorse with the little streamers of ice blowing and tinkling in the wind, as though he could penetrate below the earth, and through it, to where the Indians were hiding, for it had occurred to him long ago that their silence was ominous, as ominous as the storm brewing in the heavens. And so, to keep his courage up, he whistled a bar or two, and looked out upon the white plains with a humorous pucker of his lips, nodding to his adjutant and at the same time rubbing his gloved hands together.

"We'll scorch them," he said, smiling at his adjutant. "Yes, captain, we'll scorch them. I reckon Mr. Otis must be the happiest old scarecrow on this earth now."

The two cavalry columns were still thundering across the plain, and the small snow was still falling, and the colonel was watching the advance of his cavalry through glasses when he observed what appeared to be small red flames leaping out of the snow. For a moment these red flames were completely inexplicable, but a moment later he heard the crackle of loud rifle fire, and instinctively he began shouting at the top of his voice: "Be careful, Hale. They're entrenched." A look of extraordinary surprise crossed his features. It occurred to him that he had underestimated the distance which separated him from the Indians. They were perhaps two miles away when he had thought they were only a mile away. Also, they must have known through their own scouts that the army was advancing, and so they were prepared, or perhaps they had heard his army coming through the snow. "Hale! Where are you?" he shouted, and he turned once again to look at his adjutant, who had turned pale with shock and whose lips were trembling. There was no sign that the Indians had broken. There, on the horizon, under the low bluffs, the blue-coated cavalry were pitching and wheeling like toy soldiers on a board which has suddenly been shivered with a blow. They were not advancing any more. They were staggering back, and their own fire was desultory while the Indian fire seemed to be concerted, so that you heard occasional shots evidently fired by the white men, and then there would be concerted volleys from the Indians. It was as though somewhere in the hollow, among the small coulees, there was a man who was signalling when the Indians should fire and when they should desist from firing.

Trembling, the colonel began to canter ahead. Some riderless horses were escaping from the melee, and whenever he saw these riderless horses he tugged at the bridle, and his mouth flew open. He had taken immense pains to form his line correctly, with the Seventh Cavalry on the right and the Second on the left, and his center formed with mounted infantrymen riding on captured Sioux ponies. Then what had gone wrong? He kept thinking of Captain Hale, red-faced, with impudent blue eyes and a slouch hat perched on one side, riding his grey horse Rover, the most mettlesome of all the greys in the column, and it was impossible to believe that the young captain had survived the charge. The snow had stopped now, and low clouds were racing across the sky, and a terrible grating sound came from the dead grass as it waved in the wind. He remembered Lem Otis racing past him, with the Cheyennes on either side, and the Cheyennes had thrown off their blankets and were almost naked except for the lightning-like stripes of yellow paint on their chests and thighs. "What an extraordinary morning it is," the colonel sighed, and turned his face away from the blue rambling line of horsemen who were riding back across the plain even before he ordered the bugler to blow the recall. He could not believe what he saw. He could only wait there, trembling, for the survivors to return and regroup.

"The center is holding, sir," the adjutant said. "Thank God for the center."

"Yes, indeed, thank God for them," the colonel breathed again, turning slightly to the right where he could see his infantrymen deployed on a little knoll overlooking the Indian camp. It was the Seventh Cavalry which had taken the brunt of the Indian fire. Now he regretted that he ordered the bugler to blow the recall. There was still hope that the line might hold. The Second was sweeping round the Indian camp and driving a wedge between the crazy pattern of tepees and the pony herd. Miles waited. It was all confusion. The sound of firing was dying down, but the cavalry and infantry were still on the rim overlooking the Indian camp, though there were fifty horses plunging riderless on the plain. Less than twenty minutes before Miles had watched his cheering troops as he lifted his white-gloved hand high above his head and shouted: "Attack!" Well, they had attacked and ridden forward in style, shouting at the top of their voices, looking wonderfully young and fresh in the morning light, each man attended by a white plume of breath, and he remembered how some antelopes had scurried away, and how the smoke rose blue from the Indian fires; but now there was no more smoke, and only in the center was there any firing. He dug his spurs into his black mare and raced towards the rim. A young lieutenant, his face bleeding, came riding up, and without saluting the colonel said: "Sir, I'm the only damned man of the Seventh Cavalry who wears shoulder straps alive!"

"You've done well," the colonel answered, but he was no longer looking at the lieutenant. He was trying to form a picture of the Indian defenses as they lay in that crescent-shaped hollow at Eagle Creek, among the winding coulees and the rotten earth thick with ice and snow. The wind was whistling in his ears. The young officer had swung his horse round, and was returning to join his comrades at the rim, but the horse refused to go, and shook and neighed so loudly that the lieutenant kept continually striking it, and even then it moved forward by inches.

"Where the devil's my bugler?" Miles shouted, looking round among the soft scurries of snow whipped off the earth by the wind for the familiar face of the boy who usually rode beside him. Then seeing the youngster riding twenty yards away on the left on a Sioux pony, he shouted: "Blow the deploy by the right flank."

The boy smiled, raised his right hand in salute, lifted the bugle to his lips and then turned with an astonished look at the colonel, and suddenly the bugle seemed to jump out of his hand.

"I can't blow, sir," the boy shouted in a high thin wavering voice.

"Why the devil can't you blow?"

"I'm shot, sir," the boy shouted, and fell forward over the pony's neck.

The colonel turned to his adjutant.

"Get one of the sergeants to take the boy to cover," he said gently.

"There's only one sergeant here, sir," the adjutant replied, "and he's dead."

The sergeant had been killed with a bullet through his forehead even while the adjutant was speaking.

The colonel swung round and galloped to the rear. He was not afraid of dying, and he would gladly have thrown himself at the rim, but he knew that the army would have become completely disorganized if he was killed. He knew, too, that the Indians had already sighted him and they were aiming more accurately than he had ever known Indians to aim. As he was riding away, a lieutenant sent to report to him from the Seventh Cavalry kept saying: "It's just murder, just murder."

"Did you get up close, lieutenant?"

"Yes, sir."

"Then tell me this. They knew we were coming, didn't they?"

"Yes, sir, they must have known. Some of the lodges were struck. I reckon they were just about to send their women out and run for the border when we came up. It's murder, sir. Pure murder. We ought to regroup, sir. We can't fight them as we are."

"You'll have to learn how to fight them," the colonel said, and gave orders that the howitzer and Napoleon guns should be brought up to the ridge northwest of the Indian village. Some firing broke out on the right, and at the same moment he heard the piercing death wail of a woman somewhere in the camp. "Well, we're getting at them," he said, and the blood began to return to his face.

All morning the firing went on, and the white men held the rim, but no further advance was made. As reports came in, Miles came to the conclusion there was nothing to be done but to invest the camp on three sides. If necessary they could be bled to death with the help of the guns.

"It's the only way," the colonel said. "We've got them at our mercy, and by God we'll keep them until they surrender."

In the early morning when the three columns converged on the camp Joseph was riding slowly towards the pony herd. He did not know that Miles had found his trail. He knew only that it was time to drive further north, and he wanted to make sure that the herd was in condition for the journey. While the snow fell, he was aware of the extraordinary quietness which had settled on the camp half a mile away, and he thought this quietness was some trick of the wind or of the snow. He remembered praying, as he often prayed, for the safety of his tribe, and he remembered looking back and seeing the blue smoke rising through the snow. Suddenly, while he was talking with the herd boys, he saw something which resembled a huge herd of buffaloes bearing down on the herd, and then there was the sound of firing. Altogether there were perhaps sixty herd boys with the ponies. Most of them were unarmed. They looked dazed when they heard the firing.

"Race for the tepees," Joseph shouted, but it was too late, for the cavalry were charging through the herd, shooting at the boys, shouting at the top of their voices.

Joseph knew now what the cavalry were up to. They would try to capture the ponies, for without the ponies the Indians had no way of moving fast, and the ponies were half their wealth. If they lost the ponies, they would have to dig themselves in.

Snow was flying, and he saw the ponies milling in confusion, and the boys huddling together, trying to make the ponies race for the tepees, but the cavalry already ringed them round. Joseph dug his heels into his horse, and raced for the hollow. When he reached the tepees, his blanket was torn to ribbons, his horse wounded and both feathers of his scalp lock were shot away.

Looking Glass had seen the cavalry coming through the snow and had organized defense lines. Braves were digging shelter pits, squaws were crawling up with ammunition. All round the rim the Indians in their snow-covered blankets were firing steadily at the white men. Only in one place had the white men reached the tepees. Looking Glass was bellowing orders, uttering piercing warning cries, jumping up and down, waving his arms and cursing as he had never cursed before. There were too many blood-soaked women sprawling among the tepees.

With a magazine rifle in his hand Joseph crawled towards four braves crouched behind a dead pony. Blood poured from a wound in the pony's belly. Joseph found himself crawling over the body of a dead brave: it was so warm that he gasped. He rubbed the snow off the forehead of the dead brave, and then pushed forward. He could see better now. He could hear the shouts and sudden screams of the whites, but the Indians were strangely silent, and most of them were lying flat on their bellies with their faces turned towards the enemy, grey against the snow, and each brave shot carefully, at long intervals, pressing the trigger only when he was sure of his man. When he reached the four braves sheltering behind the pony, Joseph waited for a moment, then rose quickly to his knees to get a glimpse of the enemy lines. A bullet whistled past one of his braids. He dropped down into the snow, but he knew now from the single glance that he was heavily outnumbered. There were cavalrymen on the right who had staked their horses and were digging rifle pits with knives and tin cups and flattened saucepans, and some were hiding behind their dead animals. There were many dead among them, but they were holding their ground. The Indians had not succeeded in pushing them back. It was bitterly cold, and the whites were shivering, and they had no taste for fighting on the rim, but they were there, and wherever the Indians showed weakness, they would be able to climb down into the valley in the shelter of the coulees, for there never was a hollow with such a jagged outline and there were places where they could easily slip down unobserved. A brave whispered: "Go back, go back." Joseph paid no attention. He fired once at a cavalry officer whose horse was spinning round, and then at an infantryman who was crawling across the plain from one frosted sagebrush to another, and all the time he was conscious, not of the enemy, but of the anguish in his own heart. They were so close to freedom, and so far. The braves were treating him with extraordinary respect. They would pause and gaze at him as they loaded their rifles, and in their eyes he thought he detected a strange sympathy, and this sympathy was unnerving. He said: "Tonight we shall slip away. Remember that. Those hawks shall not tear us to pieces with their talons." Then very sharply, because at last he had read the unspoken words written on their eyes, he said: "Where is Alokut? Where is the one who laughs like the summer clouds?" There was no answer, but one of the braves, younger than the others, turned his head towards the north of the camp, and there was no welcoming smile on his lips, no expression on his face, not even the expression appropriate for sorrow. "The eagles—" Joseph began, and then was silent.

Behind him, deep down in the canyon hollow, there came a shriek of despair, not unlike a death wail. He turned round. From the direction of the tepees they were waving to him and making signs that Looking Glass was dead. He began to crawl away from the dead pony, and then he sprang to his feet and raced towards the tepees. Looking Glass was lying spread-eagled in the snow: a bullet had smashed through the looking glass he wore on his forehead and broken into his skull. From that moment Joseph knew the direction of the battle was in his hands, and in his hands alone.

All through the morning from his battle post beside the tepees Joseph gave orders. By signals and by shouting he kept the defense lines thrusting at the enemy. Braves came slithering across the snow with reports; occasionally a brave would come riding across the valley, holding onto his pony's mane and hanging against the pony's side so that the white men would think it was simply a pony running loose. By the end of the morning the troopers were turning back from the rim, but there was another charge in the afternoon. The charge was thrown back, and now there was no more than desultory fire along the rim. From a wounded trooper it was learned that Old Man With One Arm was still many miles away: it was Bear Coat Miles who was leading the attack.

When darkness fell Joseph sent three braves through the lines with orders to reach Sitting Bull and ask for help.

He had fallen asleep and now he was awake, and the snow was still falling, and there were still some scattered rifle shots echoing against the bluffs, making a sound like the falling of an icicle, very clear and sharp, and afterwards there were long silences broken by whimpers of pain from a bluecoat or an Indian lost in one of the coulees, but these sounds were less frequent now. Once or twice there was a coyote-howl from the direction of the bluffs: and listening to these howls, Joseph smiled, for there was energy in the sounds and they were full-blooded and must have come from the young braves. Then, while he was straining ahead trying to look out across the darkness in the direction of Bear Coat's tents, he saw an orange glow lighting up the tepees and the women who stood at sentry-go outside them, and he was glad there were no cries of pain when the shell exploded far away in the direction of the bluffs.

Pulling his striped blanket over his head, with the Winchester in his hand, he made his way along the coulee until he came to the place where Alokut was lying in a little hollow scraped out by the women's knives. He could not see Alokut: he could only discern faintly the outline of a frosted face powdered with snow, a thing that glowed as though a small candle lay inside, and then the candle would flicker and come to life and fade. It was very still and warm in this hollow, for no wind came here. He put his warm hand on the cold, snowy hand of his brother and said: "The eagles have flown, and this feather has fallen from the heavens. May the Great Spirit protect the feather." He choked back his sobs, afraid that some of the braves would hear him, then bowed his head and rested it against Alokut's breast, hoping against hope to hear the heart beating; and it was strange to him that

Alokut was so silent. He stared at the falling snow, the huddled braves lying on buffalo robes, their faces pointed to the sky, and somewhere among the bullet-riddled tepees and the shelter pits the children were crying out against the cold, for no fires could be lit. "A snow ago we were together," he groaned aloud, "and now Looking Glass and Alokut have been taken from me."

Down in the valley some women were searching for buffalo chips, feeling for them with their moccasined feet, and others were tending the wounded. In the darkness Joseph passed a squaw giving water to a white trooper, who kept shouting: "Water! Water!" It was a word Joseph knew, and it alarmed him that a man could shout so loud when he was so near to death. In the hollow under the low clouds shapes moved with a small glow, but when the blizzard came about three o'clock there was only darkness, the snow thudding to earth, and the sleet following. Everywhere there were men and women huddled in blankets, shivering in the cold. That night five inches of snow fell, and the high wind whistled like a prolonged scream against the stunted pines of the bluffs.

The next day there was little fighting. It seemed that Bear Coat was determined to freeze the Indians into surrender. The cold drifts fell, and there was hardly any earth to be seen anywhere: only the thick white coat of snow, the dead lying under snow blankets, the whole valley turning into ice. In the white tepees the children wailed all day, but when the Napoleon gun was brought closer and shells were lobbed into the camp, hurling children and squaws into the air, there was no more sobbing. Quietly the Indians collected the dead, and covered them with snow.

That night it was reported to Joseph that thirteen magazine rifles had been taken off the dead and wounded troopers who fell or made their way into the rim. Later in the night, when the buried village was hushed and there was no more fighting, White Bird and Joseph held a council of war. They had expected aid from Sitting Bull. They thought it would be rushed to them, but no messenger had come in. Could they make a dash for safety? The braves who lay in their thin blankets in the snow said they had strength enough for the journey; they had no need for food; they could drive themselves another forty miles with the few ponies they still possessed, but how could they bring their jerked buffalo meat? how could they bring the women and papooses? how would they know when they had reached King George's country when they were travelling through a snowstorm? There were deep lines on Joseph's face, and there was a strange tenderness in his voice when he said: "Then we must stay—we must stay to the very end."

When dawn broke the whole valley seemed to have disappeared, and there was no sign of the soldiers. They had withdrawn to their fires far across the plain, leaving only scouts and a thin ring of troopers behind, but the twelve-pounder gun, used now as a mortar, with the muzzle elevated at a high angle, was lobbing bombshells into the hollow. Five more braves were killed, and three more women. Worse still, the Indians were at the end of their resources and fired at anything that moved: they killed three of their own braves, mistaking them for troopers or Cheyennes.

At noon a lieutenant on a black horse came to the edge of the rim, bearing a white flag on a pole. To an Indian girl hiding among stacked tepee-poles, he said that Colonel Miles wished to talk with Joseph. An hour later, when Joseph came up the rise, the white flag had disappeared, but the lieutenant was still sitting there on his horse. With Joseph were three young braves. Behind the lieutenant was Lem Otis. They rode in silence to the colonel's tent a mile away. A small charcoal fire was glowing there. Colonel Miles smiled, showing his teeth, standing outside the tent, his long blue coat with the brass buttons and the shoulder straps immaculate, untouched by the snow.

"Come," he said. "Come by the fire. Let us talk this matter over. We are sensible men."

With his head bowed Joseph followed the colonel into the tent. It occurred to him that the colonel was smiling a little too readily, as though he wanted to ingratiate himself or prove his affection for the Indians; and while Lem translated, and the younger officers crowded round, Joseph stood quite still, listening for voices, watching, hoping that by some gesture, some accent of his voice, the colonel would betray his true feelings.

"I have come because you sent a white flag," Joseph said quietly, and his face glowed like bronze in the light of the charcoal fire.

"You have come because you are an honorable man, and have fought bravely," the colonel went on, and he was smiling pleasantly, stripping his white gloves from his hands, leaning forward a little on the campstool, gazing up at Joseph who stood beside the tent pole. "Let us have an end to this matter. Surrender. Put yourself at my mercy. I shall treat you well. There is warmth and food here. Take this warmth and food to your squaws. Do you not believe I shall treat you well?"

"Will you let us return to Wallowa?"

"No."

"Then where will you send us?"

"I promise you I will have you sent back to the reservation at Lapwai."

"When?"

"As soon as it can be arranged. By spring you will be back in Lapwai. All you have to do is to surrender your weapons—nothing else. From the moment your weapons are stacked, food will be rushed to your people. Your squaws will not have to cry any more. I have heard them crying. Stack your weapons, and there will be an end to the battle."

"I will surrender half my weapons—not all. We shall need our rifles on the reservation. White men will attack us. They will always attack us. Do you expect us to go unarmed?"

"New rifles will be given you when you reach the reservation."

"If I give up my rifle, I give up my life."

"You must listen carefully. I have offered you the terms of surrender. I cannot accept conditions—you must surrender unconditionally, and in exchange I promise you that everything possible will be done for your people."

"I must have half of my weapons."

The colonel drew a large red handkerchief from his pocket and brushed it over his face. It was very warm in the tent. He was out of patience. In front of him, like a great bronze lamp, the face of the chieftain was shining. Lem was smiling. He was translating very carefully and accurately, and from time to time the colonel nodded approvingly in his direction.

"Then you refuse?" he said at last.

"I do not refuse to surrender. I refuse to give up more than half of my weapons."

The soft voice of Joseph, which sounded like the wind waving on summer grass, a very rich and pleasant voice even when you could not understand a single word which came from his lips, infuriated the colonel. He knew that Howard was coming up. He was worried at the thought of Sitting Bull sitting in Canada less than two days' march away, a man who would think nothing of sending a thousand braves over the border to rescue Joseph. He thought, too, of the generalship which he desired above all things. If Joseph surrendered to him, it was likely that he would be a general within a few weeks, a few months at most. Then why these delays? Could not Joseph see the advantages of surrendering to him? Hadn't he promised that Joseph would be returned to the reservation? Here was a poor devil of an Indian who did not recognize bounty when it was thrown at him. All the time Joseph was calmly regarding the colonel. He saw how the thick red lips trembled and curled under the heavy downward-brushed mustache. He was aware of an eagerness which was strangely menacing, strangely quick. Somewhere behind the expressed words of the colonel other words lay hidden in ambush. Once more the colonel drew the immense pocket handkerchief out of his coat where he had impatiently stuffed it, and slowly wiped the sweat away from his face.

"Will you listen to me?" the colonel asked sharply.

"I will listen to you, but I must have half my weapons," Joseph said. "Neither more nor less—it must be a half."

"You are mad to think such a thing!" the colonel shouted.

He shouted something to the officers. A moment later troopers came rushing into the tent, with ropes. They quickly bound Joseph's hands and feet, then rolled him in a double blanket, so that his hands, his legs and his whole body were pinioned, and he could stand upright only because he was being supported by the troopers.

"Take him to the servants' tents!" the colonel shouted. "Take him out of here!"

Joseph's eyes were closed. He thought of the lieutenant with the white flag, the long ride to the tent, the face of Lem. It was his own fault! He should have known they would trap him. Now they would send the lieutenant to the rim, and Lem Otis would shout that Joseph had surrendered. Four soldiers were carrying him, as they would carry a log. He was a chieftain, and they dared to carry him like this. It would be better to die, better to stop breathing by an act of the will. Once he groaned, and the troopers paused, thinking he was ill, but on the gaunt and painted face there was no expression. They threw him on a mattress in a tent belonging to the doctor's orderly.

An hour later one of Miles' lieutenants, sent out with a reconnoitering party, was captured by the Indians and held a prisoner.

During the afternoon firing broke out again. There was no wind, no snow was falling, and once a faint yellow sun shone through the low clouds. Indians on the bluff had followed Joseph's movements through glasses. They saw Joseph enter the tent, and less than an hour later they had seen something dragged out of the tent, and there was no sign of Joseph, who had promised to give a signal. They discussed what they had seen, whispering together. White Bird told them to wait an hour. Perhaps some accident had happened; perhaps Joseph and Bear Coat were still discussing the terms of surrender. Meanwhile the captured officer was placed in a shelter pit and guarded by squaws.

All through the long afternoon there was desultory firing. Once the Indians attempted a sortie in the direction of Bear Coat's tent, but they were pushed back. Three bombshells from the Napoleon gun burst over the remaining tepees, burying four women in the shelter pits and killing their children. There was now no food left in the camp. Towards evening a messenger with a white flag was sent to the colonel's tent with a scrawled message from the captured officer. The colonel had not known that one of his own officers was captured, and sent for Joseph who was brought to the tent with his hands tied behind his back. With a razor the colonel cut through the ropes.

"I shall have to send you back," he murmured, his face reddening. "You have captured one of my men. I shall send you back in exchange for him."

"Why?"

"It is what has to be. I must save his life."

"Even if you killed me, my braves would not harm him."

"You say that, but how can I be sure? No, it is best to exchange prisoners."

"Was I a prisoner? I came under a white flag."

"We shall not discuss technicalities now, Joseph. Go back under a white flag, and let me have Lieutenant Jerome safe and sound. Do you still refuse to surrender?"

"I refuse, unless I can keep half of my weapons."

The colonel made a little gesture of mock despair. He felt more powerful than ever. The Cheyennes had reported that the Indians were weakening: in a few hours they would be forced to surrender or accept a massacre.

With a group of young officers, and with Lem Otis riding at the head, Joseph rode back to the brim. Darkness was coming down. The white flag was whipping in the wind. At the edge of the hollow Joseph bellowed at the top of his lungs: "Let the white officer go free." The lieutenant emerged from the shelter pit, shook the icy snow from his uniform and began to scramble up the slope. When he reached the group of officers the exchange was solemnly made, and Joseph rode slowly down to the village, his head bent low, his hands folded on the pommel.

When the officers had all gone, Lem remained behind. He had brought his rifle with him. He dropped down in a snow hollow and meditated, while the blue shadows raced across the valley. The strange incident in the colonel's tent when the chieftain was bound hand and foot came back to him in bright and minute detail; it pleased him to remember how once Joseph had shuddered, as though a great fear had come to him. How are the mighty fallen! Far in the distance among the swirling snow shadows he thought he could see Joseph in his striped blanket among a circle of young braves crouching at his feet. He could not see clearly. His one remaining eye was running. During the day he could see well enough, but in the evenings he had always had trouble with his eyes, and now, after the long gruelling journey across the Rockies, after following Joseph until the man was trapped in a little pit near the Canadian border, it seemed that he must accustom himself to blindness soon. Well, he had shown his strength. He had torn an eyeball out by the roots. The Cheyennes worshipped him, and the colonel trusted him, but why had the silly colonel spoken of sending Joseph back to Lapwai? Were all the hard-fought battles in vain? Would Joseph accomplish in defeat all he had hoped to accomplish? There was no sense in it. He must be killed, and then the strength of those savages would be utterly destroyed. It was very silent now, the only sound coming from the worried gusts of snow brushing off the sagebrushes. The Indians were lighting fires. They seemed to think the battle was over. It was the first time they had been able to light fires for three days. Darkness was lapping all around, but he could still see the chieftain in the light of the fires.

When Lem slowly raised his rifle to his shoulder, he was in a strangely elated mood. He would kill Joseph and have done with it. He would kill the chieftain honorably, while they were still fighting. Joseph was standing there, talking to the braves, with dead ponies all round him and the tepees behind him. It was so simple that the very idea of killing Joseph now made him laugh, and he wondered why he had not thought of it before. He ran his hand along the barrel of the Winchester and then spat on the barrel to give it luck. He wanted to sing hymns. He was as deliriously happy as he had ever been. He did not know that the valley and all the gullies contained subterranean dwelling places, communicating galleries and a host of hiding places, and that the Indians could observe every inch of the rim from concealed positions. He did not know that Shades of Night had been watching him closely. He would not have recognized Shades of Night if he had seen her, for she was hardly more than a skeleton of herself, and she was shivering with clenched teeth and praying, and her fingers were numb with cold. Suddenly she fired. For a brief interval Lem was conscious of a blinding light beating like wings against the walls of his skull. He groaned: "Dear Moll, dear Shades of Night," and when the waving lights faded away he thought he saw their faces clearly, and when he rolled off the rim and his body went bounding down the slope he thought he was running down the hill which led to Wallowa Lake. He wanted to cry out with joy because he had so suddenly been returned to his own home. He wanted to laugh and tell stories and hold some woman, Moll or Shades of Night or another, in his arms. When Shades of Night found him, he was lying sprawled over a boulder at the bottom, and his broken face was pointed to the sky. She crouched over him to see whether he was dead. He whispered: "Holy, holy, holy, Lord God Almighty," and then his whole body gave a little convulsive leap and he lay still.

His red beard and the white bandage over one eye caught the fading light, and when all the valley was lost in shadow Shades of Night thought they were still shining there.

XXXV

From Where the Sun Now Stands

"WE have the Indians coralled yonder, general," Miles said when Howard came up with his column. "They're firing from holes and trenches, but there isn't much strength in them. We've been firing into them steadily all day, and I reckon we'll keep firing all night unless they surrender. They're stubborn brutes, general."

"I always said they were," the general answered, and he was glad to see the red glow of the campfires surrounding the tents. The general turned to his adjutant: "Well, Stevens, we've made it just in time."

They went into the colonel's tent where a feast was being prepared for them. The general was hungry, worn out by the long march. It was late in the evening, and he had seen the flashes of rifles from the rifle pits on both sides as he came riding across the plain. Sitting in the warmth of the tent, with the charcoal fire blazing, listening to the pleasant crackle of rifle fire in the distance, the general smiled at the young colonel and said: "I know you are ambitious for a star. Well, you'll get one. There's no doubt about it. I'll leave the command to you. We'll have a surrender tomorrow, and I shall not bring up the main body of my troops until afterwards."

The colonel smiled, offered the general a glass of wine and then drank his health. The firing was going on, but you could expect it to go on at intervals until the very moment of surrender. Joseph could not last out much longer. Somewhere down there, in that rabbit warren of a valley, his braves were slowly being cut to pieces. He was glad the wind had drifted to the north, because the sound of the women chanting the death wail always disturbed him. He ran his finger along the rim of his wineglass and said: "It's a great honor, general, and you may be sure I won't forget it. I forgot to tell you, general, that I have had a short talk with Chief Joseph. I promised him that if he surrendered I would do everything possible to ensure his safe return to Lapwai."

"That was honorable of you."

"But he refused to surrender. Said he would surrender half of his weapons, but not all of them. I took the occasion to detain him for a little while, but he would not change his opinion. Now of course he will be forced to surrender under any terms we offer. Will there be a trial, general?"

"No, I'm against putting him on trial. He has fought honorably most of the time. Though I hate to, I have to admit he has been a resourceful commander. I hope myself that he will be allowed to return to Lapwai, but of course it is hardly within our department to determine what will eventually happen to him."

Shortly afterwards, tired by the journey, the general and the adjutant went to the tent which had been set aside for them. Stevens said: "I feel you have been very impulsive, sir."

"Why?"

"Because you refused to accept the command. The articles of war say that when two commands meet, the senior officer must assume command of all. I feel sure your generosity will be misunderstood. You have followed Joseph for sixteen hundred miles, and Miles has followed for a bare three hundred."

"Well, he has coralled Joseph. He deserves an act of generosity, Mr. Stevens. Don't you agree?"

"I don't trust Miles," Stevens said quietly, turning his head away.

"Then you are being extremely ungenerous. I trust Miles implicitly. During the Civil War he was my adjutant, just as you are now my adjutant, and the truth is I would trust him with my life and it pleases me to perform a small act of generosity."

They went to sleep and were awakened at dawn by bugle calls. The firing was still going on, and Stevens remembered that he had been awakened by volleys of rifle shots several times during the night. Early in the morning the general sent a message to Joseph saying that further resistance could only lead to hardship. If necessary, the general was prepared to hurl his whole column against the Indian rifle pits. Joseph replied that he would surrender during the afternoon when the dead were buried.

Late in the afternoon he rode slowly up the rise with the wind in his face, accompanied by four young chiefs, two on each side, leaning heavily against his knees. As he rode Joseph was aware that a sudden silence had descended on the battlefield. He was hardly aware of the young chiefs who came with him: they were less to him than Alokut, who seemed to be riding at his side. His Winchester lay across his knees, and his hands were crossed over his saddle horn, and when he looked up his eyes were so misty with tears that he could not see the boulders which lay beside the path or the shape of the ridge ahead. Only the speckled pony with its red tail hung with streamers of eagle feathers and the furry black mane glittering with ribbons looked fresh; the clothes of the chieftain and his assistants were tattered, and the squaws and braves who followed were naked under their torn blankets, and their lips were blue and their hands shook with cold.

In front of him as he rode hung the great plume of bluish smoke from the nostrils of the pony. The smoke delighted him; it was life, and death was everywhere. So he rode up on the evening of defeat, with the stars coming out of the cold heavens where only a few clouds remained. The reddish glow of the sunset was already turning to a vaporous yellow, and the shadows were thickening.

"Where are they? Are they over there?" Joseph muttered, pointing to a knob of rock on the rise; but no one answered, and he knew he had confused the enemy with some stones.

Blinded by tears, sometimes muttering to himself, he now pressed his knees more firmly in the sides of the pony, and because he knew they would take the pony away, he had half a mind to gallop across the plains on it for the last time, paying no attention at all to the officers who were awaiting him; and if they shot at him as he fled across the plains, so much the better. Then he remembered the procession of warriors coming on foot behind him, and wondered why he had weakened so.

The snow melted on the pony's mane and glistened, and once the pony shook its head and all the spray flew off, and this explosion of spray glistening in the fading sunlight pleased him. His head was bent so far forward that he could touch the mane with his lips, almost bury his face in that rich silky mane which stirred and quivered with life and reflected in its black depths all the remaining light in the heavens. "It is good," he said, and for the last time that day a fleeting smile crossed the dark, graven face.

When he breasted the rise and saw the plain stretching in front of him, the chieftains who had accompanied him up the slope drew back. A group of officers was standing close to the advance rifle pits. They resembled a small heap of black rocks. There were dead horses lying on the earth, and these he saw more clearly than he saw the officers, and the stench came to his nostrils. He saw that the hawks had pecked at the skins of the horses. The officers, who had been expecting Joseph for a long time and could not understand his unaccountable delay, were surprised that he came alone, and seemed so uncertain of himself, and had difficulty in managing his pony. Those who had seen Joseph at Lapwai could hardly recognize him. He was thinner, greyer, curiously lonely and out of place. Was this skeleton the man they had fought over nearly two thousand miles of backbreaking forests and roads and flooded rivers? He wore no feathered headdress, only a beaded ribbon across his forehead and his scalp lock was tied with a twist of otter fur. His hair hung down in thick braids, and he wore the kind of cheap buckskin leggings that his braves wore, and there was a grey woolen shawl like a cape blowing from his shoulders. He held himself erect, and there was a ghost of a smile on his lips, but no one could tell what the smile meant. When he was some ten paces away from the officers he raised his hand in salute, patted the pony's mane, whispered something to it and dismounted. Even then he did not come forward. First, he removed the shawl from his shoulders and draped it round his waist, then he held up his Winchester and gazed at it for three or four seconds, and his lips were moving as though he was talking to it. There was a kind of defiance in his slow graceful movements. He would take his own time. The officers, who were standing with their backs to the sun, did not realize that he was waiting until the sun's rim had disappeared below the horizon. He was waiting for that mysterious moment when the sun had altogether disappeared from the earth.

At the exact moment when the sun went down he walked forward alone towards the man in the faded blue military coat whose empty sleeve was pinned to his side, whose long iron-grey beard was being whipped in the wind and whose blue eyes had never for a moment left Joseph since the chieftain came over the rise. There was no smile on General Howard's lips. He looked like a man who hates himself. In this he was unlike Miles, who was smiling with quiet derision and pride, occasionally stroking his mustache upwards with the back of his hand. Howard was rock-firm. He seemed to have lost all sense of time and place: he was looking at Joseph because there was nothing else in all that wind-swept land except the figure of Joseph who walked so majestically towards him, and all the time Howard knew there was something wrong, and the order of military protocol was being disobeyed. It was not towards him but towards Colonel Miles that Joseph should have been marching. And then, too, Howard was conscious of the unexpected sound of someone wailing in the darkness which was beginning to settle over the land, but no one was wailing. The sound came from the Indians coming up the slope behind Joseph, and was compounded of their heavy breathing, the rustle of their frozen clothes and the soft padding of their moccasins on the ice. Now, one by one, the Indians were coming up over the rim, but as soon as they reached the rim they stood silent, watching Joseph.

Joseph stood five paces in front of Howard, the Winchester in the crook of his right arm. Silently he offered it to Howard, who made a quick gesture of his thumb in the direction of Miles. At first Joseph did not understand the gesture. He had offered the rifle muzzle first to Howard. He now reversed it, and still offered it, asking himself what had happened that the general should refuse it. Was the long stiff journey up from the valley in vain? Were there to be more conditions, more discussions? Was the surrender to be refused? There was a hard glint in Joseph's large black eyes when he saw Miles waving to him impatiently. So he would have to surrender to Bear Coat, who had entered the fight only in the last five days, and then only by accident. He would have preferred to offer the Winchester to Howard, for then at least he would be acting as a chieftain surrendering his weapon to another chieftain.

Quickly, with an astonishing abrupt gesture, a terrible fixed look on his face, Joseph thrust the Winchester into the hands of Miles, whose arms were outstretched to receive it. To do this he turned slightly on his heels. Afterwards he turned to face Howard, because he could not bear to look upon the childish satisfaction on the face of Miles.

The sun was now sinking quickly, and all the plain was creeping with blue shadows. Out of the shadows officers were coming forward. Among them Joseph saw a young lieutenant whose eyebrows were sunburned yellow, and whose small drooping mustache was of the same bright yellow color. The young lieutenant was opening a notebook, waiting for the chieftain to speak, smiling above the poised pencil, and when an interpreter came forward Joseph lifted up his hand in the direction of the sunset and began talking in his piercingly sweet voice heavy with sorrow.

"Tell General Howard that I know his heart," he said, facing the interpreter, and then paused, waiting for the interpreter to finish translating the words into English. "Tell him that what he told me before I have in my heart. I am tired of fighting. Our chiefs are killed. Looking Glass is dead. Alokut is dead. The old warriors are dead. It is the young who say yes or no. He who led the young men is dead. It is cold and we have no blankets. The little children are freezing to death. My people—some of them—have run away to the hills, and have no blankets, no food. No one knows where they are—perhaps freezing to death. I want to have time to look for my children, and see how many of them I can find. Maybe I shall find them among the dead. Hear me, my chiefs. My heart is sick and sad. From where the sun now stands Joseph will fight no more forever."

Some officers, coming forward to shake Joseph's hand when he was finished, looked carefully into his face to see whether he meant what he said, but they saw only a dark mask of bronze and two eyes blazing in the dark. At last Joseph turned away, drawing the blanket he had been wearing round his waist over his head; then for the first time they realized why he had not worn the blanket over his shoulders. They saw five bullet holes in the blanket, and there were the scars of fresh wounds on his forehead and wrists.

The surrender was now nearly over. Howard was whispering to Miles who was waving a slip of paper in his gloved hand. Apparently he had thought of asking Joseph to sign an article of surrender. The Winchester was now in the hands of his adjutant. Miles stood there smiling, his coat blowing open, his slouch hat perched jauntily on the right side of his head. The last stragglers from below were coming up the rise.

"What are your orders?" Stevens turned smartly to the general. The young lieutenant tried to catch Joseph's eye, but there was no hint of recognition.

"Well, I had not thought of giving orders," the general answered gravely. "This is up to Miles. No, I will give an order, Stevens. You will take Chief Joseph as a prisoner of war into the camp. You will see that he is well treated—not annoyed in any way, and you will carefully guard him in case any effort is made to enable him to escape."

The words were translated to Joseph. Miles was watching his black charger, which was being brought up to him. The young lieutenant was smiling, and Howard was looking at his watch. Already the crowd of Indians on the rim was disappearing into the pools of black shadow.

Far away to the left Joseph could see the tents with lamps burning inside, and he wondered why he had not noticed them before.

"You must come with me now," the young lieutenant was saying. "It is only a little way."

They walked in silence towards the tents which seemed so distant but were in fact less than ten minutes' walk away. Miles on his black charger rode past them, waving his hand in salute; and Joseph noticed that the young lieutenant bridled, clenched his fists and looked sternly at the colonel as though he wanted in some way to show disrespect for this man who had deliberately held back so that he could ride past them when they were on their way to the tent. Then the colonel disappeared in the darkness, and there was only the hammering of the horse's hooves on the icy ground.

"The tent is for you," the young lieutenant said when they were standing inside. "If there is anything you want, anyone you wish to see, any messages you are thinking of sending, then let me know. There is not much comfort here, but we shall try to make you comfortable. Is there anything you want now?"

Joseph said nothing. He looked round the bare tent, the kerosene lamp, the bare truck bed with the mattress stuffed with an inch of straw, the saddle hanging on the tent pole and the grey canvas underfoot. The young lieutenant was saying: "The general and all the soldiers under him wish you well. They hope your troubles are over, and you will rest and regain your strength."

Still Joseph said nothing. The darkness was crowding in from outside, and the kerosene lamp was swinging in the wintry wind which came through the open flap. The lieutenant shivered. It occurred to him that everything he had said was inadequate. He asked whether Joseph wanted food, but there was no answer. As though in a dream Joseph was staring in the direction of the bluffs, and sometimes his large brown hands would stray over the blanket, and when his fingers found the bullet holes they would pause. After a while the lieutenant withdrew, and Joseph was left alone with his own sombre thoughts. A gun carriage with squeaking axles rolled down the lane between the tents. A mist was creeping along the plain. Standing at his full height, so that the feather of his scalp lock was bent by touching the canvas, Joseph remained standing, staring into the night; then very quietly he closed the tent flap, turned the kerosene lamp low and drew the blanket over his head.

XXXVI

The Blazing Fires

GENERAL Howard sat on the edge of his camp bed, listening to the sounds which came welling out of the night. There were many sounds, but there was not one which gave him any pleasure. He thought of the dead and the dying, and then of the long pursuit, and of all the adventures on the way, but his mind kept returning to the moment when Chief Joseph came up the rise on horseback. By some trick of the light he had seemed larger than life, a huge man carved against the landscape, terrible in his dignity and in his sadness. There was something accusing in the look Joseph had given him. He stared round the tent, at the small folding table and the leather pouch which contained his maps, his diary and all the orders issued since he left Lapwai. There was no comfort in the barrenness of the tent. "War—war—there's no end to it," he said aloud, and then he drew a sheet of paper towards him and began to write:

Headquarters Department of the Columbia
In the Field, Battlefield of Eagle
Creek, near Bear Paw Mountains
Montana, October 5, 1877

The Secretary of War,
Washington, D. C

Sir:

I have the honor to report that Chief Joseph, after a bitterly engaged contest lasting five days, agreed to surrender to our forces at 2.20 P.M this day; about 4 P.M. the chieftain, accompanied by the remnants of his people, with their arms, came up the ravines. The majority of their ponies, numbering seven hundred, were captured—

He could not go on. He sat there, staring at the flame of the kerosene lamp, the shadows on the wall, the papers rustling on his table. Once more he saw the chief coming up the rise. The headache which had been ready to pounce on him all day as last caught up with him. He screwed up his eyes with pain, buried his face in his hand, and when he heard someone tripping over the tent guys, he shouted: "What's the use? Don't you know your way around?"

"No, sir."

"Oh, it's you—Stevens. Come in, Keff. I'm writing my report, and I have a damned headache. Have you seen Joseph?"

"He's asleep."

"You're sure?"

"No, I'm not sure. He was lying down on the bed with his blanket wrapped round his face. I slipped in, because for one moment I thought he might have killed himself, but he was breathing regularly. The kerosene lamp was burning, and I turned it out."

"That was when?"

"A few minutes ago."

"Poor devil, he needs to sleep," the general said, and then smiled wrily.

There wasn't a man in the camp who didn't need to sleep except perhaps Colonel Miles, who was intoxicated with his own glory. The general glared down at the lead pellets and the papers on the folding table. "Poor devil, poor devil," he muttered several times. There were red rims round his eyes, and the beard was rough, as it always was when he was disturbed. Then the general began to tug at the mustache ends, as he cocked his eyebrows and glared accusingly at Stevens.

"I hope you didn't enjoy this damned war," he said sharply. "It wasn't anything that redounds to the credit of our arms. I tell you, I am mortally tired of the whole business. I hope Joseph goes back to Lapwai. I'll do everything I can to see that he does, but in Washington they do things according to their way—it's not my way. I'm glad Joseph is sleeping." After a pause the general went on: "Did you take down Joseph's speech at the surrender?"

"Yes, sir."

"Then I shall be beholden to you if you will give me a copy."

Stevens tore two hastily written sheets from his notebook. The general glared, evidently having trouble in reading it.

"I never learned how to write a decent hand," the lieutenant explained .

"I daresay you never will now. Have to learn these things in school."

The general wanted to talk about simple, harmless things; he wanted to forget the long pursuit and the battles. But he could not forget. The knowledge that the journey was over, that nothing could be done to alter the pages of history, that he was envious of Joseph and had no real trust in Miles, all these things made him for some reason miserable and conscious of his own abiding loneliness, and suddenly, not knowing what he was saying, he exclaimed: "I couldn't help it, could I? It just had to be done, didn't it?" He turned his face away, and from the shadows Stevens heard him saying: "If we had left them in Wallowa, it wouldn't have done any harm. We haven't written a glorious page in the Army's history, I'm afraid. We could have done better, and best of all if we had let him slip into Canada. I suppose we will have to learn mercy—even the Army will have to learn that. It's not my fault that it had to happen."

When Stevens left the tent, he was sure General Howard would soon fall to his knees.

Outside, the snow was still coming down, but very lightly. The Indian women were still chanting round the fires, warming themselves, holding their thin brown arms to the flames. Sometimes, when the wind came along the gullies, it brought with it the putrefying sweet smell of the dead who remained unburied on the frozen earth.

Colonel Miles was standing outside his tent, smiling, pleased with himself and his conduct of the army. He had lost some of his best officers, but the price was worth while. Stevens was about to pass him and make his way towards the Indians crouching beside the fires when the colonel called him back.

"Is the general asleep, Mr. Stevens?"

"I reckon he is."

"Then I won't disturb him," the colonel went on. "Worn out with excitement, eh?"

"I wouldn't say General Howard is worn out, sir. Will the Indians return to Lapwai, sir? I hope they will. I do pray we can help them go back."

The colonel stiffened to attention. The face, so calm and reposed before, suddenly bristled with anger, and the heavy jaw was thrust out.

"Mr. Stevens, we have fought those devils hard for five days, and all you can think of is how soon we can get them back to the pleasant pasture lands of Lapwai! I am not at all sure they will be allowed to return to Lapwai. It's a matter for the Department of the Interior. They must be punished somehow, and I wouldn't be surprised if they were sent to the Indian Territory to cool their heels for a while. You take your battles very coolly, young man, but you didn't fight this one. If you had fought these red devils, you'd have a different idea about the proper disposition of them. I've given half their pony herd to the Cheyennes and the half-breeds who fought with us. Joseph thought he was clever—"

"He had dignity, sir, and he fought bravely, and he was good to his people, sir."

There was no reply from the colonel. Abruptly he turned into his tent, and disappeared. Stevens was left with the snow, the campfires and the Indian women, who sang in low mournful voices. Creamy smoke rose from the blazing fires, and there was always a little sputter when the snow fell in the flames.

Stevens wandered among the fires, counting the survivors. They were less than three hundred now—three hundred men, women and papooses, who had defied the main strength of the United States Army. He looked for Melting Icefloes, Red Moccasin Top and Bird-with-one-eye, but he was told they were dead, had died long ago at the battle of Big Hole. He was about to turn away and go to his tent when he caught sight of Shades of Night. She was so thin, so faded that at first he thought he had seen an old woman. She had drawn a blanket over her head, but he recognized the turn of her shoulders and the way she lifted her head, and he saw the glint of the circlet of glass she wore. He sat down beside her, whispering her name. Frightened, she turned, and her mouth opened and she gave a low moan and said: "Why are you here?"

"I am here to help."

"You cannot help us now. It is too late. We are asking the help of the spirits, but they say terrible things—"

"What kind of things?"

"They say we shall never return to Wallowa. We shall go down a river, and many more will die."

She turned away. The chanting went on. Stevens discerned within the chanting voices a strange undercurrent of sound which did not seem to come from the singers: it was as though the voice came from elsewhere, singing at a different tempo, at a different place, in a different language, about different things. Was this the voice of the spirits? He did not know. He said: "Whatever happens you will be in the hands of those who love and respect your people. Do you believe me?"

"Yes, I believe you," Shades of Night answered, and then she began to sway with her eyes closed, and she was singing again, and after a short while Stevens rose and went to his tent.

The End of the Story

A MIST hung over the Missouri, eddying and swirling, and sometimes through the mist there would come boiling tongues of sunlight. It was dawn now, and from the sagebrush island where they had moored the flatboat for the night they could see how the mist was slowly being sucked towards the sun. Stevens had spent the night on the island, listening to the lapping of the river and the wind in the sagebrush, the cries of the night birds and the drumming of the deer on the distant shore. He heard the scuffling of the beavers and the soft talk of the Indian women who had slept on the flatboat, and he was glad he was not with them, because he always wanted to throw his arms round Shades of Night, and when he did, the women squealed with laughter.

He rose and washed himself in the ice-cold river. He hated the river which had gouged its way through the soaring rocks; hated it for its fierce strength; hated it because it was taking the Indians south, far from Wallowa; hated it because it was white with ice floes, and where there were no ice floes there were huge rope-like webs made from the bodies of dead grasshoppers, and you had to cut your way through them with the sidesweeps.

He stood there under a tangled willow, listening to the distant howling of wolves and coyotes, and the soughing of the waves. He could see nothing, only the whiteness all around him, the mist clotted and swirling and touched with the sunrise. Then once more, as so often during the journey down-river, he heard a wonderfully clear whistling sound which seemed to come from all directions at once, now remote, now close at hand. The strange whistling hung in the air. It came, he told himself, from the cliffs. A moment later it came from another direction altogether, more plaintive, more piercing than ever. The sound chilled his blood. Plunging through the sage, making his way with difficulty, because the mist lay so thick around the island, he went to find Shades of Night. He knew she was on the flatboat. Most of the women spent the night on the island, but some had remained to care for the wounded braves who could not be moved. Now the cooking-fires were burning on the boat, and he could see Shades of Night with a red glow on her face from the fire. She was boiling salt pork and coffee, and the smell of coffee beans hung heavy in the wintry air. Some women were coming along the bank in Indian file, huddled in their striped blankets: children were prancing along the shore, rampaging through the thick white milky mist with bows and arrows, after beavers. Already three beavers had been tossed limply on the boat. Skinned, they would be thrown into the pot for the evening meal.

"You cold?" Shades of Night said, warming herself over the smoking coals.

"Yes, cold," he answered, watching her breath turn into a long white plume, then melting into the smoke of the fire. "The damned howling went on last night."

"What howling?" Shades of Night asked innocently.

"I've told you about the howling. If you can't hear it, you must be deaf. It goes on all night and gets on my nerves. It's like the coyote-howl, only worse, and there's more of it, and God knows where it comes from. A man has no peace when he listens to these howlings."

He began to stuff tobacco into his pipe. She kept glancing up at him. She wore a cap of beaver skins, two skins wrapped together, which she wore for some reason at an angle, and the two tails of the beavers hung over her ears, so that when she laughed, the tails swung like short pigtails. She screwed up her eyes because the smoke was getting into them, and said: "What is this howling you are always talking about? Does it come from the heart?"

He thought she had gone insane. Time out of number, he had described those terrible cries, and now she was asking whether the sounds came from the heart.

"It has nothing to do with the heart," he said stubbornly.

She dipped a tin cup into the boiling coffee. Already the other Indians were crowding round the fire.

"You are sure, Stevens?"

"Yes, quite sure. Also, I do not like being called Stevens."

"That is what you say."

"Nevertheless I do not like it, Shades of Night."

"Do you think I like being called Shades of Night? I am not darkness. I am sunlight. No, I am sometimes sunlight. This morning I think I am sunlight, but this afternoon—"

"Would you prefer to be called Morning Glory?"

"No, I would prefer to be called Pteu-mox-kha-she-ni-lekh-ho-pa-ni. That is my name. You mustn't laugh when I say my name. It means 'she who rises early and has dew on her eyes.' It is not true either, but it belongs to me."

Suddenly Stevens heard the distant howling again. He shivered slightly, spilling some of his coffee. What puzzled him was that none of the Indians seemed to be in the least alarmed by the sound, and would even smile when they heard it, although they were always whispering together and discussing the other sounds they heard.

"It's the sound of the male elk calling," Shades of Night said, laughing.

He did not believe her at first, but all the other Indians nodded and began imitating the sound, laughing as though they had no care in the world. Already their flesh was filling out on their bones. Health was slowly coming back to them. They would go to Indian Territory, and then perhaps, when some assistant secretary remembered them, they might be allowed to return to Wallowa.

At noon the sky was blue, the sun was shining and the water birds rose in the sky. The great arching crags on either side were lost in the golden vapor which seemed to be let loose from the sun. There were no more howlings of wolves and coyotes, no more plaintive cries of the nighthawks, no more ropes of grasshoppers in midstream. The rocks on either side shone like beaten bronze, and soon they came to a widening of the river. Birds flocked in thousands overhead, and the river roared, and the flatboat drove steadily downstream. Shades of Night and Keff Stevens were together in the forepeak of the boat, and sometimes they would turn to one another, looking at each other as they had never looked upon any person before. There in front of them, broad, mysterious and powerful, with the huge white muscles rippling through the blue flesh, wrinkled near the shore and smooth as ice in midstream, as imponderable and strange as destiny itself, lay the river. "As lovely as Wallowa," Shades of Night said, and then, resting her head against Keff's shoulder, she smiled to herself.

THE END